SEE HER BURN

A totally gripping chilling crime thriller

Please note this book was first published as
The Dispossessed

MARGARET MURPHY

Detective Jeff Rickman Book 1

Revised edition 2020
Joffe Books, London
www.joffebooks.com

**Please join our mailing list for free Kindle books
and new releases.**

ISBN 978-1-78931-450-2

The Murphy Clan — thanks for everything

CHAPTER ONE

Jeff Rickman watched the blood seeping from him and was hit by a wave of nausea. Saliva flooded his mouth and he forced his gaze away from the steady, sickening pulse up to the high hammer-beam vault of the church. The building reeked of old wood, candlewax and incense: the odour of sanctity that years of neglect and even deconsecration could not displace.

From the gothic arch of the west window the resurrected Christ smiled down at him, his arms open in welcome, palms upturned. October sunshine dazzled through the stained glass and red light spilled radiant from Christ's wounds.

Rickman began to feel a detachment, a light-headed clarity. Each dusty mote in the shafts of evening sunlight became a particle of dancing light, the shift and settle of timbers seemed to follow the tracking of the sun's rays, and the inching of the sun across the waxed floor was discernible to him. He closed his eyes and fancied he could almost hear the sighs and whispers of generations of penitents.

The pulse throbbed thickly in his throat and Rickman opened his eyes, unable to ignore the steady loss of blood. Swallowing hard, he fought the sickness, focusing instead on the pink granite pillar three feet away. In its polished surface he discovered flecks of white and gold and grey among the pink crystals. He looked downward to the carved marble vine leaves at the base and upward to the grey clusters of grapes at the head of the column, pale against the vivid warmth of the granite. Gradually, the nausea subsided.

It's all about blood, he thought; the giving and taking of it. Religion was founded on it and steeped in it. Church was all very well, but blood ties were the strongest, they said: the ties of family and of nation. Not for Rickman, though. For him, family was no more than a name, and one that could not be relied upon at that: Rickman, Reichmann, or Richter — one theory even held that the family name was originally Lichtmann — the combination of an ancestral lisp and an immigration official's indolence had resulted in the current spelling distortion — or so the story went.

Friendship had always meant far more to Rickman than church or family or nation. He turned his head a little. Next to him, close enough to touch, was Lee Foster. He lay with his left arm flung out and his right crooked over his eyes. Rickman had known Foster a long time and had worked closely with him over the past two years. He knew that this ordeal was far worse for Foster than it was for him. Foster would never have set foot inside this building if Rickman hadn't bullied him into it. Neither man looked at the other, nor spoke. They bled silently, each preoccupied with his own thoughts.

A light tap on his shoulder. A dark-haired woman in a white lab coat stood over him. 'You're done,' she said, clamping and disconnecting the tube attached to Rickman's arm and skilfully removing the shunt from it.

'I'm blaming you for this, Jeff,' Foster said.

Rickman turned to him. Tie loosened, shoes tucked under the trolley, Foster still managed to look smart.

'You volunteered for this, Lee — remember?'

'Yeah, well, if I ever volunteer for anything again,' Foster said, his voice slightly muffled by his shirtsleeve, 'Lock me up till the urge goes away, okay?'

'We're thinking of having the next session at police headquarters,' the woman said. 'If Inspector Rickman can fix it for us to use the cells, you could kill two birds with one stone.'

She smiled at Rickman and he felt a momentary quickening of his pulse. She was pale — invalid pale, as if she had spent all of the summer indoors — but her skin had a luminous quality, and her eyes, large and long-lashed, were the colour of polished oak in sunshine. She finished taping Rickman's arm and moved on to Foster.

Rickman noticed that Foster had arranged his right arm so that it wouldn't flatten his hair. Foster's hair was carefully tousled, as always; he gelled and sculpted it till it gleamed in dark-brown spikes. Lee Foster was apt to be vain — a characteristic that both amused and infuriated women.

'Be gentle,' he said, 'I hate needles. *He* threatened to tell the whole station if I didn't do this,' he went on, peeping out from under his arm. 'That's despicable, that, isn't it? Using a man's phobia to blackmail him.'

'You wouldn't believe he used to be a marine, would you?' Rickman said.

'Go 'ead, rub it in,' Foster said. 'Expose all my little foibles to ridicule.'

Amusement sparkled in the woman's eyes, but she didn't comment, instead allowing them to argue back and forth while she clamped off the blood flow and disconnected the tube.

'Best you don't watch this bit,' she said, when she had finished. 'I'm about to take the shunt out.'

'Nobody takes the shunt out of Lee Foster,' he said, lifting his arm from his face and turning his smile onto full beam. 'That's my name, by the way.'

She leaned closer and whispered, 'You're not my type.'

He struggled onto one elbow. 'It wasn't a marriage proposal,' he replied. Then, 'What is your type?'

Both she and Rickman heard the plaintive note in Foster's voice, and they exchanged a quick, amused glance. Foster misunderstood.

'Him?' he exclaimed. 'The rugged Roman profile was all very well in *Gladiator*, but we're in the twenty-first century now, love.'

'Funny,' she shot back, 'I keep getting a whiff of caveman. Just so you know — the shunt's the bit with the needle attached. But if you want to watch, it's up to you . . .'

'I thought you nurses were supposed to reassure your patients,' he said, still trying it on, but Rickman saw he had lost some colour.

'I'm not a nurse, I'm a phlebotomist and you're not a patient, you're a donor,' she said. 'Now — are you going to close your eyes?'

'I'd rather look into yours.'

Those eyes . . . They crinkled at the corners, and Rickman was reminded for a moment of someone, but the likeness was gone before he had the chance to fix it in his mind, leaving only a vaguely disturbing after-image.

'You want to look in my eyes?' she asked.

The wide-eyed innocence in Foster's dark blue eyes made him look younger than his thirty years. He gave her his sick-puppy smile and gazed adoringly at her. She stared back at him, her mouth turning up into the suggestion of a smile, then she gave a little tug and Foster yelled.

'That didn't hurt a bit, did it?' She lifted his hand and placed the first two fingers over the cotton-wool ball in the bend of his arm. 'Press firmly,' she said.

'Press firmly?' Foster scowled. 'I might just press charges.'

She chuckled, taping the dressing in place.

'Don't lift anything heavier than a pint for the next hour or so, okay?'

Foster shook his head doubtfully. 'I think I need watching,' he said. 'By a professional.' He paused a second. 'When do you get off?'

The wintry pallor of the woman's skin suffused momentarily with annoyance. '*Where* do you?' she asked.

CHAPTER TWO

There was a chill in the air. Grace Chandler hesitated on the doorstep, wondering whether to go back inside for a jacket.

The sun was just visible as a milky disc behind a thin cloud layer. Grace decided to take a chance on it breaking through. She skipped down the steps, feeling a thrill of excitement at the freshness of the morning and the promise of fine weather. She dumped her briefcase in the boot of the car and tucked her handbag behind her seat, within reach.

Mossley Hill to Liverpool city centre was a twenty-minute drive, but she was late, and the rush hour had begun, which could double her journey time.

She turned the car toward Sefton Park and skirted the top of the lake, following the kidney-shaped contours of the park along with a steady stream of rat-runners who were also trying to avoid the traffic lights and hold-ups on the main roads.

As she drove, she daydreamed pleasantly, thinking of Jeff sitting in the bedroom armchair as she towelled dry after her shower, love and lust in his hazel eyes.

For a few minutes she had pretended not to notice; he was already washed and shaved, smartly dressed, ready for work. A colleague described Jeff as looking like a bruiser in a suit: his nose had been broken at some time and badly reset, and he had accumulated a number of scars, one of them bisecting his right eyebrow. He wore his chestnut-brown hair short, as did most police officers she had met, and she supposed that anyone seeing him for the first time might mistake him for a tough nut. If he was tough, Grace never saw it in him, but she found reassurance in his strength of character as well as his physical strength.

'See anything you like?' she asked, with a sideways glance at him.

He smiled. 'Oh, yeah.'

He caught her hand as she crossed to the dressing table, pulling her onto his lap to kiss her lips, her throat, her breasts. Then he lifted her and carried her to the bed. Her fingers found the buckle of his belt and she sighed, rising to meet him as he went south.

* * *

The sun was stronger already. In the five minutes it had taken her to reach Sefton Park it had burned off the misty layer of cloud and now filtered through the sycamores and horse-chestnuts around the perimeter, dappling the honey-coloured shingle on the pavements and warming the frontages of the Victorian mansions that formed the crust of the inner gem: the geode of grass and trees and water that Grace thought of as the lungs and heart of the city.

Traffic was backed up at the main road and she flicked her indicator right, jinking across a gap in the stream of cars and escaping the jam into one of the avenues. It was narrow and cars parked along both kerbs constricted it further. She edged into a gap to let an oncoming car through. Thirty yards from the end of the road, a bin lorry was idling, skewed at an angle to the kerb. A bit of a squeeze, but room to pass. Suddenly, the lorry pulled out, blocking the way through. The driver looked at her in his mirror; she could almost see the glint in his eye.

'Damn,' she muttered, leaning forward to switch the radio on. A cool rap version of 'Summertime' blasted out and she settled back in her seat, ready for the long haul.

The outriders dragged two bins over and hooked them to the apparatus. The accumulated stench of decayed food, sweet and sickening, belched out from the rear of the lorry. Bags and loose rubbish tipped into the filthy cavity, sending a bubble of foul air so thick she could almost see it.

'Thanks, fellas,' Grace muttered, shutting off the fan.

The lorry lurched forward three yards and then shuddered to a stop.

'Damn it!' She yanked on the handbrake with more force than was necessary and glared at the driver; he stared back at her in his wing-mirror.

Two more bins were brought, and the empties trundled back to the kerb side. The hydraulic lift whined and grumbled, lifting the two bins. Suddenly, the inane prattle of the presenter became unbearable; Grace felt in the door pocket for a CD and came up with Peggy Lee. She looked down to slot the CD in the player then sat back to enjoy it as the bins tipped their contents into the cavity of the lorry. Bags, newspapers, empty cartons, potato peelings. The contents of the bin on the left remained stubbornly in place, then a square of carpet fell out.

After it—

A body.

A woman. Naked. Head-first. Her hair a rich brown, streaked with slime. Green eyes. Bright, luminous green. Her arm fell across her face, as if in a defensive gesture. A butter wrapper had stuck to her left buttock. Her inner thighs glistened red. Grace registered horror and pity and outrage. The body slid with a slithering thud into the maw of the lorry. Then, from the base of the bin, a gelatinous red-black slick. Blood.

* * *

Constables Allen and Tunstall were the first on the scene. They were arguing as they pulled in head-to-head with the bin lorry. Tunstall was the more experienced officer. A big man with broad shoulders and an even broader Lancashire accent, he was not going to be talked round.

'I've told you once — no,' he said. 'Only one of us goes near the body — "keep your scene clean". You know the rule.'

'Come on, mate, it's my first suspicious death,' Allen said.

They got out of the car, Allen still arguing, but Tunstall interrupted: 'Shut up, will you, and get the Crime Scene Kit out the back.'

Allen grumbled but he cheered up when Tunstall told him he could tape off the area. 'What are you gonna do?' he demanded.

'Confirm we've got a crime scene—'

'Take a squint at the body, you mean.'

Tunstall ignored the interruption. 'Then I'll call for a police surgeon, SIO and CSIs.'

'CSIs?' Allen repeated.

'Crime Scene Investigators.'

'Isn't that what the Yanks call them?'

'It's what *we* call them, now. Haven't you done the forensics course yet?'

'The basic training, yeah.'

'Well,' Tunstall said, 'When you're all grown up, they'll let you go on a proper course with the big boys, and they'll tell you that SOCOs went out with the old cast of *The Bill*.'

Tunstall got his look at the body before taking the names of witnesses and then reported back to the sergeant on duty at Toxteth Station. 'I'll need a police surgeon and SOC — CSIs,' he corrected himself quickly. 'What about the SIO?'

'That's up to the Major Incident Team. No need for you to worry about that, Tunstall.'

'No, I mean, will he come out, like?'

'What for?' the sergeant asked.

Tunstall wasn't sure how to answer that. Senior Investigating Officers came out because that was their job, wasn't it?

'Aren't you lads up to the job?' the sergeant asked.

'Well, yeah, but it's not like we're CID, is it? I mean, I don't want to sound silly, Sarge, but won't they want to — you know — investigate?'

'There's nothing they can do till after the CSIs have done their bit. It's your scene, Tunstall. You don't let anyone onto it who doesn't need to be there. If a senior officer does show up, you can bet it's just for a nosy at the body. Make him wait till the CSIs have finished.'

'Right-oh . . .' Tunstall still wasn't sure about keeping an SIO behind the line, but if the sarge said it was all right . . .

'Tell me about the scene,' the sergeant said.

Tunstall glanced over at PC Allen. 'We've taped from the lorry back to the house where the bins were collected from.'

'The house is scene as well,' the sergeant said. 'Have you established a common approach path?'

Tunstall hadn't thought of that. 'Allen's supposed to be dealing with access, Sarge.'

'Allen hasn't been on the job long enough to know how to tie his bootlaces,' the sergeant said. 'Sort it. Stop anyone using the front door, if you can.'

Tunstall solved the problem by getting Allen to knock on doors and ask people to use the fire escape to come and go from the premises. The ground-floor flats had no option but to come out through the front of the house.

'Did you tell them to stay indoors unless it's urgent?' Tunstall asked when Allen returned.

Allen grinned. 'Don't worry about that, mate,' he said. 'Most of them girls work nights, if you know what I mean.'

'Oh,' Tunstall said. The wheels and cogs ground a bit, then he repeated, 'Oh!', this time with more comprehension. 'If they're working girls, we'd better get someone round the back, taking names in case they slope off.'

'Well don't look at me,' Allen said, ready to fight for the right to stay out front.

Two squad cars pulled up, one either end of the road and Tunstall and Allen smirked at each other. 'Sorted,' they said in unison.

Within ten minutes, the road was cordoned off and an officer posted at the foot of the fire escape.

* * *

The police surgeon was allowed through on foot. He climbed into his white oversuit next to one of the police cars. He clipped his ID tag to his suit and slipped on his overshoes before walking on. As he passed the front of the squad car, he noticed a woman sitting in the back seat. A small woman in her mid-thirties; her hair was shoulder-length, softly layered, strawberry-blonde, and she wore a red tunic top over slim-fitting trousers.

'Grace?'

The car door was open, so she must have heard, but she didn't respond at first.

'Grace, are you—?' He looked at the silent bin lorry and the binmen standing in a queasy cluster near the cab. 'Was it you who found her?'

Grace slowly lifted her gaze to him. Her face was pale and her hair tousled, as if she had been compulsively running her fingers through it.

'She's just a child,' Grace said, the statement almost a question. Her blue eyes were troubled, uncomprehending. 'She can't be more than seventeen years old.'

'Did you touch the body?'

Grace shook her head, and immediately swallowed, as if the movement had made her nauseous.

The police surgeon pulled on a pair of gloves and slipped a mask over his mouth and nose before pulling up the hood of his suit. There seemed little point, given the potential for cross-contamination on this one, but it was procedure, and he liked procedure: it gave order to a chaotic world.

He walked to the bin lorry, nodding to one of the officers on duty. It didn't take long. He returned as a large van rumbled up the street, nudging its way through the crowd that had gathered at the tape.

'The CSIs will take it from here,' he said.

CHAPTER THREE

The Toxteth CID office was busy. An armed robbery, a break-in at a primary school, a stolen car found burned out in Granby Street, and a number of thefts of student mobile phones.

'If they didn't carry the damn things like fashion accessories, they wouldn't get them stolen,' Sergeant Foster grumbled. 'Haven't they had the "Street Safe" talk, yet?'

Lee Foster shared office space with Inspector Jeff Rickman, behind a glass and hardboard partition at the far end of the room.

'I'd've thought chatting up all those wide-eyed Freshers would appeal to you,' Rickman said, glancing up from a budget report he had been struggling with for days. Foster was lean and tanned after a holiday white-water rafting in the Canadian Rockies, his cobalt-blue eyes startling against the tan. Rickman wondered in passing how many conquests he had made on the trip and whether the lack of a hairdryer and freeze gel had cramped his style.

Foster smiled. 'I prefer a woman with a bit of experience.'

'You're joking, aren't you? Any woman with experience would know to steer clear,' Rickman said.

Foster took the jibe in good part. 'It's my personal tragedy — doomed to be misunderstood.'

'Your personal tragedy,' Rickman said, 'is your lack of subtlety.'

Foster nodded, thoughtfully. Taking a slip of paper from his pocket, he unfolded it and held it up between his index and median fingers. 'You're probably right.'

'What's that?'

Foster smiled. There was something voracious in that smile which made Rickman say, 'Not the phlebotomist?'

'Home phone number. Not every girl goes for the strong silent type, you know, Jeff.'

Rickman couldn't help but smile. 'Lucky for you they don't, eh, Lee? Anyway, you know what they say.'

'About what?'

'Still waters,' Rickman said, tapping the side of his nose. 'They run deep.'

Foster laughed. 'More like *muddy* waters in your case.'

The phone rang and Rickman picked up.

'Don't know why we can't just give them a crime number for the insurance and file this pile of junk in the bin,' Foster muttered, thumbing through the report slips. 'It's not like we're gonna find anything as portable as a mobile. And even if we did, how're you gonna identify them? 'Cos it's not like—'

Rickman cupped his hand over the mouthpiece. 'Shut up, will you?'

Foster flicked through the crime reports in silence, listening with half an ear to Rickman's telephone conversation and feeling a mounting excitement.

'Leave that,' Rickman said as he hung up.

Foster dropped the crime reports without a second thought. 'Where are we off to, Boss?' This was business, and a degree of formality was called for.

'Looks like we've got a murder,' Rickman said.

'Ooh, goody. A murder scene.' Foster snagged his sunglasses from where he had hooked them over the handle of his coffee mug. An outline sketch of an island and the logo: 'A gift from Plum Island Animal Disease Centre' ensured that Foster's mug rarely went astray.

Rickman gave the merest shake of his head.

Foster's shoulders drooped. 'No murder scene?'

'We'd only be in the way,' Rickman said, as if talking to a disappointed adolescent. 'As soon as the scene's been processed we'll move in with a team.'

'All the interesting stuff will be gone by then,' Foster said, with a sigh. But Rickman never budged when it came to maintaining the forensic integrity of a scene. He shrugged. 'So, like I said: where are we off to?'

'Management meeting.'

It was enough to make Foster feel wistful about the pink flimsies stacked on his desk, each one a reported theft of a mobile phone.

They went through to the conference room, which was grander in name than in reality. It was an oblong space with grey carpet and plasterboard walls. The walls were painted white, there was a whiteboard and a felt-covered notice board side by side on the back wall. The windows were small and ineffective, so fluorescent strip-lights hummed constantly, giving the room a garish cast and the men assembled an unhealthy grey colour.

Detective Chief Inspector Hinchcliffe had come from HQ for the meeting; he was a tall, rather ascetic-looking man with grey hair and deep frown-lines between his eyebrows. Rickman knew him by reputation only. Hinchcliffe introduced himself and nodded to Foster.

'I think you know Tony Mayle,' Hinchcliffe said.

Mayle was the crime scene coordinator. Just coming up to his mid-forties, he was an ex-cop: six years in uniform, ten as a Detective Sergeant in CID. He had trained as a SOCO and, as the Scientific Support Unit became increasingly civilian-staffed, he took his police pension and studied for a degree in forensic science before returning as a crime scene manager. He had the steady gaze and unflappable composure of an experienced officer. These things, combined with his scientific detachment and observational skills, made him the best CSI Rickman knew.

The introductions made, they sat around the conference table while Mayle ran through the details.

'A young white female,' he said. 'The body was hidden in a wheelie-bin in one of the avenues off Ullet Road; it was discovered when the bins were emptied this morning. There was massive haemorrhaging from the groin area at the top of the left leg. Looks like she bled out inside the bin.'

A silence, each man thinking how much blood that would involve.

'The Home Office pathologist might be able to get here to do the post-mortem this afternoon, if he can reschedule his appointments.'

'Any signs of restraint?' Rickman asked.

'Nothing obvious, but they might have been removed after she died.'

'Or she was drugged,' Hinchcliffe suggested.

'Photos?' Rickman asked.

'I'll get copies to you as soon as the Imaging Department has processed them,' Mayle said. 'Should be within the hour. Technical Support say the video copies will be ready by four p.m.'

'How many crime scenes?' Rickman asked.

'The bin lorry — we're bringing that in for a thorough going-over. The bin, obviously. It looks likely she lived in the house the bin was collected from, so we're treating that as a scene as well.'

The risk of cross-contamination meant that each scene would need a different set of CSIs. This was already looking costly.

As Rickman made notes, Hinchcliffe said, 'One of the girls reported that the occupant of the flat next door hasn't returned home since last night.'

'Why not get her to have a look at the body?' Foster asked.

'Contamination,' Mayle said. 'I don't want anyone near the victim till we've got all the DNA swabs we're likely to need.'

'Give Foster a call when you're done,' Hinchcliffe told him. 'He can bring the neighbour in to identify the body.'

'Do we have a name?' Rickman asked.

Hinchcliffe shook his head. 'The other girls say they knew her only by sight.'

'There are a lot of sex workers in the house,' Mayle added. 'We do have other evidence,' he went on. 'Blood spatter in the hallway. Could be old, though. And blood on clothing we found inside her flat.'

'Worth getting a forensic scientist in to look at the blood spatter?' Rickman asked.

'Not until we know if it's hers. It could be from a Saturday night brawl, for all we know.'

'And the blood on the clothing — what's the turna-round on DNA, now?' It was changing all the time.

'For a major crime — seven days,' Mayle said. 'But the lab could do it in twenty-four hours, if you pay premium rate.'

'Jeff?' Hinchcliffe prompted.

'It's not my call, sir,' Rickman said, 'But I'd say let's see what we've got before we start spending big.' He worked through the facts so far in his mind. 'If we can get a visual identification, it'll save time. I suggest we interview the witnesses and everyone who lives in the house — see where that takes us.'

Hinchcliffe nodded approval. 'In fact, it *is* your call — at least for the moment. I'm going to be tied up for a few days — queries about disclosure on the Mathew Street shooting.' A turf war had blown up six months earlier between rival drugs gangs supplying the city-centre clubs; it culminated in the shooting of one of the gang leaders in a city-centre pub.

'You're appointing me Senior Investigating Officer?' Resources had been stretched since the shooting, with a number of subsidiary investigations resulting from Hinchcliffe's enquiries, but Rickman hadn't been expecting this.

'You passed your Chief Inspector board exams a couple of months ago, didn't you?' Hinchcliffe asked.

'Yes, sir.' Rickman glanced at Foster, who raised his eyebrows.

'Okay. You'll be Acting DCI. You will report directly to me, and when I'm not available, to the Detective Superintendent. This is temporary,' Hinchcliffe warned, 'only until I've cleared things up with the CPS on this other thing.'

'Fine by me,' Rickman said, mentally rubbing his hands, ready for the challenge. 'When can you let us have access to the house?' he asked Mayle.

'We'll be out of your way within the hour.'

'Named witnesses?'

'So far, you're looking at the binmen and driver, and a woman who got stuck behind the lorry. Should be a good witness — she's a doctor.'

Rickman felt a spasm of alarm. 'A doctor? D'you have a name?'

'It'll be in the scene log,' Mayle said.

'Someone you know?' Hinchcliffe asked.

Rickman didn't answer immediately. He knew Grace sometimes cut through the avenues to get to work, but he did not want to mess up this opportunity. He might have passed his DCI board, but he was still a DI — and DIs were not routinely put in charge of major investigations. But if Hinchcliffe thought his objectivity was in any way compromised, he would pull him off the case. 'Shouldn't think so, sir,' he said.

Hinchcliffe eyed him suspiciously for a moment, then said, 'In that case, you'd better get down to Edge Hill Station — I've arranged for a Major Incident Room to be set up there for you.'

In the event, they delayed the move for more than an hour: Rickman had to reassign some of his more pressing tasks to junior officers and cancel a couple of meetings. More urgently, he had to get in touch with Grace, and he could do that with greater privacy in his own office.

* * *

While Foster put together an enquiry team, Rickman called the hospital.

'Anything?' Foster asked, between calls.

'She's left the hospital. She works in a clinic, afternoons,' Rickman explained. Grace worked part-time as an A&E consultant and part-time in a GP practice, heading the refugee support team. 'Her mobile is switched off and the clinic phone is permanently engaged.'

'She's busy — probably the best thing for her.'

'You're probably right . . .'

Foster sighed. 'You'd best get down there.'

Rickman hesitated. Evading DCI Hinchcliffe's question was bad enough, but it was really pushing his luck going AWOL at the start of a major investigation. He should be organising the team, ordering in equipment, developing an investigative strategy, not skiving off to check on his girlfriend.

'You'll be fit for nothing while you're worrying over Grace,' Foster insisted. 'I can get you on your mobile. If the boss asks, you're on your way over to the scene.' He gave one of his wolfish smiles. 'I'll meet you there if you like.' It seemed that Foster was determined to get his look at it.

'Thanks, Lee,' Rickman said, grabbing his jacket from his chair.

'You all right, mate?' Foster asked. 'Only it's hard to tell.' It was one a constant source of mutual baiting: Foster's transparency versus Rickman's impenetrability.

'She shouldn't have to deal with this crap,' Rickman said at last.

'None of us should, mate,' Foster said.

* * *

The GP practice was a low-rise, purpose-built building just off Princes Road. A pitched roof and bright red window frames made it look more like a playschool than a municipal building, while cotoneaster and pyracantha tumbling over the one-foot-high brick wall at the entrance softened the hard architectural edges. The bushes were full of orange and red berries — together with an assortment of sweet wrappers and the odd supermarket carrier bag. The tarmac had been dug up in places to accommodate steel bollards after a ram-raid attack a year previously, and the windows were protected by matching red shutters that were rolled down each evening.

Inspector Rickman presented his ID at reception — an octagonal cubicle housing the switchboard and records, which dominated the centre of the building. The woman directed him to the left, past a row of people of various nationalities, all waiting to see Dr Chandler.

He loitered until the door opened and stepped up as Grace came to call her next patient.

Her expression of professional welcome was soured somewhat when she saw him. 'I'm in *clinic*, Jeff,' she said, quietly.

'So I see.' She looked pale, her skin milk-white against the coppery blonde of her hair, and her blue eyes shone with an almost preternatural light. Rickman recognised it as the look of someone who has been too close to death. For a moment he thought she would send him away. Then she stepped aside and ushered him into her surgery.

The room bore unmistakable signs of Grace's humanising influence: a Jack and the Beanstalk wall chart for measuring children's heights; a painting Rickman recognised as one of Grace's own watercolours. Behind her desk, a corkboard was layered with hundreds of photographs: children, adults, family groups — birthdays, christenings, picnics.

In a chair to the side of Grace's desk, a slim, sallow-skinned woman studied him. She had a long face with high cheekbones and dark, wary eyes. Her dark, almost black, hair was pulled back from her face and tied in a simple ponytail.

'I'm sorry,' he said. 'I didn't know you had a patient with you.'

'This is Natalja Sremać,' Grace said. 'My interpreter.'

18

Rickman offered his hand.

Natalja stood in one smooth movement. She was tall — five foot ten, maybe, and long-limbed. She barely touched his hand; hers was clammy.

'Grace has spoken a lot about you,' he said.

'You will want privacy.' Her voice was deep, heavily accented — middle European.

Grace smiled at her. 'He's just fussing,' she said.

Natalja returned the smile. She had a wide, full-lipped mouth, but the smile seemed edgy. It faltered and failed, and she became flustered. 'I need cigarette,' she said. 'I'll be outside.'

She closed the door softly behind her and Grace folded her arms. 'You scared her off.'

'What did I say?' He spread his hands in a gesture of injured innocence.

'You didn't have to *say* anything,' Grace said.

'She's your friend. You've known her, what? Six — seven years?'

'Seven.'

'Yet I've never met her.'

'She's shy.'

'And I'm curious.'

'You were sizing her up.'

Rickman puffed air between his lips. 'What can I tell you? I'm a cop.'

'First. And last.'

He saw a twinkle of humour in her eyes and took it as a sign that he it was safe to return to the reason for his visit. 'I was worried about you.'

Grace rallied with a surprise attack. 'You come here, disrupting my clinic, frightening my translator, looking like a cop—'

'Yeah? What does a cop look like?'

The ghost of a smile played on her lips. 'You,' she said.

'I thought you said I look like a boxer,' Rickman shot back.

'*Failed* boxer.' She was smiling for real, now. 'Too many wounds to have been a successful scrapper.' She explored the scar on his chin and the white line bisecting his eyebrow with her fingertips.

He caught her hand and looked into her face. 'Are you all right?'

'I'm fine,' she said, firmly, but she wouldn't look at him.

He searched her face and she sighed. 'I've seen bodies before, Jeff. I've operated on them. Cut them open. I've even dissected them, when I was a student.'

'You've never discovered one before though, have you?' he said.

He saw a shimmer of tears in her eyes. She looked so pale, and the frown-line between her eyebrows seemed more pronounced than usual. She cleared her throat and said again, 'I'm fine.'

'Well, you should know—' He took a breath. 'I'm heading the investigation.' Rickman held her hand a while longer.

She nodded, her frown deepening, as if she was having trouble taking it in. At length, she said, 'You're heading the investigation,' as if trying to make the words sink in. Then she seemed to shake herself, becoming suddenly brisk and businesslike. 'That being the case, we can talk about this later.'

He looked at her hand in his, so small, so capable. 'I should've listened to Lee Foster,' he said. 'He told me you'd be okay.'

'He's a wise and wonderful detective sergeant,' she said, smiling.

'Now I *know* you're not being serious.' Rickman bent to kiss her. Her lips felt cold.

* * *

'He's gone.'

Natalja was sitting on the low wall that bordered the car park at the back of the clinic. The air was still and heavy, after the chilly morning, and hazy sunshine glinted from the car roofs.

'Excuse me?'

Natalja looked hunched and anxious, her face gaunt and sallow. Grace felt ashamed for having made light of her fear of the police, and she used a diversionary tactic. 'Let me have one of those,' she said.

'You want a cigarette?' Natalja said. 'I didn't know you smoked.'

Grace sat next to her on the wall. 'You didn't know me in my dissolute youth. Fifteen years on and I still get the craving.'

Natalja handed Grace the pack, together with her lighter, and watched with curiosity as Grace lit up.

'Are you all right?' she asked.

Grace frowned. 'Jeff just asked that.'

Natalja waited for an answer. Receiving none, she prompted, 'Well?'

'I'm not sure,' Grace replied. It was easier to be honest with Natalja than with Jeff. 'I feel numb, mostly.' She glanced up into Natalja's concerned face, aware that she would have seen far worse in Croatia. 'It was the . . .' What was the word? 'The *disrespect* that got to me. How could they treat another human being with so little respect?'

'By not seeing her as a human being.' All the light went out of Natlaja's eyes and she looked away, grinding her cigarette under her heel as she stood. 'Mrs Duboisson next,' she said.

Grace raised her face to the warm autumnal sun. A sparrow cheeped monotonously in the sycamore beyond the car park. 'Mrs Duboisson,' she repeated, and sighed. Seven years they had known each other — worked together, shopped and lunched, and had girly nights out together, and yet Natalja still backed away from talking about her past. Grace had seen it before in trauma victims: a misplaced shame for the degradation they had suffered. Survivor guilt. She felt it a personal failure that she had never been able to convince Natalja that she was not to blame.

21

CHAPTER FOUR

Sergeant Foster pulled up several doors down from the house. A section of the street was still taped off and finding a space was even more of a pain than usual. Tony Mayle had called him from the SSU: they had all the samples they needed; the girl's body was available for identification.

He flashed his warrant card and was waved through the crime scene tapes. Outside the house, a big ruddy-faced constable stood duty. Foster put his hands on his hips and squinted up at the building. The upper windows lacked curtains or blinds. Holes were patched with cardboard and Sellotape, and a grimy piece of sheeting had been stretched across one of the first-floor windows and nailed in place. It was impossible to tell the original colour of the paintwork, since most of it had flaked off. The front step was lumpy and cracked with not one of the original red tiles intact. The garden consisted of a single overgrown buddleia that had forced its way through the badly laid concrete. A few late butterflies probed the flowers, searching for nectar.

'Nice, in't it?' Tunstall said.

Widnes accent, Foster thought. *Woolly back.*

'Prime development site this, mate,' Foster said.

Tunstall glanced over his shoulder, a doubtful look on his face. 'You reckon?'

'If I had the money, I'd put in a bid meself.' He gave the massive buddleia and the rusting motorbike leaking oil under the front window a critical glance. ''Course you'd have to fumigate before you even started demolition.'

'Nah,' Tunstall said. 'Vermin'd want summat cleaner.'

Inside, the house smelled of damp, more than anything: damp plaster and rotting wood. The hall was dark and he had to tread carefully to avoid tripping over tears and holes worn in the lino. He found the light switch — a crude timer device — and walked up to the first floor. The light clicked off as he reached the top step and he had to press the timer again.

Police tape was tacked across the door to the left of the landing. Foster knocked at the door next to it and waited. He heard muffled footsteps, felt them vibrate along the fragile joists.

'Yeah?' A high-pitched voice, a little coarsened by cigarette smoke and too many nights spent working outdoors.

'Police, Miss Carr.'

A pause. Then, 'So?'

Great — a cooperative type. 'Can you open up? I'd like a word.'

The chain went on and then the door opened a few inches, exposing an eye and a nose. The eye was grey-blue and faded, the mouth a thin slash of pink. Foster showed his warrant card and introduced himself.

'Yeah?' she said again.

'Can I come in?' he said. 'Only I feel a bit of a dickhead talking through your crack.'

The eye darkened. 'That's all I need, a smart-arsed bloody copper.'

'Either we talk now, or I come back during office hours and we talk down the station,' he said, adding, 'That's *your* office hours, not mine.'

23

She muttered something under her breath, then the door closed briefly, and he heard the chain rattle off the latch. The nose and mouth were attached to a tired face, almost as washed-out as the denim blue of her eyes. Her skin was lined from too much smoking, too much hardship, but she couldn't have been more than thirty. She was wearing a pink fluffy towelling robe and her hair, just shampooed, hung in dark dripping curls.

The door opened close to the edge of one wall. A queen-size bed took up most of the floor space. A sink and a two-ring stove occupied the far corner, to the right of the window.

'You are Trina Carr?'

She answered with a slight lift of the head. 'You can sit over there.' She pointed to a bright pink inflatable armchair by the window. There was a lot of pink in the room: pink paintwork, pink carpet — freshly hoovered — clean pink sheets on the bed. Even the fairy-lights wrapped around the headboard were pink.

The thought of wedging himself into a bubble of squeaking, farting plastic did not appeal, and Foster declined. 'Why don't I . . .' He walked to the far side of the bed and carefully moved a menagerie of stuffed toys from her bedside chair.

She watched him sit as if convinced that the chair would give way under his weight.

'Nice place,' he said. 'Very . . . pink.'

'What's wrong with pink?' she demanded.

'Nothing,' Foster said. 'It's a feminine colour, isn't it?'

This seemed to mollify her, and she sat on the bed, leaning a little towards him, revealing more of her cleavage than was necessary. '*I* like it,' she said.

Foster decided to capitalise on his advantage and went for flattery. 'You keep a clean house.'

Trina sat up, offended, immediately on the attack. 'What did you expect? A filthy doss with slime on the sheets and used johnnies in the ashtrays?'

Foster held up his hands, leaning back a little in his chair, placatory, defensive. 'All I'm saying is it can't be easy in this place.'

She remained bolt upright, but a wary acceptance showed in her face.

'All I'm saying . . .' he said again, his tone soothing.

'Yeah, well, try telling that to the landlord.'

'You want to talk to the housing associations,' he suggested. 'They've got some nice properties in the city centre.'

She snorted. 'Had a housing association flat once. They don't take too kindly to working girls.'

'You could always change jobs.'

'Like I've got a choice.'

'There's always a choice,' Foster said. He saw she was going all huffy on him again, so he pushed on with his next question. 'Do a lot of the girls bring their tricks here?'

'You'd have to ask them,' she said.

Foster resisted the temptation to roll his eyes and said, 'What about you?'

She shrugged. 'I bring a few home — if they're clean and they're paying top whack.'

'Thin walls,' Foster said. 'You must hear them coming and going — 'scuse the pun.'

'It's not a brothel, if that's what you're saying.' He thought he had offended her again, but she went on, 'I've worked in a brothel. It takes organisation: staff for the phone, reception, a rota for the girls, commission for the owner. Old Preston, the landlord, couldn't organise a cock-up in a — well, in a brothel — 'scuse the pun.'

Foster smiled. He liked her style, but if she was trying to steer him off the topic, to bamboozle him with her charming chatter on the logistical problems of running a knocking shop, she was sweet-talking the wrong guy.

'What time did you get home?' he asked.

'When?'

'Last night.'

She shrugged. 'Depends. I was in and out all night.'

Foster refrained from jokes involving actresses and bishops — just. 'With some of your clean punters?'

She frowned, not understanding.

'You brought them back here.'

'Oh,' she said. 'Yeah.'

'Did you hear anything?'

She looked uncomfortable. 'Like what?'

'Oh, I don't know,' Foster said, finally losing patience. 'What sort of sounds d'you think a girl makes when she's being bled to death?'

Trina flinched. She got up from the bed and went to the mantelshelf for her cigarettes and lighter. She didn't light up immediately, but fiddled with the packet, opening and closing it.

'She was new.'

'Yeah?'

'When you're new, sometimes . . .'

'Sometimes?' he encouraged.

She took a breath that sounded almost like a sob. 'I might've heard her crying.' She looked at him as though pleading for understanding.

'When?'

'Just after half-two, when I come home for a break.'

'Alone?'

She stared at him. 'Alone, all right? Look — I was sick of standing out there, freezing me tits off, so I come home for a warm and a cup of coffee.'

'I'm not your pimp, girl,' Foster said. 'I'm not accusing you of slacking — I just need to know if we've got any other witnesses to interview.'

'No punters,' she said firmly. 'I was on me own.'

'What about your neighbour? Was anyone with her?'

'How would I know?'

He rapped hard on the wall behind her bed. 'This piece of crap must provide about as much noise insulation as a shower curtain.' He repeated the question, separating each word: 'Did you hear anyone with her?'

Trina looked down at the clean pink carpet. 'I might've heard a man's voice — but he was just talking. He wasn't — it didn't sound like — like he was hurting her.'

'Okay. So what did you do?'

Trina took out a cigarette and lit it. 'She was always crying. It's something you go through.' She avoided his gaze. 'After a bit it's not so bad.'

'What,' Foster said again, 'did you do?'

She turned to the window and opened it, blowing cigarette smoke into the icy air. 'I put on a CD, racked up the sound.'

Foster stared at her back. After a few seconds she turned on him, eyes blazing. 'Don't you judge me!' she shouted. A tear quivered on her lower lid. 'If I'd've known what was — that she was—' The tear spilt onto her cheek. She wiped it away with a shaking hand.

'You thought this man was a punter,' Foster said.

'What was I supposed to think?'

'And she brought men back?'

'She was only here a few days.'

'And you didn't know her name?'

'I told you, didn't I? *God*!' She threw her cigarette out of the window and fetched a tissue from the bedside table.

'Where was she from?'

She wiped her nose. 'How would I know? I'm not her mother, am I?'

'Right now, Trina, you're the closest to next of kin she's got,' Foster said, lifting his eyebrows and waiting for her to get the point.

When finally she did, all the aggressive tension left her and her shoulders slumped. 'Ah, come on, lad — I've given the plods a description already.'

Foster wrinkled his nose. 'Sorry, love. Not enough,' he said. 'We need a positive ID.'

'No,' Her voice took on a high-pitched, panicky tone. 'You can't make me. I don't even know her.'

'But you know what she looks like. You can tell us if it is the girl from next door.'

'I'm working tonight . . .' she said, in a last desperate attempt to avoid the trip to the mortuary.

'Not a problem,' Foster said. 'I'll be finished here in about an hour. I'll take you — drop you off wherever you're working after. How's that?'

She stared resentfully at him. 'Got a choice, have I?'

He smiled back. 'None whatsoever.'

CHAPTER FIVE

The Incident Room at Edge Hill Police Station was already up and running by the time Rickman arrived. He drove past the two-storey building of muddy brick. The shops opposite were mostly abandoned. In the middle of the row, the fading yellow frontage of Wavertree Bikes, on the adjacent corner, white lettering against a black background, the proud logo of another failed optimist: 'Specialists in furniture and luxury interiors'. The entire row was shuttered and the upper windows bricked up.

The car park was at the back. A school minibus huddled among the police vehicles for safety. Rickman unscrewed the radio aerial and flung it into the boot of his car — a high wall and security cameras kept the cars relatively safe from theft and vandalism, but in an area like this, you didn't take chances. He walked around to the front of the building. The planting areas, marked out by low brick walls, had been filled with tarmac, and now sprouted weeds. He showed his warrant card and was buzzed through to the offices to the left of reception.

A few extra desks had been moved in to the Incident Room and every inch of space was filled with computer equipment and filing cabinets and bodies. He paused for a moment, enjoying the quiet hum of a Major Incident Room warming up for the start of an enquiry.

A tall blonde brushed past him and began a discussion with another female officer about the results of the house-to-house. Several people were engaged in telephone conversations, asking questions, making notes. A man Rickman vaguely recognised as a DC from the south of the city was scrolling down a screen listing missing persons reports. His phone rang and he picked up the receiver, talking as he continued his computer search.

Rickman saw Foster at the far side of the room, writing up details of the dead woman on the whiteboard, below a crime scene photograph he'd tacked up with Blu-tack. He wound his way through the chicane of tables and chairs to where Foster was standing. At six-foot-four Rickman was an imposing figure and it took only a few moments for a hush to fall, as fingers ceased tapping at keyboards and phone conversations were ended.

Rickman read eagerness and excitement on some of the faces, raw ambition on others. When he had everybody's attention, he began.

'You've all had a preliminary briefing: female victim, probably teenage. No name as yet—' He glanced at Foster for confirmation, who gave a slight shake of his head.

'The Forensic Science Service has collected evidence from the scene,' he said, 'but it could be some time before the results come in, so we need to prioritise. Number one priority is witnesses. This is a transient population — if we don't catch them fast, we'll lose them.

'Next, the victim: her name, her friends — if she had any — contacts, habits, and most particularly, her movements in the hours before she was murdered.'

'There's only one thing that lot'll open their gobs for, and they expect payment for it,' Foster said.

Rickman was used to Foster's less than tactful approach. He raised an eyebrow at him and said, 'Go easy — but be persistent. One girl has been killed, others might be at risk; see if that gets through to them. We need an ID on the girl.'

He located the officer he had seen scrolling down the list of missing persons and asked him for an update.

'Nothing so far, Boss,' he said. 'But I've only had time to go back a couple of weeks. How far d'you want me to go?'

Rickman thought about this one. The victim had no friends at the house — at least no one who would admit to being her friend. This was unusual: the girls usually looked out for each other.

'Has anyone spoken to the landlord?'

The tall blonde Rickman had noticed earlier spoke up. 'Naomi Hart, sir. The landlord's name is Preston.' She wore her hair in a twist, accentuating the length and curve of her neck. Rickman noticed the men on the team noticing her.

'It's like you said,' Hart went on. 'It's a transient population. The girl on the rent-book has vanished. He says it's not uncommon for tenants to hand over the rent-book to a friend — saves the hassle of finding a place. He doesn't care so long as they pay on time.'

'Did she?' Rickman asked.

'He didn't get the chance to find out. She hadn't been in a full week.'

'Her neighbour confirms that,' Foster chipped in.

'Go back to the landlord,' Rickman told DC Hart. 'Remind him of his legal responsibilities. See if you can find the previous tenant — maybe she knew the victim.'

Rickman turned back to the officer searching the missing persons database. 'Try the last three months on MisPer — you'll just have to go on the physical description and approximate age. We need an identification fast.'

'If she *is* a Tom, chances are she'll be on the DNA database,' Foster said.

Rickman thought about it. 'I'll ask for premium service on the victim's DNA profile and the blood found on clothing at her flat. If we get lucky, the killer might just have left blood at the scene.'

There were nods of approval, newbies took assiduous notes, summarising the key points of the briefing, which reminded Rickman. 'Pocket notebooks are all very well in the field, but any notes are part of the evidence; you'll want to keep a fairly detailed record of your enquiries updated on a day-to-day basis,' he advised. 'Since your scratchings could be used as an exhibit by learned counsel, it might be best not to use your notebook for your weekly shopping list . . .' He watched, amused, as the younger officers dutifully made note of the need for a notebook.

'Tonight, I want a team of officers interviewing girls in Hope Street, Mount Street, Falkner Square — any of the likely spots: if she was on the game, someone must know her. Was she new on the street? Was she freelance? If not, who was her pimp? He could be our main suspect.'

'If she's new,' Foster said, 'could be *nobody* knows her.'

'Which is why we keep on checking with missing persons. We might have a name by tomorrow, if the DNA results score a hit, but we need as much background on the victim as we can gather. If you want to find your killer, know your victim.'

Some of the older hands nodded approbation at the wisdom of this police adage.

'Who's on house-to-house?'

The DC in charge stood up. 'We started with the house itself,' he said. 'Most of the girls were working last night, didn't get back till the early hours.'

'I want exact times — when they left, when they returned to the house — that way we can narrow down the time of death a bit. What about the neighbour?' he asked.

'She heard crying in the night,' Foster answered. 'Half-two in the morning. She didn't think to report it, of course.'

'What did she do?'

'Turned up the stereo, waited till it was quiet, then went back out to work.'

A few people exchanged glances, shaking their heads in disbelief.

'Did she notice anything unusual? Visitors — strange cars in the road?' Rickman asked.

'There's strange cars outside that house day and night, Boss,' Foster said. 'But she did say it was odd the bins were already out when she got back around half-five this morning. Apparently, she usually has to do it.'

'So the killer put the bins out. Any fingerprints?'

'Plenty,' Foster said. 'Nothing useful, like. Mostly the girls'. A couple from the binmen — who, incidentally, did a pretty good impression of the three wise monkeys.'

Rickman pounced on this. 'Are they hiding something?'

Foster shrugged. 'Nah, just bloody useless.'

'All right.' Rickman thought he had a fairly good overall picture of the investigation as it stood. Time to impart some information of his own. 'Preliminary findings on the PM are inconclusive.' There were one or two gasps of surprise. They all knew how the girl had been found, and Tunstall had described in stomach-churning detail the mass of partly congealed blood that had slid from the bin into the lorry.

Tunstall had been seconded to the team. He put his hand up, like a schoolboy. 'I don't want to sound silly, sir, but you don't need a doctor to tell you she bled to death. That bin lorry were like something out of *Carrie*.'

A few people chuckled, but Rickman silenced them with a frown. 'There are newly trained officers on this team, looking to make their mark,' he said, 'and experienced officers who no doubt think they've seen it all before.' He swept the room, taking in each and every one of them. 'I want this clear from the outset: we play this by the book. We work on facts — not assumptions, or gut feelings or appearances.'

'Sir,' Tunstall said, shrinking in his chair.

'The pathologist isn't happy to pronounce on cause of death until he's had the toxicology reports,' Rickman said. 'Drugs may have been a factor. Fortunately,' he added, 'Tunstall and Allen kept the area clean, so the CSIs got the best shot they could at profiling a naturally messy scene.' He wanted to make the point, not to squash the constable on his first outing to a Major Incident Room.

An officer in uniform from the communications room came to the door and mimed 'Phone.'

Rickman spoke over the heads of the gathering. 'Tell them I'll call back.'

The constable grasped the back of his neck 'It's the hospital, Boss. They say it's urgent.'

Grace. He experienced a sudden falling sensation.

People swivelled in their chairs. Rickman resisted an impulse to rush for the door and instead addressed the group, bringing the focus back to the purpose of their meeting. 'Any questions or comments should be directed to Sergeant Foster,' he said. 'Remember, everyone has something to contribute to this enquiry. And the only stupid question is the one you don't ask.'

He made his way outside.

'Sorry, sir,' the constable said, 'I thought you'd want to take it.'

'You did the right thing,' Rickman said, feeling the muscles tighten in his jaw and neck. 'Can you put them through to my office?' He didn't want anyone listening in. Grace had seemed all right when he saw her, but what if she had gone into shock? Many of these officers didn't know him: they needed to think that their boss was cool-headed, that he had his mind firmly fixed on the investigation. He could trust Foster to handle the Q&A like the showman he was, all Rickman had to do was keep up the illusion of serenity.

He strode to the office that had been set aside for him and waited for the phone to ring, snatching it up immediately.

'Inspector Rickman?' The accent was foreign, possibly Asian.

'What's the problem?'

'You *are* Jeffrey Rickman?'

His full name. *Jesus,* this was the how cops spoke when they went to make an arrest. Or to break bad news.

'I am Detective Inspector Jeff Rickman,' he said, his voice taut with anxiety. 'Now what do you want?' *She was so pale when I left her,* he thought, and remembering their last kiss, *her lips were so cold.*

'It's your brother, Inspector Rickman.'

For a moment, the statement made no sense whatever. *Brother?* He stared at the receiver. Then, like a digital signal coming up to strength, the blocks of colour clicking into place, he saw the picture, clear and uncompromising.

'Inspector?'

Rickman realised that an answer was required and, putting the receiver back to his ear, he said, 'Who is this?'

'My name is Doctor Pratesh,' the voice said. 'Your brother was brought into the Royal University Hospital.'

'My brother . . .' It didn't seem any more real even when he said it aloud.

'Mr Simon Rickman?'

'That's his name all right.'

'He was admitted—'

'Why have you contacted me?' Rickman interrupted. Anxiety had given way to suspicion and suspicion to irritation.

'Why?' Pratesh repeated, shocked. 'Because you are his brother.'

'Is that what he said? That you should contact me because I'm his brother?'

'That's more or less it, yes,' Pratesh said. His bewilderment was evident.

'Sorry, Doctor Pratesh. That cuts no ice.' He began to hang up, but the doctor's voice, raised in agitation, made him reconsider.

'Sir,' he said, 'you haven't asked what is wrong with Simon.'

First-name terms, Rickman noted. It had to be serious if they felt free to call you by your first name. Either you were terminally ill or too out of it to protest at the informality.

'I haven't asked, Doctor Pratesh, because I don't want to know.' Rickman replaced the receiver.

CHAPTER SIX

Grace dumped her briefcase, kicked off her shoes and dropped her keys in the bowl on the hallstand. The scent of ginger and frying vegetables wafted from the kitchen. She had inherited this house from her parents and sometimes, especially at this time of year, when the evenings were chilly and she stepped from the paved driveway into warmth and cooking smells, she felt the anticipatory excitement of a child returning from school. Eidetic recall: emotions and pictures flooded back to her; good memories, untainted by the equivocation that came with adulthood and a more realistic view of the world.

'Jeff?'

She padded to the kitchen. It still made her heart leap when she saw him, even after three years of seeing him almost every day. She only had to catch a glimpse of that slightly marred Roman profile, or to hear him humming to himself while he listened to the radio, and she felt a shiver of delight. Watching him cook was always a special pleasure. She'd had the cooker hood installed, along with the new kitchen, a year before they met; it was positioned for someone of average height, so Jeff had to stoop slightly to see what he was doing.

Normally, he was reserved, even undemonstrative, but when he was cooking, he chopped and fried and seasoned as if it was an expressive art, banging about the place with the panache of a professional. It brought out the performer in him like nothing else did, and she loved him for it.

His dark-chestnut hair was slightly tousled as if he had dragged the T-shirt he wore over his head in a hurry, and his upper arms flexed as he tossed the food in a sauté pan. He seemed to sense her watching him and turned, still shaking and tossing the food in the pan.

'You missed your true profession,' Grace said.

He smiled. She couldn't gauge it: bitter, maybe? Maybe even a little angry? The warm hazel of his eyes sparked liked charged amber at such times; she looked into his eyes and thought she caught a flash of electrical energy.

Jeff often cooked when he was angry. All that sound and fury, he said, got it out of his system. He turned back to the hob and she thought, *Or worried*. Sometimes he cooked when he was worried, too.

'Good day?' he asked.

'Oh, you know. Same old. Except I saw a dead girl tipped into a bin lorry on the way to work.'

'That'd take the shine off.'

He knew better than to smother her with concern; particularly, she realised with a pang of guilt, after her cool reception at the clinic.

'You're early,' Grace said.

He said, 'Hmm,' and she knew they would return to this again later.

The kitchen was too big for the two of them; it was proportioned for older times, when houses like this were peopled by large families, with a staff to fill them and take care of them. Grace loved it, even so. She'd had the floor recovered with pink quarry tiles. The cupboards were old pine, glowing warm against the chilly utility of a steel cooking range and hood. The centre of the floor space was taken up by an old oak table. It had been there when her parents moved in, in nineteen fifty, and had no doubt stood in the kitchen for seventy more years before that. Now it was white as bone and dipped a little in the middle from over a hundred years of use. When she remembered, Grace rubbed oil into it, but it soaked in and vanished like a rain shower into cracked clay.

They sat at this table to eat their meal, as she had done every day since she was a child, except for a few years after graduation, when first she spent a year in Kenya doing VSO work, and afterwards bought a flat in the city centre, to be near the hospital and the night life. She returned home at the age of twenty-nine, after her father fell ill with the cancer that would claim his life in eight short months. Her mother died four years later, leaving the house to Grace, and it had never occurred to her to sell: this was home — it always had been, and always would be. She hoped to have children in this house, and though they had discussed it only in passing, she knew that Jeff wanted it, too.

She watched as he tipped the final ingredients into the pan and it hissed ostentatiously: king prawns and asparagus — no red meat, Grace noted. Though he still hadn't taken her up on her reference to the events of the morning, he was nevertheless sensitive to her feelings.

A glass, then another, of wine and she was ready to talk. She couldn't bring herself to tackle it full-on, so she asked him again, 'Why *are* you so early?'

'Couldn't keep away from you.'

Her turn to say, 'Hmm . . .'

'Sorry I frightened Natalja away.'

Grace shrugged. 'She didn't go far.'

A comfortable pause followed. They both knew she would get to the point eventually, and Jeff, it seemed, was willing to wait until the moment she felt ready.

'Natalja's been through a lot.'

'I imagine she has.'

They looked at each other over their empty plates. He didn't push her, he simply waited, giving her the space to say what she had to say — what she needed to say — and at last she spoke.

'I keep seeing her.'

She sipped her wine too quickly, feeling herself slipping from the pleasant warmth of slight intoxication to something far less comfortable.

'She's falling. I want to catch her, to stop her—' She shuddered, hearing again the slither and thud as the body fell into the filthy cavern of the lorry.

Jeff reached across and took her hand. She looked up at him, almost startled to find him there.

'The police surgeon — he's a clinician at the hospital — he asked me had I touched her. There was a butter wrapper . . . I wanted to—' She looked into his face, trying to make him understand. Rickman stroked her hand and listened, waiting for the rest. 'They left her with nothing, Jeff. Not even her dignity.'

Then she was crying, unable to stop.

He gathered her in his arms and they stood in the kitchen, surrounded by the remnants of their meal, while Grace wept, her face pressed into his chest, and he stroked her hair. The heat of her distress burned her skin, and she was almost surprised that he didn't pull back. They stood for some time, holding each other, until her tears subsided, and with it the pain. She felt empty, but empty was good, because she had been filled with an outrage, a hurt and an anger that were too much to bear.

They washed the dishes, passing plates hand to hand, not speaking until gradually, Grace felt a calm settle on her. When Jeff stacked the last dish in the cupboard, she reached up and kissed one fuzzy earlobe and asked, 'Are you *ever* going to tell me why you were home early?'

He sighed, knowing that she wouldn't let up until she knew. 'Over a glass of wine,' he said, and kissed her on the lips. 'Mmm . . . warm.'

'I should hope so.' She had forgotten already how cold she had felt all day, how she had cursed her impulsiveness in leaving her jacket at home. It was a chill like a fever; it rattled her teeth and made her hands shake. She blamed the autumn chill, or the air-conditioning, but she would not admit that she was in shock. Now, at home, the chill was gone, and she felt warm, protected by his presence.

* * *

Jeff brought the glasses through while Grace put a Norah Jones CD in the player, lit a few candles and then curled up on the sofa. He sat next to her, listening to the music, his wine glass in one hand dangling over the arm of the sofa, his eyes closed. His long legs were sprawled out across the rug, his feet were bare.

Grace watched him a while; he took an occasional sip of wine, but the tension never left his shoulders and a muscle jumped compulsively in his jaw. After a while, she prodded him with her toe. 'C'mon,' she said. She was really feeling the effects of the wine now. ''Fess up.'

He glanced at her, his eyelids drooping. 'I got a call from the Royal.'

Grace frowned. 'A colleague?' she asked.

'My brother.'

A silence. When Grace finally spoke, he heard the shock and hurt in her voice. 'You said you had no family.'

The muscle in his jaw jumped again. 'I don't.'

'But—'

'He left when I was ten years old, Grace. I haven't seen him in twenty-five years.'

Complicated family histories. Grace knew all about that. But twenty-five years wasn't enough to pick apart the knots of family ties, was it? She set aside her unease that he had lied to her, and asked, 'What did he want?'

'I don't know. A doctor phoned me. Said that Simon named me as next of kin.'

Grace blinked. Jeff had a brother, and the brother had a name. Simon. She tried it out in her head. Simon Rickman.

'He wants to see me.'

'You mean you haven't been in already?'

'*Twenty-five years*, Grace,' he repeated, his eyes dark and fathomless. 'What the hell could he possibly want?'

She stared at a candle flame filtered through the red wine in her glass, thinking how little she knew about his family background. Absent father, mother dead of a heart attack aged forty-five. She took a sip of wine, looking at him over the rim of her glass. 'Only one way to find out,' she said.

CHAPTER SEVEN

Grace had made it sound so simple. But Rickman sat in his car for an hour, still undecided. The hospital car park was deserted; visiting time long over, only the night staff and security remained. The A&E department ran as an autonomous unit at night. Of course, Grace had wanted to come with him. 'Moral support,' she had said.

But he wanted to do this alone. Minimal contact, a clear message that any family ties between him and Simon had long since been severed. Grace would not understand that, and Rickman didn't want her to witness any ugly scenes; she was exhausted and had been through enough for one day — for a whole month of days.

Twenty-five years. Simon disappeared for two thirds of his life and now he wanted to walk back in, like he'd just popped round the corner for a packet of fags.

Rickman weighed up the possibilities: had he come to apologise? Rickman had known men wait a long time — even twenty-five years — for money, or revenge; he had seen them fight for justice, for the satisfaction of being vindicated. But to wait twenty-five years to make an apology? No.

He tested his own feelings: concern? How could he feel concern for a man he didn't know? Had he come just to tell

Simon what he thought of him? That wasn't his style. Anger was there; he denied its presence, even though he could feel it as a hot mass, growing in size, building pressure under his rib cage. Finally, it was curiosity that made him get out of the car.

His breath smoked and his footsteps rang out on the cold ground. A lone mongrel, scavenging on the remnants of a discarded chip-packet, lifted its head. Its eyes shone like yellow glass in the artificial light. It stared at him for a moment, then skulked way, tail dipped and head lowered.

Security let him through when he showed his warrant card. He took the lift to the fourth floor and stepped out onto an empty landing; grey polished tiles and pearl-grey walls, a whiff of disinfectant and medical grade alcohol, and absolute silence. The floor felt unstable beneath him, and he went to the window, more to steady his nerves than to get his bearings.

Below, the parking bays were stitched like cartoon scars across the concrete. Beyond the hospital grounds, the Radio City tower, crowned with radio and phone antennae, was lit by spotlights, blues and purples and greens, constantly shifting and blurring as if to some unheard musical beat. The waterfront wasn't visible from this angle, but the bone-white concrete of the Catholic Cathedral, its lantern tower lit for some special occasion, shone in the middle distance, a squat reflection of the Radio City building. Suddenly impatient, Rickman pushed away from the safety rail and headed for the double doors into the Head Injuries Unit.

A subtle rush of sound replaced the silence of the hallway: the hiss and suck of a respirator; the faint click and whirr of pumps pushing measured doses of drugs and plasma into patients. To his left, the subdued voices of two nurses. The nurses' station itself was deserted. As he skimmed the list of rooms and names, a door opened and he heard quick footsteps heading towards him.

A woman: European-looking, tall and elegant, dressed in a brown calf-length suede coat and knee-length boots, dark hair with highlights of gold and copper. She carried herself with an easy grace and she reeked of money.

She looked upset. Seeing Rickman, she stopped and subjected him to a thorough and critical scrutiny. 'You must be Jeff.' Her voice was cultured, English, Rickman noted with some surprise. There was no warmth in the greeting.

'I'm Jeff Rickman,' he said. 'Who are you?'

She didn't answer, only stared at him, her eyes brimming with tears. They were beautiful eyes, large and brown, but they were filled with bitterness.

'He'll be delighted to see you,' she said. 'You're all he's spoken of since he came round.'

'Look,' Rickman said, 'I don't know what this is about . . .'

'Why should you? I don't — and I've been married to him for twenty years. Go and talk to your big brother. Tell him how much you've missed him.' She pushed past him, hurrying for the doors.

'Mrs Rickman?' One of the nurses, come to find out what all the commotion was about. 'Oh,' she said, hesitating. Then she seemed to recover herself and continued towards him. 'He's through the second door on the right,' she said, jerking her head in the direction of the room Mrs Rickman had come from.

'Who?'

'Your brother.'

It seemed that this evening, Rickman needed no introduction. Yet he and Simon had never been alike. *Grace*, he thought, smoothing the way for him with a phone call. He gave a mental shrug.

The door to the private room stood slightly ajar. He pushed it wider, still undecided. Inside, a man paced with agitated determination. He was tall — almost as tall as Rickman, but leaner, rangier. He had high, flat Germanic cheekbones, and thick eyebrows that had faded over the years from lemon yellow to a more distinguished silver. His pacing had a compulsive quality, a furious edginess, and Rickman felt a sudden stab of emotion. It was like watching his father. In the seventies, their father had worn his hair long and curling, and Simon's was now short and salt-and-pepper grey, but the tension in the shoulders, the constant nervy need to be on the move, even the slight lope in the stride gave an eerie likeness.

From time to time, as he paced, Simon's head shook slightly, as if he was engaged in an internal debate and had found some facet of the argument he couldn't countenance.

* * *

Simon was pacing because if he didn't, he would go insane. The top of his head would shatter like an eggshell and his brains would spatter the walls. The whole *world* would explode. That's how it felt, being told crazy things by people who looked serious and caring and responsible, people who wore hospital uniforms. Except they were telling you crazy things and expecting you to accept what they were saying and then stopped you from leaving when you wanted out.

It wasn't a prison — at least, he didn't think so — since there were no bars on the windows and the door was open, so how could it be a prison if they didn't lock the cell doors? On the other hand, it could be a madhouse: he knew there was another word — a better word, but words were elusive: they teased just beyond his grasp. He kept getting this picture of himself trying to reach the top shelf of the kitchen cupboard at home, knowing that was where Dad kept his tobacco and papers, and sometimes they were so close he felt them brush the tips of his fingers, but he could never quite reach them. Anyway, if it was a madhouse, they didn't always lock the doors, did they? Except maybe at night; but it was dark outside, so it must be night and the door was open — but maybe that was because the woman had been in, keeping an eye on him.

That woman. *Jesus!* He pushed his hand through his hair, but it was all wrong — too short. His was long and curly except they said that was a long time ago, and when he said, 'Have I been asleep that long — kind of asleep, only not a good kind of sleep?' They said no, it's only been a week. Which was stupid, because obviously it couldn't have been.

He massaged his temples, trying to make his brain work, but it was like thinking through cotton wool, like wading through treacle, like when you have a cold and you're all stuffed up and can't breathe, only this is your *mind*, and it won't work properly, and if your mind doesn't work, what are you? A loony? Someone to be locked up for everybody's safety?

He'd gone off again — gone off at a tangent, she kept saying. She? Everything was slightly off, like a dream, but if this was a dream he would have woken up by now, wouldn't he? He tried to concentrate. The woman — that was it — he'd been thinking about the woman. She'd left a picture of the two of them on the — the thing — by the bed. What was the thing called? Box thing, with a door. Anyway, she said the picture was of her and him when they got married. It did look a bit like him — more like Dad, but modern-looking. The woman — she said her name was Tanya — Tanya was a looker. Old, but still foxy, but it wasn't possible, was it, that he'd forget his own wedding? And anyway, the guy in the picture — the guy they said was him — was so *old*. If he really was that old, he'd missed half his life.

Then they took him to a mirror and he freaked, because that was Dad looking back at him, only a bit older and without the beard.

'No, Simon,' they said in their reasonable, professional voices. 'That's your reflection. That is you in the mirror.'

He had been in a coma. *Coma!* That was the word. Been in a coma and he had some kind of amnesia. People were always going into a coma in films. Only when they woke up they just had a bit of a headache and they had to be careful not to sit up too fast and then they were fine. But he wasn't fine. It had been days and still he wasn't fine. So he asked for Jeff. Well, actually, he asked for Mum first, but they said she died a long time ago, and that was a shock, because it felt like she should be around, especially now, when he really needed her. He had cried then. The fear took him, pinning his arms and pressing on his chest, till he couldn't move, couldn't think, till he begged just to be left alone.

He kept forgetting and asking for her at first, but he had it straight now. Mum was dead. It was just him and Jeff. Jeff would be able to fill in the gaps. Also, if Jeff was old, he'd believe it — that he was old too — and he must have forgotten the rest. Jeff would be there to fill him in about the bits he'd forgotten, and everything would be fine because him and Jeff were always tight. 'Tight as ticks,' Mum always said. Though he never really knew what that meant. He would ask Jeff when he came.

Abruptly, he stopped and turned. Jeff!

* * *

The physical impression of their father shattered for an instant and Rickman saw Simon as he had been twenty-five years ago, in the summer of nineteen seventy-nine. A skinny youth with long, tousled blond hair and a liking for torn jeans, swaggering a little in the dyed black army greatcoat he'd bought from the Army & Navy surplus store across the road from Lewis's. Rickman was looking into the kingfisher-blue eyes of his seventeen-year-old brother — the person he loved and trusted most in all the world. The old anxiety was there, but so was the strange defiance and the almost manic enthusiasm and energy.

'Man, am I glad to see you!' Simon rushed forward, grinning like his jaw would break.

Rickman stopped him with a look. It had taken thirteen years of hard police work to perfect that look, walking the toughest beats in Toxteth, patrolling the wastelands of Speke and Bootle, later as a CID officer investigating dealers and pimps, gang killings and organised crime, eyeball to eyeball with hard cases and psychopaths.

The grin sickened and died, and Simon stood with his arms limp at his sides, a stricken look on his face. And there he was again, their father — more tanned and lined, for sure, less soft around the middle. But the injured look, the puzzled expression that said, *What did I do?* These were mannerisms Simon had learned from their father.

'Jeff?' he said.

Rickman felt sorry for him and then furious that he should feel anything at all. 'What do you want, Simon?'

'Nothing, I—'

Simon's electric-blue eyes clouded and Rickman sighed. This wasn't going to be as straightforward as he'd expected.

'Your doctor said you were asking to see me.'

'Yes.' He frowned, as if trying to remember the conversation.

'Why?'

'You're my brother, Jeff. I just — I wanted to see my brother.'

'It took you a while.' Again, the frown, the pause as if thinking, far from being an automatic process, required intense concentration and absolute stillness.

'Soon as I woke up,' Simon said at last. 'I was in a . . .' His lips pressed together as he tried to retrieve the word and Rickman got another flash: his father at forty, staring into space as if he might snatch the word he was struggling for out of the air.

'I've been in a sleep,' Simon said, obviously embarrassed at failing to find the right word. Rickman saw the little head-shake he had noticed earlier. 'Words . . . Like fishes. Slippery . . . Deep asleep?' He was asking for a prompt.

'Coma,' Rickman said.

Simon nodded. 'Coma,' he repeated, trying to commit it to memory. 'It was a car crash.' His hand strayed to the crown of his head. 'I don't remember.' He frowned with the effort of trying. Then he looked at Rickman and his face cleared; he even smiled a little. 'Remember you, though.'

'Great,' Rickman said. '*Now* you remember me.'

Simon missed the irony. 'I rember—' He shook his head impatiently. 'I *remember* everything, Jeff,' he corrected himself.

'Everything?'

Rickman looked into his brother's face. He saw a flicker of something: guilt? recognition? and then Rickman said, 'If you remember everything, you'll know why I'm walking out of here.'

* * *

Then Jeff was gone and he didn't know how it happened. He'd forgotten to ask him all the things he'd meant to ask, like did Jeff remember him getting married and was the woman in the picture really his wife and why couldn't he think of the right words for things like — like coma. See — he did know it. But what was the good in remembering a word five minutes too late?

Jeff was mad at him, that was for certain and he didn't know why that was, either. Maybe he'd had a row with Jeff and that's why he'd crashed his car. They were always fighting. He gave his head a little shake: they were always fighting *as kids*. They weren't kids anymore, because Jeff was old now.

Despite what they had told him — despite the evidence of his own reflection looking back at him from the mirror — Simon had half expected to see *his* Jeff walk through the door. Ten-year-old Jeff with pockets full of secret treasures: rubber bands, a pocket torch, the silver pen knife Simon had bought him for his ninth birthday, and hidden from Mum, so she wouldn't confiscate it. Jeff with the scabby knees and big ideas. Not this *old* Jeff, this big, frightening Jeff who seemed so angry and who sounded so much like Dad.

The Jeff who had come to see him was all grown up. Which meant that what the doctors said was true: he, Simon, really was forty-one. He looked in the mirror over the hand-basin and saw, with fresh horror, his father's face staring back at him, his father's eyes, anxious, angry, afraid.

He heard a rushing sound in his ears and failed to recognise the roar of his own blood, pulsing madly. But he felt the fear; he knew that all right.

He wanted to run after Jeff, to say sorry — just so they could be friends again — so he wouldn't be alone. But the world seemed bigger, more hostile, terribly changed during the lost years between his youth and this grotesque maturity and he could not find the courage to step over the threshold.

* * *

Rickman saw Simon's wife at the entrance to the foyer. She was smoking a cigarette and the security guard was pretending not to notice, which was difficult, since he could barely keep his eyes off her. Rickman could see why: her natural beauty was enhanced by a poise that made him wonder if she had been a model. Perhaps that was how she and Simon had met.

Seeing him, she threw the cigarette out of the door and hurried over. She was lightly tanned, and her dark-brown eyes shimmered with intelligence.

'Look,' she said. 'I'm sorry about . . .' She waved her hand, inviting him to fill in the rest. 'It's just that since he came out of the coma, he's been obsessed, going on and on about you.'

'He said he doesn't remember the crash.'

A harried, desperate look crossed her face. 'He doesn't remember *anything*. Between childhood and waking up in the hospital — it's all a blank.'

Shocked, Rickman asked, 'Is it permanent?'

She raised her shoulders in a gesture of helplessness. 'They call it post-traumatic amnesia. It usually wears off, but some people . . .' Her eyes filled with tears again and she frowned, looking over his shoulder, trying to regain control. 'He treats me like a stranger — I swear he has more affection for the nursing staff. We have two boys. He won't see them. He won't see his own *children*— Oh, God!' She put her hand to her mouth and sobbed.

Rickman took her by the arm and guided her to a seat. She rummaged in her handbag, her hands trembling as she retrieved a tissue and dabbed at her eyes and nose.

'I'm sorry,' she said, 'It's just so—'

'You've had a terrible shock,' Rickman said, wanting to say more, but feeling more like a stranger than ever.

She composed herself, determined to explain. 'I've nobody to turn to, you see.'

'How old are the boys?' He felt awkward calling these strangers 'my nephews'.

'Jeff is seventeen and Fergus is twelve.'

'Oh,' Rickman said. *He named his son Jeff.* 'But they must be missing school.'

'Yes, I should send them back — they board at the British International School in Milan — but they want to see their father before they go, and he still refuses to see them.'

'I'd like to meet them,' Rickman said.

She seemed surprised and delighted. 'That would be — I know the boys would like that.' Fresh tears brimmed in her eyes and she retrieved a tissue from her handbag. 'God,' she said, 'It's a wonder I'm not wrinkled like a prune with all this crying.

'For a week we didn't know if he'd survive, and then to find he doesn't know me . . . It wouldn't be so bad, but my parents are old and unwell — they can't travel all the way from Cornwall.' She stopped and a tear tracked slowly down her cheek.

'You live in Cornwall?'

She shook her head. 'Milan — that's where Simon's business is based. But my parents live in Cornwall — that's where I was brought up.'

'So why were you in Liverpool?' She seemed a little startled by the question, and Rickman realised that he had sounded sharp and he smiled apologetically. 'My partner says I don't have conversations, I conduct interrogations.'

She returned the smile, apparently reassured by this personal admission. 'We came on business,' she said. 'Simon said it would be a chance for the boys to see his childhood home on business expenses. He runs an export company — clothing and leather goods, mostly.'

'I know.' Rickman saw the question in her eyes and shrugged. 'There was an article in one of the Sunday supplements.'

She nodded, watching him solemnly, her eyes magnified by the tears standing in them. 'I know you two were estranged,' she said, watching carefully for his reaction.

'He told you that?'

She nodded. 'Before the accident. Now, all he remembers are the good times.'

Convenient, Rickman thought. 'Did he tell you why we're — estranged?' It was a dispassionate word, unencumbered with the emotion he was surprised that he still felt.

Her eyes searched his. 'He told me it was his fault.' A silence grew between them. She fiddled with the strap of her handbag, finally digging out another cigarette. 'Will you come back?' she asked.

'I don't know.' It was a truthful answer, but brutal. Rickman saw her tense and regretted his bluntness. 'If you need anything—' He took a business card and wrote his home address and phone number on the back. 'Anything at all — a place to stay,' he added impulsively.

She smiled. 'I wouldn't dream of imposing on your hospitality. We're staying at the Marriott Hotel for the moment. It's central, and it's comfortable. If we're here much longer, I'll see about leasing a house.'

'Look—' He realised he still didn't know her name.

'Tanya,' she said.

'Tanya,' Rickman repeated. 'My argument isn't with you.'

She offered him a slim, cool hand. 'I know. And I hope you do come back. He may not deserve it, but . . .' She smiled softly. 'I think he's been lonely for you. I think — ' she hesitated. ' — whatever it was . . . I think he regrets what happened between you.'

CHAPTER EIGHT

Grace woke with a start as Rickman tiptoed into their bed-room. The reading-lamp was on and the paperback she had been reading tumbled to the floor with a thump.

'Shh . . .' Rickman said, kissing her forehead and slipping the book onto the pile on her bedside table.

She rubbed a hand over her face. 'God, Jeff, I'm sorry. I wanted to wait up for you. What happened?' she asked, her voice slurred with sleep. 'How is he?'

'He's fine,' Rickman said. 'We'll talk about it tomorrow.' She looked sick with exhaustion, and Rickman wondered if it was delayed shock.

'But Jeff—'

'Tomorrow,' he said, smoothing her hair.

She murmured something incoherent and drifted off again.

Rickman lay awake all night. Grace was restless, struggling and twitching, sometimes gasping in distress, and he spent much of the time soothing and talking to her softly. At last, she seemed to drift into a dreamless sleep and he lay beside her, listening to her breathing. At around four a.m., he gave up on sleep and sat in a chair in the morning-room, watching for the first glimmer of dawn so that he could make breakfast.

He brought Grace toast and coffee in bed. They avoided the contentious topics of his brother and her experiences of the previous day, but he noticed her stealing glances at him when she thought he wasn't looking.

While she showered, he stared out of the bedroom window onto the garden. They had planted a birch sapling when he moved in almost three years ago. Now, trembling on the brink of leaf fall, every leaf an intense, buttery yellow, it glowed like a patch of sunlight on the grass.

'Are you ready, yet?' Grace asked.

He turned to face her. She was wrapped in a bath-sheet, her skin pink from the heat of the shower, ready to carry the burden of his family problems on her narrow shoulders, and he marvelled that he was with her — that this lovely creature had chosen him.

'Ready for what?' he asked.

'To talk.'

He took a breath, ready to postpone the discussion but Grace held up her hand. 'I'm a patient person,' she said. 'And it's not that common to be simultaneously patient *and* doctor. I have my limits, however.' She smiled a little, to show him that she was prepared to give him time, but he read in her expression that this, too, had its limits.

'Simon has post-traumatic amnesia,' he said.

'How bad is it?'

'Cataclysmic.'

She watched for any sign of emotion, and seeing none, said, 'Kind of makes it all a bit pointless, doesn't it — you bearing a grudge against him?'

'We didn't . . .' These were feelings he had kept buried for years. It was a protective mechanism and his brother's return had torn open scars he thought had long healed. He took another gulp of air.

'This isn't a family tiff,' he said at last. 'It's not about sibling rivalry or petty jealousies.'

She waited, holding him in her gaze, her eyes so blue and clear, so trusting that he felt almost incapacitated by his love for her.

54

'I do want to tell you, Grace . . .'

'But you've kept this to yourself for twenty-five years and you're frightened to let the genie out of the bottle.'

He paused, then nodded.

She slipped her arms around him, her hair still wet, her body warm and perfumed from the shower. 'You know where I am if you need me.'

He looked down at her. 'But you'll be in clinic, Doctor,' he said.

She smiled. Grace had never minded being teased. 'Just so long as you refrain from interrogating my patients and intimidating my interpreter.'

'Will *you* be all right?' he asked. It was only a day since she had discovered a murder, and yet she was thinking of his problems, concerned about his feelings.

'Do I *look* all right?' She stood back for him to get a better look, and truth be told, she looked more than all right: her skin seemed suffused with a soft light, her eyes a clear sky-blue, despite her troubled sleep, and her hair, still damp from the shower, seemed to have taken a russet autumnal glow, glossy and rich.

'Grace—'

She put a finger to his lips. 'Stop *worrying.*'

He couldn't do that, but he saw the need to stop asking, so she dressed and finished drying her hair and they left the house in their separate cars, in a friendly, if wary silence.

* * *

The Incident Room was filled to capacity. Many of the desks were cluttered with cups smelling of the combination of plastic and coffee peculiar to vending machines. It was just seven-thirty and improvised breakfasts of fast-food take-outs, sandwiches and chocolate bars were being eaten. One or two of the women had gone for the healthy option of fruit. Rickman felt wired: lack of sleep, cup after cup of coffee and the adrenalin high of being given his first major enquiry.

The noise level was up on the previous evening, which Rickman took as a good sign: it denoted high spirits, a level of expectation for the outcome. It also meant that the team had begun to gel; they had more to talk about than which division they had been drafted from and the first sketchy facts of the case. Today they were teammates.

To one side of the room, Rickman noticed a gloomy group: the interview team who, with Foster as team leader, had made a foray into the Liverpool 8 district to interview the working girls. They had worked until well after midnight and were back in this morning, red-eyed, and looking a little despondent.

Start with Foster's lot, then — give them the boost of knowing that their work, however fruitless, was important, and get the negative stuff out of the way early in the briefing. He called on Foster.

'Big fat nothing, Boss,' Foster said. Despite less than five hours' sleep, he was smoothly shaven and his hair was styled and sculpted to its usual perfection. He wore a short-sleeved shirt, crisply laundered and chosen to show off his tan and the well-toned muscles of his upper arms. 'She was only on the block a few days. Didn't do a hell of a lot of trade — too timid, the other girls said.

'No one saw her the night she was killed. Nobody really knew her. They never saw her with a pimp. They never asked her where she was from . . .'

'So you've been banging your heads against a brick wall.'

'I don't think it's malicious, Boss. What do you think, Naomi?'

Lee Foster didn't need support from anyone, and Rickman saw this for what it was: the sergeant putting the moves on DC Hart — letting her have her say as a gesture of friendship, in the hopes of something more than friendship.

'She never spoke to anyone, sir,' Hart said. 'I mean never. She never once opened her mouth.'

'Not to talk, anyway.' Foster just couldn't resist the innuendo. It raised a few sniggers, but Rickman saw that he'd lost any gains he'd made over the previous evening with Naomi Hart.

She glanced at him with distaste and said, 'I was thinking — maybe she's deaf or something.'

Rickman nodded. 'Worth checking with the School for the Deaf, any of the social clubs. See if they recognise her. There are pictures available for collection at the back of the room.'

The officer closest to the pile raised his arm, pointing vertically downward as people turned to check.

'Anything from Carrie's blood, Boss?' A young DC had asked the question.

Rickman turned to him. 'What did you say?'

The officer glanced at his pals, alarmed. 'I was wondering about the DNA, Boss.'

'What did you call her?' Rickman said, and the silence in the room was like the pause before a thunderclap.

The young officer shifted in his seat. 'Carrie, Boss.'

Rickman looked at him a while before speaking. 'What's your name?'

'DC Reid, Boss.' He licked his lips.

'Well, DC Reid, we don't have a name for this young woman,' he said. 'We do know that she was probably still in her teens. We know that she was deliberately and clinically bled to death and dumped like garbage.' He was thinking of Grace's tears for the girl the previous evening. There was a shame-faced hush from the team — it seemed that the young DC wasn't the only person to call the victim 'Carrie'.

'Like . . . garbage,' he repeated with deliberate emphasis. 'Now, we can't help that, but we can afford her the respect her killers denied her.'

The young officer apologised and after a shuffling of chairs and general coughing and clearing of throats, the team settled down again.

'To answer your question,' Rickman went on, 'The victim's profile does not appear on the DNA database. The results from the other bloodstains aren't back from the lab, yet. The good news is, we'll have HOLMES2 online from nine a.m. today.'

A muted cheer went up — even Foster's team brightened up a little. The HOLMES team were specialist operatives: indexers, researchers, clerks, typists. They took some of the slog out of a major enquiry for the investigative officers, collating and entering thousands of completed lines of enquiry onto the HOLMES2 computer program, and once it was filed, it could collate the information, sorting tens of thousands of cross-references in seconds. The junior ranks liked it because it prioritised actions and sifted through a mass of data that could make a human brain turn to mush. Added to this, the general view was, if HOLMES was deployed, it meant you were on an important case, and important cases made careers.

'All reports, written on correct forms — ' he held up a copy of the quadruplicate message form ' — should be taken directly to the receiver. Second floor, room 208.'

'Who's allocating jobs today, Boss?' somebody asked.

'For today, it's Sergeant Foster. The HOLMES team has already got a day's backlog to sort and index, so if there's anything you think needs immediate attention, talk to him and flag it up with the receiver as well. As of tomorrow, actions will be the responsibility of the HOLMES Action Manager.'

He waited a moment and, as there were no further questions, he gave the floor to DS Foster. The sergeant had rattled off the first three jobs before Rickman was out of the room.

Foster waited until DI Rickman was out of earshot, then turned to the young DC. 'Reid,' he said. 'You can compile a list of all the deaf social clubs. Might teach you a lesson in speak no evil.'

'*Everyone's* calling her Carrie,' DC Reid complained, all injured pride. 'Ever since Tunstall said—'

'Ah,' Foster waved a finger at him. 'But not everyone's calling her Carrie *in front of the boss*, are they?'

'No, Sarge,' Reid muttered.

Foster grinned. 'If you'd've actually watched the film you would've known better. Right at the end some daft sod thinks he'll go the cemetery, make amends — but Carrie reaches right out of the grave, grabs him by the ankles, and yanks him hell-bound.'

CHAPTER NINE

Grace pressed her fingertips to her eyelids and rested for a moment. It had been a long, hard day, haunted by after-images of her dreams in which she saw the girl falling. In the dreams, Grace was standing by the side of the lorry; she lunged forward, trying to save the girl from that bruising fall. Each time, she was too late.

Natalja reached over and squeezed her shoulder. 'It will pass,' she said.

Grace opened her eyes, but Natalja had already looked away and was gathering her things, ready to leave. That was Natalja all over: moving target, catch me if you can. She never spoke about her time in Croatia during the war, and she didn't mix with other Yugoslavs.

The internal phone rang and Grace picked up.

'Sorry, Doctor Chandler.' It was one of the receptionists. 'There's a woman in the waiting-room. She's come from the hospital. Says she's got to speak to Doctor Grace.'

'I've seen my last patient.'

'She's in a shocking state, Doctor . . .'

Grace looked at Natalja. Natalja shrugged: she didn't mind. 'What's it about, Helen?'

'I can't make head nor tail of it.' Helen's voice became muffled and Grace imagined her turning her back on the woman and cupping her hand over the phone. 'She doesn't speak much English — just keeps asking for Doctor Grace.'

Grace sighed. 'Send her through.'

Moments later, the woman burst through the door, talking rapidly, clearly distressed. It was evident from the bulge under the thin jacket she was wearing that she was about four or five months pregnant.

'She needs to calm down,' Grace said, taking the woman's hand and leading her to a chair.

'Iraqi?' Natalja said. 'Irani? Farsi?'

The woman murmured something in reply and Natalja turned to Grace. 'She's Iranian.'

'Does she speak Farsi?'

Natalja nodded.

Natalja's facility with languages was phenomenal: she spoke French and English fluently, Serbo-Croat, of course, some Albanian, Russian. She had picked up a working knowledge of Farsi from an ex-boyfriend and practised it by talking to the other interpreters on the council's books. The woman spoke fast, her eyes wide, and her words coming in breathy bursts.

'You must be calm,' Natalja said in Farsi, speaking firmly and clearly. 'You must be calm for the baby's sake.'

The woman took a few choking breaths and placed a protective hand on her belly.

Through Natalja's interpreting, Grace learned that her name was Anusheh Tabrizi. She had been in the UK for two weeks. Grace fetched her a glass of water and carried her own chair around from her side of the desk to sit beside her patient.

'Now, tell me what is the problem.'

While Natalja translated, Grace waited, all the while holding Mrs Tabrizi's hand. She kept her eyes fixed on the woman's face, making it clear that she was speaking *to* her and not *about* her. She had worked with Natalja for a long time, and the usual formalities of translation were taken as read: the pauses and the instructions to 'tell her' were unnecessary, an encumbrance they had long since dispensed with, so Grace's questions and the answers Mrs Tabrizi gave seemed easy, almost as natural as if they were conversing in a common language.

They were living in emergency accommodation while their claim for asylum was assessed. Mrs Tabrizi had begun feeling unwell. At first she thought it was something she had eaten, but then she began to bleed. Natalja listened carefully, then translated: 'Her husband was not at home — he was at an ESOL class. She couldn't reach him, so she went to the hospital.'

Mrs Tabrizi seemed so young. Her tiny face, tightly encircled in a scarf that hid her hair, was pale and anxious.

She spoke again, stopping mid-sentence, choked by sobs. When she finished speaking, she began to weep afresh.

'She says they refused to help her at the hospital,' Natalja said, puzzled. 'They say she must go to another place. Grace, she says they told her she couldn't have her baby.'

Alarm bells were beginning to ring in Grace's head. 'Where did they tell her to go instead?' Natalja asked the question and the woman pulled free of Grace, digging in her handbag as she spoke.

'They told her to find someone to translate. Her friend recommended you,' Natalja said.

After some searching, Mrs Tabrizi drew out a folded sheet of paper, offering it to Grace with a trembling hand.

'This is where the hospital say she must go,' Natalja explained.

Grace unfolded the paper and stared at it for some moments, shocked at first, then sick with sorrow for Mrs Tabrizi and furious with the doctor who sent her away with such an inadequate explanation.

'Did they have no one to translate?' she asked.

Natalja spoke briefly and listened to Mrs Tabrizi's response. 'It was an emergency,' she said. 'Nobody was available.'

'Did you not see a doctor before you came to the UK?'

She had not. Hospital services were patchy, at best, in her country and anyway, midwives did most of the birthing. Women simply didn't go to hospital to have a baby, unless there was something wrong.

Grace took the woman's hand again. 'Mrs Tabrizi, I have very bad news.'

Natalja told the woman what Grace had said, and Mrs Tabrizi cupped her belly with her free hand and spoke.

Two words. No translation was needed — the gesture and her concern were clear: she knew something was terribly wrong with her baby.

Grace nodded. 'I'm sorry.'

Mrs Tabrizi spoke. Natalja looked at Grace. 'She wants to know what is the matter with her baby,' she said.

Grace stared at her helplessly for a few seconds. How was she going to tell this woman that the baby she had cradled in her womb, that she had crooned to and loved was in fact a monstrous growth that would kill her if it wasn't removed? That there was no baby — there never had been; that the place they were sending her to was the gynaecological oncology unit?

'This letter,' she began. 'is written by the doctor who examined you. Did they show you the pictures they took?'

Mrs Tabrizi looked to Natalja to interpret. When she understood, she nodded, then spoke again, her confusion evident in her worried frown and in the little shrug as she finished what she had to say.

'She didn't understand what they were showing her, Grace,' Natalja translated.

Grace took the young woman's hands in hers again. 'You have a tumour in your womb,' she began. She explained in small steps, trying to keep her composure for the sake of the woman looking up at her, so anxious, yet with a timid hope in her eyes.

Mrs Tabrizi seemed numbed. For a long time, she didn't speak.

'They have to remove the tumour,' Grace said. Natalja's voice, soft and unobtrusive, sounded like a muttered prayer beside her

Mrs Tabrizi nodded in two jerky movements, her hand straying protectively to her belly.

Grace looked at her friend. 'Oh, God, Natalja . . .'

Natalja frowned. 'What?'

'Tell her—' Grace closed her eyes for a moment. 'Tell her that, when they remove the growth, there won't be any more babies.'

Natalja stared at her, horrified. 'I can't tell her that.'

'You must.'

'Grace, this should have been her first child. You can't expect me to tell her she won't ever have children.'

'I expect you to tell her the truth.'

Mrs Tabrizi looked from one woman to the other, witnessing the battle of wills and sensing that there was worse to come.

'Natalja, if she doesn't find out here, she'll find out when she's rushed to hospital with a massive bleed.' She paused, looking into Natalja's face, trying to make her understand there was no other way. 'Tell her, Natalja. Please.'

* * *

There was no doubt that Natalja had told Mrs Tabrizi everything: it took the best part of half an hour to calm her down. Grace called for a cab to take her back to her emergency accommodation, after Natalja had phoned to make sure that her husband had returned home. He had wanted to come out to meet his wife, but Natalja assured him that it would be quicker for him to wait for her. Mrs Tabrizi spent much of the intervening ten minutes on her mobile to her husband. Natalja, already late for a date, left it to Grace to see her off the premises.

Grace helped her to the taxi, surprised to see a man half-sitting on one of the steel bollards that protected the entrance to the clinic. She paid the driver and turned, resolving to ask the man his business. He stood as she approached. Sales rep., she thought, assessing him by his smart black overcoat and gloved hands.

'Doctor Grace?'

Her evaluation shifted: her clinic patients called her Doctor Grace, as did members of the refugee community: she took the use of her first name as a compliment, as a mark of affection. The use of the name marked this man out as a refugee just as decidedly as his accent. She recognised it as Serbo-Croat, but she was certain that she had never met him before, so, pet name or no, she was wary of him.

'I'm Doctor Grace,' she said, thinking *I've left my damned attack alarm in the consulting room.* He was tall, solidly built, smooth-skinned and dark-eyed. His hair was black and glistening in the artificial light.

'My name is Mirko Andrić.' He was young — early- to mid-twenties, she guessed, but he had the confidence and quiet authority of a much older man. His handshake was warm and firm.

'Are you ill, Mr Andrić?'

He smiled. 'I'm very well, thank you.' He gave a little bow as he answered, and Grace was disarmed by his old-fashioned courtesy. 'I was looking for your colleague.'

'Doctor Corcoran? I'm afraid he isn't here.'

'I'm sorry.' He seemed a little embarrassed. 'I think maybe I used a wrong word. I meant your assistant — Natalja Sremać.'

'No, your choice of words is fine — it was my mistake,' Grace said, looking at him more closely. Was this someone Natalja had known in Croatia? She had worked with refugees for long enough to know that not every friendly enquiry was as benign as it appeared. 'You know Natalja?'

'We are old friends.' He smiled again. His teeth were slightly crooked and he wore his hair unfashionably long, falling into a cowlick over his forehead. His face had the same marks of weariness she sometimes read in Natalja's expression; a weariness that went back to the pain and privations of the war.

'I'm afraid she's already gone,' Grace said. 'You must have just missed her.'

He looked disappointed. 'You don't have her number?'

Grace dipped her head apologetically. 'I'm afraid I can't . . .'

He held up both hands. 'Of course,' he said. 'It was stupid of me to ask. Excuse me.' He hung his head, and the cowlick fell over his eyes, giving him a look of boyish vulnerability that made her want to trust him.

'Look,' Grace said, loath to get in the way of Natalja meeting up with an old friend. 'Why don't you give me your number — maybe she'll call you.'

He swept open his overcoat and dipped smoothly into the pocket of his suit jacket, taking out a small silver case and producing his card with a flourish.

Grace took it, touched and a little amused by the swagger in the gesture. '*Verve*,' she read.

'Business solutions,' he added, pointing to the tagline beneath the firm's name.

'Oh.' Grace said, none the wiser. 'I'll be sure she gets it, Mr Andrić.'

A frown creased his brow. 'Mirko,' he said. 'Please.'

Grace smiled. 'Mirko.' She held out her hand. Underlying the warmth of his handshake there was energy, she thought. Energy and passion.

Mr Andrić had left by the time she had collected her things and locked her consulting room. She said goodnight to Helen and left her to close the shutters and activate the alarm. She walked round to the car park at the back of the clinic. The night was dark and moonless and intensely cold. The security lights clicked on as she turned the corner of the building. Only her car remained, looking shabby and forlorn nose in to the low back wall. She dumped her briefcase in the boot and slid behind the wheel.

A sudden uneasiness gripped her and she glanced in the rear-view mirror. Nothing, only the steel shutters juddering and grinding into place over the windows.

She backed out and pointed the car down Princes Boulevard, heading for home. At Ullet Road traffic lights she got that odd feeling again. The hairs rose on the back of her neck and she glanced nervously in her mirror. There was nothing to see. Nevertheless, Grace reached down into her handbag and, finding her attack alarm by touch, she was reassured as she slipped the plaited cord around her wrist.

She inched forward but was caught in the next cycle at the lights. A moment later, she sensed, rather than saw, something shift behind her seat and turned, wide-eyed. There was someone in the car with her.

Grace screamed, pulling the pin out of the alarm, triggering a wall of painful sound, pounding and reverberating against the windows and roof and doors of the car.

'Don't, Grace! It's okay. It's me!'

She screamed again, reaching to release her belt buckle and flee the car, before she recognised the figure struggling from the floor behind her seat.

Natalja.

'What the *hell* d'you think you're doing?' Grace yelled.

'Turn that damn thing off!' Natalja shouted.

Grace reached for the alarm, which screeched and flashed a warning on the seat next to her, but she knocked it to the floor and it took agonising seconds to retrieve it. They were attracting attention; the driver of the car next to her mouthed something to Grace, his concern evident. Grace shook her head, wincing with the force of sound battering her eardrums, trying to reassure him as she fumbled with the pin and tried to reinsert it. Suddenly, it was done, and the silence in the car was intense.

'Bloody hell, Natalja!' Grace shouted over the echo of the alarm's din still ringing in her ears.

'I'm *sorry*.' Natalja sat back, pushing her hair from her face and retying her ponytail.

'You nearly gave me a heart attack.'

'Grace, I—'

'I thought you were—'

Horns blared and Grace almost leapt out of her seat. The lights had changed. She engaged first gear but took her foot off the clutch too fast and stalled the car.

'Shit!' As she fumbled with the ignition, Natalja tried to explain.

'There was someone—'

The engine fired and Grace screeched through the lights as they turned red, leaving a queue of irate drivers fuming in her wake.

'What do you mean "there was someone"?' Grace demanded, half turning to look over her shoulder. 'D'you mean that man?'

Natalja nodded.

'Why the hell didn't you just tell me?'

'I *couldn't*. I saw him at the entrance and . . . I just didn't want to see him.'

'So you broke into my car.' A new wave of outrage swept through her. 'How the *hell* did you break into my car?'

'This heap of tin?' Natalja said dismissively.

'You seem to rate it as a getaway vehicle,' Grace said.

'You didn't have to make it such a big thing, okay?' Natalja shouted back.

'*I'm* making a big thing of it?' Grace carried on, turning onto Smithdown Road, wondering how, suddenly, she was in the wrong. 'What about you? I mean you creep out the back way, break into my car and hide on the floor to avoid speaking to a man who clearly knows you.' She took a breath and let it go in a long outrush. 'Are you afraid of him?'

'No.' Natalja fell silent, but Grace wasn't willing to leave it there.

'If you're not afraid of him, why not just tell him to his face — "Mirko, I don't want to see you?"'

After another brief silence, Natalja sighed. 'Because it's more complicated than that. I knew Mirko in Croatia. When people know you from home, they think there's some special — I don't know the word — like a knot.'

'Bond.'

'Bond,' Natalja repeated. Grace had never seen her write down a new word, but Natalja amassed new vocabulary with a facility that was astonishing.

They drove past the Brook House pub, and a scruffy row of café bars and pizza places and Grace asked, 'Was he from Knin?'

Natalja had escaped from Knin when the Balkan war started. It was in Croatian control now, and, as a Serb, Natalja had been forced to give up all hope of a safe return. 'Yes,' Natalja said reluctantly. 'Knin. At least that's where we met.'

Grace glanced in her mirror again. Natalja's face had the closed look she always had when Croatia or the Yugoslav conflict was mentioned. 'You don't want to talk about it,' she said.

'There's no point.'

Grace drove under the railway bridge and took the next left. 'Okay.'

Natalja leaned forward, her face close to Grace's. 'Please try to understand,' she said. 'It was a bad time for me, but it's in the past now. Best to forget.'

'Sometimes the past has a way of catching up with us,' Grace said, thinking of Jeff and his brother. Parked cars lined both sides of the street, but she found a space fifty yards from Natalja's house and pulled in at the kerb.

Natalja stared past her. 'I thought he was in London,' she said.

'Mirko?' Grace asked. 'But you haven't lived in London for years.'

'Since I came to Liverpool.'

'So how did he know where to find you?'

Natalja didn't even have to think about it. 'He has friends in the refugee community.' She lifted one shoulder. 'I'm known because I am interpreter.'

'Why do you think he's here?'

'I don't know. Business?'

Grace remembered the business card and handed it to Natalja, searching her face for signs of anxiety. She found none.

'*Verve*?' Natalja said.

'It means spirit or creative energy,' Grace said.

She was surprised to see Natalja's generous mouth break into a smile. 'Verve,' she said. 'Also, it rhymes with nerve.'

CHAPTER TEN

The doorbell rang. It was late, and Rickman wasn't expecting anyone. He peered through the spyhole at the figure shuffling from one foot to the other under the porch light and with mounting irritation he opened the door.

'What d'you want, Lee?'

Foster ignored the question and said, 'Only *you* could have a communication system based on silence.'

Rickman wasn't in the mood to see anyone from work; certainly not Foster. 'If you want to discuss some matter relating to the case, you should talk to DCI Hinchcliffe,' he said.

Foster ignored the advice. 'Why didn't you tell me?'

'Why didn't I tell you *what*?' Rickman injected a note of warning into his tone.

'That you'd been sent to the sin bin by the DCI — bin not being the best choice of words given the circumstances, I'll grant you . . .' Foster was deliberately provoking him.

'Are you gonna let me in, Boss?' Foster demanded. 'It's bloody freezing out here.'

'If I said no, would you go away?'

'Not till you tell me what's going on.'

Rickman sighed. 'I suppose you might as well come in — we were just coming to the interesting bit.'

'Ooh, goody,' Foster rubbed his hands. 'Do I get to watch?'

Rickman gave him a hard stare and Foster winced. 'I just overstepped the mark, didn't I?' He didn't wait for an answer but rattled on with barely a pause. 'Well if I did — and I'm pretty sure I did — I apologise. Sir.'

Rickman took a breath. He didn't know whether to punch Foster or laugh. In the end, he satisfied himself by saying, 'Attitude like yours, Foster, it'd be a miracle if you ever rise above the rank of sergeant.'

Foster grinned. 'Maybe, but I bet I have a few more laughs on the way than most.'

Rickman knew that he was included in Foster's miserable majority. He turned, leaving Foster to shut the front door. The sergeant clumped down the hall after him.

'We're just about to eat,' Rickman said, showing him into the dining- room.

'Hiya, Doc!' Foster said, seizing Grace in a bear hug.

Grace laughed, holding the serving spoon she had in her hand away from her to avoid dripping tomato sauce on the sergeant's clothing. 'Good to see you, too, Lee,' she said, drawing back from him a little breathless.

He held her at arm's length and looked solemnly into her face. 'How're you getting on, like, after . . .' He tilted his head. 'You know.'

Grace matched his solemnity. 'As well as can be expected,' she confided.

She saw his eye stray from her to the meal laid out on the table.

'This is nice,' he said. The table and the oak dresser and waxed wood floor gleamed in soft candlelight, while cool jazz played at a muted volume. He eyed their plates greedily. 'Don't suppose there's any of that going spare? Only I missed lunch and it looks like dinner's gonna be a chippy meal.'

'You won't be staying long enough to eat,' Rickman said.

Grace went to the dresser and fetched a plate and cutlery. 'You'll have to excuse him,' she said. 'We don't have a dog to kick.'

"S'all right, Doc,' he said. 'I never pay him no mind anyhow.'

Grace dished a portion of lasagne. 'Pour the sergeant some wine,' she said, handing Rickman a glass from the dresser and fixing him with a look that said she would brook no argument. 'Please, help yourself to salad,' she added more pleasantly, for Foster's benefit.

'Never touch the stuff,' Foster said, a look of mild alarm on his face. He jabbed at his food with his fork. 'This is great scran, though.'

'Thank the chef,' Grace said.

'I never believed him when he said he could cook.' Foster jerked his head in Rickman's direction. 'Next you'll be telling me he can sing.'

Grace chuckled. Rickman, however, did not find it funny. He stared at Foster, but the sergeant was entirely engrossed in eating the food Rickman had carefully prepared so that he could break the news to Grace gently. In the end, he conceded defeat, filled his glass to the brim and sat down to his meal.

They ate in silence for some minutes, only asking for bread or salad to be passed from one side of the table to the other.

It was Foster, never one to be abashed in such circumstances, who eventually broached the tricky subject of his visit. 'So,' he said between mouthfuls, 'What was the interesting bit you were just getting to?'

Rickman glanced at Grace.

'As I recall, you were just about to tell me why you'd been suspended,' Grace said, pausing between mouthfuls.

'Not suspended, Doc,' Foster corrected her through a mouthful of food, 'Compassionate leave.'

'You didn't see Hinchcliffe's face,' Rickman growled. 'There was no compassion in it.'

* * *

Rickman had gone straight from the evening debrief to DCI Hinchcliffe's office. He had asked to see the Policy Book:

Rickman's record of decision-making since the start of the enquiry. Hinchcliffe sat behind his desk looking grey and tired.

Hinchcliffe was a tidy, fastidious man who never managed to look neat. He was tall and large-limbed, slightly clumsy, faintly embarrassed by his clumsiness. Despite this, he had a clear-up rate that was the envy of the Merseyside Force. His documentation, from discovery to court, was immaculate; the continuity of every piece of evidence, every recorded interview fully accounted for; the rationale behind every major decision transparent and carefully reasoned.

What he lacked in physical grace he more than made up for in mental acuity, and he expected the same high standards from his officers. Rickman knew what to expect: a discussion of this morning's debrief, an explanation of his decisions and a round-up of the investigation so far.

'Take a seat, Jeff,' Hinchcliffe said.

As Rickman came into the room and closed the door, he saw Mayle, the crime scene coordinator, who had been hidden from view. Rickman nodded and Mayle lifted his chin, not quite establishing eye contact. Rickman lowered himself into a chair. *Odd*, he thought. *Decidedly odd.*

'We've just received the analysis and cross-match on the blood found on the victim's clothing,' Hinchcliffe said.

'Yeah?' Rickman looked at Mayle, but he kept quiet: apparently Hinchcliffe was going to do the talking.

'No match to the victim and nothing on the DNA database.'

'Hell.' Rickman passed a hand over his face. 'We're chasing an unknown attacker of an unknown victim,' he said. 'This isn't going to be good for morale.'

'Oh, it gets worse.' Hinchcliffe's voice was soft, but Rickman heard the heat of anger in it and he looked up, surprised.

Hinchcliffe nodded to Mayle. 'As you know,' Mayle said, 'we routinely run DNA samples through the Police Elimination Database, in case of contamination.'

Rickman stared at him. 'And?' He felt Hinchcliffe's eyes on his face and turned to him. His expression was unreadable.

'They got an exact match, Inspector.'

Names and titles, Rickman thought: so important which you choose when delivering bad news.

'It matched your profile, Jeff,' Mayle said. There was regret in his voice, but Rickman's eyes remained on the DCI.

'A perfect match,' Hinchcliffe said.

'It has to be a mistake.' Rickman replayed the events and actions of the last twenty-four hours in his head, desperately trying to establish where he had messed up.

'No mistake.'

Mayle spoke up. 'We thought maybe you'd visited the scene — unintentionally contaminated the evidence.'

'I checked the scene logs myself,' Hinchcliffe said, tapping the bound A4 notebook on his desk. 'There is no record that you were anywhere near. You've a reputation for it, haven't you, Inspector? You let the CSIs get on with their job without interference.'

'That's right,' Rickman said, his voice even, although he felt sick. 'I wasn't there. Yesterday or any day.'

'Then how did your blood get onto the victim's clothing?'

'I don't know—' Rickman's mind raced — what the hell was happening? A sudden recollection: the old church, incense, blood sacrifice. 'I donated blood a few days ago,' he said, trying not to sound too desperate. 'Maybe—'

'You think you're being set up?' Hinchcliffe's incredulity was evident.

Rickman glared back at him. 'I know it.'

'Why?' Hinchcliffe demanded. 'What possible explanation could there be? You've been working on the "Street Safe" campaign for the last six months — are you suggesting that one of your teenaged muggers framed you?'

Every explanation he thought of would only incriminate him further, so Rickman said nothing.

'Go home, Jeff,' Hinchcliffe said.

'Are you suspending me?' Rickman demanded.

'We can do without the bad publicity,' Hinchcliffe answered. 'Your brother is seriously ill.'

'News travels fast,' Rickman commented, unable to keep the bitterness out of his voice.

Hinchcliffe raised an eyebrow. 'It's a police station,' he said.

Take a personal call in a police station and you might as well send the contents as a global email, because in a matter of hours everyone would know about it and have a strongly held opinion on it.

'As far as the press are concerned, you need to spend time with your sick brother,' Hinchcliffe went on. 'I'll be running the show during your "leave of absence".'

'Will you at least check the donated blood — see if any's gone missing?' Rickman asked.

Hinchcliffe stood, his patience exhausted. 'I will investigate this . . . development as thoroughly as I check every line of enquiry,' he said. 'In the meantime, you should go home.'

Rickman hauled himself out of his chair, suddenly feeling every tensed muscle, every minute of lost sleep.

* * *

Grace was watching him, her eyebrows raised her in a gesture that said clearly, *I'm waiting.*

'My DNA has turned up on the victim's clothing,' Rickman said.

Grace blinked, replacing a forkful of food onto her plate. 'She wasn't wearing any clothing.'

'The clothing was inside her flat.'

'How—?'

'I don't know, Grace.' He wanted to say more, but he didn't know where to begin.

Grace held his gaze. 'If you don't know how, then you must at least have some theory as to why.' Grace always cut straight through the crap.

He told her about the blood donor session and Grace listened in perfect stillness. When he had finished, she said, 'I have to ask again — why?'

Rickman and Foster exchanged a look. 'I've got one or two ideas,' Rickman replied.

'Oh? Have you let your boss in on these "ideas"?'

'There are things a DI with ambitions to make DCI simply doesn't tell his senior officer.'

'For instance . . .' Her voice was controlled, but he sensed her exasperation and saw a coolness in her blue eyes.

He didn't answer.

'What will you do?' Grace insisted.

Rickman looked at Foster. 'Sort it.'

'Well, I hate to butt in on your games, boys.' Grace stood up from the table and moved to the door. Rickman could see that she was angry and hurt, and he felt an answering stab of pain in his chest and guts. How the hell did get himself into this mess? He waited until he heard the kitchen door close, then swallowed a mouthful of wine.

'She doesn't know?' Foster asked.

'No.'

Foster pushed a hand through his hair. 'Jeez, man! You should've told her.'

'How could I, Lee? How could I explain to her why I . . .' He couldn't finish. They both knew what he had done — hadn't Foster helped him to clean up the mess, afterwards?

'I didn't kill that girl,' Rickman said.

'I *know* that, don't I?'

Rickman felt a slow burn of shame for the insult to Foster's intelligence.

'Look, Lee, I'm sorry.'

'I should think so, an' all, mate. I've known you since my first major investigation — what was that — five years ago? We've shared an office for two years. You helped me through the sergeant's board. Got drunk with me when my mum died. Sorted the bloody funeral when I couldn't get my head round it. I know you better than you know yourself, mate. You bide by the rules, you don't like mess and you're shit-hot on forensics. You're not gonna leave a great fat clue at the scene, are you?'

Rickman laughed.

'What?'

He scratched his eyebrow. 'I thought maybe you took me to be too moral to bed and then murder a prostitute.'

Foster's eyebrows twitched. 'Like you said yourself, Boss. Still waters…'

Rickman sucked his teeth. He had asked for that. 'What's the word on the team?' he asked.

'The DCI gave us all the official story — your brother being ill and that, but people started wondering why the tests hadn't come back on the DNA.' Foster clapped his hand to the back of his neck, embarrassed. 'Then someone who knows someone at the labs made a call, and it's been pretty much the gossip down the pub tonight.'

'Shit . . .' Rickman passed a hand over his eyes. He poured more wine into Foster's glass. 'I'm going to need some help with this, Lee.'

Foster smiled crookedly at him. 'Why d'you think I'm here?'

CHAPTER ELEVEN

People don't like looking at corpses.

The Imaging Department had digitally altered the photographs to make it look like the girl's eyes were open, but even then, she looked dead. Half a dozen times, when DC Hart showed the picture, she had seen the look of consternation change to horror. 'My God, is she—?'

Dead? Yeah, she wanted to say. How else are you going to get a picture of an unknown murder victim? Somehow people still expected to see a blurry holiday snap, or a slightly wonky snapshot of a slightly squiffy girl at a party. When she explained that they didn't know the victim's identity, they got all flustered and angry with themselves for being so daft.

After five hours of leg work, she had spoken to four committee members of the Deaf Association, the head teachers of every Liverpool comprehensive school with provision for deaf children, and, of course, the head of the Deaf School itself. The Chairman of the Deaf Association agreed to scan the picture into their system, to see if they could come up with a match.

Hart didn't hold out much hope. The girl had come unremarked into the urban landscape and had been swallowed whole by it, disappearing as silently as she had come.

In the Incident Room a number of officers had returned to write up reports, some were making phone calls, a few chatted quietly over cups of coffee. The whiteboard still looked sparse: the crime scene photo alongside the victim's photograph, digitally doctored for public consumption, and when she was last seen — that was about all they had, apart from her address. Carrie — they all called her Carrie, now Rickman wasn't around to complain — was as formless as a shadow. Rickman might disapprove of the nickname they had given her, but for the team, the name made her more real — more *substantial*, more human.

Halfway through writing up her report, Hart's mailbox beeped. She had new mail. Smoothing a hank of pale blonde hair behind one ear, she grabbed the mouse and opened her mailbox

> **From:** *J McCormack* **To:** *DC Naomi Hart*
> **Subject:** *Search of database*
>
> *I've checked using different fields: eye colour, approx. age, hair colour etc., then did a vis. match with members' photos.*
> *I'm sorry, she's not on our files.*
>
> *Let me know if there's anything else I can do.*
> *Jason*

'Bloody hell,' DC Hart muttered, then went back to her report.

'No joy?'

She swivelled her chair to look at Sergeant Foster. He was a few paces away and she suspected that he had been watching her for some time.

'No, Sarge,' she said, turning her back on him in a deliberate gesture.

'This might cheer you up.' He moved around to the front of her desk and skimmed a fax sheet on top of her report. 'Lab results,' he said.

DC Hart picked up the sheet. Most of it was technical stuff she didn't understand, but the summary was clear:
they'd got Carrie typed as Middle Eastern nationality, possibly mixed race. 'That helps,' she said.

'Explains why she didn't do much talking.'

She gave him a hard stare and he said, 'What?'

'Is this a peace offering, Sarge?' She kept a lid on her
anger, but she wouldn't let him get off so easily.

Foster's eyebrows went up a bit, then he said, 'You're
not still mad at me for that little crack I made?'

She didn't answer and he said, 'Come on, Naomi — it's
just a bit of humour — rally the troops and all that.'

'You mean "rally the lads".' He looked surprised and she
half expected him to come back with some remark about her
being a feminist.

Foster opened his mouth, then shut it again. Then he
took a breath. 'Maybe I was a bit out of order,' he said.

'The way she died,' Hart said. She looked past him for
a few seconds. 'It was ugly.'

'It's never pretty,' Foster said.

'No,' she agreed. 'But it doesn't come much uglier.' She
shifted her gaze to his face. 'We can't make it right. But like
the boss said, we can show her some respect, can't we?'

He nodded slowly. 'Yeah,' he said. 'Yeah, we can.'

Neither spoke, and an uncomfortable silence grew. 'One
of us should leave,' Hart said. 'And this is my desk.'

Foster roused himself. 'Right.'

He made to pick up the slip of paper, but Hart stopped
him. She had never seen him chastened; she thought it suited
him much better than his normal, macho act.

'I've got some contacts,' she said. 'Refugee charities, that
kind of thing. Leave it with me, I'll see what I can do.'

'Brill,' Foster said. 'Take it to the HOLMES room with
your report when you've finished. Tell the Action Manager
what you just told me. You might want to contact NASS and
Immigration as well.' The National Asylum Support Service
was responsible for providing financial support as well as

accommodation for asylum seekers while their applications were being considered.

'Get him to put one of the newbies onto the phone work — you don't want to waste your time listening to musak while they keep you on hold for eternity.'

Hart couldn't help smiling.

'What're you grinning at?' he demanded.

'Nothing, Sarge. I'm just seeing a new side to you.' This Lee Foster she thought she could learn to like.

CHAPTER TWELVE

The hospital car park was full when Rickman arrived: afternoon out-patient clinics and ward visitors competing for limited space. If he hadn't been blocked in, nose-to-tail by two other drivers anxious to make it to the kiosk, he would have turned back. Then it was his turn to pay and he thought, *What the hell?* It wasn't like he had anything else to do.

Time had stretched interminably during his enforced idleness. He had busied himself with weekend tasks, raking leaf fall from the back lawn, mending the garden gate and washing his car by lunchtime. Through all of it, trying to think of a way to tell Grace what he couldn't tell the DCI, but succeeding only in finding excuses for not telling her. They had parted that morning with no more than a polite goodbye. He saw puzzlement and hurt in her eyes, but he couldn't find the words to reassure her — to make it right.

He listened to *The World at One* on Radio Four, munching through a ham sandwich without tasting it, watching leaves slowly blanket the lawn again. The trees had been tenacious of their summer green, but two nights of frost had set the autumn bonfires alight. The leaves smouldered orange, gold and blood-red, a false heat in this dismal October afternoon.

They floated sodden from the maple and the beech tree at the boundary fence, already rotting where they fell.

Grace would not be home before six-thirty, the enquiry was out of bounds and he hadn't the patience to read. He went through to the sitting-room and flicked angrily through the channels. Every one of them seemed to feature unhappy families: chat shows, soaps, the afternoon film, all seemed steeped in familial misery.

It was a close-run thing between making the trip to the hospital and going to the pub and getting blind drunk. But such choices were never as close as Rickman thought: he'd always had an aversion to drunks and drunkenness, finding the former too easily roused to rage, and the loss of control caused by the latter too unsettling.

Clouds huddled low, enfolding the city in a false twilight and he had driven to the city centre in sombre mood. He turned left under the barrier and found a space in the middle of a row, squeezed between a four-by-four and an old Renault which had been parked at an awkward angle.

He took the concrete steps down to the side entrance and along the grey-tiled corridor to the lifts at the centre of the building. He had believed that all family ties were severed when his mother died. He was just twenty, then, and months away from his finals. He had joined the Force as a graduate, and from that moment, the police became his family, his social life, the centre of his world. Did he really want to take on a new family, one that had all the complications of guilt and unsettled scores?

He didn't know, and while he wavered, undecided, he rode the lift to the fourth floor and walked through the ward doors. Other visitors followed him out of the lift, carrying flowers and gifts of food. A television boomed further down the corridor, the nurses were gathered in the glass square that served as an office, out of the way of patients and the demands of relatives.

In one of the rooms, two men in dressing-gowns sat hunched over a game of draughts. They glanced up at him and Rickman saw in the anxiety and frustration of their expressions that they didn't know how to take the next move. The rules of this simple game, like the complex rules of life, were beyond them now. The most distressing thing was, they knew it.

He averted his eyes, quickening his pace a little. He heard his brother's voice, raised in excitement. There was a compulsiveness about it, and an agitation, as if he needed to talk, as if his life or his sanity depended on it. Rickman had seen this occasionally in assault victims, and more often in witnesses to violent crime. They relived the horror over and over, blaming themselves for not having intervened, justifying their lack of intervention, going round and round until he interrupted to reassure them: There was nothing they could have done; it wasn't their fault, Most of the time, it was true. It was never enough, but it gave a little solace.

He stood a few paces from the door, trying to listen to what Simon was saying. Was he asking for reassurance? Was it the burden of his guilt that kept him from resting? He turned as Rickman reached the door, tense with resolute concentration. When he saw Rickman, Simon stopped talking and stood still. For a few moments, he stared as if trying to focus on his face.

* * *

He kept telling them, but they wouldn't listen. He told them they'd made a mistake, but they seemed so sure they were right, and the woman — Tanya — she kept coming in like she belonged there. All his waking hours, the terror of what he didn't remember — the huge black hole in his memory — threatened to overwhelm him.

Tanya frightened him: her expectations, her emotional demands were too much to cope with. He had told them over and over, it should be Jeff sitting in that chair, not some stranger. Little Jeff with a pile of *Superman* comics, because Superman was his favourite. Simon had always

85

favoured *Batman* for the gadgets and gismos and Bruce Wayne seemed somehow more grown up — more *real* than Superman. Batman was strong, sure, but he was human, and he used his brains as much as anything to beat the bad guys, and that appealed to Simon. He used to call Jeff 'Robin' when he was little and Jeff got mad because he wanted to be big and strong, like Superman, not some skinny kid like Robin. Which he was, of course — a skinny kid. He was little and weak and he hated that — hated being weak — but he was brave, Simon remembered; Jeff had always been brave.

He stopped. Tried to concentrate. There was something trying to surface, some memory. But he didn't know what to concentrate *on*. It was just a feeling . . . like he'd forgotten something important.

Then he saw Jeff — an older Jeff — Jeff as a man. They had told him he'd forgotten things — years and years — which he didn't believe. But now, seeing this old Jeff, he had to believe. And though it was sad Jeff had got so old without him noticing, he was glad to see him. Jeff had come, like he knew he would. He felt his face split into a grin and he took a step forward.

'Jeff!'

* * *

Rickman held his brother off with a handshake. He looked to Tanya for an explanation.

'He doesn't remember,' she said. 'He's forgotten you were here before.'

'I did not forget!' Simon yelled, suddenly trembling with fury. 'I remember things you never even knew.'

Tanya shrank back in her chair, shocked and frightened.

Rickman spoke softly, knowing that his voice would get through to Simon. 'What do you remember, Simon?'

Simon turned. He seemed shaken, but also disorientated, as if he didn't know the cause of his agitation. Could his memory be so faulty that he'd forgotten already why he had screamed at Tanya?

He began talking about their childish games, the den they had built in the woods at Croxteth Park; the dam they had constructed in the stream; their night-time flits to explore the dark streets while others slept, and Rickman felt a quickening of his pulse. These memories had a power over him; he found himself responding despite himself, found himself softening towards his brother.

Simon told the stories in exquisite detail, recalling the pearly mists that swirled around their ankles on early summer days in the park; how once they lay down on the sodden grass and tried to count the shimmering gems of dew weighing down the tips of every bent blade, wishing they were diamonds so that they could stuff their pockets and take them home. His brother grew calm as he recounted their childish fantasies and, at length, he lapsed into silence, a small smile playing on his lips and the light of those sunny days shining in his blue eyes. Rickman realised with a shock that Simon hadn't simply calmed down, he hadn't only forgotten why he had raged at Tanya; he had forgotten raging at her at all.

* * *

'I was in a crash,' Simon said. *'No. That's wrong.* Not crash.'

'No, Simon,' Rickman said. 'You're right. You were in a crash.'

'I know that. I know I was.' Jeff was looking at him like he was crazy. God . . . why couldn't he explain? It wasn't wrong that he'd been in a crash, because obviously, he had — what was wrong was he'd meant to say he'd been in a *coma*, but 'crash' just came out like he had no control over his mouth. Words kept doing that: either they weren't there at all, or the wrong ones came out. It was bad enough having no control of the material world — of the doctors and the people who came to see him. But it filled him with dread to think that his mind was so . . .

The word that finally came to him was 'deranged'.

He watched Jeff's mouth carefully, because it was hard to hear what people were saying unless you watched their lips. Jeff explained that he knew about what had happened, because had been to see him the day before. Simon believed Jeff, but he simply couldn't remember.

'Coma,' he said, when he finally sorted out in his head the words and the order. 'Not crash.' Which was the wrong thing to say, because Jeff looked at him like he was crazy again.

He wanted to know about the things he'd forgotten, but Jeff must have something wrong with his memory as well, because he kept saying *he* didn't know. He said, 'Ask your wife.' But Tanya didn't *feel* like his wife. What could he ask her?

'Are you mad at me, Jeff?' he asked.

'No, Simon, I'm not mad at you.'

He asked Jeff questions about himself, because he needed to know about Jeff's life — what he had done with it. He asked about Jeff's job and if he was married and how many children he had. He couldn't remember what Jeff said about the last two things, but the woman got some photographs out and said they were holiday snaps of his children. At first, he thought she meant Jeff's children, because one of the boys in the picture looked just like Jeff. But these were colour snaps, and their dad never took anything but black-and-white, so it definitely wasn't Jeff. Still, the boy did look just like Jeff when he was little, only in colour. His hair a tangle of chestnut-brown curls, the hazel eyes wary, perhaps even haunted, the skinny elbows and knees — were Jeff. The young Jeff. Not the hard-eyed grown-up Jeff. Tanya said his name was Fergus and Fergus was their child — hers and Simon's. He couldn't think about that now, and he had to tell her to be quiet because it felt like his head was coming off.

Jeff stayed for quite a while, even though he was a policeman and there was a murder he had to — to . . . The word had gone — when the police talk to people and ask questions and find out who's done a crime. Jeff was doing that. God, it was so *humiliating*, this loss of language.

'So,' Simon said. 'You're a bizzy.' It was what they had called cops as kids.

'I prefer "police officer",' Jeff said, but he smiled a little, like he didn't really mind.

'What I mean is—' Simon shrugged, suddenly feeling shy. 'You got to be Superman after all — fighting evil, saving the innocent.'

'I wish it was that simple.' Jeff didn't talk much, but when he said things you felt like they meant something. It was just hard to work out what.

Jeff had always been a better listener than a talker. He listened like he expected *your* words to mean something as well — something more than just the words — and sometimes Simon saw something behind the man-face of his brother: an after-image of the young Jeff, always serious and quiet. He would write down that Jeff had visited, to remind himself, so he'd know next time.

'I used to call him "my little bother",' he told Tanya, more to prove he could remember things than because he wanted Tanya to know. '*He* said that made me his *big* bother.' He smiled and for some reason tears came into his eyes. Appalled, he turned away from them and went to the window; he cried so easily since the accident, it was embarrassing.

When Jeff finally said he had to go, Simon watched him walk out of the room and he felt a little tremor, as if a small earthquake had nudged the foundation of the building, momentarily turning the concrete floor to jelly. Jeff didn't look weak anymore. He didn't look like he needed Batman to watch his back.

CHAPTER THIRTEEN

It had been a day of triumphs and frustrations. The DNA results on the murder victim had brought them several steps closer to finding her true identity but dealing with Immigration and the National Asylum Support Service was proving more difficult than any of them had anticipated. Software problems, backlogs, overwork, understaffing were all trotted out as excuses why they couldn't help to track down the girl's name.

After a late briefing with a bad-tempered and harassed-looking DCI Hinchcliffe, Foster suggested the day team should go to Picton Road for a pint. By ten o'clock, about twelve had gathered. The landlord sent out to the chippy for food to save on drinking time, and they settled in the snug, after one or two of the local scallies decided they weren't in favour of sharing it with bizzies.

DC Hart had picked Reid as her newbie, and she had given him the job of contacting NASS for help in identifying the victim. He had been cut off twice during a forty-five-minute hold and both times it had been 'impossible' to reconnect him to the person he had previously been speaking to.

Reid held forth while Hart got the drinks in. 'I says, "Give me the complaints department." She says, "We haven't got a complaints department." So *I* says—'

'Well you bloody well should have!' they all chorused in unison.

'An hour and a half.' He shook his head. 'They don't even play you music, so you'd know if you've been cut off.'

'My guess is she hung up as soon as you opened your mouth,' Hart said, setting down a pint in front of him. 'Hearing you, she probably thought, "This clown doesn't even speak English."' Reid had a broad accent with catarrhal 'c's and no 'h's at all.

'Oh, yeah, thanks, Nay,' he said.

Naomi swiped his pint from his hand even as he pursed his lips for the first sip. 'Na–o–mi,' she said. 'Three syllables. Can you do that, Andy? Can you?' She was smiling, but there was a veiled threat in the way she held the pint that Andy might just find his drink in his lap if he didn't comply.

Jeers went up as he repeated her name and won his prize of a pint.

She ruffled his hair and sat down to her own drink. 'I had to set the DCI on them in the end,' she said.

Foster came over from the bar with a tray of drinks and slid them onto the table. 'He was not happy,' he said.

'So when do we get to know?' someone asked.

Foster shrugged. 'They've got her age, description and race. You'd think they'd just stick it in their database and run a search, wouldn't you?'

'But . . .' Hart said.

'But — they said it might take a few days, 'cos some of the documentation hasn't been entered into the computers yet.'

'You *wa'*?' Andy Reid again. 'What if we went round saying "We did arrest a few scallies around Kensington on the night in question, your honour, but we can't produce them in court, like, 'cos we haven't got round to the paperwork." I mean — do me a favour . . .'

'He's got a point,' Foster said, sinking half his pint. There was general agreement, and Foster was hopeful he would conclude the business of the evening without much hassle; but the conversation drifted away from the investigation to football, the telly, only drifting back to work when somebody mentioned the dismal lack of overtime allowed in the investigation budget.

Respect for Sergeant Foster's feelings had kept them away from the topic of Rickman's suspension up to that point, but an hour of drinking blurred the boundaries. Added to this, it became apparent that Foster wasn't going to do the tactful thing and turn in for an early night. So, haltingly at first, the conversation turned to the gossip of the day.

Foster kept quiet, letting them warm up for a bit. There was no good in him putting in his two penn'orth if it stopped them dead. After the food was eaten and cleared away, people could give their full attention to the matter, and more of them added their own insights and speculations. Gradually, their embarrassment at speaking in front of Rickman's friend faded and people became more outspoken.

Foster forbore when someone said, 'No smoke without fire'. He bit his tongue when another member of the team called Rickman 'a dark horse'. Rickman often criticised him for speaking before he thought, but Foster knew that Rickman's habit of careful reflection sometimes made him look passionless, even manipulative — which was funny, given the present circumstances. He sipped his pint slowly after downing the first half, waiting for the right moment to drop a hint of two that would turn the flock in the direction he had planned.

'What d'you reckon, Lee?' Naomi Hart had drunk over her usual limit and apparently felt emboldened by her earlier encounter with Foster.

Foster raised his eyebrows in question, not wanting any disapproval that might creep into his voice to spoil her flow.

'You've worked with Rickman for, what — two years? What d'you reckon to this blouse with his blood on it?'

Foster knew that if he delayed long enough, someone else would answer for him, he whiled the time away admiring the almost white blonde of Hart's hair.

'My source at the Forensic Science Unit said there was a hell of a lot of it,' someone chipped in.

'Yeah,' Reid said. 'But he's a *cop*. He's not gonna leave something that obvious at the scene, is he?'

'I was thinking that,' Foster said mildly, thinking, *Nice one, Newbie*.

'Did anyone notice if he had any cuts?' Naomi asked, her head swivelling a little loosely on her neck as she glanced around her workmates. 'I mean, if there was so much blood, where'd it come from?'

There was a general shaking of heads.

'Nosebleed?' Reid offered. 'Anyhow, it doesn't have to be visible, does it? She could have cut him anywhere — he could be hiding it under his clothes.'

Black mark against the newbie, Foster thought. 'I heard it was about half a pint.' It was a wild exaggeration, but if he planted the idea in someone else's mind, he was hopeful he wouldn't have to say it himself.

The newbie gave a low whistle. 'That's half a donor session.'

There was a pause while drink-fuddled minds chewed this over. Foster hardly daring to breathe.

'If someone got hold of one of those blood transfusion bags, from last week, it'd be easy to fake evidence,' Naomi remarked.

'Nimps,' Foster agreed, with masterful understatement. He sipped his pint and peered over the rim at the thoughtful faces of the men and women around him.

'God,' Naomi said, as the full implications of what she had said hit her. 'Any one of us could've been set up.'

Foster liked this: paranoia was great for getting the rumourmongers going. 'Someone with a grudge . . .' he added, keeping it non-specific, making it seem like he was just agreeing with the general tenet of her argument. Another pause followed, while people filled in the blanks, remembering everyone they had pissed off in the past month. The threats didn't seem quite so empty now.

'If someone on that donor team's bent, they could be selling cops' blood all over the city.' *That newbie's got imagination*, Foster thought. He got in another round of drinks to encourage them to stay and develop their conspiracy theories.

As he waited for the drinks at the bar, chatting idly with the landlord, he listened with one ear to the rumble of conversation continuing in the snug: voices raised in exclamation, vigorous assertions made, and felt a glow of satisfaction. By morning this would be all through the team, and as stated fact, instead of merely a possible explanation of how Rickman's blood got into the girl's flat. The randomness of it, a natural anxiety that it could so easily have been their blood the killer had used, would frighten people into exonerating Rickman. If they believed that it could have been any one of them, fewer people would be likely to speculate that Rickman had been set up as the result of a personal grudge. When he returned with the drinks, they barely looked up, so intense was their conversation.

He'd lay odds that Naomi Hart would be in the boss's office first chance she got, demanding to know what Hinchcliffe was doing about the possible theft of the blood.

He checked his watch. 'Gotta go.'

'You wimping out, Sarge?' Naomi asked. 'I was just gonna get another round in.'

'You're slurring, girl,' he said. 'You'd be wiser to get an early night.'

'He can't stand the pace . . .' Reid taunted.

'That remains to be seen.' Foster smiled to himself. 'Got a date, haven't I?'

'At this hour?' Naomi said. The landlord had given them a lock-in, and it was way past calling time.

'It's near midnight,' Reid squinted at his watch.

'Past your bedtime then, isn't it, Newbie?' Foster said. 'Anyway, I never said it was a night *out*.'

CHAPTER FOURTEEN

They went where they wanted, took what they wanted, whenever they felt like it and nobody could stop them. They moved fast, always on the lookout for the yellow police CCTV vans, covering their heads and faces like modern-day Ninjas.

They varied the action, so the shopkeepers and the security guards never got the measure of them, shoplifting at the corner sweet-shop one day, steaming the sports shops down the city centre once in a while for new gear. When you went mob-handed, the shop assistants didn't know who to grab first.

They called themselves the Rokeby Rats, after their junior school. They'd have to find something else next year, when they moved up to Hope Valley High. Daz suggested Valley Vermin, because Daz always liked to think ahead, and Beefy said he'd decide when he was good and ready, just so long as they didn't end up sounding like one of his sister's poncey story books. Thing was, he didn't know that rats were vermin, and Valley Vermin would have been a clever way to make the step up to Big School. But Beefy didn't like Daz being clever; it showed him up.

Daz should have been the gang leader — only Beefy had a punch like Holyfield and a temper like Tyson, whereas Daz wasn't that strong and he was a rubbish fighter, so really it was no contest. The lads felt safe with Beefy as boss, so long as he wasn't going off on one of them, that is. Anyway, next year seemed a lifetime away and right now, they were the Rats — heroes of their own action movie, warriors of the back streets, feeding on adrenalin and fast-food.

The other two members of the gang were Jez and Minky. Jez was fast — he could snatch a mobile and be a mile away in five minutes flat. They mostly sold the mobies to Beefy's big brother for a pitifully low set price. He said it was because so many of them were write-offs since phone providers brought in the deactivation service. Beefy's brother was six-foot tall and built like a brick shithouse, which gave him the advantage in most arguments. Also, he had the contacts to fence the phones, which the Rats didn't. It just about kept them in ciggies and video games, which was okay, but it was better when Jez grabbed a purse or a wallet, because there was no middleman to pay off.

Minky was Jez's little brother, and he was a pain in the arse. He was only ten — still in year five — and kind of small and weedy, both of which meant that Beefy wouldn't recognise him as a full gang member. They called him Minky on account of him still having his baby teeth. He came along because Jez didn't like leaving him at home with what was going on there, and he could be useful when there was trouble, because he looked so innocent, and he'd cry if someone so much as looked at him sideways.

They'd been in town all day and into the night, ducking in and out of the shops in St John's Precinct, robbing a few bits of jewellery, just to keep their hands in, swiping a scarf and a T-shirt off one of the market stalls in Church Street so they could make a Guy. Daz found a couple of bin-bags full of paper and stuff at the back of one of the offices in Lord Street, and they dressed them in the clothes.

They stood outside the Windsor pub in Pembroke Place for two hours, while mizzly rain turned to mist and mist thickened to a patchy fog.

'Whose idea was it to come to Pembroke?' Beefy demanded.

'*Flat* broke, more like,' Daz said. Nobody dared to remind Beefy it was his idea. They had collected just two pounds twenty-three pence, most of which Minky took, him being the only one of them that looked scrubbed clean and innocent.

Minky piped up, 'It's no wonder, is it? Our Guy's crap.'

Beefy told him to shut up, but Minky never knew when to leave it alone. He pouted a bit, and said, 'Look at it — it hasn't even got a head.'

'We could use yours.' Beefy grabbed him in a headlock and twisted a bit. 'Know why you've still got your baby teeth?' Beefy said. 'From staying on your mother's *tit* too long.'

Jez held up both hands, 'Leave it out, Beefy . . . He's just—'

Minky swung his left fist hard and connected with Beefy's balls. Jez grabbed hold of him, pulling him backwards at a run.

'Come here, you little bastard!' Beefy roared. But Jez and Minky had run out of range, and Beefy wasn't built for the chase. He attacked the Guy instead, kicking and stamping on it, tearing it to pieces in his rage.

'What're you doin'?' Daz said. 'It's completely fucked, now.'

Beefy kicked the Guy a couple more times. 'It's a useless piece of crap!' he screamed. 'And you—' He pointed at Minky, 'are dead.'

Minky was feeling brave, half-hidden behind his brother, so he yelled back, 'You'll have to catch me first, Sumo Man!'

Beefy's eyes widened and he ran at the two of them. For a second, Minky froze, then Jez jerked him by his jacket hood and they were off, pelting down past TJ's, darting down an alley that led out onto an empty plot.

A powerful *BANG!* above Jez's head. He bellowed like he'd been hit, and Minky screamed, then Jez went on the attack. He was fast. The next second, he had a banger in his hand, lit and thrown in one smooth action before Beefy had time to take cover. Bea-*u*-tiful.

'War!' Beefy yelled.

The fog was thick in pockets; it lent a realism to the fight. It swirled around them like smoke, keeping the smell of gunpowder in their nostrils for longer, startling frightened screams from people when one exploded near them. They dodged from car to car along the streets, ducking and circling, launching ambush attacks and counter-attacks till their supplies were nearly exhausted and it had turned from a fight into a game. Around them, other explosions and muted flashes from distant skirmishes around the city. They were laughing when they weren't screaming. They felt alive and strong. Anything was possible on a night like this.

Jez called a truce after he'd run out of bangers. Beefy and Daz bombarded his position, behind a row of steel bins in an alley behind the new housing on Shaw Street, till he begged for mercy, screaming with laughter.

Beefy agreed, if Jez and Minky declared undying allegiance and bowed down to the great Beefy Beale.

They were on the way home, friends again, when they saw a man walking a bit further on from them. He had his head hunched down between his shoulders and hurried along taking little steps.

'Looks like he's dying for a piss,' Jez said, and they all cracked up.

''Ey, lad?' This was Daz. He started the new game, now he'd leave the rest to Beefy.

'Hey, *Paki*!' He looked Asian, maybe Arab, but 'Paki' was as good a name as any.

The man looked over his shoulder. They could see the whites of his eyes.

'Penny for the Guy, mate?' Beefy said.

He turned away and hurried on, which really pissed Beefy off. 'Hey, lad?' he yelled. 'Had your Giro, yet? Spare a penny for the Guy?'

They had almost caught up, but he drifted in and out of focus as the fog tumbled down from the strip of terraced gardens to their right. Beefy lit a banger and held it so long they were all screaming at him to throw it. At the last moment, he lobbed it high and far. It went off right over the man's head.

'Man, that was sweet . . .' Jez murmured, filled with awe.

The man gave a terrified yell. It made the boys look at each other, a bit uneasy, the way he screamed. Beefy creased. He was laughing and choking, leaning on Jez for support. 'He thinks he's in *I*-raq,' he said. 'Hey, Saddam! Want another rocket up the arse?'

Another banger exploded to the man's right and he broke into a run. They followed him, Jez — being fastest — acting as scout. 'He's cut down Conway Street!' he shouted to the others. 'He's heading for the tennies.'

They all knew that the old tenement buildings housed the immigrants.

They belted after him, howling and baying like dogs. The man ran past the lift and flung open the fire escape door. He ran up the concrete steps with the boys snapping at his heels. A second door led onto the landing. Four front doors along the length of the building. He got to his front door and with one last frantic look over his shoulder, slotted the key in the latch and fell inside.

* * *

The man's wife had been waiting for him to return from the all-night pharmacy on London Road, with medicine for their baby. She saw the terror in his eyes and stared back at him, clutching the infant to her. 'What is it?' she gasped.

He pushed the bag containing the medicine into her hand. 'Go into the back room,' he said. 'Close the door.'

The boys hooted and howled, pressing their faces to the glass of the front door.

'Please, go away,' he said. 'My baby is sick.'

'My baby is sick!' Beefy repeated, imitating his accent. 'Goodness gracious me, my baby is sick!'

They hammered on the door, opening the letterbox and shrieking like ghouls. Daz had an idea. 'Trick or treat!' he shouted. Daz always had the best ideas. He shoved his last banger into Beefy's hand and shouted again, 'Trick or treat!'

Beefy grinned savagely and reached in his pocket for his lighter.

He shoved the lit firework through the letterbox and yelled 'Fire in the hole!' They all crouched like Vietnam Vets, hands over their ears, and listened for the satisfying *boom!* as the explosion reverberated down the hallway of the flat.

The woman screamed and the baby set up a wail. They turned to run and found their escape route cut off. Two big mean-looking men blocked the way they had come. Another man who looked more like a businessman than a hard man, stood in the way of them fleeing down the landing and out at the far end of the building. There was a three-storey drop over the balcony, so the only probable route was past the tall, smartly dressed man who looked rather mildly at them, like a bank manager contemplating a customer who had run up an unauthorised overdraft.

'Get out me way, dickhead.' Beefy was all bravado. The others watched nervously. He'd bluffed his way out of worse, and they had no choice but to put their faith in him pulling it off again.

'First, you have to go to the house and apologise,' the man said.

Beefy got two words into mimicking his accent. The man's hand flicked out sharp as a whip and dealt him a stinging blow across his head.

Shocked and furious, Beefy squared up to him. 'You can't hit me!'

'Is that right?' the man said, as if the information was of real interest to him. 'Well, I'm just a dumb immigrant, what do I know?'

'FUCK ALL!' Beefy yelled, trying to barge past.

The man smiled, pushing him with one hand. Beefy fell with surprising force, banging the base of his spine hard against the concrete. Tears of rage and humiliation filled his eyes as he fought to catch his breath. The other boys stayed quiet, hoping they wouldn't attract notice.

'You,' the man said.

Daz took a step back.

'You handed him the explosive.'

'I never!' Daz was terrified: when he looked at the quiet man, he saw the kind of man he might himself become: someone who was in control, and who knew how to control others. Worse, Daz knew what he would do next, if he had that kind of power.

'Don't lie.' The man spoke slowly, quietly, but there was danger in it. Ball-shrinking terror.

Daz shrugged, but his shoulders wouldn't respond properly, and it looked to the others like he'd flinched. 'We were just having a laugh.'

The man tilted his head. Inside the flat, the wails of the baby and the sobbing of the woman went on. 'I don't hear laughter.'

Minky started to cry softly.

'Come here,' the man said, and Daz edged reluctantly forward. 'Closer.'

He moved faster than a snake, grabbed Daz by the scruff of his neck and the seat of his pants and tipped him over the balcony.

Minky gave a piercing shriek.

For one heart-stopping moment he seemed to release his grip, then the man had Daz by the ankles, holding him out above the weedy tarmac of the forecourt. The distant ground vanished and reappeared as the fog eddied and surged. Daz tried to scream, but all they heard were breathless gasps.

'Stop it!' Minky begged. 'Please, Mister!'

The man smiled, glancing first at the two men and then at the boys. Beefy sat open-mouthed on the floor, terrified that he would be next.

The men moved forward and he shrank back. They laughed. It sounded like the low rumble of bowling balls rolling on wood.

'Just "having a laugh",' the man said.

He raised the paralysed Daz back over the rail and dropped him on the ground. 'Take them home,' he said to the other two men. He didn't look at Daz, who lay gasping and puking on the floor in front of him.

'Make sure it's the right address.'

He bent, looking into the boys' faces. 'Do you know what will happen if you tell anyone about this?'

They all nodded.

He picked on Minky. 'Explain to your friends what will happen.'

Minky said, 'I . . . I . . .' and broke down, sobbing uncontrollably.

'Okay,' the man said. 'I'll tell you. If you speak of this — to anyone.' — He emphasised the last word — 'You will die.' He stayed at a crouch, waiting until each of them looked up at him. 'Do you understand?'

They nodded.

He craned forward as if straining to listen. 'I can't hear you.'

They all answered, even Minky, who couldn't stop crying.

He straightened up, staring at them for a few moments longer, then he stepped aside.

'Bye-bye, boys,' he said. 'I'll be seeing you soon.'

CHAPTER FIFTEEN

The fog lingered all through the next day, creeping into the empty cellars of Falkner Square and Hope Street, probing the cracks and gaps of the rusted iron and sodden plyboard barricades over the windows of derelict properties in Wavertree Road and Kensington. On the Mersey, ferries chugged blindly to and fro on their twenty-minute journey from the Pier Head to Seacombe, blasting out Beatles songs into the fog until even the tourists were sick of the repetition. Further down the estuary towards the Irish Sea, the fog was a dense bank of milky white and only the mournful bellow of fog-horns kept the Isle of Man ferries at sparring distance from the Dublin Seacats.

Rickman spent the day in the attic, dusting off memories he would rather forget. When, at last, he found the leatherette album, tucked away in a cardboard box without a label, he wiped it over with one hand and stared at it for several minutes; but he could not bring himself to open it. And when he pulled the attic door closed behind him, his hands were empty.

He became aware of a distant ringing and realised that the hall phone was jangling off the hook. He sprinted down the stairs wrestling with a vague anxiety for Grace.

It was Hinchcliffe. 'Can you come in immediately?' he asked.

'I'm on compassionate leave,' Rickman reminded him.

'I'll expect you within the hour,' Hinchcliffe replied. 'Watch out for icy patches.' Then he hung up.

Rickman mused on this cryptic advice as he showered and changed. Hinchcliffe was no fool. Had he sussed Lee Foster's involvement? But when he opened the door to leave, he was hit by an icy blast of air and he saw, amused at his own paranoia, that Hinchcliffe's solicitousness had been genuine: the ground was thick with hoar frost. The trees in the front garden were edged with it. The frost grew in dazzling white needles from every bare branch and laced the margins of the few remaining leaves. Over all, lay the fog.

Rickman pulled on his gloves, but didn't bother to fasten his overcoat, relishing instead the bite of frost and the insidious probing of the saturated air. The fog parted, swirling like smoke as he trotted down the steps, curling and eddying in the vortex created by his coat-tails, then settling once more into blank white stillness.

* * *

He passed Foster on the corridor with no more than a curt 'Good afternoon.' Others stared, wondering why he was there, and quickly averted their gaze when he caught their eye. He went straight to the DCI's office.

Hinchcliffe sat behind his desk, Tony Mayle to the right of the door.

'This is like déjà vu all over again,' Rickman murmured.

Hinchcliffe, it seemed, did not appreciate the irony. He fixed Rickman with a beady eye and said, 'Come in, Inspector.' Rickman heard no apology in either his tone or his demeanour and he quelled a slight nervousness.

When he was seated, Hinchcliffe nodded to Mayle.

'We've discovered an anomaly in the bloodstains on the victim's blouse,' Mayle said.

'An anomaly . . .'

Hinchcliffe's expression was unreadable, but Rickman thought Mayle looked embarrassed, which he took as a good sign.

'It didn't come from a normal bleed,' Mayle said.

'Which is . . . anomalous,' Rickman said. It wasn't that he bore any resentment against Mayle, the CSC, was doing his job impartially, as he always did — he just wished he would get to the point.

'There is a chemical present in the sample,' Hinchcliffe said.

'EDTA,' Mayle added.

'Used in blood samples to prevent them from clotting,' Rickman said. Anyone with more than a basic forensic awareness would know that. 'Oh — and in blood donated for transfusions. Which means that the blood on the murder victim's clothing came from the donor session, like I said.'

'Which brings me back to my original question,' Hinchcliffe said, watching him closely. 'Why?'

'Maybe I was just unlucky.' He turned to Mayle. 'Did you check the donated blood? Was there any missing?'

Mayle glanced at Hinchcliffe before answering. 'Yours was down by about fifty mils,' he said. 'You can make a lot of mess with fifty mils of blood.'

'Don't I know it,' he said bitterly. 'Were any other blood bags tampered with?'

'We're checking now,' Mayle said. 'Some have already been used.'

Rickman looked at Hinchcliffe. 'Reinstate me,' he said.

'High Park Street police station, first thing tomorrow.'

Rickman shook his head. 'No.'

Hinchcliffe blinked. Before he could rouse himself to outrage at being contradicted, Rickman went on: 'Look, sir, I have to be reinstated to *this* case.'

'Out of the question,' Hinchcliffe said.

Mayle began to get up. 'I should—' He gestured toward the door.

'Sit down, Tony,' Hinchcliffe said. Mayle shot Rickman an apologetic look and took his seat again.

'Sir,' Rickman said. 'If you reassign me off this investigation it'll send the message out that there was something in this' — he waved a hand disparagingly — 'evidence; that I somehow managed to wangle a way out of it.' He looked Hinchcliffe in the eye. 'They'll think that you don't trust me.'

He was sailing close to the wind, voicing the very concerns Hinchcliffe must have, but airing them now meant that Hinchcliffe would have trouble returning to them later. Added to this was the psychological advantage gained by facing the DCI eyeball to eyeball and telling him he was wrong.

'Reinstate me,' he said again. And waited an agonising thirty seconds for a response.

* * *

He stopped by his office. Hinchcliffe had been scrupulous in redirecting his work: his in-tray was empty except for an A4 sheet with the message, printed in thirty-six point lettering, 'All paperwork for DI Rickman to be re-routed to DCI Hinchcliffe's office.'

Foster glanced up from a late lunch of corned-beef sandwiches and crisps. 'All right?' he asked. Normally, this was an all-purpose greeting, but today it was a question.

Rickman grinned, 'More than all right.' He hung his coat behind the door, then took the note from his in-tray and screwed it into a ball, dropping it into the bin. 'I'd like to call an emergency briefing. Get as many as you can — I don't want it to look like I'm sneaking in through the back gate.'

* * *

Foster spoke to the officers working from the Incident Room first. He sent someone off to the kitchen to find any loiterers.

Then he organised a phone-round the officers on house-to-house and other lines of enquiry.

The briefing was scheduled for four p.m. and the response was exceptional. Nearly everyone on days came in — not wanting to miss the outcome of this little drama.

Rickman waited until a few minutes past the time: he knew that Foster had not given a reason for the early briefing, so rumours would be rife. Equal bets on both his suspension and his exoneration, if Rickman knew cops. He just hoped they'd offered better odds on his exoneration.

He made his entrance and a hush rippled out as he passed. He saw one or two eyebrows raised, glances exchanged. Rickman knew he would have to find a way to bring the crew together; having them bickering over whether he was guilty or not simply wasn't an option. He needed them to be in accord. A quick survey of the room gave him his subject matter: an evidence bag shoved under one of the tables, reports sitting on desks when they should have been filed hours ago. Everywhere plastic cups, sweet and crisp wrappers, bins overflowing with sandwich cartons and wastepaper. If accord meant them agreeing over the fact that he was a niggling bastard, so be it.

'This room,' he said, 'is in shit order.'

He saw a resentment settling on the faces of some of the officers. These were the ones, he guessed, who had bet against him.

'We're running a major investigation in what looks like a teenager's bedroom.'

People glanced at each other. He even saw a bit of eye-rolling. Even those who had been in his favour were stung. Good. It means they wouldn't go crowing to their mates and dividing the team.

'Evidence will be bagged, labelled and logged with the Exhibits Officer on arrival — no diversions, no delays. Reports will be written up immediately you return to this office and taken to the Receiver in the HOLMES room when complete. Are we clear?'

They were.

He asked for verbal feedback on the day's actions: NASS were adamant they couldn't work any faster on identifying the girl, so the community liaison officer had been brought in to talk with refugee organisations and see if any progress could be made that way.

'Okay,' he said. 'I'll call a press conference — get an artist's impression of the girl on the regional news bulletins. Maybe that'll jog a few memories.'

'Sir?'

Rickman recognised the slightly wheezy Widnes accent of Tunstall. 'I don't want to sound silly, sir, but why don't you just use the photo?'

'Because I don't want to upset all the mums and dads watching telly with their kids at tea-time with a picture of a dead woman.'

Tunstall missed the sarcasm in Rickman's voice. 'Oh,' he said complacently. 'I see.'

Rickman hesitated. He wasn't sure how to broach the subject of his return to the investigation. He didn't want to sound defensive, but he didn't want to leave the subject open to further speculation, either.

'Sir?' It was Tunstall again. 'Are you back for good, sir?'

'Yes, Tunstall,' Rickman said.

'Only we'd heard your brother was quite poorly, sir.'

Rickman couldn't tell whether the man was a consummate actor or extremely obtuse: there was no hint of irony in his voice, not even the ghost of a smirk on his face. But the rest of the team saw the joke all right.

He had a choice: stand on his dignity and look like a pillock — or take it with good humour. Rickman answered as if the question had been ironic. 'Let's say he's making a remarkable recovery,' he said.

A few smiled. Laughter was disguised as coughs.

Tunstall, alone, did not see the joke. 'What about this blood donor thing then, sir?' he asked.

Rickman couldn't believe the man's gall. He saw a number of people shuffle uncomfortably — they thought he had gone too far. But when he looked into Tunstall's face, he saw a mild puzzlement, like he knew he'd made a gaffe, but he wasn't sure how or why. At least it gave Rickman the chance to clear the air.

'Blood *was* stolen from the donor session,' he began, choosing his words carefully. A rumble of consternation from the team meant he had to raise his voice to continue. 'The FSS and NHS Blood Donor service are investigating, but I'd like to set up a team to talk to all the staff who were there on the day — I mean everyone — from the receptionist to the van drivers.' This was met with general approval, and Rickman sensed he was onto a winner. 'Where's DC Hart?'

'Here, Boss.' Rickman located Naomi Hart at the back of the room. She had called him 'Boss', implicitly accepting his reinstatement as SIO on the investigation, and making her own alignment clear to the others on the team.

'I'd like you to head up the investigation into that nasty little scam.'

'Sure.' She seemed pleased.

It was the least he could do since, according to Foster, she had given the conspiracy theory sufficient credence to get him off the hook.

CHAPTER SIXTEEN

'Don't you worry about drinking so much coffee?' Grace asked. Natalja was on her fifth of the afternoon, with hours still to go.

'I smoke too many cigarettes to worry about a cup of coffee.' She flicked her hair back from her shoulders and looked askance at Grace. 'Anyway, you look like you could use some caffeine.'

Grace picked up the next patient's notes. 'You're probably right.' Jeff had slept badly, getting up at three a.m., not returning to bed. At breakfast, he seemed agitated, as if he was expecting something to happen at any moment. He still wasn't talking — at least not about the important things.

She sighed and reached for the phone to let the receptionist know that their short coffee break was over.

The next patient was Czech Roma. Her medical records noted her age at twenty-seven, but she looked much older, tired and worn, her face lined. Her hair, an intense black, was dry and frizzed, and she kept it pulled back from her face in a ponytail. As she spoke, with Natalja translating smoothly and unobtrusively as always, Grace noticed that the woman had been avoiding looking at her. Instead, she spoke directly to Natalja, turned a little away from Grace herself. *She's trying to block me out*, Grace thought.

'They are eight in a two-bedroom house,' Natalja said, translating from Czech. 'There is no hot water. Her baby girl is sick.'

'Is the baby here?' Grace asked. Czechs often came as a family. 'I should see her.'

Natalja translated and the woman brought her palms together, sliding one over the other as if rubbing dust from them. '*Nejsem tady na to, abych vykládala o svém miminku.*'

'She says she's not here for the baby.'

She waited and the woman spoke again.

'She's here because of her house. It's no good for eight people,' Natalja said.

Grace raised her eyebrows. 'If your baby is sick, I can help you to put pressure on the accommodation provider,' Grace said. 'But, I'm sorry, housing is not my job.'

The woman listened to Natalja's translation with increasing annoyance. Natalja seemed unwilling to translate her reply.

'Go ahead,' Grace said. 'I'm thick-skinned.'

'It was just insult.'

Grace said, 'The Asylum Support Team will be here tomorrow. You should speak to them.' She paused, while Natalja translated. 'If you are sick, I will treat you. *That* is my job.'

For the first time, the woman looked directly at Grace, as Natalja translated, her eyes black and glistening with bitter resentment.

Then she said something and Natalja responded angrily. The woman got up and walked briskly to the door.

'Wait.' Grace had realised what it was that had been troubling her. She knew this woman.

The woman stopped and turned, a look of open contempt on her face.

'Ask her if she has a little boy — a six-year-old?' Grace said.

As Natalja spoke, the woman's expression changed to one of horror. She stepped back, shaking her head.

'How is Tomàs?' Grace asked, addressing her question directly to the woman.

She blanched at the name, even before Natalja had spoken.

'Sorry,' she said in English. 'No Tomàs. You make mistake.' She walked quickly to the door and hurried outside.

Grace got up, ready to follow, but Natalja stopped her. 'Leave her, Grace,' she said.

'Don't you remember her, Natalja?' Grace grabbed the mouse excitedly and navigated through the woman's computer file, accessing each of her children's medical records in turn. 'She was here last year — or maybe eighteen months ago. But it was under a different name. Their asylum claim was refused — they were sent home.'

Natalja snatched the mouse from her. 'What does it matter if she was here before?' She lowered her voice. 'The Romas, they just want a few months to work on farms. What's so wrong with that? Nobody else wants it.'

In the past, the Czech Romas would come to England between summer and autumn, work on farms at below minimum wages for a few months and return home with enough money to feed their families for the whole winter. But it was now illegal for asylum seekers to work, and Czech Romas were routinely sent home after processing.

'I know why they come, Natalja.'

Anger flashed in her friend's dark eyes and Grace added, 'I've got nothing against her.'

'Then why are you hounding her?'

Grace was shocked. '*Hounding?*' she repeated. 'Good God, you don't think I'd report her to Immigration?'

Natalja seemed momentarily disconcerted, but she squared her shoulders and asked, 'Then why all these questions?'

'Because,' Grace said, feeling an answering flash of heat, 'her son, Tomàs, has diabetes.' She completed her search of the family file. 'None of these children is listed as having diabetes.' she said. 'If Tomàs isn't receiving treatment, he could die.'

Stricken, Natalja put her hand to her chest. 'Forgive me,' she said. 'It's just . . .' Grace felt that she was trembling on the brink of some revelation. 'The girl who was killed?'

With a thud, Grace saw the child-woman's face, the startling green eyes, the sickening mass of blood sliding out after her into the lorry. 'What about her?' Grace asked, quelling a queasy surge in her gut.

Natalja dipped her head. 'I guess it makes me nervous.'

Grace got the sense that she was being corralled away from a more sensitive topic. 'Why does it make you nervous?'

'You always have to know everything!' Natalja burst out.

Grace was stunned by the accusation. 'Natalja, you know that isn't true.'

'I need cigarette.' Natalja snatched up her jacket and handbag.

Grace got by with mime and the elementary English skills of her next two patients. She had never seen Natalja so on edge. She made several calls on her mobile while she was out in the freezing cold; Grace heard muffled snippets, all in Serbo-Croat.

Grace made a note for a health visitor to call on the Roma family and check on the children. They would need a Czech interpreter, but perhaps Natalja would not be the best person for the job.

She thought about the people she saw every day in her clinic — what they were willing to risk in order to stay together as families, what Natalja must have gone through when her parents were murdered, and she wondered about Jeff. Estranged from his brother, unwilling to help him even in extreme need.

* * *

Jeff Rickman checked in with the emergency hotline before he went home. It was nine thirty p.m. and he was

113

exhausted from lack of sleep and nervous tension, but it was great to be back on the job. He had some making up to do with Grace, he knew that — not least because that morning he had still been on compassionate leave and when Hinchcliffe had summoned him, he had left no note or message.

'What've you got?' He was speaking to an impossibly young DC with a ruddy outdoor complexion and two days' beard growth that was no more than peach-fuzz on his chin and upper lip.

'Plenty of calls, Boss. But they're all saying the same thing.' He handed Rickman a wad of papers. On each, the date, time of call, sex and in some cases the name and phone number of the caller.

Rickman skimmed the top half-dozen. Cab drivers, other working girls, residents of the flats and houses around Hope Street — they all said the victim had been touting for custom. 'It keeps coming back to the street,' he said, handing the slips back.

It keeps coming back to the street, he thought on the drive home. Street life, street values, girls who made a living on the street. Men who preyed on street girls. So, in a sense, it kept coming back to him; to a night two months previously when he had lost control and almost lost his understanding of who he was. Or perhaps the vicious unthinking creature he had become on that night was his true self. This notion had haunted him in the days and weeks since, because in all the years since his childhood he had told himself that he could change, that he didn't have to be ruled by anger, that arguments didn't always have to be settled with fists.

* * *

He dumped his keys in the bowl on the hallstand and flung his overcoat over the newel. The house was quiet.

He called upstairs. 'Grace?'

He found her lying on the sofa in the sitting-room. A medical journal lay in her lap. She looked tousled and pale and achingly vulnerable. An occasional frown troubled her brow as some passing dream disturbed her sleep.

The fire had burned low. He added a log and sat on the floor next to her, watching for a time the light playing on her face, lending it warmth. He felt a searing love for her, watching her unawares, and a fierce desire to protect her, though he didn't know from what.

After a time, she stirred and moaned.

'Shh,' he whispered, smoothing a stray lock of hair from her forehead. 'It's all right.'

She opened her eyes and the firelight danced in them as she smiled. 'Hey,' she murmured drowsily.

'Hey yourself.' He kissed her and she responded at first, but then she seemed to come to herself and pushed him away, fuddled and frowning.

'Don't come that with me, Rickman.'

'What?' he asked, widening his eyes.

'You know what.' She propped herself up on one elbow. 'I want answers, Jeff.'

'I've been reinstated . . .' He was hoping to deflect her from more difficult topics.

She grunted. 'So, your little plot with Lee Foster came off?'

He stared into the fire.

'See?' she exclaimed, fully awake, now. 'Why can't you be straight with me?'

'Because,' he said, still unable to look at her. 'I *can't* be straight with you.'

'I give up,' she said. 'I'm just an amateur. You've had years of study with professional prevaricators and liars.'

He winced. 'I've never lied to you, Grace.'

'But you haven't been entirely truthful, either.'

He couldn't argue with that. He hadn't been truthful. There were reasons, but none that he could discuss with Grace. 'I'm trying to *protect* you, Grace,' he said at last.

'From what?'

What could he say? From getting dragged into something he was ashamed of? From the dirty side of his job? Maybe ultimately from himself.

She read him perfectly. 'The Job,' she said. 'You boys and your secret societies.'

He didn't answer. If that was the worst she thought of him, he felt he had got off lightly. They didn't speak for a long time. The fire crackled and danced in the hearth, and he racked his brains for something to say that wouldn't increase the distance between them.

Grace sat up, swinging her legs onto the floor. She sat with her hands tucked under her thighs, staring at his profile as if willing him to talk to her.

'You really aren't going to tell me any more, are you?' she asked.

'It's work stuff,' he said reluctantly. 'I can't discuss it.'

'Well, make up your mind — either it's confidential or you're trying to protect me.' Her pale blue eyes darkened when she was angry, and now they were slate-blue.

'I'm sorry Grace, I don't mean to—'

'Lie to me?' she suggested.

'I was going to say "keep you in the dark".'

At length, Grace sighed. 'Your brother phoned this evening.'

'Oh,' he said, suddenly very still.

She stared at him, waiting for more. He couldn't look at her.

'He's distressed and disorientated, Jeff. He doesn't understand why his brother won't see him.'

'I have,' Rickman said through gritted teeth. 'Twice.'

'But you didn't want to.'

He smiled bitterly. 'That's another matter entirely.'

'We've all the time in the world,' she said, her voice so quiet it nearly broke his heart to hear it.

He shook his head. 'It's too complicated . . . I don't know how I feel about all of this. I don't know how much I want to say.'

'You feel you have to measure your words with me?'

'Grace, I didn't *say* that.' He reached up to touch her face, but she stood and walked away.

'The problem is, Jeff, you're not saying anything at all.'

'I've spent all my life keeping this under wraps, Grace.'

She stopped in the doorway, her back to him, but he could feel her listening with every fibre of her being.

'I don't like to even *think* about my childhood,' Rickman said. 'I dealt with it on my own, put it behind me — and now my brother who, by the way, left twenty-five years ago, suddenly wants to talk about it. Well it's too damn late.'

Grace turned to him. 'I'm not your brother, Jeff.' Two spots of high colour stood out on her cheekbones.

He felt awkward, unable to look her in the eye.

'Do you think I'll be shocked?' she asked. 'Jeff, I work with unhappy families and their unhappy children every day. It's my job to help people.'

'I'm not one of your patients, Grace.' He closed his eyes *God, why am I so clumsy?* 'I didn't mean that the way it sounded,' he said. 'I meant that I'm your partner — I want your love, not—' He had almost said 'not your professional concern' but that, too, would sound harsh, and he really didn't want to hurt Grace.

'For the record,' she said, her pretty face creased with pain. 'I do — I love you. And people who love each other help each other.'

Rickman tasted acid at the back of his throat. He began to reply but she was already gone, closing the door behind her.

CHAPTER SEVENTEEN

Grace crouched next to the weeping teenager and tried to reassure her. Around her, the quiet urgency of the Accident and Emergency Department continued unabated. Low murmurs of encouragement and comfort, sharp instructions from doctors and nurses, phones ringing, an occasional cry of pain, a sob of relief or anguish.

Kirsty Brooks had fallen from her bicycle on her way to school and smashed her front teeth. She was sixteen and her hobbies, had she been asked to list them, would be make-up, clothes, boys, pop music . . . and boys. In that order. Andy Carter, in Year Twelve, was showing an interest — a *sixth form boy hanging around the school gates so he could walk her home!* Asking could he sit with her in the school canteen. She was being *noticed*. Andy owned a motorbike and now, on the brink of real recognition, on the threshold of cool, her life was in ruins.

'I look like a bloody freak!' she shouted, her voice rising to a shriek. Mostly, the consonants were lost, her lips and tongue so swollen that it hurt just to make the plosive sounds. She groaned and put a hand to her face.

Kirsty's mother began to apologise, but Grace shook her head. She took Kirsty's hand and spoke softly but insistently, explaining what would happen when the ambulance came to take her on to the Dental Hospital. 'We got all the teeth that were knocked out,' she said. 'They can put them back in.'

'Yeah, right.' A tear of pain and self-pity tracked down her cheek.

'When the swelling has gone down, they'll put a brace on to keep them straight.'

'A brace! Oh, *God* . . .'

Fresh tears sprang to her eyes and Grace, anxious to keep her calm, said, 'Come on, I bet half the kids in your class wear braces.'

Kirsty shrugged, unwilling to concede the point — did Andy Carter go with girls who wore braces on their teeth? No chance. 'You wouldn't understand,' she said.

An ambulance pulled into the bay. Grace glanced up, but the registrar seemed to have it covered, patting her on the shoulder to tell her to carry on.

'Tom Cruise wears braces on his teeth,' she said.

'No way!'

'Way,' Grace said. 'When he gets new crowns.'

Kirsty's eyes grew round with astonishment. '*Crowns*?'

'How d'you think the Hollywood stars look so perfect?'

She thought about it for a moment, dabbing her eyes and mouth with a tissue. 'I thought they were, like — born gorgeous.'

Grace raised her eyebrows and Kirsty said, 'What?'

'Ben Affleck?' Grace's tone was conspiratorial, and Kirsty leaned forward, eager for the gossip. Grace tapped her own upper incisors. 'Capped.'

Kirsty slid her a look, her bullshit metre on full. 'Will they cap my teeth, then?'

'The chipped ones — sure. Lovely white porcelain crowns.'

Kirsty was almost serene by the time the ambulance arrived to take her around the corner to the Dental Hospital. Grace watched as the porter wheeled her patient to the ambulance and noticed a man standing by the door, a look of admiring amusement on his face. He looked distinctively European in appearance: tall, rather elegant, dressed in a long woollen overcoat. He stepped forward, pulling off his gloves, and offered his hand.

'That was impressive.'

She recognised the voice immediately. 'Mr Andrić! You look — different.'

'Mirko,' he reminded her.

'You cut your hair!' It had been cut short and choppy since she had last seen him. It gleamed rich and black, complementing the olive colouring of his skin.

'I think that it was time to move into the twenty-first century.' He ran his fingers self-consciously through his hair and smiled with disarming shyness, revealing his slightly crooked teeth.

'It suits you,' Grace said, and he gave that curious tilt of his head that hinted at the formality of a bow.

'Forgive me,' he said. 'I can see that you are busy, but I would like to speak with you a moment.'

The anxiety on his face and the diffident way in which he made the request made her think instantly of Natalja: her unease over the last few days and her outburst during clinic had preyed on Grace's mind almost as much as Jeff's continued silence.

She showed Mr Andrić through to the relatives' room. It was laid out for people in crisis: comfortable chairs, tissues, a phone with an outside line, even a coffee machine. Somewhere quiet to hear bad news. Grace banished these morbid thoughts and invited Mr Andrić to sit. He did, perched on the edge of his seat, evidently uncomfortable — perhaps, she thought, even a little nervous.

He placed his gloves on the table, giving himself time to collect his thoughts and decide how to begin.

'Doctor Grace,' he said. 'You don't know me, and I don't blame you if you are suspicious of me. But please believe when I say that I have been Natalja's friend since Croatia.'

'Of course I believe you,' Grace said. 'Natalja told me.'

Some complex emotion passed across his face: relief, perhaps even pleasure that Natalja had spoken of him. He clasped his hands, leaning forward with his forearms on his thighs. 'Natalja's family were killed.' He glanced up and Grace acknowledged that she knew this part of Natalja's story.

'She went through very bad times.' His fingers pressed hard into the backs of his hands, whitening the knuckles.

'She said you knew each other in Knin.'

'After her parents died.'

'You took care of her?'

A frown passed over his face like a spasm. 'I did what I could.'

Grace sensed that he blamed himself for some real or imagined failure of protection. 'Natalja has done really well since she came here,' she said, wanting to ease his pain.

The ghost of a smile flickered over his features and he said, 'This is good.' He hesitated, uncertain. 'You have been a friend to her, I think.'

Grace shrugged. 'I hope so.'

He looked again at his hands. 'I talked to her yesterday. She was — how can I say?' He frowned furiously, trying to find the right word.

'Agitated?' Grace suggested. It was a fair bet, given the way Natalja had been recently.

'This means nervous — shouting?'

Grace gave him a rueful grin. 'It isn't just me, then?'

He remained serious. 'She is keeping bad secrets, I think. Things she should say to a friend. Someone like you.'

Grace was touched. She had thought he was here to plead his case, or maybe to get her to plead it on his behalf, but Mirko Andrić had in fact come to find help for Natalja.

'You could be right,' she said. 'But I don't think she'll confide in me.'

'But you are her friend,' he said. 'You are *physician* — she should trust you.'

Grace winced. 'You've never heard of Doctor Shipman, I take it?'

'Excuse me?'

Many of the refugees had a respect for doctors that verged on reverence, and she felt a little mean for having been so flippant. 'It doesn't matter,' she said. 'But Natalja is a very private person. She doesn't like to talk about her past. I don't even know how she got here.'

'Oh.' He sat back, releasing his hands and resting them on the arms of the chair, repeating, 'Oh. That's a pity.'

For all his elegance and confident manner, she saw that Mirko Andrić was still a young man, wanting to help a friend, but unsure how to go about it.

'All we can do is be here if she needs someone to turn to,' Grace said.

He frowned, not entirely convinced, but anxious to do the right thing. 'You are wise, Doctor Grace,' he said.

Grace smiled, embarrassed by the flattery. 'Not wise,' she said. 'Resigned.'

He seemed puzzled and she went on, 'I mean we have to accept it. If Natalja doesn't want to talk, we can't force her.'

'No,' he said, frowning. 'I suppose.' He fell silent for a moment and Grace waited, feeling that he was building up to something. 'I think—' He seemed embarrassed. 'Natalja, she feels bad about some things she did in the past. But it was survival. I think, maybe, she sees me and it makes her remember those bad things. So—' He seemed to find the next part difficult. 'I think it's best I don't see her again, until she asks.'

Grace reached over and squeezed his hand; he seemed surprised by the contact. 'Give her time,' she said, and Andrić smiled the saddest, sweetest smile she had seen in a long while.

He left soon after that, extracting a promise from Grace that she would contact him if there was anything he could do, and pressing another business card into her hand.

* * *

Normally, Grace would drive straight over to Princes Park for her afternoon clinic, to eat her lunch in the modern, bright staffroom. Today, however, she felt incapable of making the twenty-minute car journey without a break, so she snagged a sandwich from the WVS tea bar and took it to the A&E staffroom.

Somebody had made a pot of coffee and she poured herself a cup. It was stewed and had an aftertaste of ashtrays, but she was too tired to make a fresh pot, so she sat on the tea-stained sofa in front of the portable TV and watched the regional news update through a snowstorm of interference.

She wished she knew the 'bad secrets' that Natalja was keeping. Mr Andrić knew what they were, she was sure. Perhaps if she had spoken to him a little longer, asked him to let her into his confidence . . .

Grace stopped herself. *Natalja's right*, she admonished herself. *You really do have to know everything*. She took a bite from her sandwich and said aloud, 'Mind your own damn business, Grace Chandler.'

She sat for another ten minutes, listening with half an ear to the news behind the hiss of static on the TV. She was beginning to nod off when the newsreader announced that police had identified the murder victim found in a wheel-ie-bin in the Toxteth area of Liverpool. Grace jumped to her feet, barking her shins on the coffee table and spilling coffee on the sofa, adding to its patina of splodges and drips; a silent witness to all the junior doctors working forty-eight-hour shifts, surprised from desperate sleep by their on-call pagers.

Cursing, she set her cup down and hobbled to the TV. The picture faded in and out as she fiddled with the aerial until, wild with frustration, she swivelled it almost full circle and the image cleared and settled.

'The Home Office, unaware of her death, had granted the young woman refugee status just two days ago,' the announcer explained.

A photograph replaced the studio shot and Grace stared at it, trying to match the gaunt child from the Immigration shots with the image of the murdered woman seared on her memory.

'Police report that the victim, Sophia Habib, an Afghani, disappeared from her emergency accommodation several weeks ago.'

The girl in the photograph looked half-starved, her hair was dull and mousy; she was almost unrecognisable, but for one unalterable feature: her startling green eyes. Those eyes had haunted Grace's dreams and even her waking moments ever since she had seen the girl's body fall into the filthy innards of the bin lorry. The eyes with their habitual fear testified to the torment the girl had suffered. Grace returned to the sofa, her appetite gone, her tiredness replaced by a jittery restlessness.

Where was the justice? This girl's young life had been blighted by war and brutality, and the country that should have provided sanctuary had turned her out onto the street to sell herself; robbing her of security and dignity, and ultimately of her life. She dumped the dregs of her coffee down the sink, and the rest of her sandwich in the bin, and set off for her afternoon clinic.

The sky was a solid sheet of featureless cloud, there was no wind, and the trees were almost bare of colour now. As she drove south-east on Princes Avenue, the sun seemed ready to breach the thickening pall of cloud. For decades, London planes had grown in twin rows along the central reservation, their dappled bark giving the appearance of sunshine even on the dullest day. But they had long since succumbed to disease and been replaced with more sombre limes.

Their leaves lay thick on the pressed gravel of the central reservation and in the gutters, decaying to a brown mulch. A single shaft of silvery light punctured the cloud, catching on the fallen leaves, turning muddy brown to bloody red. Then the cloud closed in and the sky went pale; as grey and still as a corpse.

Grace parked her car at the back of the clinic and walked around to the entrance. A queue of people had already formed, wanting to see her, even though her clinic was not due to start for another twenty minutes. They would look to her for help and comfort, advice and solace and she felt inadequate to the task.

Natalja was subdued at the start of the session. She kept losing track of what patients were saying and having to ask them to repeat symptoms or questions. She stumbled over her words, struggling to keep up with Grace, as if fighting an overwhelming inner turmoil.

About halfway through the afternoon, while they waited for the next patient to walk down the hallway to the consulting room, Grace touched Natalja lightly on the arm. 'Are you all right?' she asked.

'I'm perfectly—'

Grace saw her friend battle with the impulse to give a sharp response. She took a breath and began again. 'No, actually, I'm not fine.' She looked into Grace's eyes, and Grace saw reflected in them the same hurt, the same torment that she had seen in the photograph of Sophia Habib on the TV screen. 'I'm not fine,' Natalja repeated. 'But there is nothing you can do, Grace. *Nothing.*'

She took several breaths, and when she spoke again, her voice was liquid, close to tears. 'I have to deal with this myself.'

Looking into her friend's harried face, seeing the dark circles under her eyes, Grace was reminded of her advice to Mirko Andrić, only that morning. But she had always found it easier to give good advice than to take it.

'I spoke to Mirko today,' she said. 'He came to the hospital.'

Natalja flushed angrily. 'He had no *right!*'

'He's worried about you,' Grace said. 'I am, too.'

'I know how to take care of myself,' Natalja said.

'Really? D'you think that poor murdered girl knew how to take care of herself?'

The habitual wariness returned to Natalja's eyes. 'What has that got to do with me?'

'She was an asylum seeker.'

Natalja began to protest.

'I know,' Grace interrupted, 'you're not the same. You moved on. You integrated. So why are you so edgy? Why won't you talk to me?'

'This is none of your business, Grace.'

'If you know something about her death—'

A timid knock on the door preceded the appearance of a small, frightened-looking man. 'I come back?' he said.

'No.' Natalja answered before Grace could reply. 'Stay. This conversation is finished.'

Grace stared at Natalja for a moment or two, struggling with a wild compulsion to seize her friend by the shoulders and shake her. Natalja refused to meet her gaze and, after a few more moments, she offered the man her professional smile. 'Please,' she said. 'Come in.'

It cost her an almost physical effort for the rest of the session, not to keep plucking away at the loose threads of the events of the last few days, trying to establish what exactly was troubling Natalja. She was furious and confused and exasperated. And she was powerless to act.

CHAPTER EIGHTEEN

It rained that afternoon. Hard, cold rain, hour after hour without let-up. Some of the house-to-house team had been reallocated to interview asylum seekers in the emergency accommodation where Sophia Habib was supposed to have been resident; the refugee charities and Liverpool City Council were helping out with interpreters.

The Incident Room buzzed with constant activity, officers came and went, dripping and grouchy. Water pooled under jackets hung on the backs of chairs for a brief airing before the next drenching. The windows misted and the room smelled of damp clothing and stale food; queues formed outside the HOLMES room on the next floor.

Naomi Hart was waiting for a phone call. She filled the time by writing up her notebook. Around her, people followed their own lines of enquiry. The solicitor who was representing Miss Habib's claim for asylum was proving elusive.

One of the refugee charities had identified the victim, and now they had confirmation from the Home Office, as well as the National Asylum Support Service. The discovery of the victim's name had created a renewed urgency among the crew members; people were keen to make real progress. For the more ambitious among them it was like a hunger.

A burst of laughter from one corner of the room made Hart glance up; Sergeant Foster, cracking another un-PC joke. Every time she began to think she might get to like him, Foster said something that alienated and infuriated her. She returned to her notes and felt, rather than saw, him drift past her and out of the room.

Minutes later, she was at DI Rickman's office. The door stood open, and both the DI and Sergeant Foster were engrossed in paperwork. She rapped on the door frame and Rickman looked up.

'We've got a hit, Boss,' she said, trying not to sound too eager. Eager wasn't cool, and despite her reservations about Detective Sergeant Foster, she wanted him to think of her as cool.

Rickman lifted his chin, a gesture of curiosity and encouragement.

'Know someone called Jordan?' she asked.

Rickman was slow to answer. 'Alex Jordan?' he said at last.

Hart nodded. 'His sister works for the National Blood Service.'

'Yes?'

Hart felt a niggling irritation. Did he want her to spell it out for him? 'Jennifer Grant — née Jordan. She took your blood at the donor session.'

Foster hadn't looked up from his work at all, and she had to control the urge to snatch his damned reports from under his nose. Jordan's sister had set Rickman up — obviously — but neither Foster nor the DI seemed even remotely interested.

'Can we link her with the theft of the blood?' Rickman asked.

Hart felt a sinking sense of disappointment. Rickman and his obsessive attention to detail was spoiling her enjoyment of her one big break in the case. 'She didn't have exclusive access,' she admitted reluctantly. 'But given her brother's activities . . .'

Foster tossed his pen down onto the pile of papers he was reading. 'Okay,' he said. 'This is a bit like listening to one side of a phone call. How about filling in the blanks?'

'Jordan is a pimp,' Hart explained. 'He's got at least half a dozen girls working the Liverpool 7 and 8 areas.'

Foster's forehead creased momentarily, then he seemed to have a moment of blinding clarity. 'You mean *Lex* Jordan,' He exclaimed. 'Nobody but his mum calls him Alex anymore.'

'Lex, Alex — whatever,' Hart said, not even trying to hide her disappointment, now. 'Either way, it's still his sister who took your blood.'

'Who's been rattling his cage, then?' Foster asked.

'I'm about to find out,' she said. 'Want to tag along, Sarge?'

Foster favoured her with one of his vulpine grins. 'Lee Foster doesn't "tag along", Naomi.'

Hart looked from one to the other. What was this? More boys' club nonsense — don't let on the girls know how to get results? She swallowed a bubble of anger at the inequity of the system and said, 'Fine,' turning on her heel to leave.

'DC Hart,' Foster said.

'Sarge.' She made no effort at politeness.

'You've done a great job on this, hasn't she, Boss?'

'Yes,' Rickman said. 'Good work.'

Hart raised her eyebrows. *Well, that nearly choked him*, she thought.

* * *

Rickman waited until DC Hart's footsteps had retreated down the corridor. Jordan's sister. He should have seen it before; he almost did, he thought, recalling a flash of almost-recognition at the donor session.

Rickman stared at Foster in disbelief. 'Bloody hell, Foster,' he exclaimed. 'You didn't *know* she was Jordan's sister?'

Foster bristled. 'Give me some credit, Boss — no, I didn't know.' After a moment or two, he smiled to himself. 'Shame to let talent like that go to waste, though,' he said. 'Girl who can get her tongue round the word "phlebotomist" shouldn't be dropped lightly.'

'Lee, this could get you in serious trouble.'

Foster shrugged. 'I had a couple of dates with a nice woman from the Blood Service. So what? Not my fault if she turns out to be a bad 'un.'

Rickman studied Foster for a few moments. He was just about brazen enough to carry it off.

'Anyway, I'm more worried about you,' Foster said.

Rickman felt a muscle in his jaw tighten. 'Meaning?'

'It's *Jordan*, isn't it?'

Rickman didn't answer. He was seeing a warm August night, Jordan's fist raised. A woman, wide-eyed, terrified. Blood on her face, blood on Jordan's fist.

'*Lex Jordan*, Boss,' Foster repeated. 'Not exactly your keenest fan. It's looking less like coincidence and more like malicious intent now, isn't it?'

Rickman pushed his chair away from his desk and ran his fingers through his hair. 'You're right,' he said. He was sick of the deception, sick of keeping secrets, sick of sitting up at nights because worry and guilt kept him from sleep. 'Maybe if I tell Hinchcliffe the truth . . .'

'Hold on,' Foster said, getting out of his chair to shut the door. 'Tell him the *truth*? That'll just get you another suspension. Permanent this time. The girl's *dead*, Boss. You losing your job is not gonna help her or anyone else — except maybe the likes of Jordan.'

'Say we bring his sister in — face her with what I know—'

'You'd be up to your eyes in shit, and all she has to say is she doesn't know how the blood got from the donor session onto Carrie's clothes — we can't prove a thing.'

Rickman knew he was right. Between donation and the discovery that blood was missing, dozens of people would have had access to Rickman's blood. And who was to say they didn't steal the blood indiscriminately? If you were a criminal wanting to get back at the cops, any dibble's blood would do.

'Let me have a chat with her,' Foster suggested.

'No — Lee — it's not your problem.'

'Let's face it, Boss,' Foster said, 'I'm already in up to my neck. I'm just getting myself out of a jam.' At the door of the office, he stopped. 'Have you told Grace yet?'

When Rickman didn't answer, he said, 'And you're all for telling the DCI?' He shook his head. 'If it's absolution you're wanting, the Doc's got a much more forgiving nature.'

Could Grace forgive him? For not having told her in the first place, for what he had done, for what he was — no different from Lex Jordan.

* * *

Foster went straight through the Incident Room. Hart was getting ready to leave. 'Can I have a word?' he said.

'Sure.' He felt a wintry blast in the coolness of her glance. She logged off her computer and looked up at him, her arms folded.

'Fancy a coffee?'

'There's some just brewed,' she said, jerking her chin in the direction of the coffee machine.

Foster clamped a hand to the back of his neck. He didn't blame her, the way they'd blown her off about her big result. He glanced around the room. Nobody was paying them any attention. 'Need a bit of privacy,' he said.

He didn't look back to see if she was following. He knew that naked curiosity would guarantee him at least a few minutes of her time.

The kitchen was empty. Foster ducked inside, holding the door for DC Hart, then leaning against it to keep it shut.

She stared at him, her arms folded, one eyebrow fetchingly arched.

'First of all, I'm sorry about that palaver in the boss's office,' he said. 'You really did do a good job.'

Naomi was unmoved. She wasn't about to give in to a half-baked attempt at flattery. He took a breath. 'Thing is — Jordan's sister — I know her.'

'You know Jennifer Grant?'

He cleared his throat. 'In the Biblical sense.'

Hart closed her eyes. 'I should've guessed. What happened? You pissed her off and she tried to nick your blood — got the boss's instead?'

Foster had to bite down hard on a protestation that he never gave his women cause for complaint. He tried to stay with the abashed look. 'Think I could have a few words with her before you go in?'

Hart shook her head doubtfully. 'I don't know, Sarge . . .'

'Come on, Naomi — you know she's just gonna deny everything. At least I can find out if we've got anything else to worry about.'

She stared at him for a few seconds, undecided, then she said, 'On condition. Anything you do get out of her goes on my report.'

He held up both hands. 'I don't want my name anywhere near this,' he said. Which was true.

* * *

Jennifer Grant rang him a few hours after they had spoken. 'You're a miserable, conniving bastard, Foster,' she said.

'Just so long as the job's done,' Foster said. 'Or are you wasting your one phone call?' In fact, he knew that Jennifer had been released: Hart had told him that she had denied everything and there was insufficient evidence to charge her.

'You *wish*,' Jennifer said. 'I'm phoning from my flat, which, by the way, I'm having fumigated.'

'Now, I thought it was quite clean myself,' Foster said. 'A few dust devils under the bed, maybe . . .'

'It's the man-size cockroach I'm thinking about,' she said.

Foster smiled slowly, leaning back in his chair. 'You knew I was a cop right off the bat,' he said pleasantly. 'Me, I had no idea you were related to a pimping scumbag.'

'You make me sick, Foster.'

Foster's smile broadened. 'Come on, Jen, you know you liked getting sticky with me.'

'You know what, Foster? You're no better than a smutty little schoolboy.'

Foster was enjoying himself. 'Yeah,' he said. 'But tell me it wasn't good.'

CHAPTER NINETEEN

Jez had a bad feeling about this. He tried telling Beefy, but Beefy wasn't in the mood for listening and he could shout louder, shove — and punch — harder that any of them, so, as usual, Beefy won the argument.

They walked fast, like Beefy was scared he'd change his mind. Down the hill, through Whitley Gardens, the grass sopping wet, squeaking under their feet, and Beefy shoving and pushing, lashing out to give Jez a sharp smack across the back of the head, kicking his ankles to keep him moving. All the time telling him they had to stick together. They had to do this as the Rokeby Rats, or they were finished.

Daz trailed behind a few paces, ashamed or maybe frightened — probably both. Jez had learned over the last few days that fear and shame were close cousins.

Every time he tried to stop and reason, Beefy would cuff him, or punch him in the shoulder, or dig him in the back, once even grabbing his sweatshirt collar and dragging him a few yards.

They crossed Shaw Street by a huge, crenellated sandstone building which had been converted to provide expensive flats for the city's wealthy twenty-somethings. It had once been a boys' school, but that was long before the Rats had even been born.

The boys argued and scuffled, their voices loud in the darkness, rush-hour traffic right and left. The rain had finally stopped and moonlight and streetlights mingled, tingeing the standing puddles, gleaming on the wet pavements and potholed roads, reflecting headlamps and dazzling the car drivers. They cruised slowly, like kerb-crawlers, their tyres swishing wetly, sending dirty splashes in their wake.

Down a side street, first opportunity, because Beefy didn't want people to see them, to be able to identify them; but the way he was shouting, it'd be a miracle if they weren't picked up before they got the job done.

Jez recognised the street where they had first seen the illegal immigrant. 'Illegal' and 'immigrant' went together in Jez's mind; it didn't occur to him that the two might not belong together. Still, he wished they had never followed that Arab to the tenements. He wished they'd never blitzed his flat. Wished he'd never heard the screams of the woman and her baby, or worse — much worse — Daz's terrified screams, no louder than a whisper, as the foreign guy held him over a thirty-foot drop.

They were headed back to the tenements now, and more trouble: Jez felt it like a premonition, a sick feeling of impending doom.

Twenty minutes earlier he had been sitting in front of the telly watching *The Simpsons* and eating chips with Minky. Beefy had showed up — tapped on the window. When he went to the front door, Beefy had told him to get his coat, they were gonna hit the immigrants. Jez didn't want to. He told Beefy, arguing with him till his mum's feller came down the hall and booted him out the house for letting the cold in. Foot up the arse and out he went, the door slammed shut behind him.

'You got to, Jez,' Beefy said. 'We all got to. Just this one job and we're off the hook. They said they'd leave us alone if we did this one thing.'

Jez looked over his shoulder through the front-room window. Minky was well away, chortling to himself at something Bart had just said. Probably 'Eat my shorts!', which was what Jez wished he had the nerve to say to Beefy.

'Minky stays,' he said, ready to fight Beefy if it came down to it.

'Minky?' Beefy glanced past him through the window. 'Who gives a shit about Minky? He's not even in the gang.'

That decided Jez. He left without his jacket and walked the streets shivering in his school sweatshirt and pants, getting a bad feeling and knowing if he didn't do like Beefy said, he was dead.

* * *

Beefy was going on about honour and the gang — how they watched each others' backs and that. But Jez couldn't see much honour in what they were doing. Like he didn't see how prodding and shoving and bullying him into it was watching his back.

To make himself feel better, Jez called to mind the way Beefy had snivelled and begged for mercy. It didn't help as much as he would have liked, but it stopped him from crying and he had promised himself he wouldn't cry, no matter what happened.

The tenements stood on a slope overlooking Scotland Road and the Mersey Tunnel approach. They had been refurbished two years previously, but the work was shoddy, and already paint was peeling, the windows were warped and let in rain and wind. There was nowhere to hang out washing, so people used the private balconies at the back of the building. The parking bays were empty, except when someone from the refugee charities visited, or sometimes the police.

A sudden squall hit them as they crossed the pitted tarmac twenty yards from the tenements, and Jez was overwhelmed by his fear. Feeling the building's shadow fall on him was like feeling the chill of death itself.

Beefy grabbed hold of Jez's shirt, laughing a little, swinging him round for Daz to see. 'Look at Jez, man. He's shakin'.'

'I'm not shakin',' Jez shouted angrily. 'I'm friggin cold, all right?'

'All right,' Beefy said, alarmed by the noise. 'You're cold. I believe you. Now shut up, will you?'

Their instructions were clear. They had been told exactly where to go. They walked past the block where they had chased the Arab. That had been for a laugh; this was in deadly earnest.

At the end block they went up two flights. The place was deserted. Lights shone through thin curtains and they heard people talking as they passed the flat doors, sometimes a TV blasting out, but there was nobody on the doorsteps to note their presence, nobody on the landings to question them.

Second floor, third door along from the right. Number nineteen. No lights. He got that sick feeling again, and licked his lips, trying to catch Daz's eye. But Daz couldn't hold his gaze. Since the foreigner (he never thought of this man as an illegal immigrant) had done that to Daz, he was different. He could never seem to look at you straight on; it was like his eyes slid off you. He stopped having good ideas, stopped talking even. Since that night, Daz just shuffled along, doing what Beefy told him to, and whenever you did happen to catch his eye, he always looked afraid. He decided to try one last time; maybe with nobody in, Beefy would see the sense of leaving well enough alone.

'Beefy.' Jez took care to whisper.

'Wha'?'

'No lights.'

Beefy looked through the glass door. No hall light, no TV flicker. 'So?'

'So why bother?'

'Because I say so.'

'We could go down London Road, collect a bit more for Bommie Night.' Jez suggested. Hallowe'en was still not past and they had used up all their firework stocks. All except what Beefy was carrying.

Beefy grabbed him by the front of his sweatshirt and said, 'I said we'd do the job, and we're gonna do it.'

Jez had had enough. At least here Beefy'd have to be careful how much he hurt him, in case he shouted out.

'We're gonna do it because *you* say so?' he sneered, bringing his face in close. 'You're sure about that, are you Beefy?'

Beefy could have thumped him, but he didn't. He put his hand on Jez's shoulder and moved even closer. Jez, anticipating a ruck, balled his hand into a fist, but Beefy seemed in no mood to fight.

His eyes widened, showing the whites. 'He come to our house.'

Jez knew he meant the foreigner.

'He just rolled up to our house, Jez. "I've got a job for you," he says. "One little job then you won't see me again."' Beefy's eyes flicked away, like he was expecting the man to be hovering at his shoulder, ready to pick him up and pitch him over the landing wall. When he looked back at Jez there were tears in his eyes.

Jez thought again how Beefy had grovelled on his fat arse in front of the foreigner and he came to a decision. *This is it*, he thought. *This is the very last time. Me and Minky'll find some other crew. Beefy's lost it. Beefy's full of shit.*

Beefy seemed to sense the shift in power, the loss of control. 'Get out me road,' he said, shoving Jez to one side. He had the banger and his disposable lighter ready.

'Light blue touch paper and retire,' Beefy intoned, putting on a posh voice, like someone in one of those films that told you about stranger danger and crossing the road safely. 'Stand well back.'

He opened the letterbox and popped the banger through the slot, like a good neighbour delivering misdirected mail. The banger made a satisfying *boom!* in the empty hallway. Beefy was already running, his heavy footsteps thudding down the landing. Jez began to turn away, when he heard a *whoosh.* through the glass he saw a trail of pale blue fire heading almost lazily down the hall.

'What the fuck?' Jez turned to look at Daz. He had seen it, too. He watched the blue light dance through the frosted glass, his eyes beginning to register something more that the habitual fear of the last few days. They widened, and then Jez read naked terror in Daz's face.

'Come on, man,' he said, already backing away.

But Jez couldn't move.

'If they find us here, we've had it.'

Jez turned to run, spun on his left foot and turned back. He could smell the fire: gunpowder and petrol and smoke. He could feel the heat through the door. What if there were people inside? What if they were asleep, or in the back room? What if they were trapped?

'Jez!' Daz called. 'Jezzer!' Then, 'Fuck it, man I'm off!' Daz followed Beefy, heading for the nearest fire escape. Jez heard the door boom against the wall, heard the clatter of his friends' footsteps retreating down the concrete steps.

The fire began to have a sound as well as a smell. A sound like a moan, then he heard a *wumph*, just like when the boiler came on at home. He peered in at the window, but the curtains were drawn, the room in darkness. He was shaking. 'Oh, man . . .' He grabbed the sides of his head, pulling at the short fuzz of his hair. 'Oh, man . . .'

The fire seemed to turn; a tidal wave of heat billowed out from the far end of the hallway. The flames were yellow, now, and orange, no longer lazy, but hot and frantic and furious.

He hammered on the glass, but the skin of his fist sizzled and he screamed, pulling his hand away. 'Get out!' he screamed. 'Jesus! Get the fuck out of there!' He used his feet, feeling them slip as the rubber soles melted against the glass.

He thought he heard answering screams, but it was only the moan and squeal of the fire and his own voice, high and breathless.

Nobody moved in the flat, though several bodies burned. Skin melted, hair singed and flared. But nobody stirred.

Further down the landing, doors opened. A man called, 'What are you doing?', his accent thick, almost impenetrable.

'*Fuh*,' Jez gasped. '*Fuh*–fire!'

He screamed one last time for them to get out and then glass exploded — door, windows — shredding the flesh on his left cheek. A splinter lodged itself in his left shoulder. Scorching air billowed out, blowing him off his feet, throwing him backwards hard against the wall. His short fuzz of hair caught fire, frizzing and flaming. His sweatshirt, untouched from the back, was burned into holes over his chest, the rest welded to his skin. People came running, shouts went up. Screams. Screams of horror and terror and despair. Jez didn't hear them, didn't hear his own agonised screams. Jez was somewhere else: somewhere between life and death, where the biggest decision was whether to go or stay, to fight or give in. To live or die. He would come to that decision soon, but not yet. Not yet.

CHAPTER TWENTY

Jez was the main feature of the regional bulletin after the *News at Ten*. His one and only moment of fame was as the boy police were waiting to question over the deaths of four men in an arson attack. DCI Hinchcliffe organised a conference room at the Police HQ which, conveniently, was across the road from the Granada TV studios at Albert Dock. It was the only place big enough to take all the interested parties: the national press, scenting a big story, had arrived en masse on the London train, just in time for the briefing. A camera crew had been sent by the BBC from Manchester, the refugee charities were represented, as was the City Council Asylum Support Team.

DCI Hinchcliffe and DI Rickman sat side by side.

'Can we assume there's a link between these deaths and the murder of Sophia Habib, Inspector Rickman?' This question came from a *Liverpool Echo* reporter.

'We're keeping an open mind,' Rickman said, 'but for the moment we are treating them as separate incidents. DCI Hinchcliffe is in overall command of the investigations and we are in constant close contact.'

'They were in refugee accommodation,' the reporter persisted. 'It seems safe to assume they were refugees.'

'Assumptions are rarely "safe",' Rickman said dryly. 'If they *were* refugees — which, by the way, means they have a legal right to remain in the UK — they would not be living in emergency accommodation.' He was being pedantic, but Rickman knew that wrong-footing aggressive reporters was the best way to rein them in.

'The bodies were found in a flat owned by a landlord who provides emergency accommodation only for *asylum seekers* — in other words, people whose claims for the right to asylum have not yet been fully assessed. In fact, nobody should have been in that flat — the landlord says it was empty.'

'Can you comment on rumours that other refugees in the flats were harbouring illegal immigrants?'

Rickman looked at the man who had asked the question. From the accent, one of the London press. From the tone of the question, one of the tabloids. Apparently, his explanation of the distinction between asylum seekers and refugees had zipped right over the man's head. 'It isn't Police policy to comment on rumours,' he said after a moment.

He had caught the eye of another reporter in the audience and was about to take her question when Hinchcliffe leaned forward to the microphone. 'We will investigate all aspects of this tragedy,' he said. 'All lines of enquiry presented to us. But we do appeal for calm on both sides.'

Grace, watching the news on TV, saw Rickman stiffen slightly. *Sides*. She thought. *Hinchcliffe is automatically setting up barriers for people to stand either side of and hurl insults at each other.*

'A crime was committed today,' Rickman said. 'Four men are dead. I am sure I speak for all concerned when I say that we wish to see justice done.'

Hinchcliffe spoke up again. 'We will investigate these deaths thoroughly. We will be working closely with the refugee charities on this.'

'What about the boy who was injured?'

'We're waiting to talk to him,' Rickman said. 'But he has severe burns and is unconscious at present. We would ask that anyone who saw three — or possibly four — boys aged around ten or eleven near the tenement blocks in Great Homer Street, to please come forward with information.'

'Can you name the men who were killed?'

'It's too early to say,' Rickman said. 'Post-mortems will be carried out later tonight, or early tomorrow; we'll update you when we have more information.'

The news item went to an image of the burned-out flat. A crowd had gathered below, among them, a group of teenaged boys from the emergency accommodation. The editor cut from the baseball bat, swinging loosely in one boy's hand, to his angry face. 'We have the right to defend ourselves,' he said. 'We're sick of being pushed around.' He had already picked up a trace of the Liverpool accent.

There were locals in the crowd as well. 'It's not safe with them lot around,' one chisel-faced youth said, without a hint of irony.

'They pick on you for nothin,' another agreed.

'Who are "they"?' the interviewer asked.

'The immigrants. They have a go at you for just, like, walking down the street. But it's a free country, isn't it? We've got as much right to walk where we want—'

'More!' someone shouted. 'We were born here.'

'Yeah — we belong here.'

The reporter turned to camera, her face grim. 'Tensions between the local and refugee communities have mounted since the body of a young woman found in a wheelie-bin ten days ago was identified as that of Sophia Habib, an asylum seeker . . .'

'And you're not helping,' Grace said, speaking over the next introduction, reaching for the remote control to turn off the TV. She stopped when she saw a face she recognised.

'I am a refugee,' he said. Mirko Andrić looked well on TV: lean and healthy and upright compared with some of the people around him, a contrast the camera crew exploited.

'I am grateful to your country for giving me protection,' he said. 'I came during the war in Yugoslavia, because people who looked just like me wanted to kill me. They have the same blood in their veins, they speak the same language, they even lived in the same street. But they killed my friends, my family. I came to escape this persecution. For most asylum seekers, the story is the same. I earn my own money, I buy my own house. This is what most asylum seekers want: to support themselves. All I ask from this country is freedom to live in peace.'

He looked straight into the camera, and the cameraman zoomed in to tight focus momentarily before shifting back to the reporter. She felt no need to add to Andrić's comments and simply signed off, but Grace couldn't help noticing the disgruntled faces of the locals behind them. They knew when they were being insulted.

* * *

The front door slammed. Grace listened for the *chink* of keys being dropped into the bowl on the hallstand, for the sigh as Jeff shrugged off his overcoat. Familiar, reassuring sounds after what she had heard on the news — sounds that were a comfort.

Jeff came into the room. 'Hey,' he said.

She smiled up at him. He looked hollow-eyed. 'Hey yourself.'

'Food?'

'Was that an invitation or a request?'

He thought about it for a moment. 'Not sure.'

'Let's say it was both.' She held out a hand and he took it, hauling her out of her chair. 'Cheese on toast do you?'

He rubbed one hand over his face; he was so pale with exhaustion that the scar bisecting his right eyebrow stood out as a jagged silver line.

'Jeff?'

'What?'

'Cheese on toast?'

'Yeah,' he said. 'Sorry. Toast is fine.'

She gave him the once-over. 'They're right about TV putting pounds on you,' she said. 'You looked quite healthy on the box. But actually, Detective Inspector, you're positively gaunt.'

'Thank you so much,' he said. 'And it's acting Detective *Chief* Inspector.'

Grace frowned, then waved a hand dismissively. 'Whatever.'

He grunted, following her through to the kitchen and collapsing into a chair at the table. She fetched spring onions and strong, sharp cheddar, Worcester sauce and pepper. 'I didn't expect you so soon,' she said.

He peered at the digital clock on the oven. 'It's almost ten-thirty,' he said.

'And you were just on the news.'

It took him a moment to process this information, then he closed his eyes for a second. 'Oh, I see. They taped the press conference at nine o'clock.'

'In that case, what kept you?'

'I dropped in at the hospital on the way home.'

She stopped grating cheese. 'Simon?'

He frowned as if he had never heard the name. 'No. The boy. Gerard Flynn — Jez to his mates.'

'Oh.' Now was not the time to push Jeff on his troubled relationship with his brother. She set down the cheese and wiped her hands. 'How is he?'

'Dying,' Rickman said. He looked up at her and she saw a species of desperation she had never encountered in him before. He exhaled. 'He's dying, Grace.'

'Jesus . . . How old is he — ten?'

'Eleven.'

'Did he set the fire, Jeff? An eleven-year-old boy?'

'I don't know.' He picked up a chef's knife and began slicing onion with absent and almost careless skill. 'Weird thing is, some of the witnesses say he was trying to save the people inside.'

'The news report suggested it was racially motivated — first Sophia Habib, now this.'

145

He didn't answer and watching him, she realised that he hadn't heard her. They finished the preparation in silence and sat at the kitchen table to eat.

'Sophia was claiming NASS support right up to the day she died,' Rickman said.

Grace pushed her plate to one side. 'You're sure it was her?'

'I'm tired,' Rickman said. 'And my brain is working to rule: no lateral thinking, no leaps of imagination — why wouldn't it be her?'

Grace shrugged. 'There could be a million reasons. I'm just thinking *how* it could be done, not *why*.'

'All right,' Rickman said. 'I'm listening.'

'For most people, one asylum seeker is pretty much like another. If someone got hold of her vouchers . . .' She tilted her head. 'She obviously wasn't living in the NASS accommodation allocated to her.'

'No.' He chewed thoughtfully. 'She hadn't been seen for a few weeks, apart from calling in to pick up mail.'

'The National Asylum Support Service is quite clear on this,' Grace said. 'Asylum seekers have to maintain residence at the accommodation address provided, otherwise all benefits are forfeit.'

'But NASS didn't get to know about it because other asylum seekers aren't going to tell, and Sophia was cashing her vouchers and replying to mail.'

'Maybe. Or maybe someone got to her mail before she did, picked up the vouchers on her behalf.'

'It's possible,' he said.

'Where *was* she living?'

Rickman sighed, registering his bafflement. 'Beats me. She hadn't been in that shabby bedsit more than a few days. Why jeopardise her chances of being awarded status by skipping the accommodation?'

'Drugs?' Grace suggested.

'We haven't had the toxicology reports back yet, but the pathologist said there was no obvious evidence of drug abuse.'

'"Obvious" being the key word,' Grace said. 'People get addicted to smoking crack or heroin pretty fast, and there are no needle marks.'

Rickman nodded. 'I'll check on it first thing.' He finished eating. When he spoke again, he sounded awkward, perhaps even a little ashamed of himself. He placed his knife and fork carefully on his plate. 'Your friend, Natalja . . .'

'Hmm?'

'She must know people — the work she does — and she's a refugee herself.'

'You're surely not asking if she would mediate for you?'

Rickman nodded.

Grace recalled the scene Natalja had made in the surgery that day when she had mentioned Sophia Habib.

'Don't you remember how nervous she was of you, Jeff?' she asked.

'But if you explained—'

'Explained what? That you want her to inform on people who trust her?'

'You make it sound sinister.'

'It *is* sinister when immigration officers, backed by police, can knock at your door at any time — maybe even in the middle of the night — and imprison you.'

Rickman was sceptical. 'Not without cause.'

'Failing to reply to a letter? Missing an interview? I wouldn't call that "cause". Especially since the letters are written in English, so even if they are posted to the right address, chances are the recipient won't understand them.'

'That's why they are allowed legal aid,' Rickman said. 'That's what their solicitors are paid for.'

She raised her eyebrows. 'So, the solicitor makes an appointment for the week after next — if he responds at all to their phone calls — by which time, it's too late.' She paused, studying him. 'You didn't know?' she asked, surprised.

He shrugged, getting up to help her with the dishes. 'I thought the system was administered with more compassion, I suppose.'

Grace snorted. 'Compassion! When NASS allocate asylum seekers to communities around the country, they call it "cleansing". Natalja was the subject of "cleansing" in Croatia. That's fairly typical of the "compassion" in the system.'

'Okay,' he said, 'Look, I'm just trying to find a way to prevent more bloodshed.'

'I know that, Jeff,' Grace said earnestly. 'But they don't trust you. How can they? They don't even trust each other half the time.' She sighed. 'I've never really understood this quest for difference. It starts on the playground and ends on the killing fields. Family, nation, race. In the end, it's all just blood, Jeff. Compatibility or incompatibility is down to a biochemical reaction. And who cares about the race of the donor, if it saves a life?'

Rickman frowned. 'I don't see it that way,' he said. 'I think it's more about belonging. Identify with a group, you don't feel so alone. But I suppose belonging to one group or class or race or nation automatically excludes others,' he conceded.

'It sets up prejudices and fosters loyalties that aren't always honourable.' Grace agreed.

* * *

Rickman scraped his last piece of toast into the bin and stacked their plates in the dishwasher. It was impossible not to draw an uncomfortable parallel between what Grace had said and his own manipulation of circumstances over the stolen blood.

'It necessitates compromise,' he said, knowing that he was equivocating. 'Moral compromise?'

He smiled. 'And you accuse *me* of interrogating people.'

Grace didn't return his smile. 'Permission to belong brings responsibilities as well as privileges, Jeff,' she said.

'Of course,' he said, but moral decisions aren't always cut and dried.'

She slid him a sly look. 'Are we back to "the Job" again?'

He glanced at her, understanding that she was giving him the chance to come clean. 'It's not just doctors who have to respect confidentiality,' he said, smiling, turning it into a joke.

Hurt and disappointment flashed in her eyes. 'Is it really professional confidentiality,' she asked, 'or self-preservation?'

'The truth?' Rickman said. 'A bit of both.' He drew her to him and kissed her. After a moment or two she broke the kiss and laid her head on his shoulder.

'You do know you can tell me anything, don't you Jeff?'

'Absolutely,' he said.

But there were some things he would never tell her; Grace was a healer — how could he expect her to understand the mistrust and suspicion and brutality of his world? A flash of memory: his own fist raised, bloodied, powering into flesh, a spray of blood and saliva. Screams. How could he justify that kind of moral compromise?

CHAPTER TWENTY-ONE

Mirko Andrić parked in one of the residents' bays near the entrance to his rented apartment. A figure emerged from the shelter of a doorway and hurried towards him. A blustery wind tugged at the open lapels of his overcoat and blatted against his face and ears, deafening him to the sound of footsteps some way behind him. Andrić stopped to fasten his coat, then reached into his car for his briefcase. He shut the door and locked it with the remote key.

The figure came at him from his blind side, catching him as he turned toward the building. A slight movement at the periphery of his vision made him raise his hand instinctively.

His attacker swung at him again, this time connecting with stinging force.

'Jesus!' he exclaimed. 'Natalja?'

'You have no right!' she shouted.

'What is this about?' he protested, holding her wrist.

'You know very well.' She glared at him, struggling ineffectively against him.

'Is this because I spoke to Doctor Grace?' he asked. '*Oprosti mi, Tašo*,' he said, using her pet name. 'I was just—'

'*Forgive* you?' she exclaimed. 'I know what you were doing. You were trying to find out how much I had told her.'

He let go of her and she almost lost her balance. He tried to take her elbow to steady her, but she jerked free. 'You don't trust me,' she said sullenly.

'Come inside,' he said. 'Have a drink. We'll talk about it.'

She frowned at him, fighting back tears, and he moved in close again. This time she permitted him to take her by the shoulder, and he stooped to drop his briefcase before taking her in his arms. She resisted at first, but then she began to weep quietly.

'*Tašo*,' he said. 'It's been too long — much too long.'

'I can't go with you, Mirko,' she said.

Even so, she held still while he kissed her beautiful dark-brown hair. She wore it longer than when he had known her; long and curling sensuously over her shoulders. She smelled of salt air and the woody richness of autumn. Then, unexpectedly, she returned his embrace, hugging him fiercely.

After a while, she pulled back to look into his face. 'Liverpool is my home now,' she said. 'I *won't* go back to London.' In her eyes he saw the horror of the past.

London for Natalja meant Immigration, solicitors' offices and endless interviews, going over and over her story. Refusal, disbelief, more interviews until the pain was so great that she could not speak. The immigration officer's reports gave a dispassionate account of when she became tearful, when she asked for a break, when she became unresponsive.

But her voicelessness was something far more profound: she told him later that when she tried to speak, her throat seemed to constrict, and she could barely breathe. For days after these punishing interviews, he would nurse her while Natalja, mute and suffering, wrote him notes of thanks, her tears pock-marking the paper.

She said once that these episodes were like a well she had fallen into where it was dark and cold and filled with pain. The questions — having to talk about these things she could hardly bear to think of — pushed her into the well. She felt herself falling, and the darkness was real for her. Over the next few days she would have to claw her way up out of the darkness again, with only the sound of his voice to guide her. Gradually, with patience and kindness, and a huge effort of will, she recovered the power of speech.

Power of speech. Before he came to England, Mirko found this a strange expression. In Yugoslavia, as it was torn apart and redistributed, power was in physical strength — in armies and guns and money. Or so he had thought then.

In England, they ran things differently. He had been forced to listen to sneering immigration officers: puny men and stern women whose power lay, not in the strength of their sinews or their skill with a gun, but in the words of the written law. He heard Natalja try to tell her story. They took her words and turned them into sticks to beat her with; stones to drive her away.

'I'm sorry, *Tašo*,' he said. 'I was afraid. I should have trusted you.'

She took his face in her two cold hands and her eyes shone with love and regret. 'Yes, Mirko. You should have.' She stroked his cheek, where the welt had turned red and raised in the cold air. 'Grace knows that my parents were murdered, that's all. I don't want her to know more than that. You know I *can't* tell her more than that.'

He bent to kiss her and felt her respond. 'So,' he said, taking her hands and holding them in his. 'Now that we understand each other, will you come and have that drink?'

She smiled. 'No, Mirko.'

'What,' he said with self-mocking outrage, 'you don't trust me?'

She kissed him gently on the lips. 'I don't trust myself,' she said.

CHAPTER TWENTY-TWO

Rickman woke feeling cold and bereft. He reached out for Grace, but her side of the bed was empty, the sheets cool. It was still dark, and when he checked the clock on the bedside table, it read six a.m.

He rolled onto his back, wondering if he should get up to find her. He wasn't the only one having a hard time, and he knew he hadn't made it any easier for her with his evasiveness.

He sighed, sitting up and swinging his legs over the side of the bed. He couldn't tell her any more than he had already, but at least she wouldn't have to feel lonely as well as left out.

The bedroom was cool, the central heating just kicking in, so he grabbed his dressing-gown and padded out onto the landing. A low bass rumble made him stop and tilt his head to listen. Was Grace listening to the TV? Breakfast TV wasn't really her thing — all celebrity gossip and soap stars plugging the latest storyline, she said. He walked down the first three steps and paused, hearing Grace's voice as a warm, clear counterpoint. She seemed to be offering comfort.

Then the low bass kicked in again. A man's voice. There was someone in the house. Lee Foster? No. Grace would have woken him immediately she knew it was police business. A patient, then? Grace did occasionally get a visit from one of her foreign patients from the afternoon clinics, though she never could discover how they had got hold of her address. Sometimes they said the phone book, but this was impossible, since their number was unlisted. Rickman was reluctant to interrupt what might be a consultation, but he was beginning to feel the stirrings of unease. It was way too early.

The man raised his voice angrily and Rickman felt a spark of anxiety. Who the hell was in their home? His heart thumping, Rickman ran down the rest of the stairs and along the hall, bursting into the sitting-room.

They stopped as he opened the door, frozen in surprise: Grace seated, looking more than usually small and slight, her hair tangled with sleep, her face pale, hands slightly raised, patting the air as she might pat a distraught patient's hand, Simon, tall and wiry, standing over her, his finger raised. He was dressed, but the clothes were a bad fit, and Rickman wondered if he had stolen them from another patient.

'Simon?' he said. A question and a warning in his voice.

Simon dropped his arm, actually hiding his hand behind his back, like a child caught in the act of bullying. He began to smile. It was that same daffy smile he gave the last time Rickman went to see him at the hospital. And the time before. Well, Rickman wasn't in the mood for another rapturous greeting from his long-lost brother.

'What are you doing here?' he demanded.

Simon seemed nonplussed. 'I came to see you.'

'On an impulse you came to see me at six o' clock in the morning?'

Grace shot him a comical look. 'Simon arrived at five,' she said. Then, registering his outraged reaction, she added, 'You were sleeping so serenely.'

'Duck on a pond, my love,' he said, responding to her humour despite his irritation. 'Duck on a pond.'

Simon looked from one to the other as if trying to decipher a foreign language. 'I don't understand.' He sounded petulant, and his face flushed with a dark anger Rickman recognised from their childhood. It was not a pleasant recollection, and he asked with deliberate roughness, 'How did you find me?'

Simon's expression changed to one of low cunning. 'I made Tanya tell me.' He spoke his wife's name as if she was some well-meaning yet tiresome stranger.

'You *made* her?' Rickman took a step forward, but Grace intervened, standing to assert her presence.

'He *persuaded* her,' she said firmly.

Simon's head jerked in that strange head-bobbing movement that wasn't quite a nod.

'You gave Tanya your address and phone number and Simon thought he should have it too — as your brother.' She stressed the last three words and gave him a look that said *back off*.

He did, literally, feeling the anger, and with it the danger, dissipate.

'What do you want, Simon?' he asked, suddenly weary.

Simon blinked, his face a blank of child-like innocence. 'I came to see you,' he repeated. 'When you didn't come—'

'I *did* come,' Rickman broke in. 'I came to the hospital twice.'

'I know.' Simon half-smiled. He seemed happy, brimming with good news that he was eager to share.

'I remember the second time. The doctors say my working mention—' He stopped, and Rickman saw panic on his face. 'That's not right is it?' For a desperate moment he looked wildly from his brother to Grace for help.

'Memory,' Grace said gently. 'Working memory. Don't worry about the words — they'll come.'

'Working memory,' he repeated, a look of intense concentration and distress on his face. 'It's — it's improving. They say I've had some kind of amnesia. But things are coming back — not in order — I know there must be other stuff, because there are too many days.'

Rickman shook his head. 'I don't follow.'

155

'They don't all *fit*.' Simon's hands opened and closed, opened and closed, in a compulsive movement, as if he was trying to claw the words out from the place they were caged. Any excitement, and it seemed his ability to express himself clearly — even his capacity to think — deserted him.

'You were saying, Simon, that a lot of time must have passed, so you must have done other things. Things you can't remember, yet,' Grace said, her voice soothing and reassuring.

Again, Simon's head bobbed in tacit agreement. 'But I'm gonna,' he said, reverting to the childish speech patterns of their earlier meetings. 'You won't believe what I can remember.'

Rickman looked hard into his brother's face. Was Simon challenging him? Baiting him even? 'My memory's pretty good, too,' he said, quietly.

The irony in his tone seemed to pass Simon by. It wouldn't have when they were kids. Was it a symptom of his brain injury, or had he lost his capacity to laugh at himself as a consequence of age and self-importance?

'I can remember all sorts of things,' Simon went on. 'From when we were kids—'

'Come on,' Rickman interrupted, taking his brother by the elbow and steering him towards the door.

'Where are we going?'

'Back to the hospital.'

'But I was going to tell Grace—'

'You've told Grace enough already,' Rickman said. He saw Grace's eyebrows lift. Surprise? A question, perhaps — and yes, he thought, annoyance, too. Then she shrugged, as if dismissing the complex of emotions until another time.

'You might want to put some trousers on first,' she said.

Simon began laughing, and, looking down at his bare legs, Rickman had to smile. Which would have been fine — nothing like laughter for breaking the ice, after all. But Simon went on and on. Grace and Rickman exchanged a worried glance — he was becoming hysterical. It seemed that

Simon experienced emotions in the extreme: anger, sadness, frustration, joy — for Simon, there were no shades of feeling, no subtleties.

'Okay, Simon,' he said. 'We get the joke; it isn't that funny.'

'But it *is*.' Tears squirted from Simon's eyes at the hilarity of the situation. 'If you took me back to hospital like that, they'd think *you* were the patient!'

Grace lifted her shoulders and spread her hands, her eyes brimming with laughter.

Rickman let go of his brother's arm with a sigh. 'I'll go and get dressed.'

'I'll come with you.'

Grace must have seen the alarm on his face, because she said, 'Aren't you hungry, Simon? I was about to make breakfast.'

'A fry-up?'

'The works,' she said.

* * *

When Rickman came downstairs showered and shaved, Simon was pushing the remnants of his breakfast around his plate with his fork and crying disconsolately. Grace stroked his upper arm, trying to soothe him. She looked up when she heard the door open, a dismayed look on her face.

'He was telling me how close you were,' she said.

'So close he hasn't been in touch for twenty-five years,' Rickman said. Nevertheless, he felt a jab of pain below his heart.

Simon turned his tear-stained face toward his brother. 'Why do you hate me?' he asked.

Seeing the incomprehension on Simon's face, Rickman relented. 'I don't,' he said. 'I'm just—' In the end it was easier to lie. 'I'm just worried about this case. When you're ready,' he added, 'I'll give you a lift.'

Grace offered to call the hospital, take him in later at the start of her shift, but Rickman declined. She let it go, no doubt thinking that the drive into the city centre would give them time to talk.

As it turned out, Rickman barely spoke a word on the car journey, allowing his brother's constant stream of disjointed ideas and recollections to wash over him unnoted.

It was bitterly cold and when they reached the hospital Rickman took off his coat and put it around his brother's shoulders. Simon was delighted, admiring its warmth and praising it in the outlandish way that Rickman now recognised was part of his illness.

'Don't get too attached to it,' he said, dryly. 'I'll be taking it back as soon as you're safely inside.'

They walked through the revolving doors into the main entrance foyer with Simon still talking excitedly. Rickman caught sight of Tanya on the far side of the foyer, heading toward the lifts. Hearing Simon's voice, she turned, as did the two boys with her. Rickman's heart missed a beat. The older boy had his mother's oval face and dark-brown hair. He was tall and tanned and carried himself with the slightly self-conscious confidence of a young Italian. The younger boy was small and slight; his hair, shorter than in the holiday photographs Tanya had shown him, was a rich nut-brown. He couldn't see the colour of the boy's eyes from across the foyer, but they were dark and watchful. Looking at Fergus was like looking at a reflection of his twelve-year-old self.

Fergus stood awkwardly, a little apart from the other two. *That's how I must have looked when Simon walked out on me and Mum,* Rickman thought. *A skinny kid, defensive, trying to be brave; trying to be a man.* Simon saw it, too. He froze, staring at the boy.

The older boy — *Jeff Junior,* Rickman told himself — took his mother's arm, supporting her, and she hurried over to where they stood. Fergus stayed put, diffident, and perhaps a little resentful.

Tanya took Rickman's hand and kissed him quickly on the cheek. 'Thank God!' she exclaimed. Then she turned to her husband. 'Simon, we've been out of our *minds* with worry. What were you thinking?'

With the replica of Jeff as a boy out of sight, Simon forgot him. He scowled at Tanya. 'I don't know why they had to tell you.'

'You were missing — what were they supposed to do?'

'I wasn't "missing",' Simon insisted, 'I knew exactly where I was. I went to see my brother — and I don't see what business—'

'Dad?' The older boy stepped forward. His voice trembled with emotion.

Simon looked at him blankly.

'Dad, it's me, Jeff.' He was pale beneath his tan.

Simon didn't respond, only stared at the boy, and as he watched, the jerky head-nodding that Rickman had seen on their first encounter began again.

Simon's eyes flicked briefly to his brother, standing by his side, then to the boy who had called him 'Dad'. 'No,' he said. 'This isn't fair.'

'What isn't fair?' Rickman asked.

'There's too much to take in. Too much . . . stuff.' He slapped his forehead, hard, with the heel of his hand. 'Think!' he shouted. 'Just *think*!'

The boy took a step back, alarmed, and Tanya put a steadying hand on her son's arm. 'Simon,' she said. 'This is your son — you remember Jeff.'

A whimper escaped Simon. 'I can't,' he whispered. 'I can't! Stupid!' he shouted, slapping his forehead again with the heel of his hand.

Rickman glanced at Tanya, giving a small shake of his head. Now was not the time, but Tanya must have struggled with this every day since Simon's crash, sure that if he made the effort, he would recognise his sons. '*Try*, Simon,' she urged. 'Try to remember.'

Simon looked wildly at his brother. 'I *am* trying, Jeff. Honest I am, but I can't. I don't know what I did wrong.' He looked so frightened. 'Stupid,' he repeated in a whisper.

'No,' Rickman said. 'You're not. You're just sick.'

'I was in a . . .' On the brink of saying it, the word seemed to slide away from him. 'Car.' he finished.

'A crash,' Rickman said.

'Crash.' Simon seized on the word triumphantly, adding, with a furtive look at Tanya, 'In a car.' Perhaps he hoped that Tanya hadn't noticed his mental lapse.

'Yes,' Tanya agreed. 'In a car. You lost your memory. You forgot—' she swallowed. 'You forgot important things about your life. Me. Your children. Won't you say hello to Jeff?' She couldn't keep the pleading note out of her voice.

Simon glanced at his brother.

'Not me,' Rickman said. 'Your son.'

Simon shook his head slowly. 'Some kind of trick,' he muttered. 'Why are you doing this to me?'

He pushed past his wife and son. The younger boy stepped aside, a look of horror on his face. There was something in that look that stopped Simon.

'This is insane,' he said, looking from the boy to Jeff and back to the boy. 'This is a nightmare.'

'I know it's frightening—' That was as far as Tanya got.

'This is Jeff — and this is Jeff.' Simon said. 'How can he be young and old? How can old Jeff and young Jeff be standing there and here, right in front of me?'

'I'm your brother, Jeff,' Rickman said. 'And this is your son — my nephew.'

Simon began to smile and his son offered a tentative smile in return. 'Dad?' he said.

'No.' He shook his head, seemed instantly furious. 'No!' Then he raised a finger and the boy flinched. A look of cunning transformed Simon's face making it unrecognisable to his children and his wife.

'Nightmare,' he growled.

* * *

Rickman took the boys for breakfast in the staff canteen while Tanya saw that Simon returned safely to the Head Injuries Unit.

They chose their food and carried it to their table in silence.

'You look a lot like I did at twelve,' he told Fergus. 'Your dad's just confused.'

'You mean he's off his head,' Jeff said bluntly. He had his mother's dark eyes. 'It's obvious, isn't it? But will he . . . ? Is he going to stay like that?'

Rickman looked across the table at the two boys. They had been kept at a distance and reassured — told stories neither of them believed, ever since their father's accident. It was time somebody told them the truth.

'Will he recover?' he said. 'I don't know,'

The boys exchanged a look that gave Rickman a chill of recognition: he and Simon across the table when they were kids and some new disaster loomed. It said, *It's you and me, bro. You and me against the world.*

The moment passed and Fergus said, 'At least he's honest.'

'Your mother has got her strength from you two,' he said. 'She's relying on you.'

'We know that,' Jeff said.

He had offended them, and by way of apology Rickman said. 'Yeah, I guess you do.'

Jeff held his gaze for a second longer, then, satisfied that they were not being patronised, he turned to tormenting his bother. 'Should've seen your face, though.' He ruffled Fergus's hair and the younger boy flushed hotly, swiping his hand away.

'Didn't see you being so brave.'

Both acknowledged the stand-off and set to, finishing off their own food and most of Rickman's. As Fergus rubbed the last of the toast crumbs from his fingers, he asked, 'So, when I'm old will I look like you?'

Rickman fixed him with a mournful eye. 'Only if you're very, very wicked.'

Fergus wasn't sure how to react and he glanced uncertainly at his brother. Jeff gave it away, chuckling as he scooped up another mouthful of cereal.

Then Fergus said, 'Oh, ha, ha.'

But he couldn't help smiling a little and Rickman thought, *This isn't so bad. Being an uncle isn't so bad at all.*

CHAPTER TWENTY-THREE

Rickman bought a bundle of newspapers and settled down to read them in his office. By the time Foster rolled in at seven forty-five, he had worked through coverage of the arson attack in two tabloids, the three main broadsheets and the local newspaper.

'You plannin' another telly appearance?' Foster asked.

Rickman looked up, his mind still on the newspaper articles. 'Telly appearance?'

'*What the Papers Say*,' Foster said.

'Doesn't strike me as your bag, Lee — current affairs.'

Foster grinned. 'I never said I watched it, did I?' He plonked a cup of coffee onto the reports on his desk, slopping some in the process, dropped a copy of the *Sun* next to it, and shrugged off his jacket. 'Have they hung us out to dry, or what?'

Rickman sighed. 'We might have to do some damage limitation. The *Daily Post* is playing down the immigrant connection, but the others . . .'

'I wouldn't worry,' Foster said, sitting at his desk and taking a slurp of coffee. 'Most of the local yobbos can't read anyhow.'

Rickman raised his eyebrows. 'The rest of the city's population can. And the *Sun* requires a reading age of around ten years — even your average yobbo can just about manage that.'

Foster looked down at the redtop on his desk and sucked his teeth. 'S'pose I asked for that one,' he said.

* * *

They began the morning briefing with the media coverage. Headlines ranged from 'VENDETTA', and 'RACE HATE ATTACK KILLS FOUR', to the more sedate 'HALLOWE'EN PRANK ENDS IN TRAGEDY'. This last was from the *Liverpool Daily Post*. When reporters from the nationals had slipped back to London and the story was long forgotten as a national scandal, the *Post* and *Echo* would still be there at the heart of the community; they would have to live with the consequences of stirring up the hornets' nest of Immigration for the sake of sales figures. Hence their more circumspect approach.

'Community liaison officers will be briefed to work with schools and youth clubs, devising supervised activities at Hallowe'en,' Rickman said.

Hinchcliffe added, 'I'm asking for extra officers to be drafted in from other divisions to patrol emergency accommodation throughout the city — we have to nip any vigilantism in the bud.'

'Any chance of getting a statement from the lad, Boss?' Naomi Hart asked.

'I spoke to the consultant at Whiston Hospital burns unit,' he said. 'They've pushed eight litres of fluid into the boy in the last twelve hours, but it doesn't seem to be doing any good. His internal organs are packing up.

'We'll need to interview his younger brother — they're very close from what I gather. Can you set something up with the Child Protection Unit, Naomi?'

She nodded. 'Sir.'

'Okay. We're treating the arson attack as a linked incident,' Rickman went on. 'DCI Hinchcliffe is the OIC

— anything that comes to me, goes to him as well. Sir?' He stepped back, allowing Hinchcliffe to take the floor.

'We don't know for certain that there is a link between these two cases,' Hinchcliffe warned them. 'And until we have definite proof one way or the other, the line — official and in-house — is that we're keeping an open mind.'

'We do know that the four men were alive when the fire hit them,' Rickman said. He allowed the murmur of comment to die down. 'They were alive, but they made no attempt to get out.'

'Were they tied up or what?' Foster asked.

'No bindings have been found,' Rickman said.

'Drugs?' Foster suggested.

'The toxicology results should be back later today, so if they were drugged, we'll know.' He scanned the room, finally locating the man he wanted. He had positioned himself at a desk against one of the walls. It was a good choice: from here, all the team would be able to see him when he began talking.

'You all know Tony Mayle from the Scientific Support Unit,' Rickman said. Mayle nodded in acknowledgement as heads turned. 'Tony will talk us through the fire scene.'

'The fire started at the front door,' he said. His calm authority held their attention immediately. 'But the most intense heat was in the sitting-room. The men were doused in an accelerant — probably petrol. It looks like there was a trail of it from the door to the bodies.'

'So someone got the flat ready to set the fire, and our little firecracker just happened to pick on that one to chuck a banger through?' Foster said. 'It doesn't make sense.'

'There's no point in theorising ahead of the evidence,' Mayle said.

Rickman covered a smile — he couldn't have put it better himself.

'Though it does look more like murder than manslaughter. The victims had no personal belongings on them. No wallets, no mobile phones. And they were pretty much burned up, so identification will be difficult.'

'What about dental records?' Tunstall asked.

'Dental health is often a low priority for asylum seekers,' Mayle explained 'so there probably aren't any records. Anyway, it's academic — their teeth had been pulled.'

Foster swallowed. 'When you say "pulled",' he said, 'you mean by a dentist, under anaesthetic, right?'

Mayle looked at him. 'I mean with a pair of pliers. We've yet to discover if they were anaesthetised.'

There were exclamations of disgust.

'*Jesus!* Foster said, his face drained of colour. 'What the hell's goin' on?'

'I don't know,' Rickman said. 'But we're going to find out. The HOLMES team will be allocating officers to talk to Jez's parents and the headteacher of his school. Find out who his mates are, if he's been in this kind of trouble before.

'The rest of the team will continue to work on our first victim, Sophia. The feedback from her solicitor, Gregory Capstick, was unhelpful — he claims he's too busy to develop a rapport with every asylum seeker who passes through his doors. According to his paperwork, he sent out a copy of the Home Office letter granting her leave to remain yesterday. No sign of it yet at her emergency accommodation, but it may turn up. If it doesn't, we'll want to interview him again. The second PM will be done today.'

'I've got that one,' Foster said, waving an action slip. He half turned, talking over his shoulder to the rest of the team. 'I just hope they haven't got the guys from the arson attack on the slab when I get there — it'd be enough to put you off bacon toasties for life.'

A few laughed, but more groaned, complaining at his insensitivity.

The DCI fixed him with a stare and Foster subsided. 'Now,' Hinchcliffe said. 'I know there's been a lot of — let's call it chat — about the stolen blood.' They all looked back at him as if to say, *Us? Gossip?*

'There are . . . indications,' Hinchliffe went on said, choosing his words with care, 'that one or possibly two other samples of donated blood were tampered with.'

'Whose?' Foster asked.

Rickman stared at him. What the hell was he playing at?

'We need to know,' Foster protested. 'What happens if we get accused of something?' He emphasised the 'we' — garnering support from the rest of the team — and a few voices of dissent were added to his own.

When the mutterings subsided, Hinchcliffe said, 'The officers concerned have been informed, but to quell any rumours, neither of them is on this team.' Some of them were mollified: if they were in the clear, they saw no reason to worry.

Hinchcliffe went on: 'Jennifer Grant, our chief suspect, is refusing to cooperate, and without an admission, it's virtually impossible to nail her with the theft of the blood.'

'She's off the hook, then?' DC Hart asked the question. This was her baby — she had investigated the connection between blood donations and the planted evidence. She wouldn't see it dropped so easily.

Hinchcliffe looked at her. 'Not off the hook,' he said evenly. 'But if we can't prove the case—'

The response from the team was not favourable, and Hinchcliffe felt the need to qualify what he had said. 'Rest assured, we have not resulted the action.' Resulting this line of enquiry without charging Ms Grant would mean it was finished. Dead in the water. 'It's just been referred. When we have more time, we'll come back to it, but for now, I'm re-grading it to low priority.'

'Okay,' Rickman said, determined to move on. 'Does anyone have any further suggestions or comments?'

Hart was an experienced officer and would recognise that Hinchcliffe had made a concession in agreeing to refer the action instead of dropping it entirely.

'On the arson attack,' she said. 'The Community Liaison Officers might know if there's been other attacks in the area.'

'It's near bonfire night,' Tunstall said, rolling his eyes. 'Of *course* there's been other attacks — kids round Shaw Street think lobbing explosives at folk is just a bit of fun.'

'I meant other attacks on immigrants,' Hart said, unfazed. 'The local bobbies'd be able to say if the immigrants are being specifically targeted.'

'Good,' Rickman said, making a note for the Allocations Manager of the HOLMES team. 'Let's get to it.'

The team began to disperse, and Rickman caught Foster's eye as he flirted with Naomi Hart. He jerked his head towards the door and went directly to his office. Foster seemed unconcerned. He shut the door and sat at his desk, flipping idly through the day's correspondence.

'What the hell did you do?' Rickman demanded.

'I talked to her, like I said I would,' Foster said. 'Couldn't get an admission, but we never expected to, did we?'

Rickman searched his face. 'Did you tell her to tamper with the evidence?'

'We can't be sure she *did*, Boss.'

'Don't piss me about, Foster,' Rickman warned. We both know that I was the target. She stole *my* blood to implicate *me*.'

'Right.'

'Well how come there's now two more bags with less than was originally donated?'

Foster shrugged. 'Beats me.' He puzzled over it for a nanosecond. 'On the bright side, it does take the pressure off you though, doesn't it, Boss?'

'And puts pressure on two officers who have nothing at all to do with this.'

Foster looked at him as though he had suddenly dropped a hundred IQ points. 'I don't see how you make that out,' he said. 'Look, one sample down in volume could be explained away, but three? That looks like sabotage. That looks like someone maybe nicked it to put you and other officers in the shit. Which looks good for you, but the sweet thing is, Jennifer Grant can't *admit* to messing with blood donations, 'cos if she does, she loses her job and probably does a spell inside.'

'You're unbelievable.'

'You worry too much.'

'I didn't ask you to fix evidence.'

'Aren't you getting this arse-about?' Foster said. 'You're the one who got set up.'

'Actions have consequences, Lee,' Rickman said tiredly.

'You're not responsible for the death of that girl, Jeff,' Foster said, heat in his voice now. 'Some bastard is killing refugees in the city. Carrie was a refugee. Jordan's got some connection, otherwise how would he know where to plant the evidence — stolen blood — which, as it happens, his sister nicked. Maybe Jordan killed her, and maybe he didn't, but we're not gonna find out with you banged up for something you never did.'

He was breathing heavily by the end of his speech, angry and exasperated, but Rickman wanted a straight answer and he was going to get it one way or another. 'Did you tell her to tamper with the evidence?' he repeated slowly, only just keeping his temper in check.

Foster debated a moment before answering. 'I told her we were finished. I told her I knew what she'd done. I might've mentioned I was thinking of having a quiet chat with her bosses. If she got creative, that's her business. But I *never* specifically told her to tamper with the evidence.'

Rickman stared at him in disbelief. He marvelled at the simplicity of Foster's morality — for him, it really was a question of what was expedient.

* * *

It was a busy morning in Casualty: the rain of the day before had finally abated, but the roads were wet, and a dazzling blue sky, together with sudden high pressure, combined to produce a few patches of ice in sheltered spots. The icy conditions brought in a steady stream of casualties. Hip and wrist fractures, mostly; many of the admissions were elderly. There was an increase in bronchial distress, too — smokers and asthmatics for whom flu symptoms had developed into pneumonia. A few isolated cases turned up sinister shadows on X-rays; these individuals were sucked quietly into the system: blood tests or CAT scans, bronchoscopy or biopsy.

A couple of minor firework injuries came in, causing a flutter of interest and even alarm in A&E: the police had asked for staff to look out for boys who might have been with Jez Flynn at the time he sustained his injuries. The excitement quickly died down when it became apparent that the burns were too recent to be relevant, and the boys were in the wrong age bracket.

Were the papers right, Grace wondered. Were thugs targeting racial minorities in the city? The papers called it a vendetta. The murders had all the hallmarks: the stylised methods of killing — Sophia by exsanguination, the four men by immolation. If it *was* a vendetta, that would imply an internal quarrel, wouldn't it? Some kind of power-struggle among the asylum seekers — someone determined to make their mark in the refugee community. But a white English boy was now involved, and it made no sense to involve an outsider in an internal quarrel.

She was sure Natalja knew something about the girl — Natalja worked as an interpreter for the refugee charities and the City Council as well as the NHS, so even if she hadn't met Sophia personally, she would know people who had.

Several RTAs came in quick succession — the start of the thaw had made road conditions even more treacherous.

They were bloody and difficult: a girl with multiple lacerations, an eighteen-year-old boy with a compound pelvic fracture, a shunt between a bus and a lorry that resulted in twenty casualties. At the end of it, Grace went outside for a breather.

'You okay, Doc?'

'Lee,' she said. The look of concern on Sergeant Foster's face made her smile, it was so unlike his usual cheery cynicism. 'There are times I think life'd be simpler if I was a supermarket shelf-filler, where the worst news you'd ever have to give folk is that stocks of their favourite cereal have run out.'

He smiled, more to encourage her than in appreciation of the joke. 'You'd soon get bored,' he said, adding before he could stop himself, 'but I wouldn't mind seeing you in the uniform.'

She backhanded the top of his arm and he flinched exaggeratedly.

'Seriously, though — I don't know how you work here.'

'This from a man who investigates assaults and muggings and murders for a living,' she said with a smile.

'Yeah, but you could have a nice cosy surgery with nice middle-class clients instead of which you split you time between this slaughterhouse and a bunch of refugees.'

'We do save the odd patient,' Grace said dryly. 'And refugees are people, Lee. All very different, all interesting in their own way.'

'Well, yeah,' he said embarrassed to have been caught out in his prejudices by Grace. 'Goes without saying. But it can't be easy, can it?'

She smiled. 'In A&E, you get a dangerously sick or injured patient and you fix them — it's an adrenalin rush.'

'I can see that'd be good,' Foster conceded.

'Lee, saving someone's life — it's the best feeling in the world.' She shrugged. 'But there's no follow-through. You fix 'em up and move 'em out. My clinic patients, on the other hand, come and tell me their good news: a birth, a marriage — when they're given leave to remain. They bring me pictures of their kids. I feel a connection with them — and that's a different kind of buzz.'

'I wouldn't know about that,' Foster said. 'The familiar faces in our line of work aren't the kind you'd wanna build a relationship with.'

Grace nodded, understanding. 'So what brings you to the slaughterhouse?' she asked.

'Sophia,' he said, knowing better than to use Carrie's pet name outside of the Incident Room. 'Second post-mortem.

171

They're still not sure what killed her — the drugs or the leg wound.'

Grace swallowed queasily, as an image of the girl's naked body flashed as if across a screen behind her eyes.

'And the toast—' He caught himself in time, correcting to, 'The toll is rising. They're making a start on the arson victims this afternoon.'

'Are you witnessing those as well?'

He nodded. 'Ten-minute break, then back into the butcher's shop.' 'Gruesome work,' Grace said. 'Are you staying for all of them?'

'God no,' he said, paling beneath his tan. 'Least I hope not. Depends how pissed off the boss is.' He grinned sheepishly. 'He took exception to a crack I made.'

Grace smiled, shaking her head.

'Well,' Foster said, 'I should . . .' He gestured vaguely in the direction of the mortuary.

Grace asked, 'Is everything back to normal after Jeff's reinstatement?'

'Back to normal?'

'It must have been difficult for Jeff, being under a cloud like that.'

'He never was, as far as I was concerned.'

She felt his disapproval, he must consider her questions disloyal, and yet, having begun, she found it impossible to stop. 'Perhaps that's because he's confided in you.'

'Are you asking if he really was set up?'

'Was he?'

'Yeah,' Foster said. 'Yeah, he was set up.'

'So what's he's hiding from me?' Now that he had conceded this much, Grace felt sure she could get more out of him.

Foster looked away. 'You know him better than anyone, Doc.'

'The trouble is, I don't believe that,' Grace said. 'He has a brother I didn't know about — two nephews.' A shocking thought occurred to her and she asked, 'Lee, did you—?'

'No,' Foster said firmly. 'No, Grace. I didn't know about his brother, okay?' He must have seen the disbelief on her face because he added, 'You've got to understand, Doc — there's a lot of shit comes with this job. Some of it human. You need someone to watch your back.'

Grace frowned. 'And what does that entail, exactly?'

Foster didn't answer immediately, but Grace waited, looking into his face, implacable, determined.

'Ah, Jeez,' he said, running his fingers through his hair. Finding a few strands misplaced he teased them out as he thought. 'I told him he should've been straight with you.'

'About . . . ?'

Foster shook his head. 'You should ask him, Grace.'

'I have — several times.'

He took a breath and exhaled heavily through his nostrils. 'I can tell you he's done nothing wrong. He's just a bit — I dunno — a bit old-fashioned. Thinks women need protecting.'

Grace misunderstood. 'I can look after myself, Lee,' she said. 'You might want to tell him that.'

CHAPTER TWENTY-FOUR

'You seem sad today,' Natalja said.

Afternoon clinic had been running for an hour. They were busy — coughs, colds, sprains from slipping on the ice — but outside of the necessary communication on behalf of Grace's patients, they had barely spoken a word since Natalja's outburst the previous day. Grace thought she heard a hint of apology in her friend's voice.

'Bad day,' she said. 'Bus crash. A child died on my shift.' She swallowed. 'He was two years old.'

'Oh . . .' Natalja stared at a spot a short distance from her, as though she saw the tragedy reinacted. 'That's terrible. Grace, I'm so sorry.'

She touched Grace's hand and Grace felt a surge of emotion.

'Yes, it is terrible,' she said, but there was the rest of the afternoon to get through, and she had patients waiting. 'Who's next?'

'Can it wait for a minute?'

Grace looked at Natalja. Her face seemed thinner since all this had started, and her lovely almond-shaped eyes had a slight downturn at the outer edges.

Grace looked up from the computer-generated list of patients and waited.

'About yesterday,' Natalja began. 'I shouldn't have shouted at you like that.'

'Do you want to talk about it?' Grace asked, accepting her apology immediately.

Natalja blushed. 'I saw Mirko Andrić last night.' She seemed to anticipate Grace's interpretation of this and hurried on, 'We just talked. But I think everything will be okay now.'

'You've come to an understanding?' Grace asked.

'Understanding,' Natalja repeated. 'Yes.'

Her next patient was a young Lithuanian. Jokubas Petrauskas, it seemed, spoke only a smattering of English. Grace estimated his age at around twenty-five; he was small and wiry, with fair hair and grey eyes. He and sat down, unsmiling, gripping the seat of the chair with both hands. Grace introduced Natalja and explained that she would interpret from Russian to English. Most Lithuanians spoke some Russian, and Lithuanian interpreters were hard to find, so they generally accepted a Russian interpreter, but it was an uneasy compromise. He nodded acceptance, refusing to make eye contact with her.

'How can I help?' Grace asked.

'*Ya zdyess buil dva goda,*' he said.

Grace tuned out, listening instead to Natalja's interpretation as he continued. It seemed a carefully prepared speech, and he kneaded the seat edge nervously as he spoke.

'He's been here for two years, trying to get status,' Natalja said. 'He says he has obeyed all of the rules — going to English classes, not working.'

The young man went on and Grace listened with a sinking heart while Natalja relayed the message. Jokubas had been warned by this solicitor that he should prepare for repatriation. It was a story she had heard many times with minor variations; a leitmotif with the recurring theme of suffering and disappointment: people kept waiting for up to four years, only to have their claims for asylum refused. They came to her hoping for some medical loophole.

'I'm so sorry,' she said. 'I have no power over the Home Office. I can't help you.'

Natalja translated.

'*A vui mozhetye.*' Petrauskas spat back.

Natalja stared at the man and Grace wondered if he had threatened her. 'Natalja?' she said.

Natalja blinked. 'He says "But you can."'

'I'm just a doctor,' Grace said. 'If you have an illness that can't be treated in Lithuania, or maybe something that would prevent you travelling . . .'

The man stared at Natalja and she looked down at her notepad, her colour hectic, her breathing unsteady. '*Ya nye mogu vam pomoch,*' she said in an undertone.

Grace frowned. Evidently Natalja had not given a full translation. 'Could you tell him—'

But the man interrupted, speaking rapidly and sharply, excluding Grace entirely, abandoning all pretence that he had come to consult her, focusing instead on Natalja.

She responded angrily and Grace looked from one to the other for a stupefied moment before saying, 'Enough. This is a medical clinic. If you have a medical need, I will try to help. If not, I must ask you to leave.'

Jokubas stood, muttering a few more words in Russian, then he looked at Grace. 'Ask her why she's still here.' His English, though heavily accented, was fluent. 'Ask her why she is in England, when it's safe to go back to Balkan State.'

'Please leave,' Grace said, quietly, but firmly.

The man tried to stare her down, the contempt on his face poisonous, and she felt a flash of visceral fear. Then the moment passed and he turned on his heel. As he left, he grabbed one of the posters and tore it down, crumpling it in his hands and throwing it to the floor. Grace walked to the door and shut it to discourage the next patient from coming forward.

Natalja remained in her chair, staring at the blank page of her notepad.

'What was that about?' Grace asked, feeling a little shaky.

'I told you.' She didn't look up.

'You told me a small part of what was said.'

'I need a cigarette.' Natalja stood, but Grace held up her hand.

'Wait, Natalja. Don't run away from me again.'

She frowned. 'I just want cigarette.'

'You're avoiding me. What were you arguing about?'

Natalja shook her head, looking away and pressing her lips together as if she was afraid she might blurt out her secret despite herself.

'What did he mean about going back to the Balkans?'

Natalja smiled. It was sad, perhaps even a little self-mocking. 'We have a saying in the Balkans: *"Prava istina je laž."*, which means "The only truth is the lie."' She sighed. 'I don't want to lie to you, Grace. Please don't ask me questions I can't answer.'

* * *

It was mid-afternoon by the time Jeff Rickman finally found time for the damage limitation exercise he had discussed with Lee Foster. Since Mirko Andrić's performance on the regional news bulletins, everyone wanted to interview the handsome Serb who spoke from the heart. The local newspapers featured pictures of him, speaking with authority, and he was described in radio news bulletins as a spokesman for the refugees.

Rickman tracked him down to a rented loft apartment in the Albert Dock. He drove through the gates and turned left onto the cobbled public car park at the entrance to the dock complex. The sun was low behind the converted warehouses that bordered the central dock, but between the buildings he saw light glinting sharply on the water. A sailing ship was moored in one of the smaller docks next to the Pump

House and its rigging clinked and sang as the ship rode the gently rippling waves.

Andrić was expecting him. Nevertheless, Rickman had to show his warrant card to the security guard on duty in the foyer. Security, it seemed, came with the high-end rental payments. He took the lift to the top floor and stepped out onto a carpeted hallway. There were just two doors at this level, one on either side of the hall.

Andrić was alone. He greeted Rickman courteously, but seemed a little wary. Rickman reminded himself of his conversation with Grace the previous night: no doubt Andrić had good reason to mistrust the police.

They went through to a sitting-room at least thirty feet long, supported in places by columns. A series of windows gave picture-postcard views of a golden sunset across the Mersey. Solid oak floors and expensive rugs, strewn like discarded Sunday papers next to sofas built to seat five. A log fire burned in a large fireplace with a stainless-steel flue.

'Not bad for a rented apartment, huh?' Andrić asked.

'Very cosy.'

'Me, I don't like the smell of wood-smoke. It reminds me too much of the war. We hacked down the trees from parks and the streets for firewood. In Sarajevo, there was nothing left, not even a bush.'

'People will do regrettable things in difficult times,' Rickman said.

He saw a glimmer of amusement in Andrić's eyes. 'This is a strange thing to hear a policeman say.'

Rickman shifted uncomfortably. 'We're human, too.'

Andrić tilted his head in acknowledgement, not, Rickman thought, altogether convinced but sufficiently intrigued to wave him to one of the sofas.

A phone chirruped once, then the answering machine kicked in. It would ring twice more during the course of their conversation: radio and TV stations requesting interviews, no doubt. 'You have the ear of the media,' Rickman said.

Andrić glanced in the direction of the phone. 'Not so much as you, I think.' He sat opposite, cool and well-tailored in black.

'No,' Rickman said, 'you made a big impression.' Again, he saw the fleeting amusement pass over the Serb's face.

'I don't speak for others,' he said. 'I say what is in my own mind — in my own heart.'

'I'm not asking you to be a mouthpiece for the police, Mr Andrić.'

'But you don't like what I said last night.'

Rickman lifted his shoulders. 'I see your point of view . . .'

'But—'

'It would help if you took a moderate line.' He paused. 'Asylum seekers, refugees — they find it hard to talk to us, I know that, and I understand. But we *are* trying to protect people here. And we could use some cooperation.'

Andrić studied him, his eyes dark and unreadable. *He's going to say no*, Rickman thought. Andrić went to the window and stood looking out across the river towards Birkenhead and the Wirral peninsula.

'I won't be informant,' he said.

There was more to come, Rickman was sure of it. He waited, and after a brief pause, Andrić went on, 'I could maybe talk to people. Explain what you said to me. If they come forward, that's good. If they don't . . .' He shrugged, and Rickman, watching his back, got the impression of solid musculature beneath the jacket.

'Sounds reasonable,' he said. He sensed that Andrić was still undecided, and he knew that trying to persuade him further might push him into a blank refusal. So he kept quiet and let the man think. After a while, Andrić took a deep breath and puffed air between his lips.

'What do you need?' he asked.

'Sophia Habib, the girl who was murdered. We know she wasn't living in the allocated accommodation. We want to know why.'

'Have you seen emergency accommodation?' Andrić asked mildly surprised.

Rickman smiled to himself. 'Despite what you might see on TV, Detective Inspectors rarely make house calls.'

Andrić half turned from the window, a hand in his trouser pocket, insouciant, urbane. 'I'm honoured.'

Rickman allowed himself a smile.

'Mostly,' Andrić said, 'emergency accommodation is crowded and unpleasant. Sometimes it's damp, dirty, and for a girl it can also be dangerous.' In answer to Rickman's questioning look he explained, 'For every woman who comes into your country alone as asylum seeker, there are twenty men. Some of these men are very bad. Some are . . .' He took his hand from his pocket and raised it, struggling to find the word. 'Hungry? She is one woman alone. What can she do to protect herself?'

'Okay,' Rickman said, feeling that now he was getting somewhere. 'I understand why she might not want to stay put. But we need to know where she went to. Who took care of her. Who put her on the street.'

Andrić nodded without comment.

'Also, her vouchers were cashed each week, but not by her, as far as we can discover. I'd like to know who was cashing them, and why.'

'That's dangerous territory,' Andrić said, frowning.

'You know something about it?' Rickman asked a little more sharply than he had intended.

Andrić smiled. 'I didn't say that. But where there is money, there is risk.'

'All I need is a name,' Rickman said.

Andrić inclined his head. 'I will try, but I make no promises.'

CHAPTER TWENTY-FIVE

As the investigation went on, the picture was, if anything, becoming more blurred. Four more deaths, hostility on all sides: the locals, the asylum seekers and the media. Rickman had a major investigation on his hands that looked like it was near stagnation. Morale was low; it showed in the sluggish responses of officers to phones ringing, their tardiness in filing reports and picking up new actions. It told in irritable exchanges between them and in the haggard and dishevelled appearance of some of the men at the morning briefings. The women covered the shadows under their eyes with concealer, their pallor with blusher; but there was no hiding the fact that the excitement and energy at the start of the investigation had dissipated, and they were settling into the punishing routine of a long-term case going nowhere.

The ACC had stopped overtime: the division was already over budget, and any extra hours worked would be strictly on the house.

Somebody had recorded the regional news on BBC1 and ITV1 back-to-back and as people drifted into the Incident Room for the evening debrief, they gathered round, coffee mugs in hand, to watch.

North West Tonight had run an exposé on the sale of fireworks to minors. The same twelve-year-old boy, his face pixilated to prevent identification, was filmed going into one shop after another in and around the city centre. He emerged from all but two with a bag full of fireworks.

Granada Reports ran with the story that there had been twenty attacks on immigrant homes in the city since Sophia's body had been found. Stone-throwing, rubbish and excrement pushed through letterboxes, firework attacks. There were counterclaims from local residents, of immigrant youths terrorising children at bus stops and in parks.

They interviewed a Roman Catholic primary school headteacher who had banned Hallowe'en celebrations in his school, calling it an exaltation of pagan rituals and anti-Christian ideals. An ironic cheer went up at this. The interviewer quizzed him, but he stuck to his moral high ground. 'We are a Christian School,' he said. 'We will celebrate the Christian festival of All Saints Day on Monday. Those who glorify the forces of evil must face the consequences.'

'Bloody hell,' Foster said. 'It's not the police they want, it's Buffy the bloody Vampire Slayer.'

There was more laughter. It was the best thing that could have happened.

Rickman sensed the change in mood when he arrived at the briefing; it was welcome, if unexpected: House-to-House had been out for three hours between five and eight p.m., this being the best time to catch people at home. They had met with apathy and outright animosity.

'You're lucky if one in three of the buggers'll give you time of day,' Tunstall grumbled.

'And the immigrants are the worst,' someone chipped in.

'We might have some help with that,' Rickman said. He passed a video tape across to the corner of the room where the TV and VCR were set up. Foster ejected the regional news recordings and slid the new tape into the slot.

It had been filmed earlier in the day. A shot of kingfisher-blue sky behind a tenement building; cut to a close-up of the soot-blackened door and window of the balcony flat where the four men had died. A voice-over summarised the circumstances as the camera panned down to the reporter, a slim, dark-haired woman in a dark-red skirt suit.

'With me,' she continued, 'is Mirko Andrić, a spokes-person for the refugee community.' She turned slightly and the camera pulled out to include the tall, elegant figure of Andrić.

'Mr Andrić, you have experienced this kind of thing at first hand, as a Serb living in Croatia. How bad blood between neighbours can result in terrible acts of violence.'

'It doesn't help always to think about the anger,' he said. 'We are alike in many ways—'

She interrupted him. 'You came to Britain traumatised by the killings. Your own family were casualties of the war. How does it make you feel when people call you parasites, hoping to cash in on the system?'

He stared at the interviewer, affronted by the question. 'Until now, nobody has said this to me,' he said quietly.

The interviewer was speechless for a moment, and he used the opportunity to go on. 'I earn my own living. I have already made this clear. But I think it is important that I should tell people this: my family were killed in the Balkan war. Your country gave me a place to live. Food and shelter. Hope, when I had none. I will always be grateful.'

The reporter was not getting the response she wanted. 'Five people just like you are dead in what appear to be racial attacks — doesn't that concern you?'

'Of course. But I think it is too soon to accuse anyone,' he said. 'In UK, a person is innocent until he is proved guilty, yes?'

Rickman smiled to himself. Andrić knew exactly when to play the ingenue.

The reporter had all but given up, yet she made one last sally, 'What do you think of the police response to the situation?'

There was a collective intake of breath, and someone muttered 'Oh-oh...'

Andrić didn't answer immediately. After a moment or two, he said, 'I think whoever did these things is a very bad person. It's hard for the police, because he is clever. But I believe they are doing their best to catch him.'

'So you do believe that the attacks are linked,' she said, latching onto this apparent admission.

He shrugged. 'Who knows? But how will they find out unless we help them? All of us — asylum seekers, people of Liverpool, television people, radio people, journalists — everyone.'

There was another muted cheer, not quite so ironic this time. The next news item came up and Foster flicked the stop key on the remote.

'Comments?' Rickman said.

'It's gonna take more than a good word from Andrić to keep things straight Sunday night,' Foster said.

Sunday, being Hallowe'en, was likely to be risky — in the eighties, the local kids had adopted the American tradition of 'Trick or Treat', and this had evolved into the far more destructive 'Mischief Night'. Normal conventions did not apply; incidents of petty vandalism, egg-throwing and antisocial behaviour escalated beyond the resources of the police. In 2003, highly explosive fireworks had been used to blow up cars and phone kiosks, as well as to attack police stations. It seemed, though, that it was self-limiting, and after a few beleaguered weeks, things returned to normal. But with racial tensions in the city running high right now, opportunists might seize the chance to launch more attacks.

'There'll be extra bobbies deployed in the likely trouble spots, more on night duty—'

'They getting ovies, Boss?' Tunstall asked.

The corner of Rickman's mouth twitched. 'Didn't ask about overtime, Tunstall. Why? Are you getting bored working on a major investigation? Prefer to be back in uniform?'

'No, no, Boss,' Tunstall spluttered. 'It were just — idle curiosity, like.'

Rickman continued. 'The schools are laying on discos and other activities and we're advising against Trick or Treat unless children are closely supervised — there are rumours of poisoned chocolate and sweets.'

'Why mess with natural selection?' Foster muttered.

'*What?*' Any laughter was quelled before it really got started.

Foster's eyes widened. 'Bad taste, Boss,' he said, realising he'd spoken too loudly. 'I just don't know when to keep me big gob shut.'

'Learn,' Rickman said. 'Fast.' He waited until everyone was clear that he didn't find such comments amusing, then he went on: 'The results of the second PM on Sophia were inconclusive, but we do know that although she wasn't bound, she was drugged — as were the arson victims. So. Similar MO, more evidence of a possible link. And if someone is targeting immigrants in the city, we need to know why.'

'I don't want to sound silly . . .' Rickman clenched his jaw, hearing Tunstall's too-familiar refrain. 'But it's got to be racist, hasn't it?' Tunstall finished.

'Because?'

Tunstall shifted uncomfortably in his seat. 'Because they're all foreign, aren't they?'

'Yes,' Rickman said. 'But there could be specific reasons why these people were chosen. Like I said, we don't work on assumptions.' He could have illustrated the point by taking himself as an example: given the blood found on Sophia's clothing one might be forgiven for assuming that he had been in the murdered girl's flat, that he had known her, that maybe he had injured himself with the same knife that had killed her. However, he chose not to draw their attention to this set of facts.

* * *

Naomi Hart was shrugging into her overcoat as the phone rang. It was late, and only a skeleton staff remained, so

185

reluctantly, she picked up with her free hand, still trying to force the other into the sleeve of her coat.

'DC Hart.'

She listened carefully, her excitement rising, practically tearing the lining of her sleeve in her hurry to snatch up a pen and make notes. Moments later she was knocking at DI Rickman's door.

'Lex Jordan's back in the frame, Boss.'

Rickman turned his gaze on her, the skin of his scalp prickling at the sound of the pimp's name.

'Crimestoppers got a call this afternoon.'

'Anonymous?' Rickman asked.

'Code name only,' she said. 'But they've checked the story and it looks good.'

'Go on,' he said.

'Sophia was living with Jordan for a few weeks, according to the source. Then he put her to work. Looks like she was only on the street a few days when she got killed.'

Rickman took a breath. 'Okay,' he said. 'We need physical proof — a witness, if we can flush one out. I'll get an arrest warrant sorted, you call the Scientific Support, tell them to have someone on standby.'

'They're still assisting the Forensic Science Service on the arson crime scene, Boss,' she said. 'There won't be many CSIs free.'

'If they have to call someone out on their off-duty tell them to do it. I want them ready to move in as soon as Jordan is in custody. I don't want to give him the chance to get one of his girls in, cleaning up.'

He passed the information to Hinchcliffe, but it was too late to let the HOLMES team know; they had shut up shop shortly after the briefing. In the morning, he would ask for new i2 charts with the new information included. These colour-coded spider graphs could show up connections that weren't apparent from a written report; they summarised information, highlighted associated facts, simplifying the core details of the investigation.

Hinchcliffe called Rickman and Foster to his office when Jordan was brought in. The DCI had spent six hours at the Crown Court earlier in the day, waiting to give evidence on the Mathew Street shooting. He had only returned to Edge Hill a little after four-thirty p.m.

Over the last four hours, he had given a press conference, and spoken with the superintendent about co-ordinating the policing and investigative response to what the Super described as a "crisis". House-to-House would be scaled down for the next two days, until Hallowe'en was over. Community liaison officers would attend the asylum seekers' drop-in centres, to see if they could get a more positive response and glean some information for the investigation. Leave was to be cancelled until Monday. November Fifth would be dealt with after they had debriefed on Monday afternoon.

The strain was beginning to tell. Hinchcliffe's colour was high; his cheeks were stained an unhealthy plum colour, warning of high blood pressure. His hair was tousled as if he had spent the best part of the evening running his fingers through it. He had even taken the unprecedented measures of loosening his tie and popping the top button of his shirt.

'DS Foster, I want you to lead the interview,' he said.

Foster glanced uneasily at Rickman. 'Me and Jordan have got a bit of history, sir,' he said.

'What kind of history?'

'I've shopped him a few times,' Foster said. 'It could get in the way of him cooperating.'

Hinchcliffe flashed him an icy smile. 'I'm not expecting cooperation, Sergeant Foster.'

Foster coughed. 'Sir,' he said. 'But it'd be good to get more than "no comment" out of him.'

Foster was using his best manipulative strategies, but the fact that he couldn't turn the fifty-megawatt smile on the gov'nor was an enormous disadvantage. Hinchcliffe's colour was darkening dangerously, and Rickman felt compelled to intervene.

'DC Hart brought this one to me, sir,' he said. 'She's proving a useful member of the team — I think she'd make a good job of it.'

Hinchcliffe took a breath, on the brink of refusing, but Rickman spoke again. 'Sergeant Foster could sit in on the interview, speak up if he feels it's needed.'

A muscle twitched in Hinchcliffe's jaw. He looked from Rickman to Foster and back again before coming to a decision. 'I want the interview on video, as well as audio,' he said. 'Jordan's solicitor is witnessing the house search. By the time he gets here, I want the interview room set up and ready to go.'

CHAPTER TWENTY-SIX

Jeff Rickman rubbed his eyes, feeling the grit like grains of sand under his fingertips. He had almost caught up on his backlog of paperwork in a frenzy of nervous activity, while Hart interviewed Jordan. He waited a few minutes more until he was sure that Jordan was out of the building before viewing the video tape.

He dreaded seeing Lex Jordan, even on tape. On the face of it, he had nothing to fear. Jordan was just a pimp, a small-time crook with a big mouth and an ego to match — a man who had created his own twisted universe and placed himself at the centre. His reputation had been built on his brutish treatment of his girls; he kept them afraid, and fear was contagious. Other small-time crooks — satellites of this gas giant of man — respected him because he had a name for being tough and dangerous. It didn't take much to make a woman afraid of a man, though — Rickman knew that from personal experience.

In reality it wasn't Jordan that Rickman dreaded, it was being faced with his own lapse of control. Jordan had seen a part of him that he had kept buried for a long time and didn't much care to be reminded of at any time.

He stared at the videotape on his desk, labelled, dated and signed by the officers present as well as by Jordan. The pimp's signature was an elaborate flourish of loops and whorls. Rickman looked at it, feeling sick with exhaustion and self-disgust. But finally, he picked it up and took it to the Parade Room, where there was a TV and video, and where he knew he would not be disturbed.

He took a chair in the front row and pressed the start key on the remote. The caution given, Naomi Hart sat straight and confident, her forearms resting on the table, her hands loosely clasped over a buff folder embossed with the Merseyside Police Authority badge. Lee Foster sat away from the main group, trying to look relaxed. Failing.

'Tell us what you know about Sophia Habib, Lex,' Hart said.

Jordan frowned. He was dark-haired and broad, long in the body and short in the leg, with the kind of strength which, given a kinder disposition, might make a woman feel protected.

'Habib?' he said. 'Don't think I know the name, darlin'.' He had a south Liverpool drawl, slow and insinuating.

Hart lowered her chin a fraction and glared at Jordan. 'Don't call me "darlin",' she said.

He nodded. 'Fine. Just don't call me "Lex".'

Hart smiled. He hadn't rattled her. *Good for you*, Rickman thought.

'She was an asylum seeker from Afghanistan,' Hart said.

He shook his head. 'Doesn't ring any bells.' He sat back in his chair, turned slightly away from the two interviewing officers. Rickman got the impression that if it hadn't been bolted to the floor, Jordan would have tilted the chair on two legs and rested his feet on the table. As it was, he planted his feet legs wide, one foot tapping to a rhythm in his own head.

'We believe she was living with you,' Hart said.

He gave her a disbelieving look. 'Not me, love. I like my own space — know what I mean?'

'We have a witness statement that puts Sophia with you over a period of three weeks from late September to mid-October.'

Good. Let him make the denials, then hit him with the facts. That way the jury sees what a lying toe rag he really is.

Jordan smiled. His upper right canine was crooked; it crossed over the incisor, giving him the appearance of an unpredictable bulldog. 'What witness?' he said, leaning forward.

Hart maintained her relaxed pose. 'I'm not at liberty to say.'

The carnivorous grin barely flickered, but Rickman thought that Jordan was worried. Had he guessed this was a Crimestoppers call? He must be wondering which of his girls had dared to speak up against him.

'We will expect full disclosure,' Jordan's solicitor said.

Jordan's grin widened for a second. No doubt he thought that once he knew the informant's name, the problem would go away. Looking at Jordan's big, weight-lifter's hands, knowing what Jordan was capable of, Rickman felt he was probably right.

Jordan sat back, slapping the table as he slumped in his chair. 'Doesn't worry me, love. I've got nothing to hide.'

They all knew he had, but the jury would not, and if Hart didn't hit him with something fast, they would remember his words, rather than hers. 'The crime scene investigators have collected a lot of forensic evidence.' Hart leaned forward confidentially. 'You don't keep a very clean house, *Mister* Jordan.'

Jordan watched her as a cat watches a bird, but still Hart remained unimpressed. 'I think we'll get a match to Sophia in the samples the CSIs took. What do you think?'

Jordan switched off the smile. He didn't answer for a good half-minute while he mulled over what Hart had said. In a masterly demonstration of self-control, she neither prompted, nor recorded a "no comment" for the audio tapes. She simply waited, leaning on her forearms with her hands loosely clasped, her index fingers pointing to Jordan, keeping the focus on him.

'What does she look like, this Sophia?' he asked, at last.

Hart allowed this face-saving question: to the intelligent juror, it would be plain that he had known exactly who Sophia was right from the start. Hart took a photograph of their first murder victim from the document wallet under her hand and held it up. 'I am showing Mr Jordan a photograph of Miss Habib,' she said.

He pretended to study it, then shrugged. 'I see a lot of girls.'

'I bet you do.' It was the first sign of animosity Hart had shown and Rickman tensed. *Don't blow it now, Naomi. Show him how much you despise him, and you've lost him.*

He was surprised to see Jordan smile. It seemed that his self-absorption and towering arrogance had led him to misinterpret her comment as a begrudging compliment. 'If you'd showed me this at the start, I'd've said.'

Hart tilted her head: she still hadn't had a straight answer.

Jordan gave a little shrug. 'She did stay with me for a bit. Nice kid. We hit it off. She was in a bit of trouble—'

'What kind of trouble?'

'How do I know? She didn't speak English.'

'But you still managed to "hit it off".'

'We shared an international language, know what I'm saying, doll?' He grinned in a way that said, *I'm a bad old dog, but dontcha just love me?*

Foster shifted uncomfortably and Jordan stared at him, challenging him to say something. From the look on his face, Rickman guessed that Jordan's sister had told him about her fling with the Lee Foster. After a moment's indecision Lee folded his arms and fell silent.

'You're going to have to be more specific, Mr Jordan,' Hart said. 'What was the nature of your relationship with Miss Habib?'

The next few questions would be crucial: if Hart mentioned Jordan's criminal record — in particular his convictions for pimping — the video evidence would be inadmissible in court.

'You wanna know if we had sex?'

'Did you?'

Jordan smirked. 'She was an affectionate girl. She liked to show her gratitude.'

Rickman could almost see Hart counting to ten as she exhaled, letting the anger go, never taking her eyes off Jordan. 'You confirm you had sex with Miss Habib?'

'What's it got to do with you?'

'That will be for us to determine.'

Jordan glanced at his brief. He raised his eyebrows. *Your call.*

'I had sex with her, yeah. So what?'

'Do you know how old she was?'

Jordan was sufficiently unsure for the question to rattle him. Hart was doing just fine.

He blinked then said, 'Nineteen, she told me.'

Hart gazed at him a long ten seconds before she spoke. The video quality wasn't good enough to show the moisture on Jordan's upper lip, but it was plain when he wiped his mouth with the back of his hand; the man was sweating.

'She was seventeen, according to Immigration records.'

Jordan smiled, visibly relieved. 'Women — always lying about their age, aren't they?'

Hart pushed on while she had Jordan off-balance. 'Miss Habib left when?'

'Middle of the month,' Jordan said.

'The date?'

'I dunno,' Jordan said. 'I'm not the talking bloody clock.'

'Why did she leave?'

'I dunno,' he repeated. 'Like I said, she didn't speak much English.'

'She was with you for three weeks.'

He shrugged. 'Something like that.'

'And she didn't learn any English at all?'

He grinned again, showing that snaggle tooth. 'She learned a bit. What you might call specialist language.'

She let that go, and Rickman cursed with frustration.

'So, you don't know why she left?'

'Look,' he said, becoming irritated with the doggedness of her questioning. 'I woke up one day, she was gone. It happens — she was mixed up — moody.'

'You said earlier she was a nice kid.'

'She was a *teenager*. Sugar-and-spice one minute, pre-menstrual hell-cat the next.'

'Women, teenagers . . .' Hart sighed. 'They're just one big mystery to you, aren't they, Mr Jordan?'

He stared at her through half-closed eyes, then looked away, laughing to himself at some private joke.

'Were you grooming her, Mr Jordan?' His head jerked back, glaring at her, and Hart went on. 'Preparing her for the street? I mean you took her into your home, had sex with her. Taught her "specialist language". . .'

'She's running rings around him,' Rickman murmured.

Jordan's eyes bulged. He leaned towards her, and Rickman saw Foster tense, ready to react.

'Did you introduce Miss Habib to prostitution?' Hart asked.

Rickman saw the tension drain from Jordan's face, even his shoulders relaxed as he waited for Hart to wreck the interview by introducing his criminal record.

'Now why would I do that?' he asked.

'You tell me,' Hart shot back. 'Me, I always have trouble understanding why men want to live like parasites off girls.'

Rickman leaned forward: she was sailing pretty close to the wind on this one.

'And I can't imagine why you would think that of me.'

'Because, Mr Jordan,' *Don't do it, Naomi. Don't say it. Don't tell the jury he's known as a pimp.* But Naomi was a wilier fox than that. 'Miss Habib was under your protection for nearly a month,' she said. 'She lived with you, shared your bed. Days after she left your place, she was working as a prostitute. It's a question of proximity.'

Rickman exhaled, smiling broadly. Hart was quite something.

Perplexed, Jordan turned to his solicitor. 'D'you wanna translate that into English?'

'You were closest to her,' he explained.

Jordan swivelled to face DC Hart again. 'From what I heard, you don't know who she was close to. *From what I heard*, a senior officer got suspended.'

Hart didn't waver for a moment. 'You heard wrong,' she said. 'But since we're on the subject—'

He snorted. 'You're gonna start in on Jenny, aren't you? Well don't even bother.' He ticked off the points on his fingers. 'She hasn't been charged, she's not gonna be, and if she was, you wouldn't even dare put it up in front of the CPS — 'cos you know what? They'd throw that half-baked case out on its arse.'

'Blood stolen from a blood donor session led by your sister, Jenny, turned up on a blouse in Miss Habib's bedsit. Are you telling me it's just coincidence that you knew Miss Habib intimately?'

'Anyone could've stole that blood.' He turned slightly to look full into the wall-mounted camera. 'Anyone with access to the evidence could've tampered with it.'

Rickman's scalp tingled, but Hart kept cool.

'I think you asked your sister to steal the blood. I think you then used it to try to incriminate a police officer.'

'Why? What's the point?'

'To divert attention from yourself.'

'Didn't work, then, did it?'

'No,' Hart said, speaking slowly and clearly. 'It didn't.'

They went round in circles shadow-boxing for another half-hour, but Jordan was an old hand: he knew the system, how far interviewers were allowed to go under the PACE

Act, and with the clock ticking on his twenty-four hours in custody, they had been forced to let him go until the lab in Chorley came through with the analyses of the DNA samples taken from Jordan's house.

* * *

The night was freezing. The security lights at the back of the building sparkled on a crusting of frost on the windscreens of the cars parked in the safety of the walled enclosure. Beyond the glare of the lamps, Rickman caught a slight movement and turned, staring into the block of shadow hard up against the perimeter wall.

A cigarette glowed sudden and hot in the darkness and Rickman walked towards it, every nerve tense. A shape emerged from the amorphous pool of black on black. The figure of a man. He took one last drag on his cigarette and tossed it at Rickman's feet. Rickman stopped, face to face with Lex Jordan. The two men were of similar height, but Jordan was several stones heavier, much of it muscle.

'Enjoy the video?' he asked.

'It was quite a performance,' Rickman said. 'Made me wish I'd bought popcorn.'

They were in a blind spot between the security cameras. Jordan must have waited in that narrow wedge of electronic darkness, standing still in the aching cold for over an hour to avoid attracting attention, just for the opportunity to talk to Rickman. Which meant that Jordan was nervous.

'Well,' Rickman said. 'It was good of you to stick around just to ask my opinion, but it's the start of your working day, isn't it? I wouldn't want to keep you.'

'You don't look too pleased for a copper who's just got away with GBH,' Jordan said.

Blood. Screams. A girl shivering and sobbing, begging him to stop. Rickman remembered all of this and felt a burning shame.

'What's up?' Jordan said. 'Your girlfriend not giving out?'

Rickman had to curb a strong impulse to punch Jordan in the mouth. Jordan must have seen it, because he pushed a little harder. 'I could lend you one of my girls for a few hours — you look like you could do with a good shag.'

Rickman forced his hands to his sides, jamming them into the pockets of his overcoat. 'Scars've healed well,' he observed.

Jordan smiled. 'Are you threatening me, Mr Rickman?'

At that moment, Rickman knew he wouldn't fight Jordan, no matter what he said. Since boyhood he had lived by the principle that violence was for social illiterates incapable of rational argument. On the occasions that he had been forced to violence, he had used minimal force — contain and pacify had been his motto. He saw a flash of the night he had forgotten that motto — Jordan's face swollen and bloody, his eyes blackened, hands raised in a weak gesture of defence — and he was sickened by the rage he had felt.

'What are you doing here?' Rickman asked.

Jordan smiled. 'Just renewing an old acquaintance.'

'You killed her, Jordan, and I'm going to prove it.'

Jordan leaned in sharply. Rickman did not flinch. 'Wake up, Rickman — you've got no evidence, and guess what? I've got no urge to confess. Confession's for no-marks who think coming clean'll make them feel better about their sorry selves. It's a myth put about by priests and coppers: "Confession's good for the soul," they tell you. But you know what? Nine times out of ten, it just lands you in the shite.'

Jordan had been preparing that speech for an hour, and Rickman had to admit, his argument was persuasive. He had another flash of blood, bone and screams. He could own up to Hinchcliffe, "feel better" about himself, but it wouldn't get them a conviction. He could say goodbye to his promotion. And there was every chance that he would be out of a job, even if they decided not to prosecute.

CHAPTER TWENTY-SEVEN

Grace was watching a film on video, sitting cross-legged on a pile of cushions in front of their tiny portable TV, when Rickman got home.

'Gunfire and speeding cars?' he said. 'Not your usual choice of evening viewing, Doctor Chandler. Bad day at work?'

She smiled, offering him her hand and pulling him down onto the cushions with her. 'Is that a new aftershave?' she asked. 'You don't normally smell so yummy.'

'I stopped for a take-away on the way home. Chinese banquet,' he said. 'There's plenty for two if you're interested.'

'In food? Always.'

They ate from the cartons while Grace watched the end of the film.

'What is this?' Rickman asked as another bomb fell on a marketplace.

'*Welcome to Sarajevo*,' Grace said.

'Don't you get enough of this sort of thing at work?'

'It's a rough area I work in,' she said, 'But they don't actually bomb us.'

He snatched the last spring roll and said, 'Facetiousness is not your most attractive quality.'

'Neither is greed yours,' she shot back, stealing a morsel of spring roll from his chopsticks like a marauding seagull. For a moment she was silent. 'I just . . .' It seemed crass, now that she had to explain it. 'I wanted some insight into what Natalja went through.'

'Why not ask her?'

Grace dropped the spring roll back in the carton. 'Because she doesn't want to talk about it. Which is understandable — I mean, how do you explain that to somebody who wasn't there?' She nodded towards the TV set.

The scene was an exterior. Day. Many of the buildings had been pounded to rubble; those that stood were pitted and scarred like the faces of smallpox victims. Trenches connected different parts of the city and a man ran, weighed down by huge water bottles slung on a yoke across his back.

The fire had burned low and Rickman threw another log onto it.

'When they ran out of trees to cut down,' Grace said, 'They turned their books into pulp and pressed them into briquettes to burn.'

'Why do I get the feeling that hits you harder than the guy with the water bottles dodging snipers to fetch water?'

She narrowed her eyes at him. 'The destruction of books has a symbolic meaning: it's as if culture and civilisation went through a gradual melt-down along with the slow consumption of their literature.'

'Don't ever change,' Rickman said, laughing.

She dug him in the ribs. 'Patronising sod.' But she was laughing too.

They cleared away, Rickman fixed them both drinks and they sat watching the last log burn slowly to ash.

'I spoke to Mirko Andrić today,' he said. They sat on the cushions, their backs propped against the sofa, Rickman's chin resting on top of Grace's head.

'I saw him on the news. He seemed — ' Grace hesitated. ' — on song.'

'He's not the sort of man to say things he doesn't believe.'

Grace twisted to face him. 'We *all* say things we don't believe, Jeff.'

'I meant he wouldn't allow anyone to put words into his mouth.'

Grace nodded, settling into his arms again. 'You must have got through to him, then.'

Rickman kissed the top of her head. 'I asked him to make a few enquiries — find out who might have stolen Sophia's vouchers.'

'And he agreed?'

'Why shouldn't he?'

Grace took his hand in hers and stroked it, smoothing the hairs marvelling at its strength and gentleness. 'In the last six months, there have been around forty-thousand claims for asylum in the UK. If just one percent of them get ripped off, you're looking at four hundred people. Each person's paltry forty pounds a week becomes sixteen *thousand* per week overall — just about a million a year. Now *that* begins to look like big business. Business worth protecting with heavy armour.'

She felt his chin shift; he was trying to look down at her. She could visualise the frown, gouging deep lines on his forehead, wrinkling the silvery scar that bisected his right eyebrow.

'People aren't stupid,' he said. 'And they have lawyers, charities — people to advise them.'

Grace plucked at the hairs on his hand, a frown creasing her own forehead. 'If Immigration recommends a charity, you can be sure a fair proportion of the refugees will mistrust it. D'you know, at Dover, there are touts waiting in vans to ferry asylum seekers to solicitors in London. They take hungry, cold people, half-crazed by their experiences, and coerce them into signing forms for legal aid — then they do bugger-all to help them.'

Rickman made a mental note to have this checked out. 'How much of a part does the black economy play in this?' he asked.

'I treat sick people, Jeff,' she murmured, sleepy with the food and drink, and the lateness of the hour. 'I don't quiz them on their earnings — legal or illegal.'

They sat for a while, Grace snoozing, feeling her pulse gradually synchronise with the faint thud of his heartbeat, and listening to the burp and buzz of the glowing remains of the log on the fire.

She started awake when he spoke again. 'I bet your friend Natalja could tell us what we need to know.'

'What?' Grace said, her voice full of sleep, then, realising what he had said: 'We've been through this, Jeff — you can't expect me to invade her privacy to satisfy your curiosity.'

'Grace, you've just put yourself through two hours of sniper attacks and genocide — you can't tell me you're not curious.'

Grace sat up fast, clipping his chin with the top of her head. They both winced, but Grace was not in the mood to apologise. 'I'm *concerned*, Jeff. I think she needs help and I don't know how to give it.'

'D'you think I'm not concerned?' he demanded. '*Jesus*, Grace! I've five people dead, no suspects and no apparent motive. If you think I'm being intrusive, I'm sorry, but I need to find out what makes these people tick. I'm not asking you to break confidences — I'm just looking for a way in and you're not helping.'

Grace recalled her reconciliation with Natalja that afternoon, the unpleasant exchange with the Lithuanian, Natalja begging her not to ask questions. Suddenly Grace was sick of secrets and half-truths.

'You want to know what it's like finding yourself in a foreign country, in an alien culture, where people talk too fast and make no allowances?' Grace said. 'Ask your brother.'

Rickman moved away from her, getting to his feet, his face flushed with emotion. 'Grace, please don't start with this.'

'Look at it from his point of view, Jeff.' She squinted up at him, a little tipsy with drink and tiredness. 'We're in a new century, but Simon's memory ends at around nineteen eighty: the New Romantics, shoulder pads and big hair. He remembers the day John Lennon was shot but has no memory of the Berlin Wall coming down. Ask him about *Fame Academy*, he'll reel off the cast of *Fame!*. I bet he could solve a Rubik's cube blindfolded, but he doesn't know how to use his own laptop computer!'

'You don't know what you're asking,' Rickman said in a low voice.

'He's a foreigner in his own country and he needs contact with the familiar — and that means you, Jeff.'

Rickman shook his head. 'It's far more complex that you realise.'

'And yet you're asking me to "find a way in" for you with my patients.'

'It's not the same!' he exclaimed, exasperated.

'Yes, it is, Jeff. It is — exactly the same. The relationship I have with my patients is extremely finely balanced. I'm here to help people. I can't do that if they think I'll run off to the police with juicy little morsels — betraying confidences, putting them in jeopardy.'

'They *are* in jeopardy, Grace. We're trying to help.'

'I know you are, but people have long memories. They don't forgive and they don't forget, and I have to go on working with this community long after your investigation is over.'

'Five people have been murdered!' he exclaimed.

'And some of these people have come to Britain having seen whole generations of their own families murdered. It becomes a question of personal survival, and anyone who puts that at risk — even for the best of reasons — is the enemy.'

Rickman turned away. 'We're not the enemy, Grace. The police are not the enemy here.'

'Yes,' Grace said, talking to his back. 'Yes, you *are*. These men and women may have been hounded, arrested, beaten — even tortured by the police in their own country. Of *course* you're the enemy.'

He turned and looked into her face, and she saw that he was wounded by her unwillingness to trust him.

'Look at it from their point of view, Jeff. You're the policeman who was implicated in Sophia's murder. You're now leading the investigation — and you're asking them to trust you?'

Rickman looked stunned. 'What about you, Grace? Do you trust me?'

Tears welled in her eyes. She hadn't meant to say so much, but now it was said, and she might as well finish what she had started. She blinked and swallowed, steadying herself before she spoke.

'I know that you and Sergeant Foster made some kind of pact the night he came here. I know that you were reinstated soon after.'

'Jesus, Grace!' His voice was no more than a whisper.

She bit her lip. 'What am I supposed to think?' she said, forcing the words past a lump in her throat.

Rickman groped for a chair and sat down. *'Jesus, Grace!'* he repeated. 'Did you think — do you think *I* killed her?'

Grace didn't answer but the tears began to flow as she sat there, shaking with the horror of what she had accused him of, and the terror of hearing the truth.

He leaned forward in his chair, his hands clasped on his knees. 'God, what I've put you through . . .'

She looked into his eyes and saw pain and regret.

'I didn't know the girl, Grace,' he began, his tone solemn. 'I promise you — I never even met her. And I've never been in her flat — even in the course of the investigation. But the blood was there, and it had to come from somewhere.' He took a breath and exhaled slowly. 'The donor session seemed the obvious source. I needed to be sure the DCI would treat it seriously.'

He ran a hand over his face.

'I got Lee Foster to drop a few hints — get a few more people worrying about the possible repercussions — just to take the heat off me and put the focus back where it should be.'

She believed him, but even now she thought he wasn't being entirely truthful.

'Covering your back,' she said.

'What?'

'Just something Lee said.'

'We've since discovered that Sophia had been living with a — a pimp named Jordan. I think he put her on the streets, and I think he killed Sophia.'

'Why?' Grace asked. 'Why would he kill her?'

'I don't know,' he admitted.

There was something in the way he hesitated before naming Jordan that alerted her: was this the added truth he was holding back? 'Why would Jordan want to frame you?'

'We can't prove it *was* him,' Rickman said. She stirred, her irritation rising to boiling point, and he added, ' — But you're right, he is the obvious choice. And he hates cops.'

'You in particular?'

'We did have a run-in a couple of months back,' he said. 'And Jordan is the type to bear a grudge.'

'A run-in?'

'Please — don't ask me for details, Grace. It was bad, and I'm ashamed of my actions — but I can't . . .'

Grace nodded, still not entirely satisfied. 'Do you think Sophia started to question the theft of her NASS vouchers?'

Rickman shrugged. 'I wish to God I knew,' he said. 'I just hope I haven't given Jordan a "get out of jail free" card.'

CHAPTER TWENTY-EIGHT

Jokubas Petrauskas's room was on the second floor of a Victorian semi in Wavertree. It had once been a merchant banker's house: five bedrooms plus servant's quarters, three entertaining rooms, a basement kitchen and scullery leading to a small kitchen garden, now laid to grass. It wasn't bad: a bathroom on each floor, food cooked fresh three times a day in the basement kitchen — mediocre food, but edible. The rest of the house had been converted to provide fourteen small rooms, each with its own door and lock.

The room was sparsely furnished: a narrow bed, one chair, a small desk, a wardrobe whose doors would not stay closed unless you locked them. But it was no worse than back home, a little better even: at least the hot water worked, and the heating came on from eight a.m. until nine p.m. at night. Certainly, it was better than Scotland Road, where the high-density housing of the tenements drew thugs like wolves to an unguarded flock.

Despite the cold and the damp and the resentment of the locals, Jokubas *liked* living in England. He liked waking to the smell of leaf mould and damp in the autumn. He liked the colour: cars, people, shops — they all seemed brighter, mixed from a more dazzlingly palette than at home.

The street noise, the petrol fumes excited him, and the girls who laughed too loudly and wore too little both shocked and delighted him.

There was so *much* of everything. They even lit up the government buildings in the city centre at night, just to show off their beauty. He liked to look up at the night sky and see no stars because it meant extravagant lighting and opulence; it meant not having to study by candlelight, not having to put on every item of clothing you owned in order to keep warm because there had been another power cut.

In the summer he had come down to the King's Dock and sat close by the big top marquee where the pop legends came to play to wealthy audiences. Big names like Bob Dylan and Paul Simon he had heard as clearly as if he had been sitting inside the tent, breathing the same hot sultry air as the people who had paid thirty pounds for a seat.

He loved England more than the rat-faced youths who were born here. He saw them roaming in gangs for protection against others of their own type, but he also saw that membership gave them a craved-for sense of identity. He had learned many such things simply by observing, as an outsider, the way this alien culture worked. Jokubas had a thirst for the new: knowledge, experience, work. He had seen England as a land of great opportunities as well as wealth. He didn't mind that some people had more than others, because he would work hard and be one of those who had much.

He took English classes four times a week. It wasn't a requirement — he wanted to do it; in fact he would have done more if he could have found another place that would take him. Back home he had watched all the English TV shows, repeating phrases, imitating the voices. It got confusing sometimes, because there were so many different ways to pronounce things in English. But he tried hard: he wanted to fit in.

He had done everything they told him he must do: while others disappeared from the emergency accommodation for days, he returned to his little room each night.

While other guys did manual work — cash in hand — or waited tables in the city-centre restaurants, he counted the pennies from one Monday to the next, when his voucher payment was due. If they asked him why he would live poor when by their standards he could be rich, he would shrug and say, '*That's the rules.*'

They mimicked him, calling him "Mr English", but he didn't mind because it was only jealousy, and when he knew how to speak English well, he would not have to meet with these sneering and sarcastic men again: he would have English friends, and would go to English pubs to drink beer and eat chips and have conversations about football.

That was his dream before his life had been torn apart. He had been denied leave to remain.

Well, he hadn't learned English and played by the rules to be told that he must go home. He would stay no matter what it took. He would rather die than go home. If that bitch Natalja Sremać had been willing to help . . . but she wouldn't even talk to him. And if he made trouble for her, she only had herself to blame. He had tried everything else, but you can't get anyone to listen if you have no money.

His priest used to say that we are all equal in the sight of God — well, to hell with that! It wasn't God who set the rules, it was men, and equality could be bought or bargained for from those who had it in their gift. He had neither money nor contacts — but he knew names and he was sure the police would be interested. It would be risky, but hadn't he taken risks to come here in the first place?

This time he would not play by the rules. If he gave them the information he had, he would be indispensable to the British Government. Maybe they would give him Humanitarian Protection, or he had heard of something called 'witness protection' which was for people who gave evidence against dangerous criminals — maybe they would give him that. They would have to let him stay at least until the trial — and there would be a trial. What he knew would bring a lot of people down.

He turned on the radio to cover the noise of his telephone conversation, checking that the door was locked before he took out the scrap of paper with the direct-line number he had scribbled down from the TV news.

First, he dialled one-four-one: he didn't want them to trace his mobile number. He didn't want them even to be able to contact him until he was sure of a deal. 'I have information about the murders,' he said. 'I know why these people were killed.'

The officer didn't speak for a moment, and Jokubas felt an icy chill — had he misdialled? 'Are you talking about the people who died in the fire?' the man said at last.

'The fire — the girl who was killed — everything.'

'I need a name and contact number,' the man said.

'No. Not until we agree terms.'

Another long pause, then the man said, 'No reward has been offered for information, sir.'

'I don't want money. I want status.'

'You want—?'

'Immigration status. I want leave to remain,' Jokubas explained.

The man hesitated. 'Look, sir, I'm not authorised —'

'Don't you want to know who killed those people?' Jokubas demanded.

'All I'm saying is I'll have to talk to my boss. Give me a number, we'll call you back.'

'You think maybe I'm stupid?' Jokubas shouted. He was putting his life in danger and this man was playing foolish police games. 'I'll call you. In one hour. And you'd better have something for me, or you get no information.'

He pressed the 'end' key and pocketed his mobile. Bastards.

For half an hour he paced the room.

Then he heard footsteps on the stairs. Heavy, hurried. He stood in the centre of his room, frozen with terror, his heart pounding as fast as the footsteps covering the final flight of stairs. He groaned. He had said too much at the English class. Goaded beyond endurance he had spoken out.

'I know the rules,' he had shouted. 'And I know the people who break them!'

Oh God. *Oh God!* People got to know — somehow, they always got to know. Just as everyone knew that you could buy a new identity if you had enough money and the right connections, so they got to know when somebody in their house or their ESOL class had been refused asylum. It was a process of osmosis. And if you threatened the arrangers — if you spoke out against them from the misery of your heart — the information was worth money. Someone who knew someone who knew someone would tell someone, and then you were in trouble.

And now they were outside, and it was his own stupidity that had brought them to his door. They hammered with their fists, rattling the frame, shaking the plasterboard walls till he thought they would crack. 'Shut the fuck up!'

His eyes widened with horror, then he clamped both hands to his mouth to stifle a hysterical giggle. It was only the Iraqi from the room below.

'Can't you let a man sleep?'

Slowly, Jokubas let his hands down. 'Sorry,' he called, struggling with hysteria. 'Sorry. I — I'll stop.'

He could almost hear the Iraqi waiting on the other side of the door, wondering if he should take it further. Then he heard a door open and somebody spoke. His neighbour exchanged a few words with his countryman, then banged on the door one last time.

'Crazy Russian,' he growled.

Only when he heard the footsteps recede and the flat door slam down below did he finally switch off the light and go to his one straight-backed chair to sit down. He watched the traffic on the road below: a few cars, a hackney cab, once or twice a police car. The heating was off, and it was cold. Cold enough that he could see his breath, tinged orange by the streetlamps on the main road.

* * *

He didn't see them arrive — didn't hear them creeping up the stairs. Perhaps he dozed off. Or perhaps they were like the beasts of Russian myths, able to change form and shape, skulking unseen like cats in the shadows, changing back to human form when it was too late for their quarry to run.

He was on his feet before his conscious mind registered what was happening: a faint scratch and the jingle of metal on metal. Somebody was trying the lock of the door. The snick was on, but it was old and insecure; it moved slightly with every attempt to dislodge it.

Jokubas held his breath; tiptoeing to the door, he held the snick in place with his left thumb, pressing his ear to the wall to listen. Abruptly, the metallic rattling stopped. Silence.

* * *

On the other side of the wall, a man listened. He was dressed in a cloak and wore a mask over his face: a copy of Munch's 'The Scream'. After a moment or two, he nodded to his partner, who was identically dressed, and then he began tapping the wall with his fingertips, noting where the hollowness became a dull thud. He smiled to himself and reached inside his jacket. 'Trick or treat...' he crooned, his voice seductive, menacing.

'Go away!' Jokubas's voice was little more than a whisper. 'I'll call the police. Go away. Please . . .' Another silence, in which Jokubas heard only the thud of his heart, felt it throbbing against the thin plasterboard wall.

'You'd better come out.' The voice sounded as close as if he had been in the room. Jokubas jumped and gave a startled yelp. 'We only want to talk,' the man said.

'No,' Jokubas said. The tears coursed freely down his face. 'No, you don't.'

'You're right,' the man said. 'We don't. But you got no treat for us — we gotta trick you. *That's the rules.*'

'Oh, God,' Jokubas groaned. *You fool, you fool, you fool, Jokubas! Why couldn't you keep your mouth shut?*

A sharp, white flash of pain. Jokubas looked down. Blood bloomed and spread over his shirt and the wall. So hot against his skin and yet he felt cold. He tried to push away from the wall, but something stopped him. He looked again, unable to make sense of what was happening.

Outside, the man grunted, pulling hard, but the knife was jammed in the hole in the plasterboard.

Jokubas breathed in short gasps. the pain faded; everything faded except for the sound of his own breathing. The darkness in the room seemed to intensify; soon he would pass out. He managed to reach the phone in his pocket. Found triple nine by touch.

The man swore, sweating and straining to pull the knife out of the hole.

Jokubas begged for help in English and Lithuanian and Russian, his voice already faint, his strength fading.

The knife-man's partner took a step away, sweeping his cloak aside, reaching for the Luger tucked into the back of his belt, bringing it round in one smooth movement, aiming at a spot a few inches above the hilt of the knife. His partner saw him and batted his shooting arm away.

'*Ne!*' His voice was low, angry, authoritative. '*Nikakvog oružja. Ne na ovom poslu.*' He placed one foot flat against the wall and levered the knife out. It nicked Jokubas's aortic arch on the way up, sending an arc of arterial spray over the room as he fell: door, walls, ceiling. Then it lost pressure. The last thing Jokubas Petrauskas saw was a gob of his own blood, trickling down the lampshade, gathering mass and momentum.

Falling—

CHAPTER TWENTY-NINE

The children's interview suite was in a detached house in the grounds of Halewood Police Station. Designed to put children at their ease, it had been decorated and fitted out like a family home: sofas, soft furnishings, framed pictures on the walls — not quite chintzy, but not far off.

They gave child witnesses a tour of the place, showing them the kitchen and toilet facilities, as well as the recording studio adjacent to the interview room, explaining that they could take a break at any time. Parents were not allowed in the interview room, as a rule, but the children were told that Mum or Dad would only be on the other side of the glass, keeping an eye on things. Unless, of course, it was a parental abuse case. Then, things were managed quite differently.

The boys were interviewed separately, Minky being the last to arrive. He sat on his hands in the middle of the armchair that had been placed equidistant between the two small video cameras wall-mounted in the corners of the room. He examined his surroundings with wide-eyed apprehension. Minky had fair hair, which he wore a little longer than the older boys, and which today, as a special treat, his mother had gelled and blow-dried for him.

Watching the recording in a packed and eerily quiet Incident Room, Rickman was struck by the innocence in the child's face — it was a face miraculously unmarred by the brutality of his existence.

Minky chewed compulsively at the inside of his cheek, occasionally nodding in response to the Child Protection Officer's questions. The format was well established: one officer interviewing the child, the other behind the screen, checking recording levels, suggesting approaches or requiring clarification from the interviewing officer via an earpiece.

Naomi Hart had previewed the tapes, isolating interesting sections, taking notes. They had no time for undigested information: the press were baying for police blood since Jokubas's murder. The refugee community — those that weren't paralysed by the horror of the situation — were threatening retribution, even Mirko Andrić was having second thoughts. Rickman had telephoned him earlier in the day.

'If I'd never helped you,' Andrić said, 'maybe this man would be alive now.'

Maybe he would — a call had been recorded to the hotline in the early hours; a man's voice, offering information about the killings. An Eastern European accent perhaps. Jokubas Petrauskas was Lithuanian. They had requested a list of all calls made from his mobile over the past few weeks, so they would know for sure fairly soon. They found the phone at the scene. Blood on the number nine button told them that he had dialled emergency services as he died. They had requested the tape of his call, it was just possible that it might have recorded something of use, although it seemed unlikely: a verbal report from the control-room operator said the victim had screamed a few garbled words in English and 'something foreign', and then the line went dead.

The Child Protection Officer offered Minky a packet of sweets. He looked uncertainly at her and then to the two-way mirror, behind which he knew his mother was watching.

'Okay,' the CPO said, her tone encouraging. 'I'll leave them here in case you want them later.' She put the sweets down on the coffee table and continued in a conversational tone, asking Minky about his likes and dislikes, telling him about her own son, in the hope of drawing him out.

Hart referred to her notes and pressed the fast-forward key on the remote control. Speeded up, Minky's body language was even more telling: His gaze kept wandering to the table then flicking away, as if he felt there was something shameful in his greed. He looked frequently at the mirror, but they were furtive, anxious glances, and the constant self-destructive chewing of this cheek and lower lip gave him the look of a traumatised animal, compulsively repeating actions as a kind of comfort.

Rickman checked the clock counter. The interview had been running for fifteen minutes and the Child Protection Officer had got nowhere. An officer with less experience might have become frustrated, but she continued, getting monosyllabic answers, and gradually, over time, the boy's jerky, repetitive movements became less obvious: he seemed to be calming down.

Hart pressed 'play', and the sound came back in.

'My son loves *The Simpsons*,' the interviewer said. Her voice had a brassy tone — too much treble; sounds were magnified: the click of a pen, the creak of a chair.

Minky's abstracted surveillance of the room stopped and she continued. 'You know what I think, Minky? I think we should've named him Bart — the trouble he gets into.'

'That's our Jez,' he said. 'Me mum's always saying that.' Minky had a high-pitched voice, the kind that would make a good boy soprano, and he spoke with a fast, north Liverpool accent.

And they were off, talking about *The Simpsons*, comparing the characters with people Minky knew, identifying favourite episodes, and after a few more minutes, the officer came back to the point she was really interested in.

'So your Jez is like Bart, is he, Minky?'

Minky nodded enthusiastically. 'He *hates* school — he's always getting in trouble. He's had three detentions already this term.'

'Does he get into trouble out of school as well, Minky?'

He frowned a moment, swinging his feet and rocking slightly. 'Not big trouble. He's never been *done* or nothing.' He pronounced it no*think*, just as he pronounced 'something' and 'everything' as if they ended in the letter 'k'.

So far, Minky was telling the truth: Jez had had no major run-ins with the police — this had been confirmed with the local community bobbies.

'You hang around a lot together, don't you?' she asked.

'I'm in his gang—' Realising that he had let something slip, he slapped both hands to his mouth.

'The Rokeby Rats,' she said, nodding absently as if she hadn't noticed.

He took his hands away cautiously as though he was afraid that some other, more important revelation might escape him before he had the chance to stop it. 'How d'you know about the Rats?' he asked.

'Beefy told me.' He wasn't convinced and she knew to back off, instead offering him the sweets again. This time he took them.

'This is all small talk,' Hart said, skipping ahead on the tape. Minky munched fast and hard, speaking with his mouth full, evidently covering less contentious issues.

It had taken time and skill and infinite care to bring Minky back to the night of his brother's accident without frightening him into silence. The Simpsons had proved useful a second time; recalling its regular weekday slot was at six p.m., she said, 'Were you watching *The Simpsons* when Jez went out, Minky?'

He nodded, suddenly crestfallen, his hand in the bag of sweets, looking, Rickman thought, like Pooh Bear with his paw trapped in a honey pot. She helped him over this difficult moment by asking him to describe *The Simpsons* episode. He did, in great detail, telling her with some relish, 'And Bart said "Eat my shorts!"' He had the voice just right, and the Child Protection Officer laughed.

'Was Jez watching it with you?'

He looked troubled. 'For a bit.'

'And then he went out.'

He nodded.

'Did you see Jez go out?'

The boy stopped munching his sweets altogether and crouched again in the pose that screamed *I want to be invisible.*

'Minky?'

'No,' he said, his voice small, his eyes averted.

'Minky, did Jez ever do anything like this before? I mean with the fireworks?'

'No.' This time, he answered too quickly, his features composed into a facsimile of innocence that was completely unlike the first unselfconscious shot they had seen of the boy.

'You see, lots of little boys do put bangers through letterboxes . . .'

Minky's eyes widened and his nostrils flared. He seemed to be looking at something only a few feet away from him. Something that terrified him. 'We never!' he exclaimed, his voice rising in pitch.

She talked him down, telling him that she understood it was hard to talk about the night of his brother's accident, changing the subject for a while.

Hart moved the tape on to the CPO's next attempt at broaching the night of the accident. Minky seemed unhappy, but calm.

'Did you see Jez with anyone that night?' she asked.

'No.'

'What about the fat lad I seen outside the house?' A man's voice, loud, threatening. Minky flinched violently, looking wildly about the room.

Hart pressed the 'pause' button on the remote control. 'Mum's boyfriend,' she explained. 'He insisted on being in the recording studio. He pressed the intercom before they could stop him. They threw him out, but they had to suspend the interview for an hour to calm the little lad down. Mum did her best, but she only made things worse.'

Rickman remembered Jez and Minky's mother from a brief discussion they'd had when she called at the station to make a statement. She was under thirty, but her face was lined and she was red and puffy around the eyes. Her hair was tied back, her face free from make-up.

She had a smoker's voice: deep and slightly hoarse, only a year or two away from chronic bronchitis, and a nervous smile that revealed bad teeth — a tell-tale sign of methadone treatment, the sugary morphine substitute prescribed for addicts.

'They did get a bit more from him,' Hart went on, starting the tape again near its end.

'Jez never left me out,' Minky was saying, as if, against all the evidence, it couldn't have been Jez, because if he *had* decided to torch the refugees' flat, naturally he would have taken Minky along for the ride. 'We always done everything together,' Minky finished.

'Like putting fireworks through letterboxes?' the CPO asked.

The boy's eyes darted to the two-way mirror.

'It's all right, Minky. It's just your mum in there — and she wants you to tell the truth.'

Minky frowned furiously, chewing on those words as hard as he had chewed on the fruit pastilles earlier. His breathing got faster and harder, and finally, he burst into tears, repeating, 'I'm sorryMumsorryMumsorryMum . . .' over and over and over until the interview had to be terminated and the tapes switched off.

* * *

There was a breathless pause, then a muttered exchange of comments.

'Jez's clothes were mostly burned off by the blast,' Rickman said. There was a collective hiss of in-drawn breath.

'But Jez wasn't wearing much anyway — just his school trousers and sweatshirt. It was showery that night. North-westerly winds, rain and hail. Why was he out on a night like that without a jacket?'

'They're a tough breed down that end of the city,' Foster said.

Rickman shook his head. 'I think he didn't want his brother to know where he was going. I think he was protecting Minky. He went out in the freezing cold in his shirt-sleeves because he didn't want to get his little brother involved in something dangerous.'

A memory echoed back at him from the defensive walls he had built around himself: all the times Simon had dragged him out of the house to play footie in the pitch-dark; the days they had spent building dams and tree houses and dens, or walked miles to the Pier Head and back just to see the ferries docking. Simon had been protecting him, too. Simon was seven years older and yet he had never complained that his kid brother tagged along with him. He dried his tears and answered his endless questions and made sure that they were fed. Simon, in his own quiet way, had kept him from harm.

Rickman realised that the team was waiting for his lead. 'I think Jez was put up to this,' he said.

'When the CPO asked if Jez had done this sort of thing before, he said "*we* never", not "*he* never",' Foster said, developing the DI's line of reasoning.

Rickman nodded. 'He wasn't alone. The Child Protection Unit will interview the Beale boy again later today.' Beefy Beale seemed as likely a candidate as any for the 'fat lad' seen with Jez the night of the accident.

'Analysis of the boy's clothing shows firework ingredients, but no petroleum products. So, whoever set up that flat as a crematorium, it wasn't those lads. Any suggestions?'

'We need witnesses, Boss.' It was an obvious statement, but no less true for that. Without witnesses who could identify the other boys present, Jez alone would be blamed for the arson attack, and they would never know why they had chosen that particular flat and at that time.

'All right,' Rickman said. 'We start again, reverse order, re-interviewing everyone in the tenements, going in to support groups, talking to people, trying to convince them we're on their side.

'We also need to blitz the emergency accommodation where Jokubas Petrauskas was living,' he went on. 'It seems likely he was on the brink of giving us information, and that's why he was killed. Speak to everyone in the house — including ancillary staff — find out if he confided in anyone.'

'This might sound silly, Boss . . .' Tunstall, plump in a shirt a size too small for him, sat near the back of the room, his hand half-raised.

Rickman wondered if the man could ever open his mouth *without* sounding silly. He waited and Tunstall said, 'This bloke Petrauskas's been bumped off and he didn't actually get round to telling us owt. They're not gonna be queuing up for a chat after that, are they?'

'If we don't ask, we'll never know, will we Tunstall?' Rickman said. Privately he thought that Tunstall was right. Nobody was going to take the risk in the face of what had happened to Petrauskas.

The meeting broke up a few minutes later. Rickman stopped Naomi Hart on her way out. 'Good interview with Jordan last night,' he said.

The corner of her mouth twitched, but she didn't smile. He understood — it wouldn't do to have the lads see her grinning like a girly just because the boss had paid her a compliment.

'Thanks, Boss. Pity it didn't get us anything useful.'

'Time will tell,' Rickman said. 'Have you referred this to social services?' he asked, holding up the video tape.

'The boyfriend?' Hart said. 'D'you think—?'

'I know,' Rickman said. 'He's harming that boy, and it's got to stop.'

CHAPTER THIRTY

When Grace wasn't on-call, her Saturday mornings were usually spent catching up on paperwork, reading, and house-work — in that order. The freezing cold of the previous day had melted into a dreary mist, and every tree in the garden dripped mournfully.

Jeff had been called out at four a.m. Another murder, someone living in emergency accommodation. He hadn't been in touch since, and she knew from past experience that he probably wouldn't return home until late. The weather was too inclement for walking, the circumstances too wor-risome for sitting still, so she checked her emails, cleaning out weeks of messages, then she sorted through the paper post. It was mostly junk, but a couple of bills needed paying. This done, she set about tidying the house, dusting in a per-functory manner, scooping up newspapers for recycling and setting books back on shelves.

By one-thirty she had dusted the furniture, and cleaned and disinfected the kitchen and bathroom, exceeding her tolerance limits for housework by a long way. She flopped down in the sitting-room with a mug of tea and flicked on the TV for the news.

She recognised Jokubas as soon as she saw the photograph. He wore the same truculent expression as he had the day he had come to her surgery, although the picture — taken, she guessed, from his NASS identity card — revealed a defensive quality she hadn't noticed at the time. At clinic, his hostility — the very proximity of all that seething anger — was frightening; but now, looking at the photograph on the TV screen, she read grief in the lines around his mouth and anxiety in his eyes that she would never have to face and could barely imagine.

He had argued with Natalja. What was it he had said as he left? 'Ask her why she's still here.' Knin had been a Serb enclave in Croatia before the war, this much Grace knew. Natalja's parents had been killed when the Croatians liberated Knin from the Krajina Serbs in nineteen-ninety-six. One hundred-and-fifty thousand Serbs had fled Croatia in the aftermath. How could she ever be expected to go back?

For an hour, Grace fretted: if she didn't tell Jeff what she knew, she would quite possibly be impeding a police investigation into multiple murders. If she *did*, she might expose her friend to danger of one sort or another. Natalja had started working with her shortly after coming to Liverpool from London. That was in the spring of ninety-seven. She had been working in London for the charity that helped her with her claim for asylum, first as a volunteer, and later as a paid employee. Grace had asked for a reference, she recalled.

She jumped up from the sofa and ran upstairs. She kept most of her business correspondence for a minimum of five years, only getting around to sorting through the dross when her attic room became so stuffed that she couldn't find what she was looking for.

The file wasn't where she had left it: Jeff must have been in, rooting around. She went through the stacks of boxes, now out of chronological order, moving them randomly at first, until she realised that she was picking up boxes that she had already assessed and set aside. Then she went at it more methodically, even creating a pile of papers for incineration. She finally found the relevant document wallet under three years of tax records.

She took out two sheets of slightly yellowed A4 paper, stapled in the top left-hand corner, and skimmed through.

N. Sremać. Her name was followed by an extensive list of duties she had performed for the charity in London, an assessment of her competence and reliability which was extremely flattering, and at the bottom of the page, what Grace had been looking for: a contact name and phone number.

She dialled the number fast, using her mobile, her hair and hands still grimy with dust, not allowing herself time to wonder if Hilary Yarrop had changed jobs in the intervening years. She felt like a traitor, and it was almost a relief to hear the careful intonation of an answerphone message. She was on the point of hanging up when the voice said, 'If you need to contact me urgently, you can reach me on my mobile . . .'

Grace scrabbled for a pen and paper, compromising with a marker pen, and jotted the number down in thick black lettering on the back of the letter of reference. It was probably a mobile she used only for work, Grace told herself. It would no doubt be switched off at the weekend.

She keyed in the number and hit the 'call' button after only the slightest hesitation. The phone was answered after a couple of rings. The woman sounded tense, anticipating problems, and Grace was quick to introduce herself. Miss Yarrop cut off her summary CV, saying, 'I know who you are, Doctor Chandler: I read your article on primary health care and immigrant populations in *The Lancet*. It raised some important issues.'

Thank goodness she liked it, Grace thought. 'Look,' she said, 'I hate to trouble you on your day off, but—'

'It's all right,' Miss Yarrop interrupted. 'I've been following events in the newspapers.'

Grace felt another wave of relief: explaining the circumstances leading to her phone call would not have been easy.

'That's the reason I'm calling,' she said. 'My interpreter is Natalja Sremać.'

'Natalja. Yes, I remember.'

'You were her caseworker, I think.' Grace was treading carefully — client confidentiality was taken very seriously within the organisation.

'Yes,' Miss Yarrop said, a hint of reserve creeping into her voice. 'She's working for you now, as I remember. How is she?'

'Not good,' Grace said. 'I'm concerned about her. Ever since all of this started she's been really on edge.'

'Natalja is a refugee, too, Doctor Chandler. It's bound to affect her.'

'Of course,' Grace agreed, 'But it's more than that. I think she knows something.'

'About the murders?' Miss Yarrop sounded shocked. 'Have you spoken to her?'

'She refuses to discuss it.'

'And how do you think I can help?'

'You were Natalja's caseworker and—'

'We've already established that.' Grace heard a hint of anger. this was no longer a friendly exchange between fellow professionals.

'I know this is . . . irregular,' Grace said. 'But please believe me when I say I wouldn't be asking you this if I could see any other way.'

'Asking what?' Miss Yarrop said with frosty civility.

Damn.

Grace knew that Miss Yarrop would not answer her question, but she asked it anyway, because she would not put Natalja's life in danger because of a squeamish abhorrence to asking awkward questions. She sensed some deep distress in her friend; she thought that Natalja was in moral or physical danger and she couldn't allow her to go through that alone — even if that meant prying into her life.

She decided to simply ask the question outright. 'I thought you might remember something — something that would explain—'

'Natalja is no longer a client,' Miss Yarrop interrupted.

'I know,' Grace said. 'I realise that. But I'm not doing this out of curiosity. I'm trying to help her.'

'She has a right to privacy.'

'I know the rules of confidentiality,' Grace said, remaining reasonable, knowing that she had a better chance of cooperation from Miss Yarrop if she maintained a calm professional approach. 'But I believe she needs help.'

'Then speak to her.'

'I've tried.' She took a breath, then added, 'I think she's afraid to tell me what's on her mind.'

'I don't see how *I* could help,' Miss Yarrop said, her impatience evident. 'I haven't seen her in — what — nearly seven years.'

'I was hoping you could tell me something about the circumstances of her arrival in the country.'

'No.' Miss Yarrop was angry now, her tone unyielding. 'And I'm surprised at a fellow professional asking such a question.'

'I'm not planning to use it against her,' Grace said, her exasperation finally getting the better of her. 'I just want to help a young friend who I believe is in trouble she can't handle.'

'Not *so* young, surely,' Miss Yarrop said. 'And the Natalja I know is quite capable of taking care of herself.'

Grace began to speak, but Miss Yarrop raised her voice, continuing, 'I can't help you. If you want to know more about Natalja, you must speak to her.'

CHAPTER THIRTY-ONE

Reconciling the asylum seekers' demands for a higher police presence with the additional burden caused by another death was proving difficult. A few more officers with HOLMES2 training were seconded from around the authority to assist the paper flow and reduce the backlog of indexing, but beyond that, the only remedy, it seemed, was to ask the team to work longer unpaid hours.

Rickman knew that if they couldn't show some progress soon, the situation might very well escalate. The riots of eighty-one had raged within shouting distance of his home. It was warm that summer; and he had listened to the sounds of the rioting and looting, throwing the sash wide, despite his mother's admonitions to keep the window locked and the curtains closed — though he couldn't imagine what she thought they might have that was worth stealing.

Their house was minutes away from Lodge Lane, where most of the looting took place. He could hear the screams, the crash of glass and later the sirens — police, fire, ambulance — all wailing in a confusion of sound. Few of them dared to breach the barricades, and soon the smell of smoke drifted hot on the air, the looted shops burned out of spite. Wood-smoke, he smelled, and burning rubber, and once, incongruously, something like burned toast. The street lamps failed, and yet during all the hours of darkness, an orange glow lit the sky.

He had listened to his pocket radio, holding it close to his ear, so that his parents wouldn't know he was still awake; hearing the incredulity, the unmistakable fear in the reporter's voice, describing the crowds carrying off fridges, TVs, using wheelbarrows and supermarket trolleys to squeeze past the barricades.

Early next morning, he crept out of the house and walked forbidden to the shops. His eyes stung with acrid smuts falling like dirty snow from a sky that was cloudless and yet strangely lacking colour. The streets were silent; the accustomed rumble of traffic on the main road was absent. Only the constant drone of a big engine. At first he thought it was a bus, waiting for passengers, but turning the corner, he discovered that it was, not one, but three fire engines, pumping water, damping down.

He walked unsteadily over broken masonry, half-bricks and slate. The pavements glittered with glass. For months, he would be haunted by dreams in which soot-blackened windows stared at him like gouged eye sockets. Burnt-out cars, the colour of rust, rested on their sills, their wheels stolen, or their tyres burned to black smoke. He saw the tarmac melted and pitted by the heat of the fires.

Williams's bakery in the middle block, was gone, its roof collapsed, the rafters little more than charcoal. Williams who had sold cakes, home-made, sometimes lop-sided, always fabulous. Scones bursting with sultanas, cream cakes that squirted jam and cream into your cupped hand as you bit into them. The woman behind the counter — who laughed at his schoolboy greed, but always gave him the biggest rock cake, the fattest scones — gone.

Nearby, the chandler's shop, smelling of soap and dust, where his mother bought plates and breakfast bowls singly to replace those that were damaged beyond repair. Cap guns, he sold, and little twists of paper that exploded like bombs

— excellent for fighting urban warfare on dark winter streets. Fireworks in October, tinsel and glitter at the year's end, and always, in spring, a patchwork of blue and yellow flowers for bedding and bright pink button-daisies which his mother, in more optimistic moments, would plant in the narrow strip of earth under their front window.

The chandler's was looted, the window shattered, the remaining stock unrecognisable in the greasy black coating that lay over everything. Whole rows of shops stood empty, purged by fire, doomed to demolition.

It had seemed then that all his life was turmoil, as if a war was being waged and he, just eleven years old, was at its centre. He felt a pain that made him want to tear at his chest. He didn't understand it, then; it built in him over the years, sometimes fading to a dull ache, but it never left him, and it wasn't until, all those years later, he was pushed beyond his limits of endurance that he recognised this pain for what it was: impotent rage, humiliating and frustrating, that fed on itself, finally exploding in violence he could not control.

After the looting and burning they had pulled down entire blocks, levelling them and laying them to grass. He had seen it all from start to finish: the stirrings of unrest, the sporadic fights, the escalation, riots and aftermath. He didn't want to see another Toxteth — not on his watch.

* * *

Rickman went straight from his meeting with DCI Hinchcliffe into the Incident Room. Conversation dropped to a low hum and he felt all eyes on him as he walked from the door to the whiteboard at the far end of the room. The bollocking he'd given them about filing reports and logging evidence on arrival had done something to straighten out the chaos, but fifty people using the room in twelve-hour rotations meant an unavoidable accumulation of mess. Desks were piled high with paper, discarded food-wrappers and coffee-cups littered every surface, and overall, the fug of late nights and bad food.

The PM photos of Sophia Habib and the arson victims were tacked to the board, the time and date when the bodies were found, together with approximate time and cause of death written in felt pen on the whiteboard beneath. A new addition was Jokubas Petrauskas's photo, scanned from his National Asylum Support Service card and enlarged for release to the press. A second whiteboard held an i2 chart. Generated by the HOLMES2 program, these charts provide a colour-coded diagrammatic summary of the main leads and links in a major investigation.

All of the victims had two-way arrows pointing to a box entitled "Asylum seekers". A generic icon of a female in a pink top with the name "Miss Habib" below was linked by a red line to Lex Jordan, who was represented by a small male icon in what looked like a blue sweater. Another line connected the arson victims — as yet unnamed — to Gerard Flynn, aka Jez. A dotted line indicated a possible link with the Rokeby Rats — Beefy Beale's gang.

One line connected Jokubas Petrauskas to the masked men seen leaving his emergency accommodation after he had dialled triple nine. The lead on NASS voucher thefts was represented by a box. So far, the only evidence they had of this was the theft of Sophia's vouchers.

Rickman studied the chart for a few moments while people finished telephone calls and found places to stand or sit or perch. Then he turned and said, 'Right — surprise me.'

Nobody was eager to take on the challenge, and the team remained resolutely silent. At length Foster spoke up.

'Turns out I was wrong, Boss.'

'*What?*'

'There you go — I knew that'd surprise you,' Foster said.

'Would you like to get to the point, Sergeant?' Rickman said, stone-faced.

'I thought it wouldn't do no good asking the immigrants,' Foster explained. 'I was wrong.' A murmur of interest went around the room. 'We did like you said, and one name kept coming up.' He left a beat of silence. 'Lex Jordan.'

'What did they tell you about Jordan?' Rickman asked, quelling a jitter of excitement in his gut.

'He's been pestering the single women, bullying the vulnerable males.'

'What do you mean, "pestering" the women?' Rickman asked.

'Asking if they'd like to earn some easy money — more on the horizontal than on the level. Doing a bit of taxing—'

'He's been taking money from asylum seekers?' Rickman remembered what Grace had said about the potential profit to be made from the theft of NASS vouchers and he felt a surge of bitter satisfaction. 'Looks like we've got a new link between Jordan and our murder victims.'

'Yeah, Boss.' Foster made brief eye contact and Rickman understood: he was just as keen to build a case against Jordan. 'Nobody willing to make a statement, like, but the word on the street is Jordan's bad news.'

'Anything specific on Jokubas?' Rickman asked.

'Someone went to complain about the noise from Jokubas's flat at around two-thirty a.m.,' Foster said.

'He witnessed the attack?'

'Nah. He heard Jokubas's radio turned up high, and Jokubas was pacing the floor. Woke his neighbour up.'

'Have you checked the time against the call logged to the helpline?' Rickman asked.

Foster nodded. 'Half an hour before the attack. Funny thing, though — the same feller claims he didn't hear a thing when the two spooks stuck a stonking great chef's-knife through Jokubas's wall and stabbed the poor bastard through the heart.'

'Sleep of the just,' somebody commented.

'Sleep of the just terrified,' Rickman said. 'Has the emergency services tape been analysed, yet?'

'Still with the Scientific Support Unit,' Hart said.

'What about the men seen leaving the house?'

'Nothing — except they wore cloaks and "Scream" masks.'

'Okay,' Rickman said. 'We seem to be getting closer to something. I'm not sure what, yet, but something. The pathologist came up with another goody today: the arson victims had wounds to the inner thigh. The CSIs have checked the carpet from the scene and it looks like there was a lot of blood . . .'

He went to the i2 chart, while they digested the new information. 'There could be a direct link between Sophia and our arson victims,' he said, drawing a dotted line with a red marker pen between the two. 'The drugs in their blood, femoral vein opened — similar MO. Except Sophia wasn't burned.'

'And she had all her own teeth.' Though Foster joked about it, he looked sick, and Rickman recalled that he had witnessed the post-mortems of both Sophia and the arson victims.

'D'you want us to pick Jordan up?' Foster asked. 'Search his flat?'

Rickman shook his head. 'We haven't got enough to rearrest him. But I want him under surveillance. I want to know who he meets, where he goes, who his contacts are. If he so much as sneezes on a refugee, we'll have him for assault.'

* * *

It was after eleven-thirty when Rickman set off for home. A right turn at the traffic lights would take him onto Tunnel Road, and from there it was a straight run through to Sefton Park. He drove automatically, preoccupied with the case and their lack of progress. It was looking more and more like Jordan had killed Sophia. But with no motive, nobody who would admit to hearing them argue, no evidence that Sophia had acted against Jordan, they couldn't move in on him. If they could show that she had retained some of her earnings, or defied him — but nobody knew her, and it seemed that nobody cared. None of her co-workers among the street girls, nobody in the emergency accommodation had even thought to report her missing.

Jordan, it seemed, was the only person who had any real contact with her, and he had stolen the girl's money and put her to work on the street. Which made him a sleaze and a thief, but it didn't necessarily make him a killer. '*Why?*' Grace had asked. '*Why would he kill her?*'

Jordan had asked him the same question the previous night, standing in the freezing cold on the police station car park. 'Why would I kill her?'

'Maybe she heard something she wasn't meant to,' Rickman said. 'She lived with you for three weeks.'

'I *fucked* her for three weeks.'

They stood eyeball to eyeball and Rickman came within a heartbeat of taking out his frustration on the pimp. Then he saw in Jordan's eyes something he recognised: impotent rage. Rickman willed him to take a pop — just one half-arsed swing — but Jordan knew when to put a lid on his temper and instead, he smiled, tilting his head at an angle.

'Think I got carried away, told my secrets to a twenty-pound-a-trick tart?' he had asked. 'You've gotta be joking.'

What other motive was there? Rickman wondered. Jealousy? Blind rage at some error of action or thought? He had seen it before — sometimes too close for comfort. But, Rickman thought, *If he's so sure we've nothing on him, why take the trouble to wait in the freezing cold to try and convince me?*

He didn't know. But he realised with a jolt that he knew somebody who might. He slammed on the brakes and a horn blared behind him. A minicab swerved to overtake, the driver flipping him the finger as he drove past. Rickman glanced over his shoulder and executed a U-turn, driving back the way he had come, turning left onto Upper Parliament Street in drifts of gentle drizzle, the drops scarcely large enough to wet the windscreen. To his right, the massive form of the Anglican cathedral stood solid on a hilltop overlooking the steep fall to the River Mersey. A sandstone edifice built on a sandstone outcrop, base- and top-lit by spotlights, it seemed almost to grow out of the bedrock.

He parked on Hope Street, next to the railings that protected the sharp drop to the cemetery below. In Liverpool mythology, George Harrison and Paul McCartney had escaped the tedium of grammar and Latin classes playing truant from the Boys' Institute up the road among the headstones of the Victorian graveyard.

At first, he saw nothing, but he knew that they were watching. As he locked his car, a figure in shorts and a fur-collared jacket emerged from the shadows, checking him out, adjusting the fur trim so that it exposed her shoulders. There were others, too, sheltering under the trees overhanging the elegant Georgian sweep of Gambier Terrace. One girl stood in a doorway; she lit a cigarette at the moment he saw her, a calculated bit of theatre. He scanned the faces. The girl he was looking for wasn't among them.

Rickman gave them a friendly wave and they went back to whatever shelter they could find. He walked on, turning the corner into Upper Duke Street. A gust of wind blew in his face, coating it with a fine mist of droplets like a sheen of cold sweat on his skin. Fifty yards down the road, a bus shelter was lit with unforgiving light. Seated on the narrow strip of yellow plastic that served as a bench was the girl he was looking for.

Desiree sat with one leg tucked under, the other out in front, her pink stilettos giving length and tone to her calf muscles. She had thin lips and long dark hair, a little frizzed by the damp.

She stood, seeing a man approach, took a step forward, even began the preening routine for his benefit. Under her overcoat, she wore a strapless coral-coloured dress. Short-sighted and too squeamish for contact lenses, she didn't recognise him until he got within a few feet of her.

'What the hell d'you want?' she demanded.

'I just want to talk.'

'What's to do, love?' she sneered. 'Can't get it up?'

'I want to talk about Sophia,' he said.

She stared at him blankly then stalked away, heading down the incline towards the cathedral entrance.

'Desiree—'

He caught up with her at the cathedral concourse. The security guard in his brick kiosk eyed them curiously. She turned on him.

'Why d'you have to come here of all places?' she demanded, glancing past him towards the top of the hill as if expecting Jordan to appear at any moment.

'I didn't know where else to find you.'

'I must've missed you off the guest list for the house-warming,' she said, her voice brimming with contempt. 'Now piss off and leave me alone, Rickman,' she said. 'You're death on legs, you are. You're the Grim bloody Reaper.'

'I can help you,' he said, keeping his back to the road, shielding her with his body, knowing that her anxiety at being seen with him was well-founded. 'I can see you get protection—'

She laughed in his face. 'That makes me feel really safe.'

'I can stop Jordan,' he said. 'I can get him off the streets, but only with your help. You have to come in,' he insisted. 'Give a statement.'

'Statement?' she said.

'About Sophia.'

'Who?'

'Come on, Desiree — you must have known her. Jordan must've moved her in right after he kicked you out.'

'And whose fault was that, 'ey?'

'So you did know her.'

Her face was closed, her pink lips a thin line. 'Never said that, did I?'

'All right,' he said, suddenly angry and frustrated with her. 'I'll tell you about her. Her father was killed by the Taliban. Under Taliban rule, women weren't supposed to go outdoors without a male escort. Her mother was stoned to death after she went out looking for food for both of them.' He half shrugged. 'It was that or starve. Sophia was orphaned at the age of twelve. After that, we don't know for sure what happened to her, because she wouldn't tell the doctors or the caseworkers. But her medical records show that she had been raped and beaten. Over a long, *long* period of time.'

'Stop it!' She tried to get past him but he barred the way.

'Sophia Habib,' he repeated. 'She was seventeen years old. She came to the UK for help, looking for protection and she ended up with Lex Jordan, for God's sake!'

'Leave me be,' Desiree repeated, her voice weak and sick.

'Jordan killed Sophia, Desiree, and he's getting away with it.'

'I don't know nothing,' she said, passing a hand tiredly over her eyes.

'You do know,' he said, grasping her upper arms. Even through her jacket he could feel their frailty. 'You're the only one that *does*.'

She stared past him for a moment and he gave her a little shake. Slowly, she shifted her gaze to meet his, her eyes pale, washed-out. Defeated.

'I'm just a stupid cow who sells herself for cash,' she said. 'What would I know?'.

'Sophia was bled to death,' he said. 'Her vein opened up like—'

'Like a pig for slaughter?' she suggested. ' — Or a cow?'

He tightened his grip. 'Four men were doused in petrol and set alight. A boy of eleven is so badly burned he probably won't survive.'

She flinched at this and he pushed on, determined to get some human reaction from her. 'Now another man has been stabbed. It won't stop there, Desiree. *He* won't stop there.'

'You don't get it, do you?' she said. 'You had to be the knight in shining armour, didn't you? Why couldn't you keep out of it? This is all your *fault*.' She broke free of him, pushing his hands from her shoulders.

He stared at her. 'You think he killed Sophia to get back at me?' He shook his head. He could see why Jordan might want to implicate him in Sophia's murder, but surely, even Jordan wouldn't kill a woman in cold blood? No — this was too much. 'He had some kind of row with her, didn't he? That's why he killed her. She was keeping money back from him — refusing to work. He lost his temper, lashed out.'

She shook her head. 'She was terrified of him. She did anything he told her to.'

'She was a child — an innocent. She wanted to get away from him. Jordan couldn't accept that.'

'You're sounding desperate, Rickman.' She stared at him for some moments. 'Maybe he did have a reason — another reason — to kill her. But why d'you think he did it like — *like that*? It was a message to his dealers and all his girls and to me. And if you weren't so bloody thick, you'd see it was a message to you an' all, *Inspector*.'

Rickman tilted his face to the rain, gazing up at the cathedral, sick with guilt and shame. Mist drifted down, caught between shadow and light, snagged on the finials of the tower and spiralled up in wisps, curling like smoke into the night sky.

When he looked at her again, there was contempt in her eyes.

'All right,' he said. 'If it's my fault, come in with me. Tell your story. Sophia deserves justice.'

For a moment, Desiree simply stood in front of him, her arms hanging loosely by her sides. Then she stepped towards him — and brought her knee up hard into Rickman's groin.

Pain shocked through him, radiating in sickening waves from his balls to his stomach and he folded to his knees, retching. Over the gurgle of rainwater in the gutters and the swish of tyres from an occasional car, he heard her walk away, the clicking of her heels on the pavement almost an embodiment of her rage.

'You must have one hell of a hygiene problem.' It was a man's voice, middle-aged, scouse.

Rickman retched again.

''Cos, you know, she's not normally that fussy.'

Rickman swivelled his head to look up. The rain felt good on his face. Cool, soothing.

The man offered his hand. It was the security guard from the kiosk. The shuddering waves of pain had begun to subside, but Rickman wasn't yet up to the challenge of getting to his feet. 'I know it can't be an angel,' he said. 'An angel couldn't be that ugly.'

'Har-de-har,' the guard said, taking back his offered hand. 'I thought you might need some help. But if you're gonna be offensive—'

'Know her, do you?' Rickman asked, taking a handkerchief from his pocket to wipe his mouth, bracing himself with one hand on the ground as another wave of nausea hit him.

'Desiree? Nice girl.'

'No doubt you told the police what you know about her?'

The guard drew down the corners of his mouth. 'First day back. I was on leave when your lot come round, asking questions.'

My lot. The mark of Cain, the curse of teachers and cops, always to be recognised. 'What're you doing working so late?' he asked.

'I'm not the one bothering the night life,' the man said. 'I don't have to explain meself.'

Rickman gave him a look. It was hard to seem authoritative, squinting up from the ground, patches of damp ruining the knees of his suit, but he must have been sufficiently convincing because the guard sighed, explaining, 'We're on duty twenty-four/seven, every day of the year — including Christmas Day.'

'Excluding leave,' Rickman said.

'Even coppers take leave, don't they?'

Rickman struggled to his feet. He had to lean with the heels of his hands on his thighs for a while, but when he felt better, he eased to an upright position and found the photograph of Sophia in his pocket. 'What about her?' he asked, handing over the picture. 'Was she fussy who she picked up?'

The guard tilted the picture to the light. 'I seen her a couple of times. New girl. Her heart wasn't in it, if you ask me. In *fact*,' he added, putting a catarrhal emphasis on 'fact', 'if you ask me, she was crap at it. Feller kicked her out of his car right here on the steps. Said he'd seen more action from a blow-up doll. Desiree looked after her, like.'

'What?'

'Picked her up, like. Set her on her feet and dusted her off. Put a sweet little pock-mark in the door of the guy's Beamer with her stiletto an all.' He smiled at the recollection.

Rickman hobbled back to the junction and caught a glimpse of Desiree heading towards the Roman Catholic cathedral, a quarter of a mile away. Two cathedrals, and four hundred and forty yards of working girls, doing business. Girls who took MDMA to keep them going through the night, morphine for the pain. Working girls strung out like beads on a rosary between two cathedrals, either end of a street named Hope.

CHAPTER THIRTY-TWO

The house was silent except for the tick and creak of cooling floorboards. Grace must be in bed. The realisation created mixed emotions in him: he ached to tell her what he had just learned, simultaneously dreading her reaction.

Grace must have put an extra log on the fire in the sitting-room before going to bed. Behind the fireguard flames licked at the edges of the log and the room was filled with drowsy heat, yet Rickman felt cold. He went straight to the drinks cabinet and poured a large scotch, swallowing it in one punishing gulp. It burned the back of his throat and gullet, but he gained no warmth from it.

He poured another and sat in an armchair, sipping more slowly, staring into the fire and thinking about Desiree's words. 'All my fault,' he said aloud. There was no escaping his share in this and — worse — he feared that there was nothing he could do to make amends.

He woke at three-thirty a.m. with a crick in his neck. Grace stood in the doorway. Light from the hall and his blurred vision gave her a faint saintly aura, then she stepped in out of the cold and he saw that her hair was tousled and her pyjamas creased and rumpled. She looked confused and pale and grumpy.

* * *

'Where on earth—?' Grace cut herself off, noticing the whisky bottle half-empty by his feet. 'That won't do a jot of good, you know.'

Rickman pressed the ball of his hand to his eye-socket. 'I know.' He set the drink carefully on the floor and looked up at Grace. 'There's been another killing,' he said.

'It was on the news.' Grace sat on the sofa, next to his chair. She should tell him that she knew Jokubas, but she felt that she must talk to Natalja first. 'Do you know if — has it anything to do with the other murders?'

He ran a hand over his face. 'He was an asylum seeker. Knife attack.'

A bright image filled Grace's consciousness: partly congealed blood sliding from the wheelie-bin after the body of Sophia; a whiff of decomposing refuse sharpened the image, and she felt the emotional shock as strongly as when she had first experienced it. 'Have you any leads?' she asked, closing off that part of her mind.

A muscle jumped in Rickman's jaw. 'You were right,' he said. 'It looks like someone is exploiting the asylum seekers.'

She laughed. 'There's a whole damned *industry* built around the exploitation of asylum seekers: the immigration authorities, the police, voluntary organisations, interpreters, hospital, clinical and nursing staff. We're all taking a cut — benefiting from their misery — maybe with the best of motives, but . . .' She pushed her fingers through her hair, feeling desperately tired; she hadn't slept well since this started, and his long days and broken nights weren't helping.

'Will you find these people, Jeff? Can you stop the killing?'

'I don't know,' he said. 'Finding them isn't always enough. We need people to talk to us, Grace.'

She felt a stab of guilt. She knew something about one of the murder victims, something that might be helpful in finding his killers. *So tell him*, she thought. *But what if it puts Natalja in danger?* She told herself that it was only for a short while, that she would get more out of Natalja than the police ever could. It didn't make her feel any better, though.

'I'll — talk to a few people,' she said, knowing that she sounded evasive.

'That's our job, Grace. Give me the names, we'll—'

'I can't, Jeff. They—'

'I know,' he said. 'They've been through a lot. They've reason to mistrust the authorities. I understand all that, Grace. I'm just sick of hearing lies and half-truths.'

She felt a spark of anger. 'Not nice, is it?'

He closed his eyes for a moment, and Grace immediately apologised.

'I'm tired,' she explained. 'Tired and confused and—'

'No,' he said looking at his hands. 'I deserved that.' He was silent for some time, and she sensed that he was trying to work out where to begin.

'I had a ten-year-old boy put in care today,' he said. It seemed to make sense, somehow, to start with the boy.

Grace waited.

'His mother's partner insisted on attending the interview. He . . . made me uneasy.'

Grace asked the obvious question; the one he would have asked himself, if the roles were reversed. 'What made you uneasy?'

'Social services asked that.' He paused. 'I couldn't tell them. But . . .' His breathing was unsteady. 'I'm trying to tell you, Grace.'

She looked into his face; he looked pale and haunted. 'I'm listening,' she said, vowing silently that she would listen without interruption, allowing him to tell the story as he needed to tell it.

It took him a while longer to gather his thoughts and summon the strength to continue.

'You wonder why I find it hard, seeing Simon.'

She inclined her head — it was acknowledgement enough.

'He was right about the early years. We were — ' He shrugged. ' — close. Simon was my champion, my hero, my role model.' He took a gulp of air.

'My father was a violent man. He beat my mother. Went for us if we tried to get in the way. Sometimes we could stop him if he'd been drinking. But he didn't always need to have a drink in him to . . .' His finger went to the scar that bisected his eyebrow.

'In those days, it was me and Simon against the world.' He shrugged again. 'He's right about that. He's seven years older than me, so I looked on him as a grown-up — except he wasn't so old he couldn't have fun. I suppose he felt he had to look after me, me being the younger one. The good stuff in my childhood — that was down to Simon.'

He fell silent and Grace asked, 'What happened?'

'He left. He was seventeen. One summer's morning, I woke up and he was already dressed.' He looked at his hands. 'I remember the smell of ozone, the bedroom curtains stirring in a warm breeze, Simon with his army greatcoat slung over one shoulder. I remember feeling frightened.'

Grace leaned forward and took his hand.

'He had a carrier bag of clothes and a bus ticket one way to London.' He raised his shoulders and let them drop. 'Suddenly Simon wasn't there anymore. I was ten years old. I didn't know what to do.'

Grace waited for him to continue.

'It gave my father another cudgel to beat me with — Simon going away. I mean, why would he leave if I was any good?' He sighed and was quiet for a while.

'The violence escalated after Simon left. My father would wake me up, bring me downstairs to watch him "punishing" my mother.'

Grace felt a stab of horror. She saw a clear image of a ten-year-old boy in pyjamas, his eyes wide with terror. The scar over his eye new and livid. When had the other scars come, she wondered. Later, when he had tried to defend his mother?

'Did you get away from him?'

'I got too big for him to punch,' he said simply. 'By that time the drink had made him soft. I flattened him a few

241

times and after that, he stopped hitting Mum, left us alone.'
He released her hand and picked the glass up from the floor
but didn't drink, and instead stared fiercely into the pale
gold liquid.

'Why didn't you tell me, Jeff?' Grace asked. 'Did you
think I wouldn't understand?'

'No,' he said. 'I knew you would. But when is the right
time? When we first met? When I moved in here? It's not
something I'm proud of, Grace. It's not something I care to
even think about. I spent my life reinventing myself. In the
job, the less people know about your weaknesses, the better.
You get used to keeping things secret, separating your life
into compartments.' He shrugged. 'Practise enough at bury-
ing the past and secrecy becomes a habit.'

He seemed to be trying to make sense of it for himself
as well as for her.

'At first, as a kid, I fantasised that Simon would come
home one day, dressed in a suit, driving a flash car, take me
and Mum with him.

'Then something happened.' For a long time he was
silent. Then he seemed to come to a decision; he looked into
her eyes and anguish in that look made her exclaim:

'Jeff, you don't have to—'

'Let me say this, Grace,' he said. 'I need to say it, just
once.'

She nodded.

'The winter of nineteen eighty-four there was a cold
snap. The school boiler broke down and they sent us home
early. I went straight home, like I always went straight home,
because I knew Mum felt safer with me around.' His voice
had no intonation; he might have been reading aloud a particularly boring report.

'It was cold — so icy cold that I couldn't feel my fingers
jammed into the pockets of my school jacket. I fumbled with
the latch key, already thinking about what we had in to eat
— I was fourteen — permanently hungry, and the kitchen
was always my first port of call.

'The radio was turned up loud: Chaka Khan, blasting out 'I Feel for You'. Mum was always on at me to turn down the noise, that the neighbours didn't necessarily appreciate my choice of music, and I was composing a gentle tease in my head along the same lines, when it struck me as odd. Because Mum hated pop music. It made her jumpy. She never listened to anything but classical.'

Grace held her breath.

I called to her, but she didn't answer. Then I heard something: faint cries. Whispers. I broke into a run, flying at the kitchen door. It held — something was jammed up against it. A sob, a muffled scream, then I heard him, telling her to shut up.' His hands closed hard around the whisky tumbler.

'I threw myself at the door till the glass shattered and I splintered the frame,' Rickman said. 'I found him — them—' He broke off. His voice was almost toneless, only the raggedness of his breathing betrayed his extreme emotion. 'She's pulling her skirt down, trying to tell me it's all right, nothing was going on, telling me *Leave it, Jeff. It doesn't matter.*'

'Oh, Jeff . . .'

He glanced at her again.

'He's taking his time pulling up his pants. Grinning at me as if to say, and what're you gonna do about it? I can see his handprint on her face, her blouse all ripped and she's telling me it doesn't matter.'

Rickman took a breath and it caught in the back of his throat.

'What did you do?' Grace asked quietly.

'I kicked him out — I mean really,' Rickman's eyes gleamed with an unfamiliar cruelty. 'I kicked him halfway up the street. He's crawling away, trying to pull his trousers up, scraping his knees on the road and he's blubbering and begging. I told him if I ever saw him again, I'd kill him.'

Neither spoke for some time.

'I thought he was leaving her alone — there were no bruises, you see.' It was inflected as a question, an invitation to understand why he had missed the signs. 'She didn't fight him because she was too afraid. And I guess she didn't know how.'

Grace went to him and kissed his forehead. When he looked up, she saw bewilderment and outrage in his face.

'I was a skinny fourteen-year-old, Grace, and I kicked his arse out of there. Simon was seventeen when he left. Why didn't he ever stand up to Dad?'

'You said yourself, he'd deteriorated over the years,' she said. 'Perhaps he was stronger before.'

'Simon left us on our own — me and Mum. I was ten. I couldn't... My father was too strong. But Simon could have—'

'Not everyone can be courageous, Jeff,' she said.

'But why didn't he come back afterwards? Why didn't he help us out when she got sick? Why didn't he come to his own mother's funeral?'

Grace looked at him for a few moments. 'I think you know why,' she said. It was the same paralysing sense of shame that had frozen a part of Jeff, that had made him want to keep his childhood from her.

He finished the whisky in one swallow.

'And your father?'

'I don't know if he's alive or dead,' Rickman said. 'Don't know. Don't care.' He gave a short, humourless laugh. 'The social worker asked me why I felt the need to "save" the boy.'

'What did you say?'

'Well, I couldn't tell her that when I looked at Minky's mother, her face seemed to change, until I might have been looking at a photograph of my mum.' He dipped his head. 'So I asked her was I right.'

'And?'

'They found bruising, unreported fractures to the boy's ribs. And burns.' Rickman grimaced and swallowed, as if fighting nausea.

Grace exhaled. 'Where is he now?'

'In care until social services can make a full assessment.'

'You did the right thing, Jeff.'

'Yes,' he said. 'Yes,' he repeated, 'I believe I did.'

She took his hand again in hers. 'You saved him, Jeff.'

'Yeah,' he said. 'Jeff Rickman — superhero.'

* * *

For a little while they sat in silence, each with their own thoughts. Rickman had done only half of what he had sworn to do: if things were to be straight between them, he had to tell her about Jordan, about his own part in Sophia's death. After a few minutes, he cleared his throat.

'That new lead I told you about?' He shouldn't be telling her this — it was part of a police investigation, but it was also bound up in his past and Grace should know everything about him — even the worst.

'Grace—' *God, it was so hard to say.* 'There's something else.'

'What?' He thought he saw dread in her eyes.

'I think maybe Sophia died because of me.'

She looked into his face, and her grip on his hand tightened.

'The run-in I had with Jordan?'

She nodded.

'It was more than a bit of push and shove. A couple of months ago, I'd been to a meeting at HQ. You were working an extra shift on A&E, so I stayed, used the gym, took my time. Must have been after eleven p.m. when I left. It was warm, you know — shirtsleeve warm, so I got in the car, rolled down the window. I'd got as far as the Anglican cathedral.' He paused, staring into the cold ash in the fireplace. 'I heard screams.'

Blood, he remembered, pouring from her nose. And those pitiful cries, begging Jordan to stop. 'I'm sorry,' she kept saying. 'I'll be good. I'll be good, Lex, I swear.'

I shouted, 'Police! Let her go!'

Jordan had Desiree by the wrist; he looked over his shoulder, a cursory glance. Then he brought his hand round in a wide arc, closing his fist as it came to the highest point, smashing it into her mouth. Her top lip burst and blood spurted a couple of feet. Rickman saw the droplets, black in the pinkish light of the streetlamps, spatter the wall of a house, the leather of Jordan's shoe. Rickman closed his eyes against the memory.

'I identified myself as a police officer and he hit her in the mouth with the full force of his fist.' He looked into Grace's face. 'I was almost on him,' he said. 'He saw me. He knew who I was. He must have known I would arrest him, but it wasn't enough that he'd battered her face to a pulp — he'd bruised his knuckles on her teeth — she'd made a mess of his shoes with her blood, and that pissed him off. So he took off his shoe and cracked her over the head with the heel. She was sobbing, trying to protect herself with her free hand.

'I got to him as he was putting heart and soul into the second swing.'

'Jeff, was the girl Sophia?' Grace asked.

'No, it was—' He hesitated, confused for a moment. 'God, I've just realised I don't even know her real name. She goes by the name of Desiree.'

'Then I still don't see why—'

'I lost it, Grace.' he said. 'I *completely* lost it. I wanted to kill him. If Desiree hadn't pulled me off him, I think I would have. My hands were covered in blood. He was . . .' Rickman stared into the middle distance. Jordan was begging for mercy, his face a bloody pulp, and what Rickman wanted more than anything was to finish the job.

'You must have seen that sort of thing before and not lost control.' He heard the shock and disbelief in her voice.

'I know,' he said. 'I've gone over and over it. I think it all got mixed up with my father, my childhood, what he did to my mother.' He shook his head. 'I can't explain it — or excuse it.'

'And you think this man Jordan killed Sophia for — what — revenge?'

'The girl I—' He stopped, a savage smile on his face. 'I was going to say "protected" — who the hell do I think I'm kidding? Desiree — she looked after Sophia. I think they were friends.'

Grace blinked. 'Sweet Jesus . . . So he got back at the girl and you by the same terrible act. But surely, Jeff, there must have been some other reason.'

'I wish there was,' he said.

'Why didn't you come to me?' There was no accusation in the question, only concern.

He looked at his hands as if they had a life and will of their own. 'I was so ashamed, Grace. I didn't know I had that kind of hate in me.' *Not true, Rickman,* he thought. *You're still not being straight with her. You hated your father as much. If you'd been a couple of stones heavier and a year or two older, you probably would have killed him instead of booting him up the street.*

'Oh, God,' Grace said. 'I was trying to work out how you got home in that state without my noticing. But then I remembered — the night you stayed over with Lee Foster.'

Rickman nodded guiltily.

Lee Foster had looked at Rickman standing on his doorstep, blood on his hands and clothes, and in typically flippant style, he said, 'I hope the other guy looks worse.'

Rickman was shaking, almost incoherent. Foster took him inside, sent him to shower, dumped his clothes in the washer and telephoned Grace with his alibi.

'He told me you'd been on a pub crawl and got smashed.' Grace said. Then, realising the alternative meaning of the word, she added, 'I guess he thought that was funny. It was just after you'd got news of passing your DCI board. Supposedly this was your celebratory night out. He made a joke about the brass not being able to hold their ale.'

Rickman couldn't look at her. 'Grace, I'm so sorry.'

'Jordan never made a complaint?'

'That would mean cooperating with the police,' Rickman said. 'But men like Jordan always find a way to get even.'

'Jeff, you have to *tell* somebody.'

'I will. I'll talk to DCI Hinchcliffe in the morning,' he said. 'I . . . I just had to tell you, first.' It was the right thing to do. All his life, Rickman had worked by survival instinct, mostly doing the right thing, but sometimes doing only what was expedient. Grace had made him think differently. In the years since they met, he had noticed a change in himself; he had come to a realisation that you could be tough without becoming hard.

Now, she slid onto his lap and gazed into his eyes. Her fingers ran lightly over the scars on his face, the thin silver line bisecting his eyebrow, the nick in his chin when his father had thrown an ashtray at him for some transgression he couldn't remember.

Grace traced the slightly flattened contour of his nose. 'Jeff,' she said, kissing him. 'Jeff . . .'

CHAPTER THIRTY-THREE

The alarm sounded at seven a.m. Grace groaned and rolled over, wrapping one arm around Rickman and snuggling up to his back

'Don't go,' she muttered, her eyes still closed.

'I have to,' Rickman said, kissing the inside of her wrist and easing out of her embrace.

'I'll write you a note,' Grace said, frowning importantly. 'I'm a doctor — I can do this.'

He laughed, wondering how, despite everything, despite the bloody awful situation he was in, she always had the talent to make him laugh. 'I've got a briefing at eight.'

'I'm famed for the illegibility of my sick notes,' she wheedled. 'Nobody need ever know what's wrong with you.'

'What did you have in mind?' He wasn't tempted, but he was curious, just the same.

'Seasonal-dependant paroxysm of the peripheral capillaries,' she said.

'Which is?'

'Cold feet — and I'm the cure.'

'If only . . .' he said with a sigh, walking around the bed, heading for the bathroom. 'But I've a confession to make today.'

Grace pushed the hair out of her eyes and sat up, suddenly wide awake. 'God, Jeff, I'm sorry — I'm so sleep-deprived I'd forgotten.'

He leaned over and kissed her. 'Don't worry about it — I'm not.' More lies. The fact was, his stomach had been turning slow somersaults most of the night.

'I'll make breakfast,' Grace said, swinging her legs over the side of the bed.

Rickman pushed her gently back. 'I'm just about up to a shower and shave,' he said. 'Food is pretty much out of the question.'

'Jeff—'

'It's all right, Grace.' He didn't need to hear any more discussion on the subject: he had made every argument and counterargument in the long sleepless hours. 'I think I should do this,' he said.

* * *

He didn't need to hear the arguments against talking to the DCI, but he heard them anyway, once Foster sussed what was bothering him.

The debrief had been unproductive — the interviews with Jez Flynn's friends proved only that they were deeply afraid. Beefy, Minky and Daz were refusing to talk — a psychologist brought in to assess Daz was convinced that the boy was suffering from post-traumatic stress disorder. The evidence pointed toward the boys being set up to kill the four men, none of whom had yet been identified. Interviews with Jordan's girls were hardly worth the shoe leather — *Except*, Rickman thought, *an interesting conversation I had with a prostitute last night*.

He was surprised at his own eagerness to unburden himself of his guilty secret. He had said many times to suspects: 'You'll feel better if you talk about it', but he'd never actually believed it. His confession would have to be deferred, however: Hinchcliffe was unavailable. He had been called to another meeting with the Detective Superintendent and the

ACC, so Rickman's report on the results of his own unofficial enquiries would have to wait.

The team dispersed to their various tasks with little enthusiasm for the work. It would have been so easy to change their mood. *You know what, guys, I think I've discovered a big fat motive why Jordan would want to harm Sophia.*

What's that Tunstall? (In his imagination it was always Tunstall who asked the obvious questions.) *No — not drugs or money or turf wars, but revenge. Simple, ugly revenge against a cop who couldn't respect the law.*

For now, though, they would have to carry on as before. He made sure that the surveillance team was up to strength and emphasised the importance of Jordan as a suspect, but until he had spoken to Hinchcliffe, he would have to keep his own counsel. So, he returned to his office and pretended to do paperwork, while Foster watched him askance.

'What the hell is keeping him?' he said, going to the door and checking the corridor.

'Dunno, Boss.' Foster was munching through a small stack of Jaffa cakes he had filched from one of the civilian clerks, while he sweated over a report on his team's latest sweep of the L8 district. After a few more minutes of trying, he threw down his pen in disgust. 'You've got as much chance of finding a virgin on Hope Street as getting that lot to help in a police enquiry.' He eyed Rickman critically for a few moments. 'What's eating you, then?'

'Jordan,' Rickman said, without thinking.

Foster put down the remains of his third Jaffa cake. 'You're not still thinking about talking to the DCI about that, are you?'

Rickman wished he'd kept his mouth shut. He returned to his desk and shuffled a few papers. 'Best we don't talk about it,' he said.

'What — in case I get implicated in something dodgy?' Foster leaned over and swung the door of the office closed. 'He's under surveillance. Give it a day or so, we'll find something on him.'

'We already have something on him,' Rickman said. 'I want this off my conscience, Lee.'

'Sleep on it,' Foster said. 'With any luck, the urge'll go away.'

'I did,' Rickman said. 'It didn't.'

Foster ran his fingers through his hair, so distracted that he didn't realise the damage he was doing to the carefully sculpted spikes. 'There's three things you never do in life,' he said. 'Volunteer, apologise, or confess.'

It seemed strange that his closest friend and his most hated enemy were both giving him the same advice. Jordan had also said that he wouldn't back up any confession Rickman made to having assaulted him. But this was an all-for-nothing deal. If Jordan got away with Sophia's murder because Rickman had withheld information, he would be complicit in the crime.

'They say confession's good for the soul.' It was a poor attempt to inject some levity into the conversation, and it failed to make any impression on Foster.

'You know what confession's good for? Keeping priests and psychiatrists in a job.'

'And police officers,' Rickman said.

'Not if they're making the confession.'

Rickman's telephone rang and he picked up.

'Jeff?'

A woman's voice, muffled, as if she was speaking through muslin.

'Who is this?'

Foster looked over, alert, ready to take instructions. Rickman held up his hand, a signal to wait.

'Jeff, it's Tanya.' She sounded as if she had been crying. 'I — I don't know what to do . . .'

Rickman shook his head at Foster, turning away. 'Has something happened to Simon?' he asked, surprised to feel flutterings of alarm.

'He's become agitated,' she said, her voice watery with emotion. 'I wouldn't bother you, but we can't get him to calm down — he keeps asking for you.'

'You did the right thing,' Rickman said. It must have taken a lot for her to make the call: after all, he hadn't been near the hospital since Simon had come to their house, and that was what — two days ago?

'Jeff, they've had to sedate him. He thinks—' She faltered, her voice wavering on the edge of breakdown, then she steadied herself. 'He thinks he did something terrible — that's why he broke contact with home.'

'But that's—' He was about to say it was untrue, but in a sense, Simon had done something terrible: he had left a ten-year-old boy with a violent and abusive father. Abandoned him with a mother who was so traumatised and brutalised that there were days when he got home from school and found her still sitting in the same chair, surrounded by unwashed breakfast dishes, staring in horror at some awful scene replaying over and over in her mind, while the storm clouds of another gathered over the catastrophe of an unprepared meal.

'I was planning to come in later today,' he said, checking his watch. 'I'll come now.' There was no telling when Hinchcliffe would be finished and at least talking to Simon would take his mind off his own troubles for a while.

'Could you?' She sounded close to collapse. 'He might listen to you.'

'Trouble?' Foster asked as he hung up.

'Family.'

Foster snorted. 'Trouble,' he said.

'I'm sorry, Lee - I've got to do this,' Rickman told him, shrugging into his overcoat.

'No problem. I'll give you a bell when the DCI gets back.'

'Okay. Good,' Rickman said, shoving his mobile phone into his pocket, his mind already elsewhere.

* * *

It took ten minutes to reach the hospital. The queues for the car park were backed up onto Mount Vernon, so he drove full circle, ending up on Prescot Street and cut through the back way, showing his warrant card to the security guard.

Tanya was waiting for him outside the lifts on the third floor. The copper and gold in her hair a flare of autumn colour in the grey surroundings of the hospital corridor. Her eyes were red and puffy from crying and instinctively, Rickman put his arms around her. She hugged him back, breaking contact with an embarrassed laugh as if suddenly recognising that they were, in effect, strangers.

'How is he?' Rickman asked.

She shrugged. It seemed a huge effort just to lift her shoulders and let them fall. 'Still asking for you.' Rickman made a step toward the ward doors, but she stayed him with a hand on his shoulder. 'Jeff, is there anything I should know before we . . . ?'

'No,' Rickman said. Nothing he could tell Tanya. Telling Grace had been difficult enough. It would be a long time before he felt able to confide in Tanya.

* * *

Simon stood at the window, looking down at the city. He turned when Rickman stepped into the room. His eyes were huge, luminous, magnified by tears which trembled on his lower eyelids, on the point of falling.

'Jeff! I thought you'd gone.'

'I'm investigating a series of murders, Simon,' he said. 'I was with you on Friday, remember?'

Simon looked at Tanya, hopelessly lost. 'When was Friday?' he asked.

'The day before yesterday,' she said, her voice calm, despite her inner turmoil. 'Do you remember?'

He frowned, shaking his head. They kept asking him questions. Asking him to remember things when his head was full of cotton wool and he couldn't make the words come and he couldn't think because you needed words to think. And he had lost the words. He tried now because Jeff asked him to. Jeff was his brother and they had always been close and somehow, he felt he owed it to Jeff. He wasn't sure what he owed — an apology, maybe, 'cos sure as the Pope's a Catholic, he was mad about something. Simon thought that it might be something he'd said — or done.

He stopped short and looked in horror at Jeff. *I did something. I did something terrible.*

Jeff was talking.

'You came to my house,' he said. 'On Friday — the day before yesterday.'

Simon saw a flash; an image of photographic clarity. 'Trees,' he said.

'I live near Sefton Park.'

Simon felt a sharp burst of something inside him. Excitement, he thought, or happiness. 'Remember the boating lake?' he said. 'Remember we skated across when it froze, just for a dare?'

'Yes.' Something passed across his brother's face and Simon tilted his head, trying to understand. Because it looked like pain. But that was a happy memory. Wasn't it?

'Tanya says you've been upset,' Rickman added.

Simon took a deep breath and tried to concentrate. It was so hard when people didn't stick to the point. There was so much to take in: new ideas, new sounds, new people, even. When he looked out over the city, he barely recognised it — a few landmarks, yes, the two cathedrals, the Liver Buildings — but the high-rise blocks were gone, and the crumbling warehouses by the docks were converted to high-priced riverside apartments.

His head was bursting with thoughts clamouring for attention. Snippets of memory were returning, not in any helpful way, but in small, meaningless bursts, like snatches of conversation heard in a noisy dining-hall or a teacherless classroom. He shook his head. Can't think like that anymore — classrooms and stuff were for kids and he was a grown-up. They were like— He concentrated. Like blasts of sound when you tuned a radio. He smiled at Jeff. There!

He'd done it. Followed a thought through from start to finish.

Tanya exhaled slowly and her shoulders sagged a little. 'He's forgotten the question,' she explained. Rickman guessed that this was a routine they had been through many times.

'I didn't forget!' Simon protested.

'You were upset,' Tanya reminded him. 'You thought you'd done something bad.'

'I didn't. I never did anything bad, did I, Jeff?'

Two days ago, Rickman would have answered sharply — perhaps even cruelly. But that was forty-eight hours and a lifetime's experience ago.

'We all do bad things sometimes, Simon,' he said. 'Other people get hurt. We don't mean for that to happen, but . . .' Tanya was watching him closely, waiting, perhaps, for a revelation.

'But they get hurt anyway,' Rickman finished.

'I don't get it,' Simon said, sounding truculent and childish. 'Did I do something? Because if I did something, you should say. I mean how'm I gonna know if nobody *tells* me? 'Cos,' he confided with comical sincerity, 'it's not like I'm Mr Memory right now.'

'We'll talk about it later — when you're feeling better,' Rickman said.

'I want to know *now*!' Simon's truculence was in danger of turning into an all-out, foot-stamping tantrum.

Rickman began to speak but was interrupted by his mobile phone.

'The Bat Phone!' Simon giggled; his mood changed again with dizzying speed. 'Quick, Robin — to the Bat Cave!'

A nurse hurried into the room. 'You can't use that in here,' she said crossly. 'It interferes with the equipment.'

Rickman apologised, cancelling the call and turning off the phone.

'Batman was my favourite,' Simon said, apparently forgetting that he had already told them. 'Only, Jeff always wanted to be Superman.'

Rickman wondered how Tanya coped with the constant agitation, the mood swings, the forgetfulness, the endless repetition and this inane, compulsive chatter. 'I'm sorry,' He held up the phone. 'This might be important.'

'I'll walk you to the lift,' Tanya said.

As he passed, Simon touched Rickman's sleeve. His eyes were clear and lucid, tinged with sadness. 'You're not Superman, Jeff. Back then, you weren't even strong. But you were always brave.' His face crumpled. 'He was always brave,' he told Tanya.

* * *

'He seems worse,' Rickman said, as they waited for the lift.

She sighed. 'Doctor Pratesh says he's making progress, but it seems like two steps forward, one step back. It could take months. He's been offered a place on a rehab course at a specialist neurological centre in — Fazakerley, I think he said.'

Rickman nodded. 'Will you stay?'

'For as long as he tolerates me. I keep hoping he'll suddenly . . .' She shrugged. It was unrealistic to expect Simon to wake up one morning and remember her.

'How are the boys holding up?'

A smile lit up her face, sloughing off years of worry accumulated in two short weeks. 'They're driving each other crazy — but as long as they don't kill each other, we'll manage.'

'You should bring them round — have dinner with us.'

She laughed. 'That'd put a stop to their bickering — they'd have to be on their best behaviour at their uncle's house.'

Rickman felt a rush of pleasure at the thought. Tanya sensed something and said, 'I'm sorry, it must be weird, suddenly finding out about them and now having the title "uncle" thrust upon you.'

'No,' Rickman said, smiling to himself, 'No, I like it, it's good.' He kissed her lightly on the cheek and stepped in

257

the lift. 'I'll sort something out with Grace,' he said. 'I'll be in touch.'

He had his mobile switched on and had dialled Foster before the lift had reached the ground floor. He crossed the great open space of the foyer in long, purposeful strides, with the phone clamped to his ear, impatient for Foster to pick up.

'You're just in time,' Foster said. 'There's been another murder. The body's very fresh. CSI's think they can get latent prints off it.'

'Best news I've had in weeks,' Rickman said, excitement rising.

'I'm on my way over. Meet you there?' Foster suggested.

Rickman hesitated; Low Copy Number DNA sampling could be disrupted by an officer even breathing in the vicinity of sensitive material.

'Go on, Boss,' Foster urged. 'Give yourself the chance to be a proper copper for the day. You can always talk to Hinchcliffe after.'

Rickman had worked this case sixteen hours a day for over two weeks. They had made a breakthrough at last — they were about to nail Jordan — and if his career was about to go down the tubes because of Jordan, he intended to be in at the kill.

'We stay out of their way till the CSIs have done their job,' he warned.

'Scouts' honour.' He could almost see Foster raising his hand in an insincere salute.

'Give me the address,' Rickman said.

CHAPTER THIRTY-FOUR

Foster was kicking his heels outside the house when Rickman arrived.

'What's up?' Rickman asked. 'Didn't want to start without me?'

'Supersleuth here won't let me in,' Foster said, with a resentful glance at the young constable standing guard at the front door.

He stood to attention as Rickman approached.

'I'm sorry, sir—' The constable evidently thought he was in deep shit. 'The CSIs are still working up there, sir.'

Rickman smiled. 'Well done.'

The young man stared at him, waiting for the axe to fall.

'No punch line, Constable. You did the right thing — followed procedure. Can't have Sergeant Foster dropping dandruff all over the shop, contaminating the samples, can we?'

'No, sir.' The constable looked momentarily relieved, then realised the implicit criticism of Foster and glanced uneasily at him.

Rickman followed his line of sight and said, 'Cheer up, Sergeant. We'll get our look-in. But if we ever do crack this case, it'll be on the forensic evidence — so let the experts do their job, eh?' He was buoyant: being kept standing out in the cold by a police constable was a price worth paying, if they got Jordan at the end of it.

They stood in the cold, hands in coat pockets, stamping their feet to keep warm. It was a day of sunshine and cloud, and the shifting light and shadow added to their sense of urgency.

A few minutes later, one of the CSIs came out of the house carrying a box with a camera and hand-held VCR.

'How does it look?' Rickman asked.

'Like someone broke her neck,' he said.

'You got the latent lifts,' Rickman said. *Tell me you got the latent lifts.*

''Course we got 'em.' The voice came from behind them.

Rickman turned around and saw Tony Mayle coming out of the house.

'What brings a crime scene coordinator out on a dismal Sunday?' he asked.

'Same thing that brings a DI to a crime scene,' Mayle said. 'Curiosity. And my indispensable specialist skills.' Mayle was smiling, now. 'Skin lifts — not easy.'

'But you did get them.'

'Thumb and partial index on her neck. We were lucky.'

Rickman exhaled. It was about bloody time they got lucky. 'I always said you were the best CSI in the north of England.' He controlled his surging elation and asked, 'DNA?'

'She fought with her attacker,' the CSC said. 'Her fingernails might yield something useful.'

'How much longer?' Rickman was used to waiting — he counted patience as one of the essential investigative skills. But they had miles to go. And he had promises to keep, not least to Grace — he still hadn't spoken to the DCI and he couldn't face Grace until he had kept that particular promise.

'We're about to bag her,' Mayle said. 'If you want a quick look.'

'That's more like it,' Foster chipped in, his good humour restored. 'You can finish playing with her down the morgue.'

Mayle rolled his eyes and Foster said, 'What?'

'It could be your spectacular lack of tact,' Rickman said. It could just as easily be Foster's use of the term "morgue" — some specialists hated the incipient creep of American jargon.

'I'm the soul of tact, me. Now let me at her.' Foster made for the front door with unseemly enthusiasm, but the constable stopped him, filling the space with his broad bulk. 'Sorry, Sarge,' he said — although, after his earlier vindication, he looked less rueful about it this time.

'What now?' Foster demanded. 'I swear, if I don't get a shufti at an honest-to-God murder soon, I'll do one meself.' It was plain who his intended victim would be.

The constable lifted his chin, indicating something behind Foster.

The CSI had stowed his cameras and now stood at the back of the van, holding a neatly bagged oversuit in each hand. 'Can't have you gents going in improperly attired, can we?' he said.

The house was a small terrace, divided into two flats. The staircase had been boxed in, as had the downstairs hall, leaving only a small gap between the front door and two interior doors, both fitted with Yale locks.

'Anyone in the downstairs flat?' Rickman asked.

Mayle shook his head. 'The bobby tried earlier. No answer.'

They put on their suits in the communal hallway; Mayle pausing with them to change into a fresh pair of overshoes. The hall floor was uncarpeted, the floorboards painted chocolate brown and the walls magnolia. The door to the staircase stood open.

'Where is she?' Rickman asked, stepping into his zoot suit.

'Sitting-room, top of the stairs.'

'What do we know about the victim?'

'I got a name off a letter in the flat.' Mayle flicked through the notes on his clipboard. 'She worked as an interpreter for the council. Natalie . . . or—'

'Natalja?' Rickman felt prickings of alarm.

'Yeah, that's it. Natalja Sremać.'

He pronounced the 'ć' as a hard 'k'. 'Sremach,' Rickman corrected him absently. *Natalja Sremać, Grace's friend. God, how was he going to break this to her?*

'Know her, do you?' Foster asked.

'I met her once,' Rickman said, remembering the olive-skinned woman with sad, beautiful eyes and a wide smile that could not hide her anxiety.

'Makes you wonder why they'd wanna come here,' Foster said, breaking into his thoughts.

'Who?'

'Illegal immigrants — there's more sharks swimming in the Mersey than you'd ever get in Balkan waters.'

'You're the soul of compassion, Lee.' Rickman pulled on his overshoes and a pair of latex gloves. 'Miss Sremać is — or was — a refugee. Which makes her strictly legal.'

'Sorry, Boss,' Foster said, without the slightest hint of embarrassment or remorse.

They were ready, but Mayle delayed them one last time. 'Hoods, please, gents.' Foster was still dragging his over his head as he took the stairs two at a time.

'We've taken one of the door panels to the lab,' Mayle told Rickman. 'Probably get a nice shoeprint off it.'

The sofa prevented him from opening the splintered sitting-room door wide, so Foster edged past it, only looking down at the body when he was well inside the room.

He gave a muffled cry. Mayle and Rickman glanced at each other, alarmed.

Her neck was bent at a grotesque angle. Her intelligent blue eyes looked startled. 'Ah, Jesus, no . . .'

'Foster?' Rickman called.

'Jeff.' Foster spun to face the door, blundered out onto the landing. 'You can't go in there, Jeff.'

Mayle and Rickman stared at him. He looked sick, jaundiced. He swallowed. 'Get him outside,' he told Mayle.

'What the hell's the matter with you?' Rickman demanded. He stepped onto the landing, but Foster barred the way.

'Jeff—'

Rickman saw the horror on his friend's face and felt an answering stab of fear. His eyes widened and he breathed, 'No . . .'

Foster reached out to touch his shoulder, but Rickman blatted his hand away, putting Foster off-balance, taking advantage, he used his momentum to shove his friend out of the way.

The room was unnaturally quiet. He saw. A heartbeat of incomprehension. A moment of perfect stillness. Then the ground seemed to fall away and he felt himself plummeting headlong. A moan escaped him and he murmured, 'God, no . . .'

Plastic bags covered her head and hands, taped at the opening to catch whatever might fall: skin cells, hair, a fibre from her killer's clothing.

He fell to his knees and tore at the plastic, repeating, 'God *no.*'

Shocked, Mayle lunged through the doorway after him and grabbed his arm. 'What the hell are you doing?'

'Get the fuck away from me,' Rickman growled, struggling with Mayle. 'She's suffocating. She needs air.' He pulled away from Mayle. 'We have to do CPR.'

'For God's sake help me!' Mayle yelled.

Foster forced the weakness from his limbs and returned to the room. 'It's too late, Jeff,' he said, dragging Rickman away.

Mayle knelt beside her, checking for damage to the seals.

'Ah, Jesus,' Foster repeated, unable to take his eyes off the body.

'Don't you fucking touch her!' Rickman snarled, trying to break free.

Foster shoved Rickman against the wall, holding him by the shoulders. 'Jeff, listen. You've got to listen to me. She's dead,' Foster said. The words sounded alien and cruel to him. 'Grace is dead.'

Rickman stopped struggling. He stared at Foster.

Behind them, Mayle said, 'Oh, God — is this Doctor Chandler?'

'We have to help her,' Rickman said, pleading, searching Foster's face for some sign that this was a mistake. *It was a mistake, wasn't it? Had to be. Because this was too awful — too horrible to be real. Grace was in bed when he left the house. She was fine. Grace was at home.*

'We can't help her, Jeff,' Foster said. 'Grace is—'

Rickman slammed Foster hard in the chest with both hands. 'No!' he yelled. 'Don't you fucking say that. She's not dead. Grace is not—'

He lunged forward but Foster caught his elbow and swung him round as he tried to pass. Rickman took Foster by the throat and both men lost their balance, crashing into the bookcase. Books and ornaments clattered to the floor.

Mayle came at him, punching Rickman between the shoulder-blades. Winded, he released his grasp. Mayle shoved him towards the door and Rickman staggered out onto the landing. The CSI made to follow, but Foster held up one hand, the other curled protectively around his throat.

'Let him go,' he choked.

Mayle stared after Rickman. 'Jeez, Foster, I swear I didn't know.'

Rickman managed the first few stairs, then his legs gave way and he collapsed on one of the risers and put his head in his hands.

Foster and Mayle stood looking down at him, not knowing what to do. After a moment, the young constable opened the front door and peered in.

'Is everything all right?' he asked.

'It's fine,' Foster said. 'Go back outside.'

The constable shot Rickman a frightened look and then hurriedly closed the door.

Foster waited a couple of minutes. A CSI appeared briefly from the bedroom at the front of the house, but Mayle warned him off with a slight shake of the head and he disappeared back into the room. Behind them, Grace's body lay just inside the sitting-room. Neither man went near her, nor even glanced in the direction of the doorway. It would seem somehow indecent with Rickman still in the house.

'Boss,' Foster said, when he thought that Rickman was calmer.

Rickman's head came up, but he didn't turn. 'Don't,' he said. 'Don't say a word.' His voice was choked with rage and despair.

He stood, unzipped his protective suit, took his mobile phone from his pocket and switched it off. When, at last, he turned to face to them, his eyes were dead, devoid of all emotion.

'Take care of her.' There was a hint of a question, an ocean of sorrow in his voice.

Mayle nodded.

Foster shuffled from one foot to the other, wanting to say something. But there was nothing he could say that would help or console.

After a time, Rickman shifted his gaze to the sergeant. 'You haven't seen me,' he said.

Foster took a breath to speak, but Rickman held up one trembling finger to silence him. 'You haven't seen me, Foster. I wasn't here.'

CHAPTER THIRTY-FIVE

Jordan lived in a three-storey Georgian property in Falkner Street, minutes from his girls' main working area — not exactly living over the shop, but as close as Jordan could get without being arrested for running a brothel.

Rickman did a quick recce as he drew up outside: cars were parked nose-to-tail from the Catherine Street to the Hope Street end; outside the student café bar and gallery they were even double-parked — the downside of urban regeneration. Rickman parked his Vauxhall Vectra parallel to a battered Citroen with a University staff sticker and took one last look. As far as he could see, there were no police. Which meant either that Jordan wasn't home, or that the surveillance team were better than he gave them credit for.

The front steps were clean and swept, the original foot-scraper, still in place, was newly painted, as was the big black front door. Rickman rattled the knocker and waited. After half a minute he knocked again, and the letterbox flicked lightly inwards as if somebody had opened one of the interior doors.

Footsteps clattered down the stairs and he clenched his fist, ready. The door opened and he stepped forward, drawing back his fist, dropping it only at the last moment. It was a girl. Dark skinned and pretty, standing five-foot-nothing in her peach-coloured nightgown and kitten-heel slippers. She gave a small gasp of surprise and fell back a step, allowing Rickman to shoulder the door open.

'Hey!' She sounded indignant, but also a little scared.

'Where is he?' he demanded.

'Where's who? And who the hell is asking?'

'Got you well trained, hasn't he? Denials first, personal safety second.'

'You get out of here!' she screamed.

'Or what? You'll call the police?' He bent down, bringing his face level with hers. 'News flash, sweetheart — I am the police.'

She started crying, giving herself up to it like a child, the tears streaming down her face, her hands hanging by her sides. She looked no more than sixteen.

He checked the two sitting-rooms to the right of the hallway, then moved on to the kitchen and checked the back door; it was locked. 'He wouldn't be hiding upstairs, would he? Leaving a little girl to deal with all this aggro?'

'I'm not a little girl!' she screamed through her tears. 'Just you *wait* till he gets home.'

Rickman went into the hall. She didn't follow him, and he listened for a few moments as she spoke into her mobile phone. The gist of it was that some big bastard had barged into his house and was refusing to leave. Jordan must have given her an instruction, because she came cautiously to the kitchen door and peered into the hall, giving a little shriek when she saw Rickman still standing there.

She listened again, then held the phone out for Rickman. 'He wants to talk to you.'

Rickman took the phone, then smiled, switching it off without listening. 'Mobile phones,' he said. 'Bane of modern life.'

'What do you *want?*' the girl wailed.

'I want to see Jordan face to face. I'm going to kill the sadistic, blood-sucking, murdering bastard.'

As he turned to go upstairs, Rickman caught a metallic glint at the edge of his vision and swung back. The blade sliced the air inches from his face. He caught girl by the wrist and twisted till she screamed and dropped the knife. He held her while he picked it up and pocketed it.

The girl squirmed, weeping. 'Please,' she said. 'Don't hurt me.'

Shocked, Rickman let go of her. She nursed her left wrist in her right hand and Rickman noticed for the first time an ugly bracelet of blackened bruises around her wrist.

'We're not all like Jordan,' he said.

She stared at him sullenly, her eyes still oozing tears.

'Know what happened to his last girl?' Rickman asked. When she didn't reply, he said, 'She ended up in a wheelie-bin, naked, bled to death.'

Her eyes widened and she clutched her nightgown tighter at the neck. She was too young, as yet, to have mastered the art of deception, and Rickman could read every thought that passed through her mind in those few short seconds.

First, she was frightened: she knew that Jordan was capable of bad things — the bruises on her wrist were testament to his bad temper. Then she wondered if Rickman was lying — trying to frighten her. Finally, her eyes flicked to the staircase as she wondered if she could get away from Jordan and be safe.

'I can get you out,' Rickman said. 'Find you a place in a hostel.'

It was the wrong thing to say: he guessed that she had lived in hostels before and had not relished the experience.

'Ooh, goody,' she said. 'A real big move up in the world.'

Rickman smiled. 'A cosy corner in a septic tank would be a step up from living with Jordan.'

She folded her arms. 'Think I'll take my chances, thanks.'

Rickman shrugged, moving to the stairs. 'Suit yourself. But don't say I didn't warn you.'

The girl followed him from room to room and floor to floor making no attempt to stop him any longer. Of course, he found nothing: the CSIs had been through the place when they established a link with Sophia Habib, so Rickman really didn't expect to discover vital evidence in his cursory examination of the house. The search was illegal, anyway, so anything he did find would be inadmissible as evidence. But the constant action prevented him from thinking. And thinking brought fresh waves of pain as debilitating and exhausting as physical pain.

'What's your name?' he asked, looking up to find her watching him. He changed his mind immediately, holding up his hand to stop her. 'No, don't bother. It'd be a lie. And it really doesn't matter — he'll change it again when he puts you on the street.'

'He won't!' she shouted. 'Lex loves me!'

He tapped his wrist, indicating the bruises on hers. 'That what he told you when he gave you those?'

She stared at him, the fury and hatred on her face a reflection of her understanding of the truth in what he was saying.

'He tells all his girls that he loves them,' Rickman said. 'Ask Desiree. She was his girl, once. I think she was with him the longest — a whole six months. His attention span gets shorter as he gets older. My guess is he'll have you on the block before Christmas.'

He moved to the window. Police sirens whooped in the distance, but still no sign of Jordan.

'Ask Desiree about Jordan's undying love. You've got a lot in common — you even look a little alike. You could swap stories, compare bruises.'

'You . . . bastard,' she hissed, tears filling her eyes again. 'You bloody . . . bastard.' He had spoiled the dream for her. Taken away the few weeks of happiness she would have enjoyed being spoiled and petted and pampered. Jordan had lied to her and she had believed him because it was better than believing the truth. But once you stop believing, you can't recapture that innocence.

The sirens were louder, now. Catherine Street, he guessed. He prayed they would pass by, give him just a few minutes alone with Jordan, that was all he needed.

The girl noticed him listening. Her shoulders sagged then she hurried to the window. The lights of a squad car flashed below. 'Oh, what?' she wailed, turning to Rickman. 'You've brung the bizzies down on us, now. He'll bloody kill me.'

'He doesn't have to know,' Rickman urged. The need for revenge burned in him like a fever. 'Just tell me where he is, I'll do the rest.'

The girl backed away from him. 'Are you mad or what?'

They heard footsteps on the stairs, then Foster burst through the door. The girl ran to him. 'He's bloody psycho, that one,' she said, moving behind Foster and out onto the landing. 'He's gonna kill Lex.'

Foster's tone was apologetic. 'You shouldn't be here,' he said.

Rickman gritted his teeth. 'I told you—' He refocused beyond Foster. DCI Hinchcliffe stood in the doorway, formal as an undertaker in his black cashmere overcoat and gloves. He looked around the room as if to reassure himself that nothing had been damaged.

Rickman switched his gaze to Foster. *So much for loyalty.*

'You need to go home, Jeff,' Hinchcliffe said. There was no anger in his voice, only mild reproof and something stronger, maybe compassion.

'I can't—' Rickman broke off. Some words are dangerous. Words like *I can't* have so many connotations. *I can't* — face going home. *I can't* — believe she's dead. *I can't* — understand why anyone would want to break something so beautiful. *I can't* — stop, or I'll fall apart.

He began again. 'I'm needed here, sir.' Safer territory: the job, the investigation, finding Grace's killer.

'No,' Hinchcliffe said.

'Sir—'

'You can't be on this case, Jeff.'

That word again. *Can't.* 'What am I supposed to do?' he demanded. 'Go home and—' *Think about Grace lying on the cold floor of Natalja's flat, being treated like any other corpse in any other investigation?* For now, he could keep the awful image of her plastic-shrouded face at bay, but how would he avoid seeing her at home, where every room of the house held memories of her?

'I can't—' He paused, forcing down the constriction in his throat that threatened to choke him. 'I can't — go home.'

'Don't you have friends, family?'

Rickman stared at him. It was almost funny. The few friends he had were on the Force. The only family he had was a brother he hadn't known in adulthood, who was trapped in the nineteen eighties, and was effectively half-crazy. Or maybe the DCI was suggesting that he should open up to his sister-in-law — a woman he had known for a matter of weeks and met precisely three times.

Hinchcliffe put a hand on his shoulder and Rickman flinched. He needed action. He needed to break some heads, instead of which, the DCI was offering him sympathy. It was too much to take. He walked out, leaving Hinchcliffe to placate the girl.

CHAPTER THIRTY-SIX

Around the Incident Room, people were huddled in small groups, talking in quiet, shocked voices. There was work to be done and DCI Hinchcliffe needed the team behind him, not paralysed by the terrible news of Grace Chandler's death. He took in all the emotion, the horror, the incipient helplessness of his officers, then launched into the room.

'You're all aware why I've called this emergency debrief,' he said, talking loud and fast. 'I am now the SIO on this case.' There was a rumble of disquiet, and he added, 'But let me dispel one rumour immediately: DI Rickman is *not* suspended. He is on compassionate leave.'

A few officers exchanged glances. Someone muttered, 'What, again?'

'The early reaction from the media today was critical,' he went on. 'One commentator described the investigation as "a shambles" — well, I suppose it doesn't inspire confidence, replacing the SIO in the middle of the case. I've since spoken to the news editors of the local press, radio and TV, explaining the situation, and their position has softened considerably.

'The BBC regional news desk will be running a short feature on Doctor Chandler's work. Local radio has reported her murder and her relationship to DI Rickman. We're already getting messages of condolence — let's see if we can change those to offers of help.'

This didn't go down well: evidently some of the team felt that it smacked of cynicism. 'I know,' he said. 'I don't like it any more than you do, but we owe it to Doctor Chandler — as well as DI Rickman — to find her killers. And I don't need to tell you that the first twenty-four hours are crucial.'

A begrudging acceptance of the reality of the situation by the same people who had shown disapproval satisfied Hinchcliffe that he had got through.

'Doctor Chandler was well-liked in the refugee community,' he said. 'I'm told that she was known universally as "Doctor Grace". Use the name, play on their gratitude, their affection or their guilt — do whatever the hell it takes to find who killed her.'

'What about the Sremać woman,' DC Hart asked. 'Is she a suspect?'

'Anything is possible. She is missing, which could mean that she attacked Doctor Chandler and then fled, or it could mean that she, herself, is in danger. One fact to consider is that Natalja Sremać is not a particularly big woman, and it must have taken considerable strength to break the doctor's neck.'

'So we treat her as a potential victim?' somebody asked.

'Until we have evidence to the contrary, yes.'

'We're spreading ourselves awful thin, Boss.' Just about everyone in the room turned to DS Foster. He looked drawn, more subdued than any of them had ever seen him. His voice was hoarse: his larynx had been bruised when Rickman grabbed him by the throat. 'If you want us to prioritise this, we're gonna have to pull people off other lines of enquiry.'

Hinchcliffe looked over his head to the back of the room. 'Gary—' A light-skinned Asian stood up. They all recognised him as the HOLMES Office Manager.

'We've re-prioritised actions,' he said. 'The top two aims obviously being to establish Natalja Sremać's whereabouts

273

and find Doctor Chandler's killer. To this end, we'll have more operatives taking incoming calls. If you've been on house-to-house, that may have changed — we've rejigged the team. Those of you who have already made links with the asylum seekers and refugee charity workers will remain on that work, but all questions will now be focused on Natalja and Doctor Chandler.'

'Why the rejig?' The DS in charge of house-to-house had spoken up, and he sounded a little aggrieved.

Hinchcliffe took the question. 'House-to-House have done a brilliant job, in very difficult circumstances,' he said, keen to keep them on side. 'The reorganisation has been made necessary by the first bit of good news we've had all week: we've got extra allocation — fifteen more officers by the twenty-thirty briefing tonight.'

A low cheer greeted this news, half-hearted, ironic.

'Boss?' A hush fell, as the team deferred again to DS Foster. His neck was livid with red marks, rapidly turning to blue-black. He swallowed with some difficulty, then said, 'DI Rickman seemed to think Lex Jordan was a prime suspect.' Subdued he might be, but not beyond stirring up mischief, Hinchcliffe reflected.

'As you are all aware, Jordan is under surveillance,' he said. '*However*: he has brought a complaint against DI Rickman.' There were groans and exclamations of disgust, but Hinchcliffe carried on, raising his voice over their pro-tests. 'Of course I'll do all I can to protect Jeff, but Jordan is within his legal rights — and as far as he's concerned, we're taking his complaint seriously.'

'*What?*' Hart was on her feet, but Foster pulled her back into her seat.

'As far as he's concerned,' Hinchcliffe repeated with emphasis. 'If Jordan's off his guard, he's more likely to do something useful. Something the surveillance team can act on.'

Hart relaxed, even looked a little apologetic. Hinchcliffe raised his eyebrows, allowing the merest hint of humour to register on his face. 'More than anything,' he said, 'Mr Jordan needs to feel secure.'

* * *

It didn't take much to persuade Mirko Andrić to mediate for them. Admittedly, he was disconcerted at first, arguing that he had barely known Grace, that somebody who could do her justice should make the appeal on her behalf.

'You know her place in the hearts of refugees,' Hinchcliffe countered. 'If I or one of her colleagues were to speak up for "Doctor Chandler", it'd sound like the authorities of a foreign — even hostile — country, lecturing to them. But if you speak up for "Doctor *Grace*" — well,' he shrugged, 'it's plain that you have considerable influence, Mr Andrić. People will listen to you.'

Their meeting was held in a conference room in the big, mud-coloured police headquarters in the city centre. Hinchcliffe was preparing for a press conference timed to catch the evening news.

Andrić looked doubtful. 'I've tried, Chief Inspector.' His shoulder lifted barely a centimetre. 'But they don't listen. Six people already are dead, but they don't help you.'

'What about Natalja?' Hinchcliffe asked.

The Serb looked at Hinchcliffe without answering.

'We found your business card in her purse,' Hinchcliffe said. 'And a photograph of the two of you on her bookshelf. I'd guess it was taken a few years ago, but you did know her, didn't you?'

A shadow of pain passed over Andrić's face. 'Why do you talk as if she's dead already?'

'I'm sorry,' Hinchcliffe said. 'We hope she is alive. The sooner we find her, the better her chances are.'

Andrić tilted his head back and looked at the ceiling, his arms folded. He exhaled, and when he looked at Hinchcliffe again, he seemed resigned. 'I'll do what I can,' he said.

He was miked up and ready to go at the press conference an hour later. Looking sombre and handsome, his eyes dark and glittering under the television spotlights, he spoke without notes, talking to camera like a professional. 'I met Doctor Grace only twice.' His expression softened. 'The first words she spoke to me was she asking me if she could help. I think that was a special part of Doctor Grace — her gift — to want to help people. It doesn't matter to her what race or religion. She helped people because they needed help, and she could give it.'

'What would you say to those who think the asylum seekers should arm themselves?' It was just a voice in a solid bank of faces: the conference had been set up in one of the lecture theatres at HQ, and every one of the two hundred seats was taken.

'Blood has been spilt,' Andrić said. 'And some are saying "blood for blood", but Doctor Grace didn't care about that. Blood ties didn't mean a thing to her — except, maybe that you have to match blood for a transfusion.' He gave a self-deprecating smile, and the assembled press and media responded warmly.

'So, I say to those people, it doesn't matter that *he* is Kurd and *he* is Iraqi. I myself am Serb, but you wouldn't know if I was Croat.' He shrugged. 'What I'm saying is, the differences — they're small. They don't matter. What matters is we should help each other, because this is bad situation.' He fell silent, troubled by his own thoughts, frustrated, it seemed by his inability to express them.

'Mr Andrić — would you like to say something to Miss Sremać?'

Andrić didn't respond immediately; a worried frown creased his forehead and he stared absently in the general direction of the questioner.

'Sir — do you believe she's still alive?' the reporter persisted.

'I have to believe that,' he replied, a little sharply. 'I know it.'

'Miss Sremać is a friend of Mr Andrić,' Hinchcliffe said, concerned that he had asked too much of the man.

'I know Natalja since Croatia,' he said. 'I met her when—' He broke off, scanning the faces of the assembled media, ranged in rows like an audience watching a drama on a stage. 'Her family was murdered, She was all alone — fifteen years old, and all alone in a war.'

Hinchcliffe approved, he was painting a picture of a real person, someone who had suffered much, someone who was vulnerable, who deserved a break in a life that had already seen too much death, too much horror.

Andrić looked directly to camera. 'Talk to her . . .' he said. 'Natalja speaks four, maybe five languages. It should be possible, shouldn't it, to find words to . . .' he faltered. 'To communicate.'

CHAPTER THIRTY-SEVEN

Jeff Rickman walked blindly for hours, haunted by the image of Grace, her face sheathed in suffocating plastic. If he had said something to her before he had left that morning, perhaps she wouldn't have gone to see Natalja. Had there been some clue in their conversation the previous night? He went over and over it in his head; but they had talked mostly about him, his problems, his guilt, his need to confess. If he hadn't been so obsessed with telling Hinchcliffe about his altercation with Jordan . . . It all seemed so trivial, so inconsequential, now.

Christ! Why had he chosen last night of all nights to unburden himself? Another, horrible thought followed on, winding him: had it been something he said that had persuaded Grace to visit her friend?

'You all right, love?'

He heard the woman's voice, but it didn't register that she was talking to him.

'Is there anything I can do?' she persisted.

He looked down at her, a small woman of sixty or so. Round and tightly wrapped in a headscarf and woollen coat, she reminded him of a Russian doll.

'I'm fine,' he said.

She wasn't so easily put off. 'I mean, you wouldn't be thinking of taking a dive in that, would you?'

He stared at her, puzzled, then glancing over his shoulder, with a shock of realisation he saw that he had wandered down to the Pier Head. He summoned a smile from somewhere, hoped it would convince.

'Just taking the air,' he said.

She looked doubtful. 'So long as you're all right.'

He felt a debilitating surge of emotion. 'I'll be getting off home, soon,' he said. 'You needn't worry about me.'

She hovered uncertainly, but Rickman turned away to lean on the rail at the end of the Pier, and after a few moments he heard her shuffling footsteps retreating into the darkness.

The wind, though not strong, was bitter as broken promises. To the north, the white concrete facades of the Liver Buildings were lit by a greenish light. He walked, keeping the river on his left, past the warehouse conversions: Jesse Hartley's dark, brick-built storage houses transformed into brightly lit loft apartments in gated developments for wealthy young business types, footballers and soap stars. Beyond them, the mouth of the estuary, where the stroppy Mersey waters meet the mutinous Irish Sea. And darkness.

Rickman faced into the wind. It numbed his body, and that was a welcome relief, for the pain he felt was physical, and yet his mind would not be quiet; his thoughts persisted in their self-destructive course, unassuaged by cold or exhaustion. He had acted blindly and stupidly. Now the surveillance team would be briefed to watch for him, alert to possible trouble.

He couldn't remember returning home; only became aware, suddenly, that his house keys were in his hand. He locked the car and shambled towards the house.

'You're a hard man to find.'

Rickman wheeled and the figure took a step back, his face registering alarm. 'Jesus, Foster! You shouldn't sneak up on a man like that.'

'Sorry, Boss. You're not wrong, though — I couldn't take much more punishment.' His voice was so damaged, he could barely whisper. He tried one of his trademark grins but abandoned it as a doomed venture before he really got any wattage behind it.

Rickman said, 'Look, Lee, I—' He put his hand to his own throat.

'Forget it,' Foster said, 'it'll do me good to give me gob a rest.' They stood on the doorstep, an awkward silence increasing the distance between them. 'I want you to know,' Foster said, 'I never grassed you up to the DCI.'

'I wouldn't blame you if you had.'

'But I never.'

They held eye contact for a few seconds, then Rickman nodded. 'You weren't the only one there, Lee. I shouldn't have jumped to conclusions.'

Foster lifted his chin in the direction of the front door. 'Aren't you gonna invite me in, then?'

Rickman looked at the keys in his hand. He didn't think he could do this.

Foster took the keys from him, opening the front door and then stepping aside. Rickman hesitated a second or two longer, then walked into the house. The burglar alarm was just inside the door into the hall. He tapped in the number, and in a steep moment of dizzying emotion — the first of many — he realised that Grace must have set it before she left the house on that final, fatal journey.

'I need a drink,' he murmured, his voice hoarse with emotion. Foster followed him through to the sitting-room at the back of the house. The central-heating timer had clicked off and the house was cooling. The fireplace was swept and stacked with logs, ready to be lit and Rickman felt another sick thud: Grace again, planning a romantic evening for the two of them.

He went to the drinks cabinet and poured two whiskies, handing one of them to Foster.

'How are you?' Foster asked.

'Numb.' Which wasn't quite true. 'Hopefully uncon-scious in an hour or so.' Rickman tipped his glass to the light; a film of the liquid adhered to the sides. Sign of a good whisky. It was just about the only piece of advice his father had ever given him.

He took a swallow, feeling punishing pleasure in its scourging progress from throat to stomach. He hadn't eaten all day and the alcohol had an immediate effect, anaesthetis-ing, warming.

'You might want to go easy on that,' Foster said, taking a seat. 'Wouldn't want you to get stopped by Traffic — you know they'd book their own granny for reckless driving of an invalid carriage.'

Rickman took another swallow. 'I'm not planning on going out.' Something in Foster's eyes caught his attention. 'Am I?'

Foster took a tentative sip of his drink, wincing as he swallowed. 'I shouldn't be doing this,' he said, and Rickman wondered if he meant drinking whisky or talking to a DI who had been kicked off a murder case.

'I'm on painkillers,' Foster explained, putting a hand to his throat. 'But Jeez — a man needs something to lubricate the voice box.'

Rickman took the armchair, sagging into it without tak-ing off his coat. He hadn't appreciated until now just how tired he was. He didn't think he could sleep, but he didn't really feel like filling the silence with idle chat, either.

'Lee, I appreciate your coming round, but if there's a point to all this, d'you think you could get to it?'

'Turn you mobie on,' Foster said.

'What?'

'I took a call for you 'bout an hour ago. Some operator who wasn't up to speed on the case put the call through to your desk.'

'And?'

Foster checked his watch. 'He should be ringing any minute now.'

'He?'

'Turn the fucker on, will you?'

Rickman complied, intrigued — grateful to feel anything other than sick emptiness. 'Satisfied?' he said. 'Now explain.'

'The caller said he had information about the murders of the asylum seekers.'

'And?'

'And nothing. He won't talk to anyone but you.'

'Well give me *something*, Lee. Was he young? Old? British? Foreign?'

'Foreign. Definitely. Palestinian, maybe. Or Iraqi.' He shrugged. 'All them towel-heads sound the same to me.'

Rickman felt a sudden dangerous burst of outrage. 'God almighty, Foster! Haven't you learned *anything* from all this?'

Foster said nothing.

Rickman set down his glass, fighting to contain his anger. He needed to lash out, to pay back some of the hurt he was feeling, but he wouldn't take it out on Foster. He wouldn't become like his father. He had spent half his life battling the inherited demon of his father's temper; he wasn't going to give in to it now.

'You gave this man my number?' His voice sounded all right to him.

Foster nodded. 'I told him to ring after eleven. Reckoned I'd've found you by then.'

Rickman didn't tell Foster how close he had come to not returning home at all. The house belonged to Grace; it was hers in ways he was yet to discover. Each room contained memories of her childhood, youth and adulthood; their three years together. The place was redolent with her spirit. How could he ever bear to stay here?

'This caller — did he give a name?' he asked.

'Nah. If you ask me, he's the cautious type.'

Rickman checked his watch. Eleven-ten. Maybe the informant had called already and bottled out when Rickman's phone was off-line. He was debating whether to pick up his drink and continue his course to oblivion, when his phone rang.

'You are Detective Inspector Rickman?' The man spoke without preamble. His voice was hard, high-pitched. Iranian, maybe, Rickman thought.

'I am DI Rickman,' he said. 'Do you want to tell me your name?'

'Not yet. I have information.'

'What kind of information?'

'Not over the phone. Meet me.'

'All right,' Rickman said. He reached into his pocket for a notebook and pen. 'Where?'

'Dover.'

'*Dover?*' Across from him, Foster raised his eyebrows in question. 'Dover is six hours' drive from here. Why should I drive six hours to meet someone who won't give me a name or tell me what information he has to offer?'

The man coughed nervously. 'Is very dangerous for me,' he said. Rickman could almost see him cupping his hand over the mouthpiece. 'I know why those people died.'

'Which people?'

'You know which people.'

'You'll have to give me something more.'

'No. How do I know you are Inspector Rickman? I want to see your face. You come, or I hang up now — you don't hear from me again.'

'Okay,' Rickman soothed. 'Okay.' It wasn't like he had anything else to do. 'Where in Dover?'

He made a few notes then ended the call.

'So?' Foster asked.

'I could tell you, but then I'd have to . . .' The significance of the words suddenly hit him and he broke off, dismayed.

'How will you recognise him?' Foster asked, trying to take Rickman's attention away from what he had almost said. 'Blue carnation in his buttonhole, or what?'

Rickman gave him a comical look. 'He said he would recognise me.'

'That's what comes of being on the telly. Are you going, then?'

'Yes,' Rickman said. 'I think he's genuine. Despite the melodrama, I think maybe he does know something.'

'Let's hope so, eh?' Foster said. 'Let's hope so, for all our sakes.'

CHAPTER THIRTY-EIGHT

Heavy rain and gusting winds made driving difficult. Rickman was glad of the distraction: radio music only jangled his nerves, and the sonorous voices of the worthies on Radio Four were dangerously soporific. He felt disconnected from the rest of the world, quarantined by the bubble of warmth inside his car; the darkness and the rain only increased his sense of isolation.

He slipped from motorway to motorway, traversing a featureless black landscape. Only at Birmingham were there recognisable landmarks: the electric-blue lights of the leisure complex, and the RAC control centre, its glass front like the prow of a ship, breasting the rain that swept in waves against it. Then on, to blank roadways and impenetrable darkness.

At Northampton, he stopped for coffee. The motorway services were empty and over-bright, the shops closed, and all but the main restaurant shuttered. The few people around walked the wide foyers foggy-eyed and disorientated: a few couples; a family group; a gang of four lads. Rickman stood out among them, travelling alone.

He sat staring at his own reflection in a rain-spattered window. In the distance, occasional convoys of lorries swept by on the motorway like trains passing on an invisible line.

Fleeting glimpses of Grace's face, superimposed on his, made him catch his breath and reach out more than once. Always sheathed in plastic, as he had last seen her, eyes closed, pale beyond endurance; and he wondered if he would ever be able to think of her again without that terrible image coming unbidden to his mind.

By four a.m., he had reached the M25 and already traffic was beginning to build. The roads were drying, now, the winds moderating, and he skirted London swiftly, queuing only briefly at the Dartford Crossing, then on, unhindered, to the M20. This part of the journey, though the quietest, was the most treacherous: here he negotiated a landscape as blank and black as any he had seen. Few towns, large unlit sections that seemed to pull on his tired eyes. The road rushed up to meet him, mile after mile; only short stretches of roadworks provided any variety or relief from the unchanging darkness.

He veered off onto the A20 for the last stage of his journey, hitting pockets of low-lying mist almost immediately. He slowed down, feeling his tiredness, now. At the roundabout on the brow of the hill leading down to Dover he turned off, taking the winding road to Dover Castle, finally coming to rest in the car park below the entrance. Here, he got out to stretch his legs, climbing the steps onto the road leading to the castle portcullis. It was six-thirty, and still dark. A mist hung in threads lower down the hill, visible as pearly skeins in the artificial lighting. As he returned to his car, a dark-coloured Audi turned in and parked next to his Vectra. Rickman wondered if he had passed the car earlier, perhaps waiting in a lay-by, watching for him?

He approached slowly: his impression of the man over the phone was that he was nervous, liable to bolt if he thought the conditions weren't right. He waited on the steps giving the driver the chance to get a good look at him. After a pause, the man got out of the car, glancing around at the building behind them and at the road above, before approaching Rickman.

He was small, mid- to late-twenties, of slight build and a rather hawkish appearance; he moved with an edgy energy, offering his hand to Rickman, but not giving his name.

'We must go somewhere else,' he said. 'We take your car.' He went immediately to Rickman's car and slid into the passenger seat.

After a moment, Rickman shrugged and followed him. 'Where to?' he asked.

'Anywhere away from Dover.'

Rickman pointed the car back the way he had come. At the roundabout, he turned right, heading for Deal and the coast. Traffic was light, as yet, the weekenders having returned to London the previous night, and the locals, bar a few fishermen, were only just beginning to stir.

'So,' Rickman said. 'D'you have a name?'

'Names are not real,' he said. 'This is real — me, talking to you now.'

'And how do I know this is real?' Rickman asked.

He felt the man's raking scrutiny and glanced at him. His passenger looked away. 'I will give you proof,' he said.

Rickman parked opposite a row of shops just as the first glimmer of light touched the horizon. They crossed the road and took the path down towards the beach. It was disconcertingly quiet: no suck and hiss of waves on shingle, no gull's cry; and Rickman realised that the shoreline itself was invisible, that it must be hidden by a steep bank of the tiny pinkish pebbles that came right up to the long grey path that ran parallel to the sea.

The smell of frying bacon on the cold air led them to a small café in what was little more than a hut near the shore. It was busy, even at this early hour. There was a hush as they walked in, a tall, pale-skinned tourist and his small, foreign-looking companion; but after a few curious looks the men went back to their breakfasts and their conversations.

His informant scanned the faces without embarrassment; only when he was satisfied there was nobody he knew among the diners did he move from the door to a free table.

He drank strong tea and ate a round of toast while Rickman devoured bacon, eggs, beans and fried bread, surprised that he had any appetite at all.

'Are we going to talk?' Rickman asked. 'Or did I drive three hundred miles just so you could watch me get egg on my chin?'

The man glanced over his shoulder, then leaned forward. 'Do you know what a fake ID can raise?' he asked. 'Do you know how much people are willing to pay for the privilege of living in your country?' His voice was high and rather percussive, but he kept it below the general level of noise in the café, and Rickman had to strain to hear.

He didn't wait for Rickman to reply, but instead asked another question. 'Do you know what ILR is?'

'Indefinite leave to remain,' Rickman said.

'A refugee granted ILR can stay for as long as they like,' the man said. 'After a few years, someone with ILR can apply for a British passport. That's worth a lot of money — maybe even thirty thousand pounds. Some people take the money and move on — apply somewhere else in your country — even move on to a different country.' He paused. 'Some just . . . disappear.'

Rickman put down his knife and fork. 'Killed?' he asked.

The man's look was as eloquent as words: *What do you think?*

'You said you'd give me proof,' Rickman reminded him. The young man seemed to be grappling with fear and indecision, and for a second or two Rickman thought his first really promising witness might run for the door. Then he saw a new resolve in the man's eyes.

He took a photograph out of his wallet, handing it to Rickman almost shyly. Rickman took it. A young man, olive-skinned like his informant, with large brown eyes and a gentle expression, anxious and a little sad. It looked like it had been taken in a photo booth.

Rickman looked at him in question.

'This is Arash Taqvai,' the man said, his voice softening for the first time in their conversation. 'We were friends.' He struggled for a moment, trying to find the right words. 'In my country, such friendships are illegal. In my country, the law says that such friends must be killed.' He could not meet Rickman's gaze. 'We were arrested.' He stared at the tabletop ashamed, it seemed, to have to admit to his humiliation at the hands of others. 'We were tortured.' He fiddled with the salt cellar for a moment, then burst out — 'I don't know how they knew — we were so discreet, you see.'

He was silent for some minutes, and Rickman saw that he was struggling to regain control.

Finally, he sniffed, wiped his face with his hand and said, 'That time, they let us go — they had no proof. But Arash and me, we are afraid next time they will kill us. So we came here. Of course we were careful. Nobody knew we were friends. We even registered at different times, different places, so nobody would suspect. But as soon as we had status, we were going to find a flat together.'

He fell silent. Without its natural animation and the nervous tension that seemed habitual in the man, his face showed the lines of pain, old and new.

'You lost touch?' Rickman asked.

'We spoke every day!' the young man responded angrily. 'We cared about each other. Sometimes, we would meet — away from people, where no questions would be asked.

'When Arash got ILR we were so happy, but . . .' He inclined his head.

'He disappeared,' Rickman said.

'Six months ago. I made enquiries — said Arash was my cousin — but I was told Arash did not want to see me. He was well and happy, and he had a new life.' He shook his head. 'I knew this could not be my Arash. When I got status, I tracked him down. I was right. This man was not my Arash.'

He showed Rickman another photograph. 'I took a picture,' he said.

Rickman held the two images side by side. There was a passing resemblance, but the two men were different, there was no question.

'Why are you telling me this? I'm not even on the case anymore.'

'Your woman — she was killed, yes?'

Rickman leaned back in his chair and studied the man opposite. 'Think we have a common bond, do you?' he asked, his voice hard.

The man met his gaze, his eyes shining with tears. 'I think you know what it is to lose somebody you love.' He hesitated, as if concerned that he had spoken too freely already, then he braced himself and added with bitter passion, 'Arash should be avenged.'

And by association, so should Grace. Rickman closed his eyes, trying to force the image of Grace, dead, from his mind. For a fleeting moment he saw her half-smile as she offered to write him a sick note. *God! if he had accepted, she would still be alive today.*

He clenched his fist, digging his nails into his palms. When he felt safe to speak, he said, 'May I keep this?' He held up the picture of Arash. The man nodded. And Rickman added, 'How will I get it back to you?'

He shrugged. 'I have copies.'

It was worth a try. 'You said copies? You have others?'

'All the same,' the man said.

Not one, but many, as if the sheer volume of images could remake his lost lover. Rickman slipped the two photographs into his notebook: Arash and the impostor who had stolen his identity.

'I'll need a name,' he said. 'Someone at the top.'

The younger man smiled. It looked like something he did infrequently. 'These people are like ghosts,' he said. 'You don't see them unless they come for you.'

'No,' Rickman said. 'They're people. Flesh and blood. And they will bleed if you cut them.'

The young man's nervous agitation returned. 'I . . .' He raised his shoulders in a gesture of resignation and apology. 'I wish I could help. But I'm not a brave man, Mr Rickman.'

Rickman didn't look away. 'You came here, today. That was an act of bravery.' The man licked his lips and looked out of the steamy café window. The day had dawned, grey, uncompromising. The sea and sky welded into a solid sheet, the only colour was the pink and gold of the shingle which stretched thirty or more yards before it shelved suddenly down to the sea.

Rickman saw, in the man's anxious, restless searching of the landscape, an echo of the boy Minky, when they had asked him about the night of his brother's accident. He had the same look of a trapped animal, desperate to escape.

'Just give me a name,' Rickman said.

The man pressed his lips together and shook his head wordlessly, as if frightened that if he spoke, he might give something away.

'Okay. What if *I* say a name?' Rickman asked. Another headshake. 'Lex Jordan?' he persisted. 'Is that who you're afraid of?'

CHAPTER THIRTY-NINE

When DCI Hinchcliffe arrived at the early morning briefing he was greeted by the combined scents of freshly ground coffee and warm, yeasty Danish pastries. A group of officers crowded around one of the desks and an electronic version of 'Happy Birthday' played at high speed.

Hinchcliffe cleared his throat and the officers dispersed, smiling, leaving an embarrassed DC Hart surrounded by birthday cards and with a half-eaten pastry in her hand.

'It's a bit of a landmark birthday, sir,' she said, blushing.

'Big three-oh,' somebody contributed.

'Many happy returns,' Hinchcliffe said, moving swiftly to his usual spot by the whiteboard.

Foster reached across from the other side of her desk and took a pastry from the box. 'It's downhill all the way from here.' His voice was still weak, though less hoarse, and the bruising on his neck had become a mottled black and purple.

Hart flashed him a smile. 'You should know, Sarge.'

Foster tapped his chest with his fist, indicating that he was wounded by the remark, but he ate the pastry cheerfully enough, washing it down with hot coffee.

Hinchcliffe called the meeting to order and the team settled down. Most of the officers had to stand — with sixty-plus on the team there was barely enough room for them when they were split into rotating shifts; all together, the room was filled to over-capacity. Hinchcliffe made a note to explore other possibilities: a church hall, maybe, or a pub function room.

'First off,' he said. 'I'd like to hear from the night team. What sort of response have we had to the TV appeal?'

A young, sandy-haired man stood up. 'Over two hundred calls, so far,' he said. 'A few names put forward. People are keen to help. We've had sightings of Natalja from all over the city: Aigburth, Everton, Sefton Park, all the way down to the Albert Dock.'

'Wherever she is, Natalja Sremać has vital information. Victim or villain, she knows something — and I want to know what that is. Now, you heard the numbers — two hundred calls,' Hinchcliffe repeated. 'Two hundred new actions. The HOLMES team are prioritising the work, so if you're not already working on something, see the Action Manager after this briefing.'

He made eye contact with Mayle who had been sitting quietly near the front of the room. 'Tony Mayle is a crime scene coordinator with the Scientific Support Unit,' he said for the benefit of the newly drafted officers. 'I've invited him here to review the forensic evidence so far.'

* * *

Mayle stood. He had worked with a lot of the men and women in the room over the years — both as a serving officer, and in his new role as a crime scene coordinator. Most would have heard a version of the events of the previous day: how DI Rickman had been put in the awful position of seeing the woman he loved, ready to be bagged and transported to the mortuary. They would also have heard about Rickman's visit to Jordan's house. Mayle had enough experience in the job to know that some of them would blame him for what had happened. It didn't trouble him, but he knew that Hinchcliffe was using this opportunity to show that he had faith in the Scientific Support Unit, and to give Mayle the chance to regain the team's confidence.

'We got a couple of good prints from the latent lifts on Doctor Chandler's skin,' he said. 'We ran it through NAFIS, but we couldn't get a match.'

'How hard did you try?' There were rumblings of agreement with the disgruntled questioner. Since its inception, the National Automated Fingerprint Identification Service had made fingerprint matching and identification incredibly easy and fast, but it did have weaknesses, the most important being false negatives.

'We ran it three times,' Mayle said. This was standard procedure. 'Then we rescanned and did it all over again, three times each at local, regional and national levels. It's a good lift — but the killer isn't in the system. When you find the man the prints belong to — it almost certainly is a man, judging by the size of the thumb print — we'll give you a match.'

They didn't like it, but they had to accept it. It wasn't his intention to send them away disgruntled with the Scientific Support Unit: it might make them sloppy in preserving and reporting possible forensic evidence — so he was pleased to be able to give them something more positive.

'We're still waiting on the DNA results from Doctor Chandler's murder scene,' he said. 'But we do have some good news on one of the arson victims. The lab at Chorley has produced a fairly complete profile. It matches a sample in the DNA database.'

A rustle of paper indicated the interest of the team as forty or more turned pages in their notebooks and began writing. This was more like it. Until now, the only name they had was Sophia's. But put that with another and another and a pattern might just emerge, then they could exert pressure on the people most likely to have answers to their questions.

'His name is Zarif Mahmood,' Mayle said, pausing to spell the name. 'He's an Iranian asylum seeker. Entered the country December two-thousand-two.'

'What's his form?' Hinchcliffe asked.

'D and D, begging. Nothing major league.'

'Where was he arrested?' Hart asked.

'Dover.'

'What's he doing in Liverpool?'

'Could be he was dispersed here,' Hinchcliffe suggested. 'Or he might have gone walkabout without the Asylum Support Service knowing — we need to find out which.'

'Did he have family here?' Hart asked. 'We could maybe get something out of them.'

'Good idea. Get on to Immigration. Get them to check his background. Meanwhile, I'll ask local TV and radio to give his name out.'

'That won't be much good if he's supposed to be living in Dover,' Foster said.

'No, it won't. So as soon as we have a photo, we'll try to get it on national news. Somebody must know these men. Somebody must care what happened to them.'

As they spilled into the glittering November sunshine — the idealists and the ambitious, the fresh-faced newcomers and the craggy old hands, the soft-hearted and the cynics — all had one goal in mind: to find Grace Chandler's killer and bring him to justice.

This single-minded resolve was for DI Rickman's sake; out of respect for him and sympathy with his loss. But it was also for themselves: why work to put away the villains, the thieves and the muggers, the violent men of the city, if they couldn't keep safe those they held most dear?

* * *

Foster interviewed Grace's colleagues at the hospital during the morning, continuing through lunch, and he would have gone on through the afternoon to the evening if he hadn't received a phone call that brought him back to base.

He pulled into the high-walled car park at Edge Hill Police Station at just after two p.m. Ten minutes later,

Rickman's car swept through the steel gates and slid into place beside him. Rickman got out stiff-legged and sick-looking. He was unshaven and red-eyed; his skin so grey with tiredness that the scars on his face stood out as silver lines.

'Bloody hell, Boss,' Foster said. 'You look like shit.'

Rickman smiled thinly. 'Thanks for that, Lee.'

Realisation dawned on Foster and he said, 'You've never gone and done the round trip in one go? If you were a lorry driver, I'd have to book you.'

'If I was a lorry driver, Grace would probably be alive today.'

Foster winced at this and Rickman said, 'Sorry, Lee. Jeez — I don't know what's wrong with me.' He took a moment to gather himself together, saying, 'I hope you don't mind me dragging you off enquiries. I thought you'd want to hear what I got from our mystery caller.' He glanced up at the security cameras. 'And I wasn't sure they'd let me in after yesterday's . . .' He seemed lost for words. 'After yesterday,' he corrected himself.

'Bloody hell, Boss, most of us were right with you on that one.'

They walked to the rear entrance and Rickman keyed in the pass number to open the security door. 'Any developments?' he asked.

Foster's lip curled into a sneer. 'Jordan's being a very good boy — for now. But he's on twenty-four-hour surveillance. We'll get him.'

It didn't seem like that was particularly good news to the DI, but Foster for once managed to refrain from voicing his immediate thoughts and instead maintained a discreet silence.

Hinchcliffe was in his office, jacket off, absorbed in paperwork. He looked up, a frown etching the lines in his forehead a couple of millimetres deeper. 'Jeff?' he said. His tone was not welcoming.

'I got a call last night,' Rickman began.

'You are off this case. You cannot be seen investigating or discussing the investigation: any perceived interference from you could undermine the impartiality of this enquiry.'

'Sir—'

'Didn't you hear what I just said?' Hinchcliffe demanded, his voice raised angrily. 'What the hell are you thinking, traipsing into my office—'

Rickman took out his notebook and retrieved the two photographs. Handling them carefully by the edges, he placed them side by side on Hinchcliffe's desk.

'What's this?' he asked.

'Possible victim,' Rickman said, pointing to the photograph of Arash, 'And the man who bought his identity.'

Hinchcliffe moved to pick them up and Rickman stopped him with a sharp, 'Sir!'

Hinchcliffe's hand hovered over the pictures.

'They need fingerprinting,' Rickman explained.

Hinchcliffe sat back in his chair.

'The man who gave me those wouldn't tell me his name,' Rickman said. He handed Foster a slip of paper from his notebook. 'His car's ID number — probably false — the guy was paranoid.'

'With cause?' Hinchcliffe asked, interested, now.

'Could be.'

They listened closely as he gave them the full story, omitting only his question at the end of the meeting.

'So they take the identity of somebody who has a legitimate claim to remain in the UK and — then what? Are we talking about multiple killings, Jeff?' Hinchcliffe asked.

'I don't think even he knew for sure — but he believes his friend is dead.'

'Who would have access to information on the processing of claims? Who would know that an asylum seeker had been given refugee status?'

'Other asylum seekers?' Rickman suggested.

'Refugee charities,' Foster said.

'Or solicitors.' This came from Hinchcliffe.

Rickman's brain was not working at full capacity, so it took him a moment to respond to this. 'Grace told me—' Even speaking her name was difficult: his chest clenched, his throat tightened, and he felt as if the breath had been knocked out of him. He leaned against the DCI's desk, waiting for the spasm to pass.

'Jeff—' Hinchcliffe half stood, concern registering in the lines on his face, but Rickman waved him away, and after a couple of moments he continued.

'Some London solicitors have a rep for rounding up asylum seekers straight off the boat. They pick them up from Immigration and take them in minibuses to London, where they're coerced into signing up with Shyster, Conman and Fleece for the duration of their claim.'

'Lucrative, I should think,' Hinchcliffe said. 'Ethically dubious, certainly, but not, to my knowledge, illegal.'

'A lot of claimants who hook up with these crooks are refused asylum,' Rickman explained. 'The Refugee Council assumes it's because their legal representation is lazy and incompetent — but what if they *are* processing claims correctly, getting successful outcomes and just not passing on the good news to their clients?'

Hinchcliffe ran a hand over his face, then fell into a repetitive movement, tracing a line from cheekbone to jaw as he thought.

'We know that Miss Habib had been granted refugee status,' Rickman said. When Hinchcliffe still did not reply, he burst out, 'Well at least *look* at the others — what harm can it do?'

Hinchcliffe reached for his telephone and punched in a number. 'Have Immigration come back with the information we requested, yet?' he asked.

There was a pause as he listened to the answer, then he said, 'While you're at it, check with the Exhibits Officer, get hold of any paperwork on the first victim.'

'And Jokubas,' Rickman said.

Hinchcliffe glanced at him frowning, but he added, 'And Jokubas Petrauskas.' He hung up. 'Miss Habib's solicitor . . .' He thumbed through the top few sheets on his desk, till he found the name. 'Mr Capstick — has been less than efficient,' he told them.

'You're thinking that he's disguising obstruction as incompetence?' Rickman asked.

Hinchcliffe tilted his head. 'Could be.'

DC Hart came to the door minutes later. Seeing Rickman, an assortment of emotions flitted across her face, but she quickly took hold of herself and spoke with professional detachment. 'Zarif Mahmood, Miss Habib and Jokubas Petrauskas,' she said, placing three document wallets on the table. Foster took the top file.

'Mahmood was dispersed to York a week ago,' Hart said. 'He had no reason to be in Liverpool. In fact, they're supposed to report back to their emergency accommodation every night, so technically, he was breaking the terms of his asylum claim, just being here.'

Hinchcliffe took one of the files and handed the other to DC Hart. 'Check Miss Habib's file,' he said. 'We're looking for the law firm representing her.'

Hart seemed disconcerted that the DI should be so pointedly excluded, but Rickman seemed to take it with equanimity, so she reached past him, accepting the offered file. 'Bolland, Capstick and Blaine.' Hart and Foster spoke simultaneously.

Hinchcliffe tapped the edge of the folder he held in his hands. 'Ditto,' he said. He riffled through the papers. 'The signature on this letter is a . . . Mr Capstick.'

Foster and Hart both checked. Nodded. The same.

'It seems we have a connection.' It was deliberately understated, but all three of them were grinning. Rickman alone looked grim.

'Find out if Jokubas had a decision impending,' Hinchcliffe said. 'And we have a new name for you to check.'

Hart glanced at DI Rickman as Hinchcliffe wrote Arash Taqvai's name on a slip of paper. Rickman kept his hands in his pockets and his head down. Hinchcliffe handed her the note. 'From an anonymous source,' he said. 'Is that clear, DC Hart?'

She stood up straighter, lifting her chin. 'As crystal, sir.'

'We need to know his refugee status, whereabouts and—'

'The name of his legal representative,' Hart said. 'Yes, sir.'

Hinchcliffe waited for her to close the door, then turned to Rickman. 'Go home,' he said. 'Let us get on with the job.' He looked into Rickman's eyes, and he softened a little. 'You look terrible, Jeff. Get some sleep — I promise you we're working flat out to get a result.'

On the way back to the car park, Rickman had to run the gauntlet of sympathetic looks and muttered condolences. Foster followed him down the back stairs. A couple of used car tyres had appeared in the recess under the final flight since morning, the unclaimed bike that had been in residence for two years leaned against them.

'Keep your mobic switched on, eh?' Foster suggested.

Rickman nodded. They walked on. Rickman stumbled, then recovered. Foster was reluctant to leave him. He held the car door open as Rickman fumbled the key into the ignition.

'I could organise a lift home,' he said.

'And start a rumour that I was drunk and incapable? No thanks, Lee.'

Foster nodded. 'Okay, Boss. But do yourself a favour — if you can't sleep, get rat-arsed. It's the next best thing.'

'Speaking from experience, Lee?' Rickman asked.

For a moment Foster considered opening up, just to let Rickman know he wasn't alone. Then he smiled and said, 'Nah — hidden shallows, me.' He slammed the door and tapped on the roof of the car, leaving Rickman to his slow and painful journey home.

CHAPTER FORTY

She looked so helpless, lying there. Natalja saw herself as if from a little distance and felt a remote compassion.

Her limbs wouldn't move. She investigated the sensation with cool detachment, making exploratory attempts to lift a hand or twitch a toe. Heavy? No, she didn't feel heavy — she felt light. Insubstantial. She would not dare to try and stand, even if she could move, convinced that her legs would disintegrate.

Boneless. That's it. For a moment she relaxed, having solved the conundrum. She couldn't move because she was boneless, stranded on the bedsheets like a jellyfish beached on a sandy shore.

Dying?

Am I dying?

'*Is she?*' she asked the outer self that looked in from outside, from slightly above. *Is this what death feels like?*

She examined the feeling with detached interest. *No: this does not feel like death.*

I am dreaming. One of those strange dreams in which you try to move and cannot. Sleep paralysis. I think that's what they call it. Then she remembered: a burning sensation, a spark lighting on bare skin. *No, not a spark. A needle. That's it — a needle containing a clear liquid.* It felt hot in her veins, then a rush — like cold air on her face; like cold water running through her veins; exhilarating, like pure energy. After that –

Nothing.

She tried to rationalise. Looking at the woman on the bed she thought, *That is Natalja. Natalja is me.* She grieved for the woman on the bed. For if this was not death, then death was close, prowling at the edges of her vision. She felt it as a dark shadow.

Light danced on the ceiling, distracting her from morbid thoughts. She listened in wonder to the patterns it made: bells and laughter, joyous, ever-changing, soft as wind-chimes. Synaesthesia — the integration of the senses — she experienced light as sound, sound as colour.

Someone is in the room. She heard the colours of his coming. His footsteps were grey and gold, the colours billowed like filmy gauze. He stopped and the coloured light fell like gossamer, covering her face, moulding to the contours of her body.

This is my shroud.

He was formless, for the colours of his hair, his clothing, the sound of his movements diffracted, interfering one with another: she saw the sounds and heard the colours and neither made sense, but she didn't care — because it was *beautiful*. With this acceptance she saw it *did* make sense, since light and colour are the same, wavelengths of energy, bursting as electrical impulses in the cortex of the brain.

She reached out to touch the colour of sound: not with her hand — she watched from outside her physical self. Instead, she reached out with her mind, rapt and enraptured in the swirling mass of crimson-scarlet-ultramarine-violet-mauve-pink — and pale, pale blue, so delicate, so beautiful she thought her heart would break.

And then she was lifted. For one exhilarating moment she was weightless. She could not feel his hands on her, raising her up, propping her head on a pillow, covering her lightly with a sheet.

He left swiftly — a brilliant red-silver lightning bolt shattered the air, catching his attention and she knew at some basic level that it was a telephone ringing. It stopped.

—And she was lulled again by the silky sound of light playing on the ceiling. Windsong, birdsong, water. She plunged in.

* * *

Grace was outside her flat door.

The damn front door — left open again.

'Natalja — please, let me in.'

But she didn't want to talk. She was ashamed and afraid. She crouched on the stairs, her arms folded tightly across her chest, praying that Grace would go away, but Grace, as always, was persistent.

'Natalja, I know you're there. Please — we have to talk.'

It was Sunday, and her neighbour hated noise. 'Grace, for pity's sake—'

'I'm not leaving.' She rapped on the door with her knuckles. 'Jokubas is dead, Natalja. What are you waiting for? Somebody else to die?'

'Go *away*, Grace!' she shouted.

From behind Grace she heard a man's voice, harsh from too much cigarette-smoking. 'Hey — "From Russia With Love" — how's about keepin' it down a bit? England's a Christian country you know — and Sunday's a day of rest.'

Grace began to apologise and Natalja had to act. She ran down the remaining stairs to her flat door and pushed it open, dragging Grace inside before she could say another apologetic word. Then she stepped out into the communal hall.

Her neighbour was standing at his own front door, unshaven and scruffy. She drew herself up to her full height. 'You don't look ready for church, *comrade*.'

He fell back a step, surprised: she had never before responded to his insults. Emboldened, she went on, 'And

303

Jesus said, "Love thy neighbour as thyself."' She was losing it; her voice was rising and she was becoming so angry she knew she might say something she later regretted, but she didn't care — in fact she began to revel in the feeling. 'But you know what?' she said, shouting in his miserable face. 'I think maybe even Jesus would see it differently if he had a fat, stupid SCOUSER for a neighbour!'

She slammed her flat door with a resounding bang and turned to see Grace staring at her with a mixture of shock and admiration on her face.

'That was . . . unexpected,' she said.

Natalja shrugged. 'What's the expression? It's been simmering in the pot for a while.'

'Close enough,' Grace said.

They went up to her flat. Natalja's neighbour left minutes later. Natalja was making tea; she heard the first slam. Pause. Nothing. 'He left the front door open,' she said. 'Again.'

'Shall I. . . .?' Grace asked, thumbing over her shoulder.

'Doesn't matter. He'll probably be back in five minutes and leave it open. Again.' She handed Grace a mug of tea and they took it through to the sitting-room at the back of the house.

'I like what you've done with this room,' Grace said.

Natalja tingled with pleasure. This was the largest room in the flat and her favourite. She had recently redecorated in cream, beige and red. She had shelving built into one alcove for her books. A TV and sound system occupied the space near the window. A long, low coffee table stood in front of the sofa.

'What about Alf Garnett downstairs?' Grace asked.

'Excuse me?'

'Mr "From Russia With Love"?'

Natalja snorted. 'He's a racist bigot, but he's also greedy. He's a taxi driver — he's all the time working — afternoons, evenings, holidays,' She gave a half-smile. 'So you see he's really good neighbour.'

Grace laughed.

For a few unrealistic minutes Natalja thought she might drink her tea and leave, but when Grace got hold of something she didn't let go. Natalja knew the moment had come when Grace set down her mug on the table, placing it carefully in the centre of the little glass coaster. People did such things to put off something unpleasant: something they knew they must say.

'What were you arguing about with Jokubas?' Grace asked again.

'I don't know what you mean.'

Grace looked at her with a sadness that was more wounding than sharp words or anger. 'When he left my consulting room, he said, "Ask her why she's here, when it's safe to go back to the Balkan State." Something like that.'

Natalja shrugged, unable, for the moment, to meet Grace's eye. 'He's crazy.'

'He *was*, maybe. But I think he was more desperate and afraid. Why did he seek you out?'

'Like I said.'

'He was crazy.' Grace spoke softly. 'Well I simply don't believe that, Natalja. Shall I tell you why?'

'No.' She looked at Grace now. She didn't want to hear any theories, and she didn't want to lose Grace's good opinion. 'Please, Grace. Don't. Nothing good can come of this. Nothing.'

Grace sighed. 'I spoke to Hilary Yarrop, yesterday.'

Natalja's heart leapt. It raced in her chest, battering against her ribs, but she had learned to hide her feelings and when she spoke, her voice was calm.

'She is a colleague of yours?' she asked.

'In a manner of speaking. You don't remember her?'

Natalja raised her eyebrows, giving a helpless shrug. Another skill she had learned was not to give in too easily — that people often pretend to know more than they really do.

'She wrote your reference,' Grace said.

'It was a long time ago . . .' She made herself look at Grace with curiosity, a hint of puzzlement.

'She was your caseworker when you came into the country, Natalja. People don't forget their caseworker.' She was irritated, frustrated, and this time Natalja did not reply.

But she felt her friend's eyes on her and knew what was coming.

After a little while, Grace sighed again. 'Miss Yarrop was surprised when I suggested that you were young — perhaps vulnerable. So I checked the records — you're wearing well for a woman of thirty-seven.'

Natalja said, 'I can't talk about this. Please believe, I'm trying to protect you.'

Grace shook her head, smiling. 'It's odd,' she said, 'how the people I care about most seem to think they can protect me by lying to me.'

'You should leave now,' Natalja said.

Grace stood. 'All right,' she said. 'I'll go. But I'm going straight to Jeff to tell him everything I know—'

Natalja jumped to her feet, blocking the door. 'Wait,' she said.

Grace stood before her. And waited. It was a powerful thing, her ability to wait — to create a silence. Natalja had seen it so many times in surgery: the patient who didn't know how to articulate their trouble, and Grace, waiting for them to find the words. Paying them the courtesy of time to think. Refugees were rarely afforded such consideration. She herself had been rushed through the system, words supplied for her when she couldn't articulate. Spaces left blank on her immigration questionnaire glared out from the form, an accusation and an affirmation that she had no plausible answer.

She had waited months to tell her story, but the immigration officer was a busy man — when she tried to explain, he grew impatient. He wanted to fill in the blanks on the form, not to know what had happened to her. Details got in the way. Time was of the essence. She was told to be quick, be succinct. Give just enough detail and tell what happened in chronological order. They didn't appreciate that there was no logic — temporal or otherwise — in the hatred that made the soldiers kill her parents. Her story was not so easily told that it would fit in the blank spaces on a form. A refugee's story, she wanted to tell him, is full of anguish and shame. It takes time to tell — time and patience, and respectful silence on the listener's part. Grace knew this, without having to be told.

But this was a different kind of silence, the type where secrets became unbearable burdens, the unspoken words a betrayal. This idea came as a shock: how could *not* speaking be a betrayal? But when she thought about it, she knew that it was quite simple — her silence was a betrayal of the trust Grace had put in her over all the years they had worked together and been friends.

'I'll explain,' she said. 'But please, sit down.' When Grace was seated, she resumed her place in the armchair.

'Before I tell you the rest, you must understand how frightened I was.' It seemed strange that it was suddenly so important to her that Grace should understand, when she had spent so much time — so much energy — building the lie.

'Knin, where I was born, was mainly Serb. It was a small town, everybody together, working, going to school — everything. When the war started, my parents got very scared. They told me I shouldn't go out — even to school. I told them we have to live. We can't stay home all the time, shaking when someone knocks on the door.' She smiled wearily. 'I was young. I thought I knew everything.' She took a deep breath and exhaled, 'I got so *mad* at them!'

For a while she didn't speak, and Grace did that wonderful thing again, of waiting, knowing that if she was patient, the story would be told. After a time, Natalja said, 'One night, we had an argument. Same as usual. I wanted to go out, they wanted me to stay home. Papa sent me to my room. I could hear them in the kitchen talking, talking. Endless talk about the war. Maybe it would be over soon. Should we go visit my uncle in Zadar? Yes — no — maybe. They couldn't make up their minds. My father said the UN would stop the killing, but my mother said we should get out, to hell with the UN.

'I couldn't stand it anymore. I put on my black jeans and a black shirt and I sneaked out. I thought I was James Bond!' She laughed at her own naivety, but had to stop, because it was so close to becoming tears, and she needed to finish the story.

'I went to my friend's house. We played records, goofed around, painting our nails and doing each other's hair. Girl stuff. Innocent. Foolish.

'I was so *frightened* going home. I kept thinking what if Papa checked my room? But then I told myself I didn't care. I was young and life seemed mysterious and exciting — like anything might happen. Knin is an industrial town — it's not pretty at all — but it was warm that night, and there was a scent in the air: roses, I think, or maybe honeysuckle, and to me it seemed like the most wonderful place on earth.

'It was only a short walk home, and I kept to the shadows. Our front door was open. I knew something was wrong and I started to run, but something told me not to go straight in. Instead, I went to the back of the house. I knew every inch of our garden and I could be quiet as a cat. I peeped around the corner of the house.

'There was a man. A soldier. Standing at the back door and peeing in the garden. He turned towards me and, my God! I nearly screamed. I covered my mouth with my hands and I closed my eyes and I prayed to God. I though my heart would burst it was beating so fast. Then another man called him, and he went back inside.' She shook her head. Her throat had suddenly narrowed and she couldn't talk.

Grace said, 'Your parents were in the house?'

Natalja nodded. 'I heard sobbing. Then a man's voice, begging. I didn't recognise it at first, but then I realised it was Papa.' She swallowed. 'Do you know what it is like to hear your father begging for mercy?'

In Grace's face she saw concern and sympathy.

'Never had I heard him sound so afraid. And . . .' She withdrew her gaze and stared instead at her hands which were red from the constant kneading and twisting she had subjected them to during the last few minutes.

'I ran away.' Her voice was scarcely more than a whisper, so ashamed was she of her own cowardice. 'I ran away and left Mama and Papa to the soldiers.'

Grace leaned forward and took her hand. 'Natalja, it wasn't your fault. If you had stayed, they would have killed you, too.'

Natalja sighed. 'I know. But a part of me still says I should have tried to help. I wanted to scream! I wanted to break everything . . .' She smiled sadly. 'But what could I do that was so terrible? I was only a little girl. The soldiers had big guns and tanks and bombs. What could I break that the soldiers hadn't already broken?'

'What did you do?' Grace asked.

'I went to my friend's house. They took me in for the night. They were too frightened to take me to my home. But they tried to telephone. The line was dead. When we went there the next day, Mama and Papa were gone. There was blood everywhere, and everything was smashed. But they were gone.'

She stared into the pale afternoon sunlight, remembering the awful sight of blood — on the kitchen table, on the floors, even up the walls. They had emptied the fridge of food and drink and crushed it into a mess of blood and milk and soda-pops.

'Did your friends take care of you?'

Natalja smiled. 'They didn't dare. They helped me to pack a few things and advised me to find my uncle in Zadar. He was my mother's brother. But he and my mother didn't get on well and anyway, it was easier to travel east, then.

'That was when I met Mirko. He's a Serb.' She saw a question on Grace's face. Natalja was a Serb: it was most likely that she would be helped by a fellow Serb. But Grace had heard in Natalja's voice her surprise that Andrić had put himself at risk for her. She pushed on before Grace could speak:

'I got to England and they gave me Exceptional leave to remain in nineteen ninety-two.'

Grace frowned. The dates were wrong. Natalja had told her that she escaped Knin in ninety-six.

'They let me stay in London,' Natalja went on. 'I went to school for one year, then got a job doing translation work for one of the refugee charities. But in 1996, the Croatian Army recaptured Knin. When my case was reviewed, I was told it was safe for me to return home.'

'How could they think that?' Grace asked. 'It would be more dangerous than ever for a Serb, going back to Knin under Croatian control. I mean –wouldn't it?'

'For a Serb, yes,' Natalja said carefully.

Grace's eyes widened as she realised the truth. 'You're not a Serb.'

'I'm Croatian.'

Grace frowned, 'I don't . . . I'm sorry, Natalja, I don't—'

'That's not my name.'

Grace stared at her for — *God*, it seemed like it was for such a *long* time.

'I never really knew you, did I?' Grace said, a dawning sense of shock on her face. 'I don't even know your real name.'

'You know me more than anyone else,' she said quietly. The murder of her parents had opened a void within her. A great empty space that had swallowed her life whole, destroying any trust she once had in the goodness of others. But she trusted Grace, as much as she could ever trust anyone.

Grace stared out of the window for a few moments. Natalja saw a shard of lemon-coloured light, reflected from one of the windows of the houses opposite, shimmering on the tears standing in Grace's eyes. She would have done anything to take away that hurt. When, at last, Grace spoke, it seemed to cost her a huge effort.

'So you invented this new person.'

'I had nobody in Knin, nothing to go back to: no family, no friends, no home. What was I supposed to do? They wanted to send me back to a place of horror. I — I *couldn't* go back.'

'What did you do?'

Grace was waiting for an answer. Always so *good* at waiting. Natalja decided she would not lie. 'I knew somebody — he had got refugee status for others. I went to him. He arranged everything, gave me a new identity — as a Serb. You have a word for that, I think — irony? It would be safe for me, as a Croatian, to return, but not for a Serb. So, the people who killed my parents would save me from going back. He got the documents, he made sure I was granted indefinite leave to remain. I got the I!' She was crying. 'That's what we called it, "The I".' She laughed through her tears and wiped her nose. 'I had to change my name, but so what? It's not like I had any family who might try to find me.'

This hit her harder than she expected, and she began to sob. Grace tried to comfort her but Natalja shook her off, angry with herself for breaking down, and angry with Grace for not understanding what she was trying to tell her.

'Don't you see?' she demanded. 'I'm responsible.'

'For what?' Grace asked, exasperated and confused. Then she blinked, and Natalja thought that perhaps she was beginning to make the connections.

'They choose people who are afraid and helpless,' she said. 'People who are alone. If they don't have family, there's nobody to complain when they're gone.'

'Are you saying that people were—?' Grace hesitated, but Natalja set her face grim and hard against her horror and outrage. Grace wanted the story — well it didn't have any nice endings or heroic acts. This was her reality. This was what she had lived with for nearly eight years. 'My God, Natalja. Are you saying that people were killed?'

'I don't know!' Natalja burst out. 'I told myself it was a business transaction — that he had paid for the documents. Truly, I didn't care how he did it — I just wanted . . .' she shrugged helplessly. 'I wanted to stay. But when those people were killed . . .' She gave up on explanations. There were no explanations for what she had done. There could never be. She wept silently.

Grace sat stunned for a few moments, then she said, 'Jokubas asked for your help, didn't he? When he came to the clinic — he asked for help?'

Natalja nodded, wiping tears from her face with the heel of her hand. 'Jokubas Petrauskas wanted me to arrange for him to meet with the man who helped me. I couldn't do it.' She laughed, almost choked by bitterness and tears. 'What a hypocrite! I did it for myself, but I couldn't put others at risk for Jokubas's sake. Not me! I didn't want it on my conscience.'

CHAPTER FORTY-ONE

'Arash Taqvai,' DC Hart said, handing the fax sheet to DCI Hinchcliffe with a flourish. 'Granted indefinite leave to remain, June this year. Last known address Bristol. Solicitor—'

'Bolland, Capstick and Blaine,' Hinchcliffe read from the sheet.

Hart looked disappointed that he had stolen her punch-line. To make up for it, he asked, 'What about the other two?'

She smiled a big, beaming *I'm about to make your day* smile. 'Mahmood was known as a pamphleteer against the regime in Iran. He went into hiding after a friend was murdered — turned up here. He had a strong case, according to the person I spoke to at Immigration. Jokubas was about to be given ILR: the decision was in the pipeline — he would have heard within the week.'

'So why,' Hinchcliffe mused, 'Did Mr Capstick, of Bolland, Capstick and Blaine tell him to prepare for repatriation?'

'Dunno, Boss.'

He smiled. 'Let's find out, shall we?'

'I'll ask Avon and Somerset Police to check out Taqvai's last known address as well, shall I?' she asked.

'Not yet.' Hinchcliffe didn't want anyone alerted to the fact that they were under scrutiny. 'Let's start with the sharks and work down to the tiddlers. It might be wise to ask Dover CID to move in as fast and as quietly as they can. I want Capstick's computer, backup disks, paperwork — the lot.'

'Might be a touch difficult keeping it quiet when a pan-technicon pulls up outside the firm's offices for that lot,' Hart said.

'I take your point, but if the other two partners are legit, they might help us with the details.'

Hart's expression was pained. Lawyers — why would they want to help the police?

'No,' Hinchcliffe said, 'I know. Let's forget I said that.'

* * *

Hinchcliffe was determined that surveillance on Jordan would be effective: no part-time surveillance; no black holes during shift-changes — he wanted Jordan watched twenty-four/seven. This meant allocating three teams of two in cars of different makes and colours on a rotation. They were in constant radio contact with each other and base. All six officers — four men and two women on the day shift — wore tiny radio mikes attached to their lapels or threaded through the sleeves of their coats.

Will Garvey was team leader, and passenger in the lead car with Brian McKenzie driving. They had just switched places with the number two car to take lead position. Garvey pressed the radio console button on the dashboard and confirmed, 'Garvey with eyeball on suspect vehicle.' He spoke without looking at the console; anyone glancing into the car would think he was engaged in a desultory conversation with the driver.

'Target heading towards Speke on Aigburth Road,' he said.

They passed the drab terraces of Dingle, the faux-Tudor library at the top of Lark Lane, the TA barracks. On the brow of the hill at Aigburth Vale they glimpsed the tops of trees, bereft of all but a few coppery leaves.

Garvey exchanged a glance with McKenzie as Jordan stopped at a set of lights just turning amber. Garvey was in his early forties. He was five-ten, average build and had medium-brown hair. His average looks gave him just the right level of anonymity for surveillance work.

'He's up to something,' McKenzie said. 'He hasn't gone above thirty all the way.'

''Course he's up to something,' Garvey agreed. 'Lex Jordan's never been outside the city centre in ten years.' He thought about it for a moment. 'Except for the odd spell in HMP Walton.'

The central reservation became grassy and tree-lined, the houses larger and more well-spaced; horse-chestnuts, stripped of their leaves weeks before the maples and limes, gave the day a wintry feel. The sun was low behind them, dazzling the rear view, which made their job easier: if Jordan did happen to check his mirror, he wouldn't see much more than a silhouette, some two or three cars distant.

'Where the hell is he going?' McKenzie asked. Liverpool Cricket Club had just slipped by on the opposite side of the road.

'Looks like we're about to find out.' Garvey pressed the button again. 'Target turning right right right, then immediate left left left into Cressington Park.'

McKenzie eased off the accelerator, allowing number three car to take pole position.

'Only one way in and one way out, so no hurry,' Garvey advised.

They held well back, one car waiting on Aigburth Road, pointing towards the city. Leaving a gap of a few seconds, the lead car followed Jordan's Mercedes through the sandstone gates of Cressington Park. Eighties architect designs stood side by side with Victorian mansions and Edwardian villas. This was where the real money lived.

Jordan pulled up outside one of the older properties: detached, three storeys, large garden, big gateposts. The lead car drove further on and parked in front of a four-wheel drive, taking advantage of its height for cover.

McKenzie backed into the driveway of a big Swiss-style lodge. Garvey glanced at him. 'Let's hope the owners are off earning the money to keep up the mortgage, eh?'

McKenzie shrugged. 'It's a good spot.'

Garvey had to agree: they could see the front door and upper windows of the target house without difficulty, while the wall of the lodge kept them pretty well hidden. He picked up his binoculars and trained them on the gateposts.

'"Rivendell",' he read. 'A bit New Age, isn't it?'

'Well they must've sold their souls to the great god Mammon,' McKenzie said, eyeing the house jealously.

'They all do in the end,' Garvey sighed.

McKenzie gave him a sharp look. Difficult to know when Garvey was joking.

Garvey radioed through the house name and number for an ID check and launched into a dreamy reminiscence. Too young to be a real hippie, he had nevertheless read *The Lord of the Rings* three times at the age of fourteen.

'You wouldn't think it to look at me now,' he said, 'But I had the lot: long hair, the flares, trench coat — What the hell is he playing at?'

Jordan had just taken a police battering ram out of the boot of his car.

'Cheeky git!' McKenzie exclaimed. 'Where'd he rob that from?'

A big black man got out of the passenger seat and they walked together to the front door of 'Rivendell', like two Uruk-hai spoiling for a fight.

Garvey grabbed the camera from the back seat and zapped off a few incriminating shots. The door flew open with the second blow of the enforcer, shattering the authentic stained-glass door lights and sending splinters of wood into the vestibule. The two men walked inside, unhurried, businesslike.

The driver's door of the lead car opened and Garvey sent a hasty instruction. 'Wait-wait-wait,' he said. Simultaneously his mobile phone chirruped in his pocket. 'Radio for instructions,' he told McKenzie, as he pressed the 'answer' button on his phone.

'Hold your positions,' the voice said. 'Do not. Repeat do NOT intervene.'

'Who is this?' Garvey demanded, ducking to check the buildings around them. A curtain twitched and a bulky figure appeared briefly, ghost-like in the shadows of an upstairs window of one of the houses opposite.

'Bloody hell,' he said.

The device in his ear blasted out: Hinchcliffe talking too loud, too close to the mike. Garvey adjusted the tiny earpiece and said. 'Sir?'

'Do not intervene,' he said. 'There is a covert oppo in progress on that address.'

'There's a B&E in progress an' all, Boss,' Garvey protested.

A window smashed and a laptop computer crashed to the block-paved driveway of Rivendell, followed smartly by a TV and a CD player.

'Make that B&E with criminal damage,' he said.

'That,' Hinchcliffe enunciated carefully, 'is the Petherington house.'

'Ah,' Garvey said.

Mr and Mrs Petherington were Cricket Club members and Rotarians. He was an investment banker, she a senior tax inspector. Their sons, Darcy and Stephen, had used their considerable social and educational opportunities to set up a small business as drug dealers.

'What d'you mean, "Ah"?' McKenzie asked.

Garvey told his team to stand down: their brief was surveillance of Jordan only, then he turned to McKenzie. 'Stephen and Darcy Petherington started out supplying club drugs: E, cocaine, Ketamine, a few dots of LSD. But they're ambitious. Word on the street is ever since Hinchcliffe closed down the Kensington mob they've been sniffing around the vacated drugs turf, growing the business in new directions, you might say.'

'Ah . . .' McKenzie echoed. It was well recognised that Hinchcliffe's previous case had created a gaping hole in the market and Darcy and Stephen — economics drop-outs, both — had studied long enough in their respective universities to learn that gaps in markets meant business opportunities.

So they listened to the sound of breaking furniture and when Jordan emerged, glassy-eyed and sweating, they got two more shots on camera and then slid back into formation, rotating the lead car every couple of miles, until they arrived back at Jordan's house.

CHAPTER FORTY-TWO

Foster was teamed with DC Hart to interview the solicitor, Gregory Capstick. The custody sergeant rang through at just before ten p.m.; Mr Capstick had been brought into the custody suite by two Dover CID officers. Foster went to see Hinchcliffe: the DCI wanted to be around when Capstick was interviewed.

He was sipping coffee from a mug stamped with the Merseyside Constabulary badge. It smelled like the real thing; it seemed that whoever had brought in the coffee maker for Hart's birthday treat had decided to leave it in the Incident Room for the time being, and everyone, from civilian staff to Hinchcliffe was enjoying it while it lasted.

'He's here?' Hinchcliffe said.

'In with his brief. We're ready to go as soon as they finish.'

Hinchcliffe took another sip of coffee. 'As long as they don't drag it out.' Although the relevant period had not begun until Capstick was logged in at Edge Hill Police Station, they had only twenty-four hours in which to question the man, and eight hours of that would be taken up with sleep time.

'Any repercussions from the incident at Cressington Park?' he asked.

Foster shrugged. 'A couple of complaints from neighbours, but Darcy and Stephen say it was a brotherly row that got out of hand.'

'Well,' Hinchcliffe said. 'That's something. We need to know if Jordan is Capstick's contact in the north. He's ambitious — the attack on the Petherington lads shows that. Let's see how far his ambition extends.'

'Right, Boss,' Foster said.

'Let me know when you're ready to begin.' A thought occurred to him. 'What about the documentation?'

'Capstick's files are travelling by police van,' Foster said. 'They've just passed the Burtonwood services — should be here in half an hour.'

'Has Hart been fully briefed?'

'Yes, Boss. One bit of bad news, though. Ashtar Taqvai's immigration file's been messed with — his photo's gone walkies.'

Hinchcliffe exhaled. His finger went to the deep crease from his cheekbone to his jaw. 'Go with what you've got. See if you can rattle him.'

The Incident Room was busier than usual. Some officers had opted to work late, knowing they had a better chance of getting a result at the start of the investigation, rather than in the weeks of slog that would follow, and Grace's murder felt like starting over. Some were there out of a superstitious notion that something would happen, that the pivotal piece of information would come on their watch. Their single, narrow aim was to find Grace's murderer. Rightly or wrongly, everything else — the other killings, the eleven-year-old boy dying in hospital of burns — took second place.

DC Reid had been given the task of checking all the numbers Grace had called from her mobile in the hours prior to her death. He had worked through several of her colleagues, all of whom were shocked and distressed by her death, but none of whom could provide any clue as to why Doctor Chandler might have called on Natalja Sremać, other than a friendly visit, on her day off.

The number he had just been given to check out was different, however. For one thing, it had been found scrawled in thick marker pen on the back of a letter they had found in Doctor Chandler's handbag. For another, the sheet of paper it was written on was a letter of reference for Natalja dated nineteen ninety-seven.

Reid made an effort to moderate his accent a little for the sake of clarity. 'Hilary Yarrop?' he said.

'Who is this?'

'Merseyside Police, Miss Yarrop,' Reid said. 'I'm sorry it's so late, but this is urgent.'

'Oh, God . . .' She sounded faint. 'Is it Natalja?'

'Natalja who?' Reid asked, careful not to give her anything — they were trying to glean information, not give it out to the public.

'Sremać,' she said. 'Doctor Chandler said she was worried about her. Has something happened to her?'

'She's disappeared, ma'am.'

'God forgive me,' she murmured. 'I'm afraid I wasn't very helpful.'

Reid said a few soothing words and asked if she had any information that could help their investigation. 'Anything Doctor Chandler said — anything out of the ordinary.'

Miss Yarrop seemed flustered. 'I'm sorry, I don't think I—' She stopped abruptly, and for a moment, Reid thought he had lost the connection.

'Ma'am,' he said. 'Miss Yarrop?'

'I've just remembered that Doctor Chandler's description of Natalja didn't tally with my recollection of her.'

'No?'

'Not at all.'

Reid was positively tingling with anticipation.

'You see, Doctor Chandler said Natalja was young and vulnerable. But Natalja Sremać was in her late-twenties when she came to the UK. She must be over thirty-five by now.'

'You're sure of this?' Reid asked.

'Of course I'm sure!' A sharp edge of authority had crept into the woman's voice. 'We worked together. I wrote her reference when she applied to Liverpool to do interpreting work. I know Natalja Sremać.'

'That's really helpful, madam,' Reid said, wanting to take some of the heat out of the exchange. 'Do you have anything we could use for comparison — a photograph, perhaps?'

'Well,' she said, suddenly doubtful. 'I'm not sure how far back our records go . . .'

Reid prepared himself for a disappointment.

'But, I think I have a snapshot from a social function Natalja came to — would that do?'

He held his breath. 'Could you maybe fax us a copy of the photograph?' he asked.

'I can do better than that — I'll scan it and send it as an email attachment, shall I?'

DC Reid stood over the computer for fifteen minutes, waiting for the *bleep* indicating new mail. When it came, the result was decisive. The woman they knew as Natalja Sremać was not the woman Miss Yarrop had worked with in the nineteen-nineties.

* * *

Foster accepted the hand-over of Capstick himself. Two officers had been sent with the solicitor, DCs Davies and Mackay. Davies was the older of the two, and he had the jaded look of a man disappointed with life. Mackay was still in his twenties. At barely five-foot-seven tall he would have failed the height requirements of more restrictive days.

Foster introduced himself. Mackay's grip was strong, and he maintained eye contact. He was stocky, but the extra weight he carried was all muscle, and Foster was in no doubt that this was a man who could handle himself in a ruck.

They signed Capstick in and he was taken to a cell by a civilian custody attendant.

'Coffee?' Foster asked.

'I'll check us in at the hotel,' Davies said. 'Don't know about you, but I'm bloody knackered.'

Mackay said, 'Go ahead. I'll take care of the formalities.'

Is that what they call them in Dover? Foster thought.

They went to the canteen and Mackay chose a beef sandwich from the vending machine, then Foster suggested they go to the Major Incident Room. 'We can get a proper coffee there,' he said. 'The stuff out of the machine is shite.'

The ghost of a smile flitted across Mackay's face.

Foster poured him a coffee and they sat at a free desk. Few people were in so late, only the late shift and one or two career-builders out to make a good impression.

'What can you tell me?' Talking was still painful and he swallowed, wincing a little.

Mackay glanced at the bruises on Foster's neck and then up to his face again, but he made no comment. He took a swig of coffee. 'He's got no previous — well you wouldn't expect a practising solicitor to have, would you?'

He burred his 'r's a bit, but Foster didn't make the mistake of labelling this steel tank of a man a country bumpkin. Mackay's hair was no more than a brownish fuzz and he had a stud in one ear. 'I checked with one of the refugee charities — off the record. Mr Capstick is considered to be a bit of a wanker.'

'Exploiter or incompetent?' Foster asked.

'Waste of space — couldn't dispute his way out of a paper bag.'

Foster raised his eyebrows.

'Since you've had him brought so far,' Mackay said, 'I assume you think otherwise.'

'We've received information that someone down your neck of the woods is selling documentation granting leave to remain.'

Mackay whistled. 'Your immigrant murders?'

'Could be. Any ideas?'

Mackay pulled at the earlobe with the stud in it. 'Mostly they keep it in the family. Chinese traffic Chinese, Kosovans take on the Eastern Europeans — mostly women for the sex trade, but a few men.'

'The only definite IDs we've got so far are an Afghan girl, an Iranian and a Lithuanian.' Foster said. Arash Taqvai wasn't on their patch, and they didn't know for sure he was dead, or if he was linked with their investigation.

'That's a pretty diverse bunch you've got there,' Mackay said. 'It's not my field, but I can make a few enquiries.'

'You might want to mention Lex Jordan — see if that jogs any memories,' Foster suggested. 'But we don't want to cause a stampede or anything.'

'Don't worry,' Mackay said. 'I'll be discreet.'

* * *

The solicitor's interview began at eleven-twenty p.m. DC Hart arrived slightly late and a little flustered, just in time for DS Foster to make the introductions and identification of voices for the tape.

Mr Capstick proved difficult. He was a smooth-skinned man with grey-blue eyes and a plummy voice which seemed at odds with his short stature and youthful looks. He wore a good suit, and although his tie had been confiscated during processing, he was every bit as smartly dressed as his legal advisor sitting beside him.

The room had been recently redecorated, and twenty years of nicotine and stale cigarette smoke had been expunged from the sound-boarding and the carpets. The walls were a pale green, the ceiling magnolia, and the interview table was sanded and so newly varnished that it still felt slightly waxy to the touch.

Foster presented him with several letters. Each was bagged and labelled. 'Can you identify the signature at the bottom of these letters, Mr Capstick?'

Capstick glanced at them. 'Those are my signatures,' he said.

Foster identified the exhibits by classification code. 'These letters are addressed to Mr Arash Taqvai, Miss Sophia Habib, Mr Zarif Mahmood and Mr Jokubas Petrauskas.'

'*Yes*,' he said, clearly irritated by the bureaucratic style of the interview.

'Every one of these letters outlines a refusal of application for asylum,' Foster said.

'Does it, really?'

'Yes.'

Capstick smirked. 'You don't strike me as being the type to worry about rejected asylum claims, Sergeant.'

Foster gritted his teeth. Sometimes the sarcastic interviewees got under his skin more than the violent ones. 'Could you confirm, sir, for the tapes, that the letters state a refusal of asylum?'

Capstick sighed, leaned forward, sifting through the letters in their plastic sleeves. His hands were small and rather square-fingered. 'Yes,' he said, 'Each of the people mentioned was refused asylum.'

'No, sir,' Foster said. 'They weren't.' He waited for a reaction, but got none, apart from a rather imperious raising of the eyebrow.

'Immigration has confirmed that Miss Habib, Mr Petrauskas and Mr Taqvai had all been granted indefinite leave to remain — granting them the right to stay in the UK indefinitely. Mr Mahmood's decision hadn't been finalised, but the immigration authorities say — and I'm quoting here — they were "minded to look favourably on his claim".'

Capstick rolled his eyes. 'If you had dealt with the immigration authorities for as many years as I have, Sergeant, you would know that they're constantly cocking up: wrong people refused, wrong people given status, letters sent to the wrong address — or not at all.' He paused to give a shudder. 'It's a bloody shambles.'

'A shambles you took advantage of,' Hart said.

Capstick's brief began to object, but Foster ignored him, placing two photographs side by side in front of the solicitor. 'Ashtar Taqvai is missing. This man' — he tapped the photograph of the impostor — 'is posing as Mr Taqvai.'

He saw a flash of anxiety, gone in an instant. Mr Capstick examined the photographs closely. When he finally looked up at the two officers, it was with amused contempt. 'This,' he said, flicking the picture of Ashtar back across the table, 'looks like something taken in a photo booth. And this—' He glanced again at Foster. 'Was this taken in the street? By whom?' When Foster didn't answer, he said, 'You really will have to do better than this, Sergeant.'

Undeterred, Foster placed the NASS photograph of the arson victim on the table. 'Zarif Mahmood,' he said. 'Dead — killed in a fire. Suspicious circumstances.' Next to it, he placed a picture of Jokubas. 'Jokubas Petrasukas. Stabbed with a long-bladed knife.' Next, Sophia. 'Miss Habib. She was seventeen or eighteen years old.' He put down the last two photographs, one, a picture of a smiling woman at a party. 'Natalja Sremać,' he said, then, pointing to the second photograph, 'This woman assumed her identity in nineteen ninety-seven. She was abducted from her flat yesterday. I don't know about you, but I keep asking myself, where is the real Natalja Sremać?'

Mr Capstick might be a solicitor, but he was not experienced in interviews during criminal investigations. He crossed one leg over the other and sat back in his chair, trying to assume a haughty disdain, but on the brink of pulling it off, his tongue shot out, nervously licking his lower lip.

'The picture of the real Miss Sremać was taken by a work colleague,' Hart said. 'We asked her to check a few administrative details. And here's an interesting coincidence — guess who was Miss Sremać's solicitor, all those years ago.' She gave him the chance to answer, but Capstick seemed momentarily speechless. 'It was you, Mr Capstick.'

Foster's scalp tingled. Hart had come up with a corker and he had to bite his lip to prevent himself from smiling.

'People have been known to disappear rather than be sent home,' Capstick said.

Hart leaned and dropped her voice confidentially. 'We know,' she said. 'We're detectives.'

'But that doesn't explain the people who've taken their places, using their documents, stealing their identities,' Foster put in.

'Supposition,' Capstick said. His face was red, and he was sweating, but his voice was calm — he would sound good on the tapes.

'We've got photographic evidence for Miss Sremać,' Foster said. 'And a reliable eyewitness. We've got Mr Mahmood's DNA on file. Say we trace him through the National Asylum Support Service, ask the bloke with his ID number and documents for a DNA sample. Think we'd get a match?'

Capstick's eyes flitted from Foster to Hart, then abruptly, he turned and whispered something to his brief.

'Mr Capstick is consulting with his solicitor,' Foster said, hoping to break their concentration. It worked. Capstick glanced back at him, rather wild-eyed. His brief requested a break and the interview was suspended at twelve-fifteen a.m.

'That'll be it for the night, won't it?' Hart asked, depressed at the lack of progress.

'We'd've had to stop soon, anyhow,' Foster said. 'When did you get that stuff on Capstick being Natalja's solicitor?'

'DC Reid gave it to me just before I came in,' she said. 'I tried to catch you, but—'

'Don't apologise,' Foster said. 'It was worth it for the look on his face. In *fact*, I'd bloody kiss you, only you'd turn around and deck me.'

She smiled, walking away. 'Maybe I would, maybe I wouldn't.'

CHAPTER FORTY-THREE

Things were different at night — more intense. There was less traffic for one thing; all the sounds and smells that were masked by the daytime noise and traffic fumes became sharper after dark. While colour faded to blacks and muddy browns, the shouts of lads out on the ale gained power, as though the night air had a special quality. Jordan loved the echo of footsteps on a cold pavement, the rush of rainwater in the gutters: secret sounds.

Sometimes, he would watch the girls queuing for the night clubs, bright and brittle as butterflies, shivering in the cold. When he was a kid his mum thought classy scents came out of a bottle with pictures of flowers on the front, but these girls wore expensive stuff — designer stuff — which followed them like a thin trail of mist on a winter night.

Nights like this, after the rain had gone, and the air was clear, he would leave the car at home and walk his beat, checking on his girls, keeping them in line. It was easier to take them by surprise when they were expecting to see the Merc; he liked to see the shock register — eyes wide, then a panicky attempt to make it right. He caught two of them lounging in a doorway, sharing a ciggie out of the cold. They did that little flutter thing — that, *omigod, he's here*, kind of thing — then put on a bit of a show for his benefit, slipping their coats off their shoulders and trotting down the steps to flash their tits at the motorists.

He split them up, moving one of them to the pub on the corner of Pilgrim Street and Mount Street. It was kicking-out time, which was good for picking up the odd foot passenger. Before he left, he gave her a little reminder that she was supposed to be working, not wasting good shagging-time — nothing too heavy, just a bit of a shove and a slap.

He had rules, and the girls knew to stick to them or face the consequences. On Huskisson Street, he saw Leah get into a Daimler. She threw him a nervous smile, as if to say, *See, Lex — I'm earning.* He was gonna have to deliver a personal message on that score. Which struck him as kind of funny, 'cos all she ever thought about, lately, was how to score her next rock of crack. A tab of E was all right, a few M&Ms to keep them buzzing through the night, even a bit of weed to mellow them out after a hard shift getting down and dirty with the clients. But no heroin and no crack — those were the rules: needle tracks were unsightly and crack just messed you up so bad you lost all self respect. For a girl on crack, the only way was down. Worse than that, it ate into his profit margins.

The Anglican cathedral loomed ahead, lit by pinkish spotlights, forming a dramatic backdrop for the girls parading the railings on the far side of the road, some of them his, a few freelance. He counted his girls: four, all looking for business like they actually enjoyed the work. They'd been warned: maybe one of the tarts he'd split up had phoned ahead on her mobie — one of the down sides of the technological revolution.

The scrub on the other side of the railings had been cleared over the past year; now a three-foot-wide shelf of concrete gave to a sheer drop down to the cathedral cemetery and gardens. The wind blew in bursts, sending clouds jostling over the face of the moon; and below, in the dark of the gardens, he heard the constant mutter of starlings roosting in the trees.

He was pleased how the Petherington thing had turned out. If the opposition was that easy every time, he'd make his first million before he was thirty. Sure, the immigration scam had threatened to turn sour, but he thought he had it back on track — now he had taught Rickman to stay out of his business. A hard lesson, the only kind people remembered. No question, though, his rep had suffered when Rickman had barged into his house, fingering his things. His new girl had been shaping up nicely till then, but she was different after Rickman's visit — hard-faced, sullen. Like he was gonna make her sell her arse on the block for twenty-five quid a poke or something, when in fact he had plans for her: escort service, the first of a string of high-class hookers — hotel business, executives. The new millennium had brought an optimism to the city: ambitious redevelopment projects, new money, inner city regeneration, and Jordan didn't intend to miss out. Suddenly angry, he thought, *Well, fuck her*. If she didn't want a taste of the high life, he'd kick her skanky arse out onto the street, soon as he got home. He felt immediately more cheerful having made the decision.

He crossed the street enjoying the sudden flurry of activity as the girls tried to impress him. He spoke to each of them, took money from a couple, meaning to check on Desiree before he went home. He stopped, lifting his nose to the air: cigarette smoke. None of the girls had a ciggie lit. He looked around. Punter waiting in the shadows for him to leave, maybe? On a cold night, you could smell it a hundred yards away. No sign. He shrugged, gave the last girl a friendly grope, then walked towards the junction.

A rat appeared, just ahead of him, squeezing its fat body between the rails, big and mean and slick with sewer filth. One of the girls saw it and let out a piercing scream, then swore, cursing the night and the city and the way of living that brought her in contact with rats and other slime. The creature seemed indifferent to the noise; it moved slowly, sniffing the ground like a dog following a trail, finally crossing the road and disappearing into a storm-drain.

Jordan couldn't see Desiree. The Smart Bus timetable board obscured his view, but she should be moving. If she was moving, he'd see her. Was she sitting down again? How many times had he said — you want to make the big bucks, you gotta work your pitch. For him, that meant walking the beat, checking his girls, seeing his pushers weren't skimming too much off — sampling the goods they should be selling. For his girls, it meant moving the merchandise, showing it to good advantage — which you could not do sitting on your saggy arse in a friggin bus shelter.

Jordan was talking himself into something here. He felt another spurt of righteous anger. Desiree had been ripe for a good slapping ever since Rickman stopped him the last time. Jordan didn't much like to think about that night, even though he had made it clear who was boss through tragic little Sophia. Sometimes he thought Desiree looked at him like she was waiting her moment. Which was why he'd put her on the block in the first place: how's a man supposed to sleep with a woman in his bed who looks at him like that?

As he got closer, he was pretty sure the bus stop was empty. Maybe she was working, after all. He felt almost disappointed. A small noise — a gasp or an exclamation — from the garden below. The cemetery was one of Desiree's favourite shagging-shops. 'Well waddaya know?' he muttered. The lazy cow was actually working. He was about to cross the road and head for home when something stopped him.

Someone had tipped off the bizzies about him and Sophia. His solicitor had got nowhere with the disclosure on that one: which meant Crimestoppers. Had to be one of the girls — had to be. Now who was it who'd clucked over Sophia like a big fat mother hen? And who was it looked at him like he was butcher's meat waiting to be carved?

'Bitch,' he snarled.

It happened from time to time: the anger in him welled, surging and boiling like porridge in a pan, and he just had to do something about it. He knew not to fight it, in fact he enjoyed feeling it build. Desiree was gonna get a kicking. A smile spread like a virus across his face: ugly and deadly.

He kept close to the railing. The cathedral security guard was talking into his radio, looking through some papers on his desk. Jordan scooted left, following the curve of the wall. The moon had come out and he could see the sweep of the footpath, heading steeply down. Maybe ten yards on, a black arch — the entrance to the tunnel through the sandstone escarpment. Either side, tight against the tunnel walls, one after another, all the way down to the garden, a procession of headstones.

She'd better be humping some stiff when he found her — and he didn't mean the cemetery kind. He'd warned her more than once about smoking on the job. 'You're not Olivia Newton John, strutting her stuff in *Grease*,' he told her. 'You're just a scouse scrubber, well past her prime.'

He walked softly, knowing how the tunnel magnified sound — he didn't want her creeping out the gate down the far end of the gardens. Groping his way along the last section of tunnel, he traced the curves of the gravestones, gritty and cold under his fingertips, finding cherubs and rose-buds plump at the corners of the stones, and once, an angel in prayer. Sea-captains and captains of industry, buried in their eightieth year, their wives dead in childbirth aged twenty-five. You must've had to be someone special to get buried in a cathedral churchyard, Jordan thought. But not so special they wouldn't dig you up and stick your stone against a wall for drunks to piss on.

At the end of the tunnel, the remains of the cemetery proper: some old crosses, a few headstones, ivy climbing up the walls to the left, every alcove bricked up against the scallies and druggies and whores. To the right, a sandstone cliff and the solid bulk of the cathedral itself.

The cathedral was lit by spotlights at night. High above the city it would be visible fifteen miles west, across the Mersey. But here, in the deep well of the gardens, with clouds flitting across the moon, it was dark. The kind of dark that made objects grainy, like a bad snapshot on a cheap camera:

he could see the pale domed Huskisson mausoleum, and the Georgian terraces on the street thirty feet above him, but little else.

He stood still near the mouth of the tunnel, waiting for the glow of a cigarette or a reflection of light from her face or clothes. A faint rustle: he glanced right and left, his eyes darting, trying to catch a movement at the edge of his vision. Nothing. Then she was there, standing on the path ten yards from him — *shining* on the path in front of him — pale and shimmering in a sudden shaft of moonlight. Mud on her shoes, right up to the tops of her killer stilettos. Her coat was open and the moonlight gave her skin a bluish cast, so she looked half-dead before he had even laid a finger on her. She had seen him, and she looked terrified.

An owl screeched. *Fuck's sake!* Jordan thought. An *owl?* He took a step towards her.

Behind him, a tall figure moved from the shadow of a carved Masonic pedestal. He raised his hand, waited for Jordan to turn and see him, then fired, twice. Head and heart.

Jordan fell.

Footsteps from above. Shouts. The starlings rose up like a cloud, wheeling and turning above them in a confusion of screams and whistles.

The man grabbed Desiree, turning and pushing her. 'That way,' he said.

A second man joined him on the path. 'Police?' he asked. The first man nodded.

On the street above them, the two officers who had been strolling arm-in-arm like a regular couple broke cover and ran, requesting backup, for the cathedral concourse. The security guard came out of the low brick building on the far side of the concourse.

'Police!' the woman yelled. 'Get inside. Stay low.'

Two cars screeched out of Huskisson Street into Hope Street in quick succession, took a wide left fishtailing into Upper Duke Street, then roared up to the front of the cathedral.

The first officers on the scene stared at the black maw of the tunnel.

'Any other way out of there?' the female officer shouted.

The security guard slid open the window of his kiosk. 'Top end,' he said, gesturing. 'St James's Street.'

The first car U-turned and screamed back the way it had come.

ARV and paramedics requested, the male officer looked at his partner. 'We're going to lose them,' he said.

* * *

Desiree ran along the path. Shadows chased her as clouds scudded over the face of the moon. She blundered on in the dark, crying, hearing approaching police sirens, knowing for sure that she would be caught.

The men either side of her fell away. She felt, rather than saw this, as an absence of comforting male bulk flanking her. She heard them heading up the slopes to the right. At this end of the gardens the cliff was not so steep, and a thin layer of soil supported spindly trees and shrubs. She ran on, heading for the tall iron gates and freedom. As she rounded the bend a car skidded around the corner into the car park.

Cursing, Desiree tried to change direction, only succeeding in falling backwards into the mud. She flung herself to the right, scrambling up the slope, grabbing at trees roots and ivy, gouging the mud itself for purchase. She felt dirt under her fingernails, and between her toes — her stilettos were ruined.

A buzz of noise became a clatter and a police helicopter shot over the top of the cathedral, swooping into the garden, its spotlight sharpening the edges of the shadows. Desiree glanced behind.

On the cliff, one of the men was caught in the glare. The police issued a warning. Desiree's former escort fired a shot and the chopper veered away. The man lost his balance and slipped back down the slope, sending stones skittering ahead of him.

Armed police in flak jackets swarmed onto the top of the escarpment on the eastern side of the gardens and the broad track of concrete on the high wall opposite, shining lights into the black sump below them. The path zig-zagged down on a thirty-degree slope to the cemetery; they crawled down it, using the mounds of ivy and the sandstone edging for cover. Shapes loomed and vanished, creating a crazy illusion of movement as torchlights and spotlights flashed on gravestones and crosses and winter-bare branches.

More police covered the north gates, their instructions to hold their position: the cemetery path would be too exposed if the gunmen managed to get some height on them — besides which, the risk of cross-fire from their own was very real in the confusion of light and noise.

One of the gunmen fired a shot. The sound bounced back off the sandstone cliff and the westerly wall, its report deafening. The gunpowder flash betrayed his position. He was on the ground, using the headstones at the edge of the path for cover. The chopper, hovering at a safer distance, issued a second warning. From their vantage point on the cliff-top, one of the officers aimed and fired. The bullet zipped past the gunman's head, chipping a draped stone urn and hurling a six-inch splinter into a tree-trunk nearby. The shape vanished, then reappeared running for the mausoleum. The chopper caught him in its spotlight. He spun round, raising his arm to shoot.

Three shots, almost simultaneous. The man fell. A flicker of brightness at the north end of the gardens caused a flurry of activity in that direction. The chopper turned about, scouring the graves. The source was located and ten torch beams trained on it. It shivered, ducked, launching itself into the air, then the startled owl skimmed silently down into the darker reaches of the cemetery.

With attention drawn from the south end, and blinded by the dazzle, nobody noticed a shadow flit across the cathedral wall.

* * *

Desiree crouched in a foetal ball, weeping soundlessly. She heard a soft footfall and tensed. A hand covered her mouth and she tried to scream, but he was strong. She felt his breath on her skin, panting. He held her until his breathing slowed and became more even, all the time soothing her and stroking her hair.

At last, he let her go and she turned to face him. He was muddy and sweating, but he seemed exhilarated, too.

'Follow me,' he whispered.

CHAPTER FORTY-FOUR

'Where's Rickman?' Hinchcliffe strode up the staircase to the second floor, pulling off his overcoat. It was half-past midnight and he had been home for precisely one hour and thirty-five minutes when the call came that Jordan had been shot.

'What?' Foster kept pace with Hinchcliffe as people flattened themselves against walls or ducked through doorways to avoid the DCI.

'Is he at home?' Hinchcliffe asked. 'Is he walking the streets? Has he been spotted near Jordan? I want to know if we can discount him, Lee.'

''Course you can discount him,' Foster said with more conviction than he felt. 'Anyway, I thought there were two attackers?' he added, glad to have something to justify his faith in Rickman. 'And what about the Petherington lads? They took a pasting from Jordan yesterday. They're after the same turf — what were they doing around half-eleven?'

Hinchcliffe eyed him with brooding speculation. 'Why don't you make it your business to find out?'

'Right,' Foster said, a touch defensively. 'I will, then.'

'And while you're at it, you can check on Rickman.'

* * *

It took him ten minutes to rouse Jeff Rickman. Foster leaned on the bell until he came to the door, confused and sleep-drugged.

'Bloody hell, Lee,' he grumbled. 'D'you know what time it is?'

'Sorry, Boss,' Foster said, searching Rickman's face. 'Didn't mean to drag you out of bed.'

'You didn't.' Rickman was fully dressed, although his clothes were rumpled and creased as if he had been sleeping in them. His brain seemed to engage with an almost visible *click* and he said, 'Has something happened? Have you found Natalja?'

'No — sorry, Boss. No, we haven't found her.'

'So why are you here?'

Foster didn't know how to tell him. finally, he blurted it out. 'Thing is,' he said. 'Jordan's been killed.'

Rickman looked at him for several seconds. 'How?'

'Shot.'

'Not a lingering painful death, then?'

'Head and heart,' Foster told him. 'Dead before he hit the deck.'

'Well, you can't have everything,' Rickman said. 'You'd better come in.'

Foster followed him through to the sitting-room at the back of the house. Rickman seemed unsteady on his feet, perhaps a little drunk — though it may have been exhaustion.

The fireplace was neatly swept and logs laid, ready to be lit, as before, but the room was cold. There were signs of Rickman's emotional turmoil. A whisky bottle lay empty on its side next to the armchair, along with a coffee mug and a plate with a half-eaten round of toast. Newspapers were scattered on the floor, many of them opened at smiling pictures of Grace, below headlines designed to elicit outrage at her death: 'THEY CALLED HER DOCTOR GRACE', 'KILLED FOR CARING', 'DID MERCY DOC KNOW TOO MUCH?' A framed photograph of Grace was propped up on a cushion on the chair, as though he had been holding it when the bell rang.

Rickman shambled to the chair and lifted the photograph, placing it back on the bookshelf and adjusting it fastidiously. 'Where'd it happen?' he asked.

'The cemetery below the Anglican cathedral.' Foster hesitated. 'You been in all night, Boss?'

Rickman turned to him. 'Think I popped him, Lee?' he asked, without rancour.

Foster felt hot and uncomfortable. 'You know I gotta ask, Boss,' he said.

Rickman sighed. 'I know. But like I said, you can't have everything.'

Foster frowned. 'I don't get you.'

'I wish it had been me, but it wasn't,' Rickman explained.

Foster nodded. 'There were two of them,' he said. 'The Armed Response Unit got one.'

'Caught or—'

'Dead,' Foster said. 'The other one got away.'

'ID?'

'None on him. They're doing fingerprint and DNA checks.' He stopped again. He hadn't broached the most difficult subject, yet. 'Jordan had a knife tucked in his trouser belt. There was blood on it. They're doing DNA profiles on that, an' all.'

Rickman looked at him.

'Only—' He was sweating. The room was like an ice box, and yet he was sweating. 'See, Jordan's girlfriend complained that you'd stole a knife from their kitchen.'

Rickman closed his eyes momentarily, smiling a little to himself. 'She said that?' He looked again at Foster. 'She said "stolen"?'

Foster nodded without taking his eyes off the DI.

Rickman got to his feet, taking Foster by surprise. He followed the DI into the hall. Rickman went to his overcoat, which was flung over the stair-rail, and rummaged in the pockets. Foster stood watching him, curious. He gripped

Foster's wrist, and turning his hand palm-up, slapped the knife handle-first into the sergeant's hand. 'She came at me with the knife,' Rickman said. 'I took it away from her. Okay?'

Foster felt a burst of hot anger. 'Look,' he said. 'I've stuck my neck out pretty far for you on this one, Jeff. I think I've got the right to ask a few questions.'

Rickman let go of Foster's wrist, looking stung and a little ashamed. 'I know, Lee,' he mumbled. 'I owe you. I'm sorry.'

Foster said, 'Yeah, well . . .' They made eye contact for the briefest moment, then both looked away.

'How did Jordan get into the gardens?' Rickman asked.

'North end, we think — by Upper Duke Street. He was found near the tunnel through the rock.'

'Didn't security see anything?'

'We're checking the CCTV, but the guard was distracted — says he didn't notice anything out of the ordinary.'

'Have you spoken to Desiree?'

'Desiree?' Foster ran through a mental checklist of the names of the girls he had interviewed in recent weeks. 'There was no Desiree.'

'You must have seen her,' Rickman insisted. 'She works the bus stop near the cathedral concourse.'

'I'm telling you, Boss, there was never anyone in that bus stop when we ran the interviews.' He thought for a moment. 'Desiree — wasn't that the girl you rescued a couple of months back? Jordan's bint?"

'Yes.' He thought about it for a few seconds. 'Look — I know she's still working — I spoke to her a couple of days ago.' He frowned. 'Saturday. It was Saturday.'

And on Sunday, Grace was murdered, Foster thought.

Rickman shook his head, as though he'd had the same thought and couldn't deal with it. Foster's mind went to his last image of Grace, dead, her face covered in a sheet of plastic.

Rickman leaned against the newel and took a few breaths, the same debilitating image in his head, no doubt, and Foster put a hand on his arm.

Rickman pushed him away. 'Give me a moment,' he said.

'Breathe, mate,' Foster said. 'Just breathe.'

'God,' Rickman said between gasps. 'It hurts even to think her name.'

'Desiree,' Rickman said, after a minute. 'Long dark hair, blue eyes. Last time I saw her she was wearing pink six-inch stilettos and a pink coat. She wears a lot of pink.'

Foster began to shake his head, then it hit him. 'Bloody hell! You don't mean Trina Carr?'

'I only know her street name,' Rickman said.

'Trina Carr,' Foster insisted. 'Lived next door to Carrie — sorry, Boss — *Sophia*. Trina's the hooker with the little pink palace — you remember.'

'Oh, shit . . .' Suddenly it all made sense: Desiree's reaction that night at the cathedral when he had pushed her about knowing Sophia, her animosity, her contempt for him. No wonder she blamed him for Sophia's murder. No wonder she gave him a knee to the balls when he told her that Sophia deserved justice.

'Trina is Desiree . . .' He blew air between his lips. He couldn't believe he had been so blind.

'Didn't you recognise her address?'

'I didn't know where she was — I didn't even know her *name,* Lee.'

'Aw Jeez,' Foster said. 'She heard Sophia crying the night she was killed. She must've known what was going down. She let that poor little tart go to her death and she did sweet FA.'

'Men like Jordan give off a whiff of fear like a moth emits pheromone,' Rickman said, thinking of his mother. 'He ruled his girls, his pushers, his hangers-on by fear — they wouldn't dare cross him.'

'It looks like our Trina did, though, doesn't it?' Foster asked. 'D'you reckon she acted as bait?'

Rickman shrugged. 'I don't know. But Jordan must have had some reason to go down into the cemetery.' He thought about it for a moment. 'Check out her flat. Talk to

341

the other girls — see if they've heard from her. Personally, I'd give her a medal for wiping a snot like Jordan off the face of the earth, but she might be in trouble.'

* * *

Mr Capstick, of Bolland, Capstick and Blaine, was less well turned-out than the previous evening. The interview began at 9.33 a.m. He had washed and shaved, but no matter how expensive the wool mix, a suit will crease when slept in. Not that he looked rested, despite eight hours of uninterrupted sleep in his cell. He appeared pale, hollow-eyed, and less youthfully fresh-faced than in the first interview.

'Tell us what you know about Lex Jordan,' Foster said.

'Lex Jordan,' Capstick repeated, screwing his eyes into slits as though the effort of concentration pained him. 'Nope. Can't help you, I'm afraid.'

'That's a shame,' Foster said. 'His mum'll be gutted. Most of Lex's mates are tarts and drug pushers.'

Capstick's greyish eyes roved from Foster's suit to his face as if to make the connection between the man and the cheapness of the cut.

'Yeah,' Hart said, taking his lead. 'It would've been nice for her to have a bit of class at the funeral.'

Foster caught a flash of something hot in Capstick's eye, quickly extinguished. He picked up the thread. 'Someone in an expensive suit who'd lay a bunch of plain white lilies on his grave.'

'I don't know what you're talking about.'

Foster thought he heard a tremor in the solicitor's plummy voice.

''Course you do,' Hart said. 'You're already linked with Miss Habib. Just one among many of your clients who've turned up dead. She stayed with Jordan for a bit after disappearing from the accommodation allocated to her by the National Asylum Support Service.'

'If you have a question, ask it,' Capstick's brief said.

'My question is, would you like to reconsider your statement that you don't know Lex Jordan?' Capstick affected a bored expression. 'In light of the fact that officers are searching your phone records and bank statements as we speak.'

Foster caught Capstick's nervous glance towards his solicitor and asked, 'Would you like to consult with your legal representative?' The little weasel was evidently frightened — of what they might know, and of what might happen to him.

Capstick seemed to get his second wind: he adopted a haughty expression and said, 'Since I've never heard of Lex Jordan, I can hardly feel the need to discuss him with my solicitor.'

A knock at the door. Foster cursed inwardly. He felt an even stronger sense of frustration when he saw Tunstall's hulking figure filling the door frame. Hart raised her eyebrows at him and Foster announced for the tape that she was leaving the room.

'Tunstall, we're in the middle of an interview!' she exclaimed, closing the door behind her.

Tunstall looked down at her, his broad face creased with embarrassment. 'I know — I'm sorry, Naomi, but I thought you'd want this.' He handed her a wad of papers — thirty or more in number, all of them itemised phone bills.

'I've highlighted the calls from Capstick to Jordan,' he said. 'Somebody else is doing Jordan's bills, else I'd've brought them an' all.'

Hart scanned the bills. Call after call was logged from Capstick's office to a Liverpool exchange number. 'That's definitely Lex's number?' she asked, immediately regretting it when she saw Tunstall's hurt expression. 'Sorry,' she said. 'Of course it is. It's just — how the hell did you find them so fast?'

He shrugged, a quick up-and-down movement, like a kid. 'Started with the most recent. Scanned them in as documents and used word search to find the numbers we're interested in.'

She grinned. 'I'd never've pegged you for a computer whiz,' she said.

'Me?' Tunstall exclaimed. 'You must be joking. No — my nephew showed me how.'

'Tunstall,' she said, 'You're a star.'

He beamed at her.

She tapped him on the arm with the sheaf of papers. 'Best not to tell the others about the nephew, though.'

Foster noted her return to the room for the tape. He also sensed her change of mood. She went through the itemised calls sheet by sheet, giving dates, times and length of call. The week of the arson attacks was particularly busy.

'You should've put old Lex on your Friends and Family list, mate,' Foster said, 'you'd've saved a packet.'

Capstick, had given up all pretence of indifference and was fiddling with the cuff of his jacket, ignoring his brief's attempts to gain his attention.

Foster stared at him for a few moments, then realised that this was part of Capstick's power game. 'Sorry, Mr Capstick,' he said. 'I know you like a direct question. Do you still deny knowing Lex Jordan?'

Capstick spoke, but so softly that Foster had to ask him to repeat his answer. He cleared his throat and began again.

'I knew him,' he said. 'But I had nothing to do with the murders. My task was to warn the—' He glanced up quickly, then away, focusing again on his jacket cuff. 'I told the . . . selected individuals that their claim for asylum was about to be turned down. Mostly they faded into the black economy.'

'And the others?' Foster asked.

'It was easier to fix up the girls.'

Hart gave a choked retort, but Foster warned her into silence with a look.

'They fixed them up with jobs in the sex industry.'

'They?'

'People like Jordan. I didn't think for one minute that my clients were coming to any harm.'

'A seventeen-year-old coerced into prostitution. And you call that "no harm"?' Hart glared at the solicitor, but he refused to meet her gaze.

'So these "selected individuals" — your clients — conveniently disappeared. Then what?' Foster asked.

'We have a waiting-list.'

Nobody spoke, and eventually, Capstick broke under the pressure of the silence. 'Since the new regulations came in, it's become far more difficult to enter the country — even more difficult to remain. Legitimate documentation is worth tens of thousands to the right buyer.'

'So you tell your client his or her claim has been refused and then you sell their ID, and with it their refugee status, to the highest bidder.'

Capstick answered with a tight, 'Yes.'

'What was your cut?' Hart asked, her voice hard.

'Fifty percent — mine was a pivotal role,' he added, as if to justify the fee.

Foster heard Capstick's brief take a sharp breath — the admission might prove very useful for the prosecution when it came to court. Foster let it go for the time being, asking, 'Where did the other fifty percent go?'

Capstick positively crouched in his seat. Every time he opened his mouth, he dug himself further in — he knew it, but couldn't find an escape route.

'Mr Capstick?'

'The arrangers,' he said reluctantly. 'People who have contacts in the refugee community as well as abroad.'

'The arrangers.' Hart's voice brimmed with contempt.

Capstick seemed surprised and a little offended by her tone.

'There's mortgage arrangers, party arrangers—' Hart went on.

'And the loan arranger,' Foster cut in, unable to resist. 'But he was on the side of the goodies.'

Hart ignored him. 'Sorry, Mr Capstick. You don't get away with calling murderers "arrangers".'

'I *told* you,' he insisted, his hands balled into fists. 'I didn't know any of — of that sort of thing went on.'

'I think you're lying,' Hart said softly.

'Being as you're so outraged by the way your honest fraud was corrupted in this shocking way, you won't mind giving us the names of the "arrangers",' Foster said.

'No.' Capstick looked horrified. 'No names — I can't give you names.'

'Can't, or won't?' Foster asked, staring at him hard until Capstick dropped his gaze.

'Mr Capstick — you're going away for a very long time. A refusal to help us with our enquiries' — He clicked his tongue — 'Not gonna look good in court.'

A muscle worked in Capstick's jaw. Foster waited while he made up his mind. 'I'll give you the names of my clients, NASS identification numbers — whatever you need.'

Foster sucked in air, blew it out in one long exhalation. 'You're offering us the names of the people you stole identities from? The people who "disappeared"?' He looked at Hart. She was too angry to see the comical side of Capstick's desperation. 'We've already got seven names,' he said. No harm in including Rickman's mystery man. 'Seven murder victims. And that's not including Natalja Sremać, who's probably been abducted, and also a doctor who worked with the refugees. I think we could find the rest easy enough — now we've got all your files.'

'Why d'you think I made all those calls to Jordan?' Capstick demanded.

'I dunno, sir. Why did you?'

'I was trying to stop the killing!'

Foster sat back in his chair and folded his arms, smiling. 'So you did know about the murders.'

Capstick did not reply.

'And Jordan was your half-share partner in crime?'

Capstick's jaw was tight enough to break a tooth.

'We need a name,' Foster said.

'No names,' Capstick repeated, his eyes showing a lot of white.

Hart and Foster exchanged a glance.

'It's gonna look better to the judge,' Foster said, 'if we can say you were cooperative.'

Capstick laughed — a high, cracked, startled shout — and then covered his mouth with one hand. He didn't speak a word after that.

CHAPTER FORTY-FIVE

Jordan's death generated a whole new set of actions. By eight p.m., the Incident Room had built to a frenetic pace. Computer keyboards rustled as officers typed up reports. Phones rang, notes were scribbled and passed across tables. Conversations were held at high decibel levels.

Hinchcliffe went unnoticed to the whiteboard; he was slightly irritated to find that some joker had drawn a gravestone and written 'RIP' under Jordan's photograph.

DC Davies, Mackay's partner, flitted from desk to desk, looking bored and tired. Mackay was on the telephone, making notes. He hung up after a moment or two and walked over to Sergeant Foster.

'A few names to be going on with,' he said. 'Me and Davies can give you a hand if you like — just cast your eye over that lot and see if anything jumps out at you.'

Hinchcliffe chose that moment to give up on dignified silence and called the meeting to order, shouting over the noise and clatter. Seconds later the room was silent: phones switched off, and computers idling, their screensavers bouncing the Merseyside Police Authority logo from edge to edge of their monitors.

He invited DC Hart to set the ball rolling.

'We've got nothing on the guy who was shot,' she said. 'No driver's licence or any other form of ID. His fingerprints aren't on NAFIS, either. The gun is unregistered. A Luger.'

'Contract killing?' Hinchcliffe asked.

She lifted one shoulder. 'It *looked* like a professional hit. Clean, quick. Just their bad luck Jordan was under police surveillance.'

'The Petherington lads have got alibis,' Foster said. 'Backed up by the A&E department at the Royal — they were kept in for observation overnight.'

'Doesn't stop them putting out a contract,' someone remarked.

'Talk to your informants, contacts — find out if there was a contract out on Jordan,' the DCI said. 'And don't overlook the refugees: Jordan was not well-liked, and it's just as likely this was a vigilante killing. Who searched his house?'

DC Garvey stood up. Jordan's death had freed the surveillance team for other duties; most of his team were subdued, even a little depressed, after the events of the previous night, but Garvey had spent a productive few hours with Jordan's new squeeze, and was positively perky, in his usual understated way.

'His girlfriend was quite helpful,' he said. 'She showed us Jordan's safe — knew the number and everything. We found a nice little stash of drugs, a sizeable wad of twenty-pound notes, and a set of NASS payment vouchers and counterfoils belonging to Sophia Habib. Also—' He checked his notebook. 'Zarif Mahmood, Farid Jafarzaden, Shahrokh Davani and Ali Nuri.'

This was greeted with exclamations and murmurs of appreciation.

'Sophia and Zarif, we know,' Hinchcliffe said. 'See what you can get out of NASS or Immigration on the other three. Good work, Garvey — you could well have discovered the names of the unidentified arson victims.' There was a spattering of applause and Garvey, deadpan, took a bow.

'It looks like Jordan was working with Capstick, selecting asylum seekers who were likely to be granted refugee status, stealing their identities and selling them to the highest bidder.' Hinchcliffe had no time for levity: he was too focused on the new information and what it might mean to the investigation. 'Ideas?'

Hart said, 'We could work through Capstick's caseload, look for single, vulnerable people with a good claim . . .' She shrugged — it was a long shot.

'It's a start,' Hinchcliffe said. 'Capstick isn't cooperating,' he told the team. 'We need a financial link with Jordan. Sift through his paperwork, bank accounts, cheques paid, phone bills. He made calls to Jordan, we know that. I want to know if Jordan reciprocated.'

'Do we know what Jordan was doing in the cemetery?' DC Reid asked.

'Drugs meet?' Garvey said.

Foster cleared his throat. 'Could be he was meeting one of his girls, Boss — Desiree,' he went on, before people started to question how he knew this. 'Her pitch is right next to the cathedral concourse.'

'And you found this out when?' Hinchcliffe asked. He had not been swept along by the euphoria of Garvey's find.

'I had a chat with one of the other girls earlier,' Foster said. 'Desiree was never there when we did the trawl-through after Sophia's murder. Early-warning system.' He held up his mobile phone. 'They call each other if there's any police action.'

Hinchcliffe was unmoved.

Foster tried again. 'Desiree worked the top of Upper Duke Street — same as Sophia. And it turns out Desiree is also known as Miss Trina Carr. The girl who had the flat next door to Sophia's.'

'And *none* of you sussed this?' Hinchcliffe demanded.

'The girls were giving us nothing, Boss,' Foster protested. 'It's only since Jordan snuffed it we've started getting a bit of cooperation. And this Desiree was never around when we did a sweep — how were we supposed to make the connection?' Hinchcliffe looked slightly mollified, and Foster forged ahead. 'When I interviewed her, Trina, aka Desiree, made out she hardly knew the dead girl. After I found out they were practically work buddies, I had a word with the security guards at the cathedral.' It was no word of a lie — after he had left Rickman, Foster went straight to the security staff. 'Seems Desiree had a soft spot for Sophia,' he finished.

'Where is she now?' Hinchcliffe asked with icy calm.

'Gone.'

'*Another* abduction?'

'One of the other girls passed her on the stairs about two in the morning. Said she was carrying a suitcase. I went around to check and she'd cleared out. There was mud on the carpet, and Desiree is very particular about hygiene.'

'I want CSIs in there now,' Hinchcliffe said.

Tony Mayle flipped open his mobile phone and made a call.

'Did you get a photograph?' Hinchcliffe asked.

'I picked one up from her flat.' Foster held up a studio shot of Desiree in soft focus.

'I want it circulated to ferry and airports.'

'Already done, Boss,' Foster said.

Hinchcliffe nodded. He would talk again to Foster about this new information, he would also ask about Rickman's whereabouts at the time of the shooting; for now, though, they needed to complete the briefing and start work.

'Tony — you got something from the tape.'

Mayle picked up a CD-ROM case from the desk he was sitting at and slotted the disk into the drive of his laptop as he spoke.

'Jokubas Petrauskas made a triple-nine call from his mobile during the attack that killed him,' he said. 'The emergency services' tape of the call gave us Petrauskas's voice and the operator, but there was something in the background. Petrauskas was distressed, so his voice was in the higher register. We tuned out the higher frequencies and enhanced the lower range. The results are on this disk.'

There was absolute silence as he clicked through the program and started the soundtrack. The first run-through was the unchanged recording: Petrauskas screaming, pleading for help. A thud.

'That's the knife going through the wall,' Mayle said.

Gurgling, then a second, softer impact as Petrauskas fell to the floor.

People looked at each other, baffled. They had heard only the voices of Petrauskas and the operator.

'This is the manipulated track,' Mayle said. He clicked the "play" icon a second time and the sound of the struggle began again. This time, Petrauskas's voice was muffled and indistinct. The background noises seemed to billow with distortion. Just after the first thud, two voices — the first no more than a booming sound at the lower reaches of their hearing, the second louder and more distinct.

'Ne! Nikakvog oružja. Ne na ovom poslu.'

'What is that?' someone asked, voicing the question in everybody's minds.

'Serbo-Croat,' Mayle said. 'He's saying, "No! No guns. Not on this job!"'

'Why no guns?' Hart asked. 'Too much noise?'

Garvey cut across this thought with the question, 'Do we know of any Balkan Mafia types moving in on the local crime scene?'

'I could check with Special Ops,' Foster suggested.

'Mirko Andrić is from that neck of the woods, in't he?' Tunstall said, pronouncing the name *Meeko Andrik.* 'He might be able to help.'

There were groans and a few chuckles at this suggestion.

'Hey, Tunstall—' Foster said. 'I've got an auntie in Widnes. D'you think your mum'd know her?'

'Sir.' There was a collective rustling as the team turned, curious to discover who the stranger was. 'DC Mackay, sir. Dover CID. Did he say Mirko Andrić?'

Hinchcliffe nodded. 'He's been helping with liaison. Do you know him?'

'Not personally, sir, but — ' he glanced at Foster. ' — I think he's on that list, Sarge.'

Foster skimmed through the list of names, trying to decipher Mackay's scrawl. Andrić was on the second sheet. 'No criminal record,' he said, reading from it. 'But suspected involvement in drugs, protection, human trafficking — you name it.'

There was a shocked silence in the room. Suddenly, the words on the tape made sense. 'No guns. Not on *this* job!' A stabbing could be a grudge attack, a robbery, aggravated burglary. But guns meant organised crime: drugs, the sex trade — heavy action.

'Is he being investigated?' Hinchcliffe.

'That's Special Ops, sir. Out of my league,' Mackay apologised.

'I'll find out,' Hinchcliffe said, his lips a thin line. Now they knew for certain that the attacks on the asylum seekers had no racial motive, beyond the sale of their identity as a commodity. And the man they had trusted and relied on for information and advice was, in all likelihood, at its very heart.

CHAPTER FORTY-SIX

Foster called in on Jeff Rickman to keep him up to date with developments. The house was cold, the fire in the sitting-room stacked with unburned logs, as before. He had bought a couple of take-away Indian meals on his way over; he placed the carrier bag in the hearth and asked, 'You turning this into a shrine, or what?'

Rickman swivelled his head to look at the sergeant, his neck a little loose, his gaze a little unfocused.

'Grace made up the fire so's you could light it, get warm, toast your toes on a cold night. Not for you to torture yourself that she's gone.'

Rickman took a step back and kicked a plate under his chair.

'You look bloody awful, Jeff,' Foster said. 'And you don't smell much better. When was the last time you showered and shaved?'

Rickman rubbed a hand over his face. The bristles had softened with length.

'Get off upstairs and sort yourself out,' Foster told him. 'I'll see if you've got anything to eat with that isn't growing fur.' He was surprised — and a little worried — that

Rickman complied: Jeff Rickman would have to be pretty far gone not even to have the strength to argue.

He surveyed the room as Rickman closed the door behind him. Half-eaten food mouldering on plates, scummy coffee mugs with a light crusting forming at the edges. Foster wasn't much for domestic comforts, but his years in the marines had instilled a habit of cleanliness and order.

He boiled water in the kettle and scraped the dishes before scalding them and then stacking them in the dishwasher. It took him a while to find the central-heating controls, tucked in a corner of the scullery off the kitchen. He switched the heating to override, grabbed a couple of clean forks and went back to the sitting-room.

The empty whisky bottle he had seen the previous day now had a companion, almost empty. He dumped both into the bin and emptied the waste into the wheelie-bin outside. He never could look at a wheelie-bin now without seeing the face of the girl he still thought of as Carrie.

* * *

When Rickman padded downstairs in a towelling robe, his hair dripping and his face smoothly shaved, the place was cleared and Foster knelt by the fireplace, blowing gently on the kindling; flames were already beginning to lick the outer contours of the stacked logs.

Rickman stepped forward, a hand outstretched, ready to stop Foster, when he realised the madness of what he was doing: thinking that by keeping the house as Grace had left it he could somehow freeze time and keep her with him.

After they had eaten, Foster told Rickman what the Dover cops knew about Andrić. For long, silent minutes Rickman stared into the fire. 'I should've checked him out,' he said at last, his voice shocked, hollow-sounding.

'You did, Jeff. He wasn't on the NCIS database. All that is known about him is folklore and rumour. He's a slippery bastard — clever.'

'I trusted him,' Rickman said.

'We all did.' Foster explained the background: the tape evidence, Capstick's admissions. 'We think Lex Jordan was creaming off some of the proceeds from the theft of asylum seekers' NASS support vouchers — which a man like Andrić wouldn't take lightly. But we think Jordan was killed for threatening the franchise — Sophia's murder brought attention to the whole scam.'

Rickman frowned. 'So why go ahead with the arson attack — that *was* Andrić's work, wasn't it?'

Foster dipped his head. 'They were drugged and bled, just like Sophia, but the fire wasn't Jordan's doing. He was just a Scouse scally whose reach was bigger than his grasp. I think Andrić used the same MO to put Lex Jordan in the frame. And the way they had their teeth pulled . . .' He shuddered. 'Whoever done that to them didn't want them identified.'

'Their identities wouldn't be worth a bean to Andrić if we knew who they were,' Rickman said, following Foster's line of reasoning. 'Put Jordan in the frame, kill him, leaving the field clear for Andrić to set up a Merseyside branch of his nasty little business.'

'Only he didn't reckon on Tunstall turning his laser-like brain on the problem.'

Rickman had to smile at the notion. 'But why four at once?' he asked. 'Was Andrić using the media's obsession with a racist motive as cover to get rid of unwanted bodies?'

'For all we know, he got a rush order for four Middle Eastern IDs,' Foster said. 'It seems likely the four victims were due to be granted refugee status, anyhow.'

'You need to talk to those boys again,' Rickman said. 'Minky and his gang.'

'We tried. They're even more terrified if anything.'

Rickman understood. Even if Andrić hadn't threatened them, they only had to turn on their radios or TVs to know there had been more killings.

'The good thing is, now we know there's a Yugoslav connection, we've asked Interpol to do a search on the fingerprints on the guy the Armed Response Unit brought down at the cemetery.'

'What about the lifts from—' Rickman couldn't finish.

'The prints we took from Grace?' Foster said.

Rickman nodded, once.

'We've sent them an' all.' They avoided looking at each other for a moment or two.

'Tony Mayle reckons they've got good DNA off some cigarette butts they found at the cemetery. We're hoping it's from the dead thug.'

'Could be local scalls doing a bit of graffiti duty, could even be Desiree — she's a smoker,' Rickman said.

Foster shrugged. 'I know, but we'd be able eliminate one or other of them — that's gotta be worth something.'

'Sure.' It was a hell of a lot more than they'd had even twenty-four hours ago. Then Rickman realised something. 'Interpol can't do DNA cross-matches,' he said, ready to sink back into despair.

'But if they identify the guy at the cemetery by his fingerprints; if they can link him to Andrić . . .'

Rickman followed Foster's line of reasoning. 'At least we'd be able to arrest Andrić on suspicion.' They had a way in. For now, that was enough.

* * *

As Foster left, sometime after midnight, Rickman asked, 'What does the DCI think of your nightly updates?'

Foster shrugged. 'It never came up,' he said.

'I see,' Rickman said. 'Look, Lee . . . I know I've been giving you a hard time, but I want you to know, I appreciate what you're doing.'

Foster had surprised him many times over the past two weeks and he surprised Rickman again. Instead of shrugging off his thanks, embarrassed by the show of emotion, he gripped Rickman's upper arm and looked into his face.

'You shouldn't be doing this alone, Jeff,' he said. 'See your family — talk to them. Let them help you.'

How could he tell Foster that his brother was a stranger — disorientated and half-crazy since his accident; his wife overburdened with worries that she might have lost the man she married as permanently and catastrophically as if his life had ended the night of the crash. How could Rickman add to her burden?

He nodded. 'I'll give it some thought,' he said.

Foster studied him for a few seconds as if trying to read him.

'You've gotta let go of the rage, Jeff. It just wears you out,' he said at last.

It occurred to Rickman that Foster might know what he was talking about; he had never really discussed his years in the marines, but he knew his friend had seen active service.

'I can't let it go, Lee. Not yet,' he said. The rage was the only thing holding him together, binding him so tight that he could pretend he was still in one piece. If he let go of the rage, he thought maybe he would shatter.

He watched Foster drive away, then trudged wearily back indoors. The smell of curry spices pervaded the house, and he took the empty cartons and trays to bin them outside. The night was dark and moonless, the sky richly studded with stars. He stood, staring up at their wistful light for a long time, until the cold seeped into his bones and, lulled by the stillness, the night sounds began to rustle around him.

Slowly, by infinitesimal degrees, he grew calm. The emotional torment of the last few days attenuated from searing heat to a dull ache that throbbed to the beat of his heart. The release of tension brought with it a great weariness; he was ready at last for sleep.

The house was filled with soporific warmth, the stairs seemed an impossible climb, but he made it, step by step, and fell into bed still dressed. He imagined that Grace was in the bathroom, scented candles burning on the windowsill, the radio playing something soft and soothing.

Brief flashes of Grace, her neck at an awkward angle; Grace, her face swathed in plastic. He twitched, groaned, forcing the image from his mind with a picture of Grace, last autumn, raking leaves from the lawn. The fierce concentration on her face had surprised him to laughter, and Grace had rugby-tackled him, tumbling him into a huge mound of red and orange and gold.

His thoughts swam, incoherent, painful, but not so punishing as before, the pain dulled by the memory of a fiercely concentrating Grace . . . Grace outraged by his laughter . . . Grace herself laughing, leaves interlaced with the fine gold threads of her hair. . . And he slept.

A dull thump.

Rickman woke immediately. What had he heard? Grace! Excited, joyful, he swung out of bed. Two steps. It hit him.

Grace is dead.

With the realisation came the image that had haunted him every minute of the hours and days since her death: Grace, her head and hands sealed in plastic bags. He doubled in pain.

Can't breathe. Not enough air.

He staggered to the bathroom and vomited in the toilet bowl. On the floor, beside the sink, a bottle of shampoo, knocked from the window ledge by the gentle stirring of the curtains. He washed his face and returned to the bedroom, but now it was too full of her presence — her make-up cluttering the dressing table, the imprint on the pillow where her head had rested, her dressing-gown flung over a chair. A novel on her dressing table, a bookmark advertising medical products keeping her place. And soft, barely tangible — the scent of her on the bedclothes, and in the very air around him.

He paced the house. With every room a new stab of pain. He couldn't get away from her — didn't want to

— and yet the pain was unbearable. The worst was thinking that she died afraid.

A guilty truth asserted itself. What he truly feared more than anything else was the possibility that Andrić would get away with it. That Grace's death would go unpunished.

CHAPTER FORTY-SEVEN

For two days Rickman remained inside the house, staying clear of the windows. The press came and went like gulls following a trawler: stir up the mud and there they were, picking over the offal for some tasty morsel. Jordan's death was the latest to bring them screaming in; speculation that Jordan had killed Grace made Rickman a target. The tabloids and the local newspaper had tried 'the death knock': words of condolence shouted through his letterbox, followed by an invitation to tell his side of the story. Notes, cards, letters and flowers they sent in the hope that he would open his door, giving them the photograph, they needed of the grieving partner. His mail piled in drifts, unopened, and he kept his landline unplugged from the wall, relying instead on his mobile.

The dawn came late on the third day, and with it a heavy yellowish swirl of cloud that lay like sulphurous smoke over the city. He slept in an armchair, his mobile phone next to him. When the phone rang it was almost seven-thirty, and jaundiced light filtered through the trees in the garden, casting an uneasy pattern on the rug at his feet.

'Boss?' it was Foster, and he sounded excited. 'We're going in.'

'What've you got?' Rickman asked.

'LCN results show the DNA on the fag-ends belonged to the shooter in the cemetery.'

Rickman's heart pounded thickly in his throat. 'How's he tied to Andrić?'

'His name is Bojan Kost. Yugoslav, from Croatia, originally. He was a no-mark thug — armed robbery, extortion, a bit of smuggling, all small-beer. The war gave him a chance to really blossom; he teamed up with Andrić around nineteen ninety-five.'

'Doing what?' Rickman asked.

'Bodyguarding, a bit of enforcing. He's done time for assault since he came here an' all.'

'Grace—' Rickman said. His throat constricted until he could barely breathe. 'His fingerprints, were they . . . ?'

'No,' Foster said firmly. 'They don't match the lifts from—' He faltered. 'From the murder scene. But listen, Jeff— '

Rickman paid close attention because Foster never used his first name when they were discussing work.

'We've got a link between Andrić and Capstick,' Foster said. 'Not much, I'll admit — just a few calls from Capstick to Andrić's mobie — but enough so's we can arrest and question the bastard.'

And enough, therefore, to fingerprint and take buccal scrapes. If Andrić or his men were identified from the DNA they had taken from under Grace's fingernails — from the fingerprints on Grace's neck . . .

'Get them all, Lee,' he said, his voice thick with emotion. 'You make damn sure you get every last one of them.'

Foster took a deep breath. 'Andrić's flat's a rental, Boss. There's nothing to stop him having another base we don't know about.' They both knew what that meant for their chances of getting Natalja out alive.

'What have you done to find out?' Rickman demanded.

'We've been monitoring his calls since he turned up as a suspect, but he's careful — a couple incoming on his mobile, nothing on his landline.'

'You need surveillance on him, Lee. Andrić's arrest might even trigger Natalja's murder.'

'The superintendent wouldn't sanction covert surveillance till we had something more definite on him. But it's set up and ready to roll soon's he's released.'

Rickman felt a sick thud. 'You're *expecting* to release him?' It shouldn't really have come as a shock: Rickman had gone over and over the situation during his enforced idleness, and whichever way he looked at it, Andrić walked free.

'It's just a precaution, Boss,' Foster soothed.

'Yeah? Think about it, Lee. You won't get him on a couple of calls to a solicitor — even a dodgy one. All he has to say is that he was asked for advice. Merseyside Police have been *relying* on his advice and support over the last few weeks — it's a matter of public record — he's been all over the news, for God's sake!'

'Maybe,' Foster said. 'But his hired thug killed Jordan — he can't get away from that.'

'Ballistics confirm he was shot by the gun they found on Kost?'

'Not yet,' Foster said, 'but—'

'You were there, Lee. You heard what the Dover police said. Andrić is Teflon-coated. I can hear him now—' Rickman stood and began pacing the room. 'Kost was settling a personal score with Jordan, working outside Andrić's knowledge — a man like that could find a dozen plausible explanations that would exonerate him.'

'What're we supposed to do, Boss?' Foster demanded, sounding more angry with himself than with Rickman. 'We're gathering the evidence—'

'The only way you'll get Andrić is if the forensic evidence ties him to one of the murders.'

'No way! Andrić is too clever to get his hands dirty.'

'Yeah,' Rickman sighed. 'We're screwed whichever way you look at it.'

* * *

363

Security was all for buzzing Mr Andrić to let him know the police wanted to speak to him. Foster assured him that wouldn't be necessary and left an officer at the security desk to guarantee that their arrival on the third floor would be a surprise.

Two officers were posted at the lift and the stairs, securing the only routes out. Foster knocked. He wore a kevlar vest under his shirt: almost as effective as the stab vests the other twelve officers wore, it had the advantage of being light and inconspicuous. So, when Andrić peered through his spyhole he saw a smiling police officer in plain clothes whom he vaguely recognised from his visits to the police station in Wavertree. Nevertheless, he was cautious: being cautious had kept him alive and out of prison, and his instincts told him to be careful.

He put the chain on before opening the door a crack. He got as far as, 'Can I help you, Off—' Then the door was forced open by the weight of five men rushing at it. The rest forced their way through after them and Andrić was flattened against the wall. In seconds he was handcuffed, and officers moved cautiously through the apartment, checking rooms.

'Where's Kost?' Foster demanded, raising his voice above the shouts of the other officers.

Andrić said, 'Who?'

Foster lifted his chin, and the officers holding Andrić turned him to face the sergeant. 'Bojan Kost. Where is he?'

Andrić allowed himself the faintest wisp of a smile. 'Taking care of business,' he said.

A man appeared in the doorway to the bathroom at the far end of the hall. He aimed a gun and simultaneously four officers raised their weapons, followed by the click of four safety catches being released.

Andrić said one word, '*Ne!*', and the man let go of the grip, allowing the gun to hang from one finger.

'Put it down!' the officers yelled. 'On the floor! Now! Put it down and step away!'

The man obeyed, taking a step back from the weapon.

'Now lie down! Do it!'

The man stood, legs slightly apart, arms folded, eyeing them impassively like a bouncer watching for troublemakers, while Andrić looked on in amusement. Foster walked up to the man. There were a few shouts of protest from the armed officers, but he ignored them.

He stood in front of Andrić's bodyguard, then stepped quickly forward and to the side of him, slipping one arm under the man's armpit, his lead leg around the back, simultaneously bringing pressure on the left shoulder and ramming his knee hard into the back of the man's leg. The bodyguard's hamstring gave, and his knee collapsed; he fell hard onto the polished floorboards.

Foster snapped on the cuffs, but the man bellowed, bucking in an attempt to throw him off.

'You can come the easy way or the hard way, mate,' Foster said, breathless with the effort of holding him. 'Makes no odds to me — we've got wheelchair access down the nick. You can walk in or we wheel you up the ramp — whichever way you wanna go.'

Andrić looked calmly around the hall at the mass of uniformed and non-uniformed police. 'Of course we'll come with you, officer. We have nothing to hide.'

The bodyguard stopped struggling immediately and Foster handed him to one of the armed officers. 'Bojan Kost?' Foster said.

The man replied with a curt, '*Ne.*'

'What is your name?'

The man smiled. Foster was convinced he'd've spat at his feet if it hadn't meant messing up his boss's oak flooring.

'Make sure you get this joker's fingerprints and run them through NAFIS,' he said.

Andrić showed no concern until he added, 'And if you can't get anything there, try Interpol.'

Andrić held Foster in his gaze, as if memorising every feature of his face. Then he switched his attention to his bodyguard. '*Nemoj ništa govoriti,*' he said.

The man barely reacted; perhaps a flicker of the eyelids, but no more.

'What did you say?' Foster asked.

Andrić smiled. 'I need translator,' he said, his accent suddenly almost impenetrable, his speech halting. 'My English — not good.'

Foster stared at him. 'You're full of shit, Andrić.'

DS Foster was last out. They had cleared and searched the rest of the apartment room by room. Each one was decorated and furnished with understated luxury — luxury Andrić could afford because he exploited and terrorised and murdered vulnerable people. And he was going to get away with it.

Andrić's gloves lay on a radiator shelf in the hallway. Not giving himself time to think, Foster took two evidence bags out of his pocket. He turned the first inside-out, using it to pick up the gloves and place them in the second bag, which he folded and sealed before slipping it into his pocket.

* * *

They held Andrić for twenty-four hours. He told them everything and nothing. He knew nothing about Natalja Sremać's disappearance, he said, although he was obviously worried.

'It's not that obvious to me — you being worried,' Foster said.

Andrić waited politely for the interpreter to translate. It was a good ploy: the translation took the heat out of any exchange simply by slowing it down. A sharp remark became ponderously slow with the buffering effect of an intermediary, and although Foster saw an occasional glint of anger, Andrić never made the mistake of answering a question without first waiting for the translation. It afforded him thinking time as well as time to cool off.

Andrić said that he ran a legitimate import-export business. Yes, he owned a little property — it was so much more reliable than the stock market, these days. He had employed

Kost because he needed the muscle: tenants in areas of London where he held property could sometimes get a little rough. He chose Serbs and Croatians because it made communication easier. Asked about Capstick, he shrugged. He might have called — Andrić couldn't remember. He had good contacts with the refugee community, people asked his advice, he did what he could to help. Even the police sometimes asked for his guidance. He stared steadily into Foster's face as he said this, maintaining eye contact, challenging Foster to deny it.

* * *

They questioned Capstick about the calls. First, he said that he couldn't recall having made them. Then he said he made dozens of calls to agencies during the course of a week.

'And what "agency" does Mr Andrić represent?' Foster asked

'He—' Capstick turned to his brief as if requesting a stage prompt from the wings. His brief raised his shoulders and spread his hands: Mr Capstick had already implicated himself so comprehensively that the solicitor clearly wondered if he served any purpose at all by being present at the interview.

'He . . . provides accommodation?' Capstick said, watching Foster's reaction carefully.

'Are you asking me or telling me?'

Affronted, Mr Capstick drew himself up, assuming the huffy and rather haughty expression he had maintained during his first interview. 'I'm *suggesting* that I might have asked Mr Andrić if he had any accommodation available for one of my clients.'

'Or maybe you were just letting him know you'd found another vulnerable refugee with a good claim.' This came from Hart.

Mr Capstick clamped his mouth tightly shut and Foster was concerned that he would refuse to talk again. Capstick talking was better than Capstick silent: at least talking there was some chance he would give them something useful — even if it was unintentional.

'Mr Andrić didn't mention you having an arrangement on accommodation,' he said.

'What *did* he say?' Capstick asked, turning so pale that his lips went white.

'You want me to tell you what Andrić told us?' Foster said, laughing a little.

Capstick wasn't so far gone that he didn't see the stupidity of his question. He kept quiet, but it was plain to all present that he would have backed up anything Andrić said.

* * *

At ten-thirty the following morning, Foster called Rickman. Bojan Kost had got away. Despite descriptions and photographs being distributed to ports and airports, he had vanished. Foster rehearsed again what he would say as the phone rang at the other end of the line. He had planned and practised this speech dozens of times in the last hour, but when Rickman picked up, he said just two words:

'Sorry, Boss.' He didn't need to say any more — Rickman knew that they must be preparing to release Andrić.

'Is Surveillance ready?' he asked.

'If he even calls the speaking clock, we'll have it on tape,' Foster said.

'Tracing?'

'That an' all. If Natalja's alive, we'll know about it.'

'Good,' Rickman said. Then again, 'Good.' Neither of them expected to find Natalja safe, but it was reassuring that everything possible was being done to protect her in the unlikely event that Andrić had kept her alive.

'How soon?' Rickman asked.

'Half an hour, tops. Boss.' Foster softened his voice a little. 'The FSU got a match on the lifts from Grace's neck.' He heard Rickman inhale sharply. 'It's the guy we arrested at Andrić's apartment. His name is Téodor Popović. They're doing a DNA match, but it's a formality. We got him, Jeff. We got Grace's killer.'

'No, you haven't, Lee,' Rickman said, quietly. 'Not yet.' They both knew he meant Andrić.

'I might be able to do something about that.' He could almost *hear* Rickman listening at the other end of the line, so intense was the silence.

'You know you said Andrić was Teflon-coated?'

'Yeah?' Rickman's voice was wary.

'Well I can be a slippery bastard an' all.'

He had held on to the gloves for a whole day, agonising over what he should do with them, forgoing sleep overnight, hoping against all hope that someone would come forward, that they would find some way to nail Andrić. The big break hadn't come. It was chickening out, he knew, to leave the final decision to Rickman, but it felt right, too. Rickman listened. He was silent for a long time. Long enough for Foster to regret what he had done a dozen times; long enough for the telephone receiver in his hand to become slick with sweat.

Then Rickman spoke.

CHAPTER FORTY-EIGHT

Prisoners were released from the custody suite through a
grey courtyard, large enough to admit a police van. Andrić
walked across the courtyard accompanied by a police constable who unlocked the outer gate which opened onto the
enclosed car park. Beyond the walls, the media were already
beginning to jostle and shout — someone had caught sight
of him.

Andrić ignored them. He stood just outside the gate,
staring into a dark corner between the courtyard and the
outer walls. The PC followed his line of sight and took a step
forward, anticipating trouble.

'Sir.' He placed a hand on Andrić's shoulder.

'It's all right, officer,' Andrić said, his fluency in
English apparently restored by his release. 'I want to talk
with him.'

The PC hovered by the gate, his hand on his baton.
Outside, the gathered media were held back by a row of uniformed officers. The corner of darkness, in the CCTV blind
spot, was also beyond their line of vision.

Rickman leaned off the wall as Andrić approached.

'Inspector,' Andrić said, bowing his head a little.

If he had a hat, he'd tip it, Rickman thought. He kept eye contact and contented himself with the neutral observation, 'They let you go.'

Andrić spoke carefully, watching for Rickman's reaction. 'Your forensic scientists showed that I had nothing to do with this terrible thing.'

'You're getting confused,' Rickman said. 'They can't place you at the scene. But that doesn't mean you had nothing to do with it.'

Andrić shrugged — helplessly, rather than dismissively. 'People believe in forensic science, Inspector. Science doesn't lie.'

'No,' Rickman agreed. 'Science is impartial. That's its great strength.'

They stared at each other for a few seconds. Over Andrić's shoulder, Rickman saw the police constable shivering in his shirt-sleeves. 'What about Natalja?' he asked.

'I wish I could tell you.'

Rickman was impressed. He hadn't said, 'I wish I knew', or 'I don't know', but '*I can't tell you*.' For a man who needed an interpreter, Andrić certainly knew how to manipulate the English language.

'Maybe Téodor Popović will tell us.'

Andrić said, 'I hope so. It's a terrible sin to have on his conscience.'

Rickman narrowed his eyes at him. 'You're a religious man, Mr Andrić?'

'Yes.'

'So you do believe in eternal hell . . .'

'For the sinner, yes.'

Another nice distinction. Rickman held him in his gaze for as long as he could maintain his self-control.

Andrić seemed to suffer some spasm of emotion. He glanced away, almost flinching for a brief moment. Then he said, 'I am sorry about Doctor Grace. It should never have happened. It was a horrible misfortune that she was in that place at that time.' It was the closest to a confession he would ever make. 'She was a good person,' he concluded.

'Yes,' Rickman said. 'Yes, she was.'

Andrić shoved his hands into his pockets. 'Well . . .' He gestured as if to leave.

'What will you do now?' Rickman asked.

'Go back to my business. Go on with my life.'

Yes, Rickman thought. *That would be easy enough.* With so much money on offer Andrić would have no trouble finding another solicitor willing to help him pick up the pieces.

Andrić turned to leave and Rickman felt a moment of panic. They weren't finished, yet. 'You know we had to arrest you?' he said, trying to hide the anxiety in his voice.

The reporters had returned to quiet conversation and it was possible to hear the traffic on Edge Lane, the rhythm of a train like a heartbeat on the railway line nearby.

Andrić turned back. 'Téodor is my employee. Of course you must suspect—'

Rickman held out a hand. For a moment, Andrić stared at it in surprise. Then he took it, as if suspecting a trap, and yet his habitual courtesy would not permit the rudeness of refusal. Then he turned and walked away.

Halfway across the car park, the media saw him and began a frenzy of shouted questions and camera flashes. Andrić turned once more and looked in puzzlement at Rickman's retreating back.

The constable let the DI through to the building without question. Foster was entertaining the custody staff with a joke. It ended with, 'But worst of all, you've let *yourself* down!' He watched Rickman from the corner of his eye as he laughed along with the custody sergeant.

'Not bad for a clean joke, eh?' he said, laughing again.

When Rickman was clear of the area, he followed. They met in the office they had shared during the course of the investigation.

'Any luck?' Foster asked.

372

Rickman held up his gloved hands. 'Let's hope it's all bad for Andrić.'

Foster took an evidence bag from his desk drawer and opened it. Rickman peeled off his black leather gloves with care and dropped them into the bag. Beneath them he wore surgical gloves. Foster sealed the bag and placed it back in the drawer for safe keeping.

Rickman thrust his hands into his pockets. 'You don't have to do this, Lee,' he said.

'No. I know that.'

'I mean it's not too late to back out.'

'Without this evidence, we're screwed,' Foster said. 'With it, Andrić is screwed. Me, I'd rather be the screw-er than the screw-ee.'

Rickman's jaw tightened. The thought of Andrić going free made him sick to the pit of his stomach; he would personally sacrifice his career, his liberty — even his life — to see Grace's killer behind bars. But he could not expect Foster to feel the same way.

'There'll be other opportunities,' he said, though even to his own ears his objections sounded feeble. 'Now we know about Andrić—'

'Now we know about him he'll go underground,' Foster interrupted. 'It's like a lucky dip for him — stick your hand in the bag, pick out a nationality. New name, new story, new life.'

Rickman opened his mouth to speak, but Foster wasn't finished. 'And whose ID will it be this time? If Andrić gets away with this, it's not just Sophia,' he said, giving her real name out of choice for the first time. 'It's not just those poor sods he burned up in that flat — it's the ten-year-old lads he got to do his dirty work, it's Minky, Natalja, Grace . . .'

Foster had articulated perfectly all the jumbled emotions and thoughts that had kept Rickman in turmoil over the last few days.

'You look surprised,' Foster said.

'No. It's just . . .'

'I never had much time for all that liberal crap.'

Foster opened and shut his desk drawer a few times, awkward, unsure how to say what was on his mind. 'Seeing Grace like that, it made me think. Them others — Sophia, Jokubas, all of them. They must have had people who cared — family, friends . . .' He stopped for a moment, struggling for control. When he spoke again, his voice was strained. 'Men like Andrić poison everything around them. And they make us a part of it.'

Rickman left the station unnoticed, five minutes later.

* * *

All Foster had to do now was wait. But waiting was not one of his strengths: it allowed too much thinking time — wondering if he was doing the right thing, worrying that he could lose his job, his whole way of life because of this.

As he worked through the day, taking statements, checking results with Mayle at the forensic labs, he argued with himself. Andrić was a killer. Without this intervention — it comforted him to call it an intervention — Andrić would get away with seven murders that they knew of: the four arson victims, Jokubas Patrauskas, Grace, and in all probability, Natalja. Maybe he was involved in Arash Taqvai's disappearance, as well. Bristol had picked up the man who was living under his name; he had all the right papers; his story matched the Immigration Department's records — he even used exact phrases they had found in Capstick's case notes. But there was no real emotion attached to his recounting of the terrible things that were supposed to have been done to him, and when he was examined by a doctor, there were no signs of torture.

Jordan had been implicated in Petrauskas's murder because the Russian's blood was on the knife-blade, while Jordan's fingerprints were on the hilt. Despite this, nobody on the team suspected Jordan of any murder other than that of Sophia.

Petrauskas was a professional killing, impersonal — merely a necessary action to achieve a goal, to keep their business safe. Jordan, on the other hand, had killed Sophia as a way of punishing Desiree and of getting back at Jeff Rickman — for him, it was personal. He had killed Sophia because she was young and vulnerable, a girl nobody cared about — an easy target for a bully and a coward, for a man who equated fear with respect.

Foster had made an arrangement with a friend in the Calls and Response Department — calls to the switchboard as well as emergency calls went through this one central office in the headquarters. The plan was that Foster would get to know before the patrol car was sent, before the call came through to DCI Hinchcliffe.

He waited all day, his nerves jangling. At every beep of his text messager it seemed his heart took a flying leap at his rib cage and clamoured to get out. It was like being on a caffeine jag: colours seemed over-bright, the sun too dazzling, the cold too intense. Distracted and irritable, he couldn't concentrate on his work.

Word came through at six p.m. Jez Flynn had died.

'Don't suppose he made a death-bed confession?'

'God, Foster, you're a callous sod!' Hart exclaimed.

'Only asking,' Foster said. 'You've gotta admit, it would help.'

She stared at him, shaking her head in disbelief. 'He never regained consciousness. Which is probably just as well, given the extent of his burns.'

'All right, Naomi, I get the picture.' Foster couldn't tell her how much that confession would have meant to him — how much he really didn't want to take the call he was waiting for.

By ten p.m., there was still no call. He was exhausted, ready for a large whisky and an early night. He drove home fantasising pleasantly on the prospect, opened the door of his flat, tossed his keys onto the work surface in his kitchen, and reached in the cupboard for a glass and the bottle of

Macallan's he saved for special occasions. He poured an inch of pale golden liquid into the glass and breathed its vapour. Rich, complicated and warm.

'*Jesus!*' His text messenger had beeped. His hand jerked so violently that he spilt some of the whisky. He licked it from his hand and checked the message. An address off Parliament Street. No greeting, no sign-off. He could be there in five minutes.

Foster snatched up his keys and drove recklessly. Nevertheless, when he arrived, a uniform was already guarding the door. The house was derelict, the windows and door sealed with perforated plates in some kind of galvanised metal. Even so, somebody had managed to force the door.

Foster showed his ID but took care not to say his name. 'What's the score?' he asked.

The constable was young; he looked nervous and unsure of himself. 'Tramp, looking for a doss,' he said. 'Found the door open.' He raised his chin and Foster turned to the marked car parked against the kerb. A pale, frightened face stared back at him from the rear passenger seat.

'We call them "homeless people", now, lad,' Foster said. Ticking off a junior officer about political correctness was stretching it a bit, given his own track record; the intention was to keep the constable off-balance, and it worked.

'Sorry, sir.'

He took this as an encouraging sign: if the bobby was calling him 'sir', rather than 'sarge', it was because he hadn't clocked his rank on the card. If he hadn't clocked the rank, chances were he hadn't clocked his name, either. He nodded, accepting the apology, then said. 'Where is she?'

'In the hall.'

'Anyone else been in?'

The constable hesitated.

'Come on, lad, we've all done it — sneaky peek at the corpse.'

'Well, only to check it was, you know — a body.'

'Did you disturb anything?'

He blushed slightly. 'I had to tear the plastic over her face.'

'Plastic?' Foster caught a searing flash of Grace, bagged up and ready to ship out to the mortuary.

'She's all wrapped up like a slab of meat,' the constable said.

Foster swallowed, putting the image out of his mind. 'Did you touch anything else?'

'No.' He seemed confident in that, and Foster was reassured.

He went to the boot of his car and pulled out a torch, oversuit, mask and overshoes. He dressed just outside the door of the house, listening to the sound of approaching sirens and trying not to rush.

'Nobody comes through that door,' he said.

The constable blinked, nodded.

'Nobody,' Foster repeated. He pulled the hood of his zoot suit over his face mask and stepped inside.

Natalja had been placed three feet inside the door, her body wrapped in heavy-gauge plastic bound with parcel tape. He allowed the torch beam to track up the torso. It was difficult to tell, but under the opalescent plastic sheet, she appeared to be naked. The beam found her face, unwrapped, framed in the raggedly torn plastic.

Her eyes were closed, her hair damp, just beginning to dry and frizz a little in contact with the chilly air. *Drowning?* he wondered. She smelled faintly of soap. She looked peaceful. The moisture on her skin lent an almost silvery sheen to her pallor, reminding Foster of snow and ice and moonlight.

He pulled on a clean pair of latex gloves and knelt beside Natalja. All day the house had stood open, but it had taken hours of darkness, the curiosity of a night creature, to discover her.

* * *

That last day, Mirko Andrić came into the bedroom, carrying a tray. He laid it on the table next to the bed and smiled at her. It was set as a honeymooner might set a breakfast tray for his new wife. A glass of orange juice, a single yellow rose, and a plate of *paprenjak* biscuits. Natalja could smell their sweet-peppery aroma; they had been her favourite treat when she was a child.

She stared at him with dull fascination. At that moment, she thought she saw in him the handsome boy who had rescued her from the soldiers in Knin. But this was not the Mirko she had known back then. This Mirko was harder, more calculating and dangerous.

The sweet, smiling boy with the heart of a warrior was gone, buried along with her parents and his, and a dozen others he had killed in the months and years after they fled Knin.

She closed her eyes, looked again, and saw a devil. The drugs made her see things that weren't there, but in some ways, they also helped her to see more clearly. In Mirko's face she could see both the boy he had been and the monster he had become. As the drugs wore off, this duality of thought became easier, almost natural. He sat on the bed next to her, smoothed a lock of hair from her face.

'*Kunem ti se, Natalijo, nisam joj nameravao učiniti ništa nažao.*' He spoke softly, with regret, explaining that he had meant Grace no harm — that her death was an accident.

Natalja said one word. '*Ubico.*' Murderer.

'*Molim te,*' he said. '*Ja te volim, Tašo,*'

She covered her ears with her hands. '*Ne!*' she screamed. 'How can you say you love me? You killed her! You killed Grace. She was my friend and you killed her.' She broke down and he tried to touch her cheek, to comfort her.

She flung his hand away, screaming at him in English and Croatian, cursing him, hitting out feebly, her arms uncoordinated, while Andrić tried to calm her, shushing and soothing her. At last, he caught her hands and held them to his chest as she wept; for a few minutes neither spoke.

At last, exhausted with weeping, she sagged in his arms, giving up the struggle. He handed her a clean handkerchief and she wiped her eyes and blew her nose.

'Here,' he said, handing her the glass. 'Drink. You'll feel better.'

She took it from him, and he watched her closely. His eyes were dark and troubled.

'Let me go home, Mirko.' The inflection made it a question. This was a mistake: in the old days she would have commanded. Mirko did not respond to pleas.

'Relax,' he said, touching the base of the glass, guiding it to her lips. 'You're upset. Drink your orange, then you can get cleaned up and I'll take you wherever you tell me.'

She drank reluctantly at first, but she was dehydrated, and the orange was cold and freshly squeezed and tasted so good.

The bathroom was beautiful; Italian marble wall tiles, the palest pink granite on the floor, polished to a glassy finish. New towels, peachy and softly fluffed, hung on the rail; new soap, exfoliator, shampoo, conditioner. Natalja stepped into the shower and let the jet punish her skin, gradually easing up the temperature until it was almost too hot to bear. She had to clear her head. Whatever Mirko planned it wasn't to let her walk out of here and into the nearest police station. He had killed Grace, just as surely as if he had put his own hands around her throat.

The drugs had dulled her emotions, just as they had heightened her senses, but now they were wearing off Natalja began to feel the pain again — to be sensible to the awful fact of Grace's death. She had often thought that it would have been easier if she had been at home when her parents' house was raided by the soldiers. She might have been spared all the guilt and pain of the years that followed.

* * *

Grace had a way of looking at you so that it seemed she could see into your soul. There was no judgement in the way she held you in her gaze; only interest and concern. She had looked at Natalja in that way on the terrible day when Mirko's men had come for her.

After minutes of silence, Grace had put down her coffee mug and asked, 'What *is* your real name?' Her eyes were solemn, a dark, dark blue.

Natalja shrugged. 'Doesn't matter — that girl is dead.'

'Surely not,' Grace said. Her voice remained gentle and Natalja was almost afraid to look again into her eyes. 'All right,' Grace said. 'You lived in London for four years. This man you knew — the one who got you your refugee status — who was he?'

Natalja bit her lip and remained silent. It shamed her to admit it, but even after all he had done, she had wanted to protect him.

'Was it Mirko Andrić? Is that why you didn't want to meet him again?'

Natalja refused to look at Grace — if Grace looked into her face she would see the truth.

Grace took a few moments. When she spoke again, it was without anger, with no trace of disapproval; she was simply explaining what she had to do. 'I have to tell the police what I know.'

Natalja turned her face away. 'Do what you think you must,' she said, unable to hide her bitterness.

'I'd like you to come with me.'

Natalja looked at her in astonishment.

'Don't you see?' Grace asked. 'You're the key, Natalja. Unless you tell the police what you know, the killing will go on.'

'No!' Natalja shouted, jumping to her feet. 'You don't understand what it was like. You don't know—'

A hammering below cut her short. 'My God,' she whispered. 'They're here.'

'Who?' Grace's eyes were wide with fear. 'Who is it, Natalja?'

Natalja snatched up the phone. It was dead. She threw it down and ran to the window. 'We have to get out,' she shouted, dragging the sash open.

Grace took hold of her arm, pulling her away. 'It's a twenty-foot drop,' she said. 'You'll kill yourself!'

The door below splintered and Grace fished in her handbag for her mobile. She had switched it off on arrival at Natalja's flat; now she struggled with it, her fingers trembling.

'Here,' she said. 'Take this. Dial emergency.' She handed Natalja the phone and tipped out her handbag, scrabbling for her attack alarm.

Natalja stared at the phone.

'What's *taking* so long?' Grace demanded; her voice was high-pitched, weak with fear.

The start-up logo crept agonisingly slowly across the menu screen, hands reaching out to clasp in a handshake. 'It's this damn phone,' Natalja shouted. 'Why can't you get a decent bloody phone?'

Heavy footsteps pounded up the stairs. Grace and Natalja worked together, pushing one of the sofas in front of the door.

At last the screen cleared and Natalja tapped in triple nine. She pressed the 'call' button as the men put their shoulders to the door and heaved. The sofa moved six inches. Grace and Natalja both screamed and shoved back. It wouldn't hold for long.

'The phone!' Grace yelled. 'Hurry!'

'Jesus, no . . .' Natalja groaned. It had come up with the message "SIM card not ready". 'Oh God,' she whispered, cancelling the number.

'Try again,' Grace said. 'I'm going to the window — use the attack alarm. Can you hold them?'

'Just GO!' Natalja shouted.

Grace ran as Natalja braced both feet pushing back with all her strength. Grace got the window open a few inches and switched on the alarm, leaving it on the window ledge. The room was filled with a deafening screeching. The men redoubled their assaults on the door, each impact moving the sofa an inch or two further and Grace covered both ears as she ran back to help Natalja.

Natalja got as far as retyping the second nine when the sofa slid across the room and the door flew open. The phone fell from her hand and cracked against the bookcase. One of the men grabbed her and forced her towards the door. Grace launched herself at him.

The man grabbed Grace by the throat, his free hand huge, obscene against the white curve of her neck. The second man grabbed the attack alarm from the windowsill and crunched it under his boot. The screeching stopped and a throbbing silence followed.

Grace reached up and Natalja screamed. The man turned his hand a fraction. A crack. Grace slumped.

'*Ti kurče, ti si je ubio.*' You killed her, you prick. The second man was dispassionate — Grace's murder was no more than an annoying complication to him.

The first man — she knew now that his name was Popović — looked at Grace's lifeless body. Then he dropped her, like she was a toy he had inadvertently broken. A wail rose in Natalja's throat, but the man clamped his hand over her mouth. They bound and gagged her and carried her outside to a waiting van.

* * *

The shower jet felt good, pounding her head and neck and spine. It frothed, the bubbles lending softness to the water. She let it play over her body, leaning with both hands against the shower wall so that the jet pummelled the tense muscles of her neck. While it cascaded over her, she breathed the steamy, soap-perfumed air.

She checked herself. *What the hell am I doing?* She killed the jet and stepped out into the bathroom, trying to regain some of the urgency, some of the anger she had felt only minutes before. The cold air felt like a sharp slap. With the shock, a flash of clarity: the drink.

She slapped her face hard — once — twice. Red welts appeared on her cheeks. The adrenalin surge gave her the will to search for something — she didn't know what — something sharp, a weapon, maybe. The cabinet yielded a packet of tissues, a spare toothbrush, aspirin, mouthwash, a bottle of men's cologne.

Do something! She had to . . . before the drugs took away her will to . . . do . . . SOMETHING.

The bottle shattered into the corner of the room, sending splinters upwards and outwards. Natalja bent and picked out a jagged shard of glass.

The smell. It was spicy; it reminded her of exotic flowers and the bitter astringency of limes, hot summer days by the sea, the smell of salt sweat and ozone on her skin. She felt warm and protected, content to stand there and breathe the scent of summer, to recall the feel of her body naked against Mirko's, his arms encircling her, holding her like she was something delicate and precious.

She stood in the bathroom with water pooling around her, a slight frown drawing a line between her eyebrows. There was something she had to do . . .

'Taso?'

She sighed and shivered. She loved it when he used her pet name. But she shouldn't love anything about him, because . . .

'You're bad,' she said. 'You, Mirko Andrić, are a bad man . . .' There was no rancour in her voice. She was saying what she believed, and yet it had no emotional colouring behind it. She wanted to act, but she had forgotten why — had even forgotten the sliver of glass in her hand. 'Too late . . .' she said sadly, as if in answer to an admonishment.

Andrić opened her hand and she stared at the coloured glass like a volunteer perplexed by a magician's trick. He took it from her palm in his gloved hands and threw it with the other fragments into the corner of the room, then wrapped her in a towel and walked her through to the bedroom.

383

'A spider,' she said, gazing at the transparent festoon, draped over every surface: floor, furniture, bedding. Then the picture shifted, like an image in an optical illusion, and she saw that it was only plastic, wrapped over and under and around everything.

Mirko wore a white one-piece oversuit, a mask over his mouth, the hood of the suit covered his hair. A shame to cover his hair; Mirko always had such beautiful hair.

'Come,' he said. His voice was gentle and sad.

'Am I sick?' she asked. She felt dizzy, but not sick. It felt good. She felt *happy*. His hands were warm and strong. Silky. She would not fall while Mirko had hold of her.

'You're not afraid, are you, Taso?'

'Afraid?' What an odd question, when she felt so relaxed and content. She twisted in his arms to look into his face. There were tears in his eyes.

'Why are you crying?' She had never seen Mirko cry before.

'You always had to do the right thing, Natalja.' His hands shifted to her neck. 'Sometimes that's not the smart thing.' He sighed, asking her forgiveness again at the last. '*Oprosti mi, Tašo.*'

CHAPTER FORTY-NINE

DS Foster took Andrić's black leather gloves from the evidence bag and put them on over his latex gloves.

'I'm sorry, Nat,' he said, unconsciously echoing Andrić's apology. He put his hands around Natalja's neck, carefully placing his thumbs over the bruises either side of her windpipe, then pressed gently. Swabbing the marks on her throat would be one of the first tasks the CSIs would perform, and when he shook Rickman's hand, Andrić had transferred enough DNA to give them a clear match.

Natalja's mouth was slightly open. He hesitated; the sirens were close now — he needed to get out, and fast.

He closed his eyes for a second and exhaled, his breath warm on the mask. 'I'm really, really sorry,' he said. Then he slid his index finger along the moist inner surface of her lip. He began to get up, looked into her face, her skin so pale he could almost see the bones beneath the skin. 'Ah, fuck it,' he muttered, and pulled a few hairs from the nape of her neck. He replaced the gloves inside the evidence bag, sealed it and slipped it inside his zoot suit.

The constable turned as he opened the front door. 'You've got a scene here, pal,' Foster said. 'This is a big one — you've heard about the refugee murders?'

The lad nodded.

'This is one of 'em. Know your procedure?'

'Well, yeah . . .' Nevertheless, he looked uncertain.

'You ask for a police surgeon and CSIs.'

'I've done that,' the constable said, a bit on the defensive.

'Good,' Foster said. 'You don't let the police surgeon mess with the body. Watch him. He should be straight in and out. All he's gotta do is declare life extinct before the CSIs start in on her. You crack open your Crime Scene Preservation Kit. Find the black book. Log everyone in and out, starting from now. And if you can't kill the urge to take another shufti at the body, for God's sake get fully kitted up.'

'What about you, sir?'

Foster raised his eyebrows. 'What about me?'

'Do I log you, like?'

Foster shrugged. 'It's up to you, lad. If you want to put me down as first officer attending . . .' He unzipped his suit and made a pantomime of searching for his warrant card.

'Yeah,' the constable said, coming over all possessive. 'But the call came out to me.'

'Like I say,' Foster said, 'It's your scene. Anyway, I've had a bellyful of murder in the last few weeks.' He left just as the first wave of cars arrived, sirens whooping and blaring, comfortable in the knowledge that his name would not appear anywhere in the scene logs, in pub discussions or in any of the folklore that inevitably grew up around the discovery of a murder victim.

* * *

Hinchcliffe made the arrest himself, as a mark of respect for Rickman. He had mugged up on the wording of the caution on his way over: the last time he had made an arrest in person was after an internal investigation three years previously, which had resulted in the prosecution of a senior officer from the south.

It was seven-thirty a.m. and still dark. Surveillance had confirmed that Andrić was alone, so they simply knocked at the door and waited for him to answer.

Andrić was relaxed — almost affable. He had been expecting a second visit ever since Natalja's body had been found. They were a day later than he had anticipated, but he didn't find that in any way troubling.

The apartment was filled with the bitter-sweet aroma of strong ground coffee and Andrić looked freshly showered and shaved. He listened politely to the wording of the caution; the DCI had engaged an interpreter, and he insisted on the translation before asking, 'Do you understand?'

'Yes,' Andrić said. 'Thank you.' He glanced down at his dressing-gown and slippers. 'You won't mind if I dress first?'

Hinchcliffe thought about it. 'Should we expect any resistance, Mr Andrić' he asked.

'It's just me,' Andrić replied. 'Do I look like I'm resisting?'

Hinchcliffe handed Andrić a warrant. 'To search the apartment,' he said. Armed officers swept the rooms, then the DCI nodded to the two officers either side of Andrić. 'Go with him,' he said.

The apartment declared safe, the CSIs came in. Tony Mayle was the first. Already wearing his overalls, he pulled on overshoes and gloves. In the hall he stopped next to an antique table and pointed to a pair of black leather gloves as Andrić was escorted, now dressed, from his bedroom.

'These yours, sir?' he asked.

Andrić looked puzzled. 'Where did you find them?'

'Right here where you left them.' Mayle indicated the table.

'No,' Andrić said, his voice suddenly hard.

'Are you saying they're not yours?'

He glared at Hinchcliffe. 'What the hell are you doing?'

Hinchcliffe stared back. 'I really don't know what you're talking about,' he said.

'We'll need them for DNA analysis.' Mayle scooped them into an evidence bag.

Andrić gave an incredulous smile. 'I've worn them — sure they'll have my DNA.'

Mayle glanced at Hinchcliffe, who gave a barely perceptible nod. 'We recovered DNA from Miss Sremać's body,' he said.

Andrić looked from one man to the other. 'That's . . . That's not possible,' he said.

'Why?' Hinchcliffe asked.

'Because—' He seemed to get a hold on himself and said, 'Because I had nothing to do with her death.'

Hinchcliffe said, 'Well we didn't say it was *your* DNA we'd found, but time will tell.'

'We also found traces of black fibres in her hair — similar to the stitching on these gloves,' Mayle remarked.

Andrić balked and the officers escorting him grabbed an arm each. 'You planted them,' Andrić said.

'No, sir. I found them. Right here.' Glancing again at the table, something caught the light and he bent to get a better look. He noticed a couple of fine hairs he had missed and bagged them separate from the gloves.

Andrić stared wildly around the hallway. Foster was just a face in the crowd, one of the mass of hard-eyed police who stared back at him without compassion or pity.

'Rickman — he must have—'

'Detective Inspector Rickman has not worked on this case since Doctor Chandler was murdered,' Hinchcliffe said. 'Sorry, Mr Andrić, there's no easy way out for you on this one.'

* * *

Rickman woke, his mind filled with a clear image of Grace. She was beside him, her body warm against his. He felt something: a presence, stronger than before, more tangible. A moment later, he remembered: Grace was gone. The pain of realisation was physical. During the investigation, while he had other thoughts to distract him, he could hold it at bay. Now, all he had was his grief. He leaned on one elbow and stared at her side of the bed, willing her shape and form into being. Failing.

He went to her wardrobe and reached down one of her dresses. She had worn it on holiday that summer. Naples. He pressed his face into its soft folds. A flashback of Grace — happy, relaxed, laughing at some joke he had made. Grace, tipsy, leaning on his arm as they walked back along the beach after an evening meal, the whispering surf beside them contributing to the intimacy of their conversation.

Again, he felt an awful breathlessness as if all the air had been sucked out of the room. He gasped, tearing at the fabric of his T-shirt, staggered to the bathroom and retched helplessly. A while later, spent and weak, he washed his face. His reflection in the mirror was grey and despairing. He was bitterly, achingly cold. He turned on the shower and stood under it for ten — fifteen minutes, thinking about what he had done.

Foster had stayed clear of Rickman immediately after Andrić's arrest: the press were still snooping around, watching Rickman's house harrying anyone who came to the door. Any contact between Rickman and the investigation might reflect badly on it, so it wasn't until three days later that Foster finally called. It was lunchtime and the day was overcast and cold. Foster didn't notice the photographer jump out of a car a little further up the road. He followed the sergeant practically to the front door of Rickman's house, timing the first click of the shutter with Rickman's appearance at the door.

Rickman flattened himself against the wall. 'Shit!'

Foster darted inside and slammed the door on the reporter's questions.

'It's all right, Boss,' Foster told him. 'The DCI sanctioned this.'

Hinchcliffe's sanction of the visit could mean only one thing: Andrić had been charged.

Rickman covered his eyes with his hand and slumped a little. Foster guided him through to the kitchen and seated him at the table, but Rickman immediately got up, pushing him away, feeling smothered by his friend's proximity — even by his concern.

Foster backed off, watching miserably while Rickman, his back turned, breathed in deep irregular sighs.

After a minute or two Rickman turned around. 'Have you eaten?' he asked.

'Don't you want to hear about the arrest?'

'I can't sit still while you tell me this,' Rickman said, the effort to keep control was exhausting in itself. 'And I can't face sitting down to a meal with only one place laid.'

Foster shrugged. 'If you wanna twist me arm,' he said.

Rickman got to work with the edible items left in the fridge, which amounted to eggs, bacon, and a few mushrooms that were just about passable. 'Go ahead,' he said. 'I'm listening.'

Foster leaned against the kitchen table, while the coffee brewed and Rickman cooked their late breakfast. 'He didn't so much as blink when Hinchcliffe cautioned him,' Foster said.

'Andrić believes in forensic evidence,' Rickman replied. 'He thought he'd taken care of all that.'

'Well he had done — hadn't he?'

Rickman thought he heard an edge to Foster's voice. He had asked a lot of his friend: perhaps too much.

For a few minutes the only sound was the hiss of frying bacon and the gurgle of the coffee maker.

'You did cover yourself?' Rickman asked.

Foster snorted. 'You're not kidding. When Mayle found them gloves, I was well out of it.'

'Did the CSIs get anything from his apartment?' Rickman asked, handing Foster a plateful of bacon, egg and mushrooms.

'You haven't got any fried bread to go with that, have you?'

Fried bread. Grace would have a fit. Rickman felt another shock — it was so easy to lapse into wondering what Grace would say or think or do, as if she was still around.

Foster tucked into his food. 'Tony Mayle reckons Andrić's bedroom and en suite have had a pretty thorough going-over in the last few days,' he said. 'New mattress on the bed, carpets steam-cleaned, paintwork washed, windows polished — he's not hopeful.'

Rickman took a seat opposite and stared at his own plate. His appetite had suddenly deserted him.

'You weren't expecting them to find something?' Foster sounded both anxious and exasperated.

'No,' Rickman said. 'No, of course not. But you know he can explain away Natalja's DNA on his gloves,' he went on. 'They perhaps met on a couple of occasions . . .'

'Yeah,' Foster said, 'But he can't account for his DNA on the bruises on her neck, can he?'

'No,' Rickman agreed. 'It would be hard for him to do that.'

Foster had put his career on the line for him. The last thing he needed to hear was Rickman's qualms on the morality of what they had done.

'Is the DCI checking into Capstick's clients?' he asked.

'Every one of his clients who's had a positive decision in the last ten years,' Foster said, stuffing a forkful of food into his mouth. 'The Home Office has promised full cooperation.'

Rickman rolled his eyes. 'God help us all.'

'One bit of good news, though. That lad — the younger brother—'

'Minky,' Rickman said.

'He's made a statement. Him and his gang got caught slinging bangers through a letterbox at one of the tenements on Scottie Road. Bloke put the fear of God into them. He's identified Andrić.'

'Did you use VIPER?'

'Yeah. Picked him out, no hesitation.'

VIPER was a relatively new system; in effect, a video ID parade stored on DVD. Vulnerable witnesses did not have to be in the building at the same time as the suspect, which made them more likely to agree to it, and it was fast

— stand-up parades could take up to three months to organise, this had taken days.

'The kid's braver than I thought,' Rickman said.

'He said his big brother always looked out for him — took the worst of any trouble they got into.'

Rickman nodded, thinking of all the beatings Simon had taken, stepping in front of him and taking the blows that were aimed at little Jeff. All the times he had proposed 'adventures', as he called them — anything to get them clear of the house, clear of danger; all the wasted years of his childhood that he had spent protecting his little brother.

'We're working on the rest of the gang,' Foster said. 'Now Minky's come forward, we'll get one or other of them to admit Andrić set up the arson attack . . .' He shrugged; he would be vindicated. They both would.

* * *

Foster had been gone only an hour, but Rickman slept in snatches, now, when the memories weren't too close to the surface, and exhaustion drove him to it. He turned off the shower and towelled himself dry. Grace would have been horrified by what he had done, but he knew he could not have lived with himself if Andrić had been allowed to go free.

Something Grace had said kept running through his head like the line of a song he couldn't shift. *Not everyone can be courageous, Jeff.* She had said it of Simon, hoping that it would help him to forgive his brother's abandonment. He had despised Simon because he hadn't had the courage to face up to their father, but Rickman understood now that it would have taken another kind of courage to trust the law to bring Mirko Andrić to justice. He had compromised his principles and placed Lee Foster in a terrible predicament because he lacked that courage.

At the head of the stairs he stopped, stared thoughtfully towards the attic door. Just inside, on a stack of box files, he found the leatherette volume. Unlabelled, undated, a version of his childhood fixed between its pages.

He left the house through the back door, but the press still managed to reel off a few shots. Others had joined the first reporter now; their photographs would show a newly determined Rickman, hurrying to his car.

'Sir? Inspector Rickman? Can you tell us how you feel about the news that Mirko Andrić has been charged?'

Rickman slowed down. He had to remind himself that he was the object of sympathy here. 'We would not have caught this man if it were not for forensic evidence,' he said. 'I am confident that the jury will show their faith in scientific procedures.'

Many who studied the photographs would speculate on the mysterious volume under his arm. A diary? they wondered — or perhaps a photo album of happier times with "Doctor Grace".

But the one image that would evoke most sympathy from the public and sell most papers was the stolen shot of Foster's arrival, portraying a worn and obviously grieving Rickman opening the door to his friend and colleague. The headline: "WE GOT HIM, GUV!" The report was given a generous four columns of copy, beginning with the news that Andrić had been charged with the murder of Natalja Sremać. It went on to outline police suspicions that he was the "Mr Big" behind a sinister trade in stolen identities.

* * *

Rickman drove directly to the hospital.

Tanya was alone in Simon's room when he arrived. When she saw him, she hurried over. 'Jeff, I'm so sorry . . . Did you get my note?'

He frowned, confused, then he realised and closed his eyes briefly. 'I'm sorry, Tanya,' he said. 'I haven't been reading my mail, the press—' He shrugged helplessly.

'Not to worry,' she said, putting her hand on his arm. 'I just wanted you to know, if there's anything we can do — me or the boys . . .'

His eyes seeped tears. It was a new experience, this family concern. They hugged awkwardly, then he held her at arm's length, clearing his throat before asking, 'How is he?'

She brightened but seemed embarrassed to be happy when Rickman was so devastated. 'He's beginning to remember things, Jeff. I don't know, but I think maybe he came back to find you — to make his peace with you. Perhaps he'll be able to tell you himself soon.'

'Perhaps,' he said. Secretly, he wished for the gift of amnesia that purged Simon of guilt and unhappy memories.

'I can't stay,' he said. 'I only came to—'

'Jeff!'

Rickman tensed. He didn't feel strong enough for another joyful reunion; his brother forgetful of all the other occasions they had seen each other in the preceding weeks. But Simon seemed bashful, almost apologetic, standing at the door as if waiting for an invitation to step inside.

'I wasn't sure you'd come back,' he said.

'Lightning visit. I brought this.' Rickman held up the leatherette volume. 'The family album — remember?'

Simon took it gingerly, turning it over and over in his hands. 'It looks so *old*,' he said, adding hastily, 'Of course, it would be, after all this time, but—' He gazed at it, a look of childish wonder and apprehension on his face. 'D'you remember how Dad used to guard it?' he said. 'We weren't allowed to touch the pages. He made us clasp our hands behind our backs so we wouldn't get our grubby prints all over it.' He glanced up at Tanya. 'He was a bloody nightmare, our dad,' he said.

Rickman and Tanya exchanged a glance. He *was* beginning to remember.

'I haven't looked at it since Mum died,' Rickman said.

'Maybe we can look at it together,' Simon suggested, his eyes lighting up.

'Maybe,' Rickman agreed. 'But not tonight, eh, Simon?'

He could see that his brother didn't understand why there must be a delay, but he took it as a sign of progress that Simon didn't argue or lose his temper. 'It might help me to remember,' he said.

Rickman put a hand on his brother's shoulder. 'That's what I thought.'

Tanya walked down to the main entrance with him.

'He seems more rational,' Rickman said.

'He is.' Her eyes shone with love and hope. 'I think we're going to take the offer of the place at the Neurology Centre.'

'Yes?'

She nodded. 'It has an international reputation — and I thought it might help to be near you.'

He didn't know how to answer, then he heard himself say, 'Yes, it might. It might just help.' He took a moment to regain his equilibrium. 'Anyway, it's time we got to know each other again,' he said.

Tanya smiled, and took his hand. He felt something break within him — a sharp pain and then a flood of warmth, and he knew that he was crying.

THE END

ACKNOWLEDGEMENTS

Sincere thanks go to Annie Ledger, Director of Migrant Helpline, and her team of dedicated and highly professional staff who work in extremely stressful conditions but still found the time to explain procedures and situations to me. They tolerated me tagging along with them and pestering them with questions, with follow-up queries and 'quick questions' and through it all remained cheerful and helpful.

To Susan Lewis and the rest of the team at Refugee Action, Liverpool: you're a great bunch of people and it was a pleasure working with you.

DCI Dave Griffin put me in touch with Hugh Owen: Cheshire Constabulary Crime Scene Investigations Manager with the Forensic Investigations team in Neston. After my day with the Scientific Support Unit, I'll never see laundry bags in quite the same light again.

I relied heavily on Misha Glenny's excellent text, *The Fall of Yugoslavia*, for the political overview of the war in the Balkans, and for the sequencing of events. *Zlata's Diary*, by Zlata Filipović gave powerful and moving insights into the conflict from the point of view of a child. I came late in the writing of this novel to Abdulrazak Gurnah's haunting novel *By the Sea*, and I was captivated by this balanced, witty, moving and incisive account of the asylum seeker's experience in Britain.

ALSO BY MARGARET MURPHY

CLARA PASCAL SERIES
Book 1: DARKNESS FALLS
Book 2: WEAVING SHADOWS

Please join our mailing list for free kindle crime thriller, detective, mystery, and romance books and new releases, as well as news on Margaret's next crime thriller!

www.joffebooks.com/contact

FREE KINDLE BOOKS

Please join our mailing list for free Kindle books
and new releases, including crime thrillers, mysteries,
romance and more, as well as news on the next book
by Margaret Murphy!
www.joffebooks.com

DO YOU LOVE FREE AND BARGAIN BOOKS?

Thank you for reading this book. If you enjoyed it
please leave feedback on Amazon, and if there is anything
we missed or you have a question about then please get in
touch. The author and publishing team appreciate your
feedback and time reading this book.

www.joffebooks.com

Follow us on Facebook, Twitter and Instagram
@joffebooks for news on Margaret Murphy's next book.

We hate typos too but sometimes they slip through.
Please send any errors you find to
corrections@joffebooks.com

We'll get them fixed ASAP. We're very grateful to
eagle-eyed readers who take the time to contact us.

Made in the USA
Monee, IL
02 October 2020

43803181R00236